BALLAD OF THE BANISHED

For more information or to book an event, contact:

authorvljansen@gmail.com

Book design by: BeYourShelf Services

Cover design by: Red Fox Creative

ISBN Paperback: 979-8-9959293-0-7

First Edition: June 2026

Author's Note

This novel contains subject matter some readers may find distressing. To avoid spoilers, a more detailed content note is provided at the back of the book.

Acknowledgments

I am forever indebted to my copy and line editor, Rachel Cook of Tapestry Writing Support and my developmental editor, Karen Hansen, for answering way too many questions and helping me shape this into something worth reading.

My cover designer, Juniper Hartmann is a goddess who can do no wrong, and I am so grateful she was patient with me through the design process.

For a brief time, over the course of a writing retreat in 2023, I was blessed with the chance to be mentored by Léna Roy, who just so happens to be my favorite author's granddaughter. I owe so much gratitude to her for what I learned in that short period.

And finally, to my wonderful husband, who has sponsored my writing adventures, listened to me rant, put up with my late-night ramblings, and just generally supported me, thank you, my love. I am forever grateful.

Chapter One

I HAD LOST count of how many times my love had died. But I couldn't leave him there, lifeless in the snow. Despite the dread that gripped me at the idea of being caught, I had to bring him back. Again. Secretly. I loved him too much to do anything else, even if it was in direct defiance of my duties as a Valkyrie.

From my vantage point on the rise above the blood-soaked battlefield, the cries of the wounded echoed in my ears. With my heart hammering against my ribs like a frantic war drum, I desperately scanned the field for Eryk's body. My fellow Valkyries moved from one corpse to the next, like ravens in the snow, and ferried each lost soul to Valhalla.

I remained frozen on the snowy hill, with my icy hands clasped behind my back. Only a lucky few had escaped a brutal death in the skirmish. Warriors from a neighboring clan had attacked in the night, and a deadly clash had ensued over something as stupid as a spit of land near the coast where the fields were fertile and the fishing was excellent. It was a stupid reason for so much bloodshed, if you asked me. The enemy had retreated finally, but not without leaving scores of dead in their wake by midday.

A man with a shock of blonde hair gathered himself up to limp away. A teenage girl with hair the red of the rising sun laid wounded, but pressed herself to her feet to make her way home. Another man, much older, mustered the strength to stand and help the ginger-haired girl.

When I was certain the other Valkyries were gone and the living warriors had all walked or crawled from the snow-covered battlefield, I knelt beside the dark-haired boy who had fallen beneath a tree at the edge of the fray. He lay face down on the ground, his curls matted with blood. A ghastly wound in his left side was deep enough to see the ribs beneath the sinew. I turned him over gently to see his mud-splattered face, peaceful in death. I could take him to Valhalla now, but if I did, we would live separate after-lives. He would spend his nights carousing and being entertained by the older Valkyries, while I stood at the side of the room, watching and singing to the warriors and gods.

I shook that thought away. He had to stay here, where I could see him during the times I could escape Valhalla without my absence being noticed. What we had was too precious to end with his death.

I placed my hand on the center of his chest and concentrated on bringing him back. After what seemed like an eternity, he gasped suddenly and struggled to sit up.

"They're gone," I said with a glance around me to ensure none had stayed behind to witness my transgression. If someone saw and told the goddess of death that I had spared a warrior from his fate, the consequences could be catastrophic.

"One of these days," Eryk rasped, "you're going to be caught. And then what, Yrsa?"

"We'll worry about that if the day comes." I tilted his dirty face back and forth to check it for wounds. He should have been dead. He *was* dead. He had died so many times now. Each time, I refused to take him to Valhalla. Each time, I brought him back to me.

"You have to be more careful." He pushed me away and forced me to meet his steely gaze. "What happens if you get caught? I'll just stay dead?"

"When the time comes, we'll worry about it then. We are being as careful as we can." I sat back on my heels. "Now, come with me. We need to leave here if we want to keep that day from coming."

I pulled Eryk to his feet and led us from the battlefield. We stepped over the bodies of his fallen fellow warriors. An icy shiver tripped down my spine as we walked past them. Eryk gave a small shudder and kept his eyes averted from the bloody battlefield. Death was simply part of being a Valkyrie, and so my own reaction was less apparent, at least outwardly. Internally, I still felt the chill of being surrounded by corpses which had once held so much life and potential.

Hand in hand, we made our way back to where Eryk left his horse before the battle. There was no time to heal him here, lest one of my sisters return and see us. Eryk mounted and then reached down a hand to drag me up into the saddle behind him. Once I was seated securely, he wheeled the horse around and galloped from the battlefield.

The security and comfort of his back against my chest as we cantered back to the village lulled me into something like a trance. I felt so safe with him; this warrior who could take down dozens of men if called upon to do so. I leaned my head against his upper back and closed my eyes as we rode, just drinking in his presence.

The warriors had driven the enemy to a battlefield half a day's ride from the tiny village Eryk called home, but we reached the rise of a hill above his village by late afternoon. Blue smoke curled from stone chimneys and oblivious, giggling children ran behind their patient mothers through the narrow village lanes. For Eryk, I was sure it was a relief to come home, but it reminded me I didn't belong with mortals anymore. Two years as a Valkyrie had made Midgard seem less and less like a place I could call home, unless I was with Eryk. Curious eyes watched Eryk and me as we rode into the village. After leaving his horse in the stable, we went to his house.

"I can't stay long," I warned him as he pulled me into his arms once the door had closed behind us. I melted into his touch, despite the knowledge that I shouldn't stay. It was torture every time I had to leave him. I loved Valhalla and my Valkyrie sisters, but my heart felt hollow and achy whenever I was parted from Eryk. "I have to go back once I heal you."

"Just for a little while," he pleaded, and then leaned in to capture my lips with his. I kissed him back as I pressed my body closer to his and wrapped my arms around his neck to hold him close. My hands tangled in his dark hair and I allowed myself to indulge in his touch. These moments were scarce and precious. And each one made me love him more.

"Do you want me to be caught?" I asked softly. "Going back after battle is how I keep our secret. You know that."

"I know, I know," he finally conceded, as he let go of me. His expression was still a little petulant, but at least he acknowledged my fears. I stepped away and smoothed my blonde curls. The beaded braids clinked together as I made sure I wasn't the slightest bit mussed. Not that anyone ever asked many questions when I returned to Valhalla after my time with Eryk. I still couldn't risk it, though. I had to be perfectly put together when I returned.

"I will see you soon, I promise. Now, sit on the bed so I can see to your side." Once he had done so, and removed his shirt, I placed my hands over his wounds and closed my eyes as light glowed between my fingers, growing ever brighter. The warmth that flooded through me when I did this was a comfort after the snowy battlefield. It was as if my hands vibrated with power and the friction warmed them.

Slowly, his muscle and sinew, blood and bone and skin, all knitted back together as the deadly wound faded. I still bandaged it, though it was unnecessary. He would have a scar, and the wound would still look fresh for a few days, but nowhere near as grisly as it had been.

"It always amazes me you can do that," Eryk said when I stepped back. He grabbed my wrist and pulled me down in his lap, kissing my temple. I laughed and tried to pull away. The sensation of being emotionally torn into pieces grew stronger every time I had to leave him. Being a Valkyrie was important to me, but I loved Eryk and would have stayed with him if I could. Staying any longer on this day was a bad idea, though, and I opened my mouth to say so before he held a finger up. "I know, I know, you must go. But it's not nightfall yet. There's still a bit of time before you have to return, right?"

"You always push things," I told him with a huff. "You were the one saying they would catch me one day. Just today, remember?"

"I know, but now I'm not at death's door, and you aren't bringing me back to life," he pointed out. "Just stay a bit longer. We can pretend like we're normal people. Please?"

"I shouldn't, Eryk." I was slowly caving, though. I loved him, and denying him such a simple happiness felt cruel. Surely a couple of hours wouldn't hurt. These were the moments I longed for. I convinced myself for a moment that no one would notice I hadn't returned right away.

"So obedient," he teased, his cheek dimpling as he smirked at me.

"It's my duty, Eryk. Just like your duty is to the jarl, and ultimately the king," I told him sharply. At his stung expression, I softened. It hurt my heart to see the pain in his eyes at my tone, and I found my resolve crumbling beneath his gaze. "I can stay a little longer, but not too much."

"I knew you'd choose right. And I'm glad you did, because I've got something special for you." Eryk reached into a table beside the bed, and pulled out a box, which he opened to reveal a torc necklace made of woven gold with dragons at each end. It must have cost a fortune, but I was too speechless to ask just how much he had spent on it. The idea that he would be so extravagant with his gifts made me feel guilty for going back to Valhalla.

When he offered it to me, I shook my head. "It's beautiful, but I can't take this. Where would I put it? I can't take it with me to Valhalla."

"Then leave it with me, and you can wear it when you visit." Eryk slipped the torc around my neck carefully and it warmed as it sat against my skin. "Let me give you gifts, Yrsa. It makes me happy."

The necklace was easily the most beautiful thing I had ever been gifted, and the fact that it was given to me by Eryk only made it more precious. It was not as delicate as the finery of Valhalla, but it was mine and it was a token of love. I bit my lip as I lifted my hand to the torc. "Thank you. But this is the last gift, yes?"

Eryk's self-satisfied smile told me he had no intention of this being the last gift.

Eryk and I curled together in one another's arms until well after midnight, fingers tangled together as we stared at the fire on the hearth. The house was our haven against the world outside. Even if it moved on without us, we wouldn't care. Our time together was limited, but we stole every moment we could and tried to savor it.

"I love you," he murmured sleepily. "I hate it every time you have to leave."

"I love you, too," I said, pressing my lips to his. "I swear my love to you on every god there is. I would do anything for you. But I can't stay forever. Even if I wanted to."

I would have no choice but to return to Valhalla soon, whether I wanted to stay or not. I had already stayed too long this time. Every night, while the others slept, I slipped back to Eryk and his warm embrace. If there were a battle from which to reap dead warriors, I would go and see to my duties there and then return to Eryk until sunset for the nightly feast in Valhalla. It was endless, and I slept little, but it didn't matter as long as I was with him.

The room had grown cold, so I extricated myself from his arms to get out of bed and stoke the fire. As I stood, a harsh wind threw the windows open. It extinguished the fire and left me standing in the dark. Eryk still lay draped across the bed, eyes wide. He was even more surprised than me.

Wings flapped and dead leaves rustled from the doorway. My heart stuttered as a familiar face stepped out of the shadows.

"Yrsa." The hollow voice sent a chill down my spine, cold as the snow that blew in from outside. "You've been disobedient."

"Mistress." My voice trembled as I spoke. I took a knee before Hel, the goddess of death. I should have heeded her commands as the overseer of the Valkyries. She ordered which warriors to deliver to their afterlife as pre-ordained by the Norns; immortal weavers who spun out the life thread of every creature. I clenched my fists at my side to keep my hands from trembling and stared at the floor between Hel's bare feet, which oozed rotting slime. The room had filled with the overwhelming odor of decay and graveyard dust.

She wouldn't just chastise me for saving Eryk; she would send him to Valhalla and we'd be separated forever. He would forget me, and eventually, if what the other Valkyries said was right, I would forget him as well.

"The Norns cut this one's lifeline many moons ago." Hel's voice was the rattle of someone close to death. Each breath sounded like it came with a struggle. "Why is he still in Midgard?"

My breath caught in my throat. My heart stopped beating entirely. How could I explain to her why I spared Eryk? Why I was there with him instead of in Valhalla?

"I love him." Tears pricked my eyes as I involuntarily uttered words she would never comprehend. "I couldn't bear to see such a noble warrior die on the battlefield."

"A noble warrior deserves an honorable death and a glorious afterlife in Valhalla. He should not be forced into an eternal life of fighting other men's battles." The goddess stared at me without malice or anger. Her eyes, which were such a dark grey they were nearly entirely black, never seemed to hold emotion. They saw far beyond what anyone else saw.

"I would rather spend eternity with her than an eternity drinking and making merry in Valhalla without her." Eryk's words earned a startled frown from both Hel and me. His brow creased with frustration as he spoke. "Do I get no choice?"

"No." Hel turned her empty gaze on him. "You don't. What the Norns have prophesied is what must happen. You cannot shirk that fate. Your death calls."

Hel would take him from me, then. The gods would likely forbid me from ever seeing him again once he was in Valhalla. If he even remembered me once he was there, we might meet eyes across the room, but we would never be able to be together as we were in Midgard. Eventually, we would forget each other and it would be as if our love never existed to begin with.

My throat tightened around tears I refused to shed before my mistress. If I thought they would move her to mercy, I might have let them fall. When the goddess raised her hand, I flinched. Would she give me a chance to say goodbye?

"I have been watching you for weeks as you paraded about in Midgard with your mortal lover. I thought in time you would come to your senses, but you never did. You remained here despite the rules, despite the knowledge that you were breaking your oaths. You have abandoned your duties, Yrsa. It is time you paid for that transgression." Hel's hollow eyes returned to my face. I shivered under her stony gaze as dread pooled in my belly. Her words were as hollow and emotionless as her eyes as she continued. "The choices you have made mean you will be exiled."

"Mistress, please. . ." I begged, my voice trailing off. I stood and stepped back until my legs hit the bed. When I reached back for Eryk's hand, it wasn't there. Swallowing hard, I forced myself to turn around. He was gone. My insides felt as if worms were eating the pit of my gut, as I turned back to face the goddess. "You've sent him to Valhalla, then?"

"No," she said with a finality that physically hurt. "I've sent him to the underworld, where he will spend eternity." Hel raised an eyebrow as I crumpled to my knees.

"You can't punish him like that for a transgression I committed, and the Norns will not let you doom someone not fated to die anyway," I said in a trembling voice. I wished it was firmer, less frightened sounding, but I was desperate and afraid, whether I wanted to admit it or not. "Please, don't leave him in the underworld for eternity. Send him to Valhalla, and I promise I will never disobey again."

"You made this choice, and he allowed you to continue it. The Norns control fate, I control death. They can come argue with me in Helheim if they don't like my determination." Hel said in that same frigid tone. "There are consequences for every action, and the consequence for these actions is a dire one. You should have chosen differently."

"Please," I begged again, falling to my knees and lowering my forehead to the floor. How could I have been so foolish? How could I have put Eryk in such a position that he would end up in the underworld? "You must give me some way to save him. I promise to take him to Valhalla if you bring him back."

Hel stared at me, unfeeling, for a long while. The silence stretched out between us with only the howling of the wind through the open window to punctuate her displeasure. Finally, she shifted and out of the corner of my eye, from where my head still touched the floor, I saw her kneel in front of me. Her icy fingers found my chin and tilted my face up to look at her.

In my two years as a Valkyrie, Hel had never once laid a hand, gentle or otherwise, on any of us. Her touch was colder than I expected, and the smell of rotting flesh permeated the air around my face. It took everything I had to keep from gagging.

"I will give you a chance. But only because you beg so prettily," she said after a moment to regard my tear-streaked face. "Traverse the Nine Realms and find the lost pieces of Freyja's armor. Then you may go to the underworld and fight for Eryk's freedom from Nastrond."

"The realm of the dishonorable dead? You can't—"

"I can do whatever I like," she hissed at me, eyes narrowing on my face.

"Can I return to Valhalla once I free him?" I clenched my hands into fists to keep them from shaking like my voice. To be separated from both Eryk and my home was truly too much to bear. And I hadn't even realized there were missing pieces of Freyja's armor. How could I begin to know how to find them?

"I said I was exiling you. What did you think I meant?" Hel's anger was palpable. Her fury settled over the room like a heavy snowfall. "I will give you a choice, though. Find the armor and bring it to me in Helheim and your warrior may be freed, but you will remain exiled. Or you may forget the quest for the armor, leave him in the underworld for eternity, and return to Valhalla yourself."

"Yes, Mistress." I bowed my head as tears coursed down my cheeks. Which was worse? Being cast out from Valhalla or Hel trapping Eryk in Nastrond?

"You have until sunset tomorrow to make your choice. You must complete the quest for the armor by midsummer." She paused, and her voice took on a gentler tone as she put her freezing hand to my hair. The smell of rotting flesh filled my nostrils again. "You are young and have not been a Valkyrie for long. I have faith you will learn from this mistake and be stronger for it."

When I lifted my face, Hel was gone.

I stayed on the floor for a long while in the silent room, with only the icy wind to keep me company. Although I shivered, I didn't close the window right away. I hoped it would numb me enough that I would be able to think of what to do next. The choice should be easy, I should know where my loyalties lay. I had made my oaths as a Valkyrie and had duties which I had sworn to uphold. But I had also sworn my love to Eryk, and I meant that just as much.

Snow drifted in to settle on the floor and across the bed. When I was finally able to move again, I crossed the room and slammed the window shut. I stoked the fire to try to bring warmth back to the small house. No matter what I did, though, it stayed frozen. My heart sat like an icy stone in my chest. Tears still fell unbidden, and I dashed them away with the back of my hand.

I'd never had a reason to travel between the other realms. The only places that were ever my concern were Asgard, where Valhalla was, and Midgard, the realm of men. I would have to find my way to the other realms, and traverse their danger, all to save Eryk. Part of me wished I had never met him, but guilty sobs immediately followed that thought.

Chapter Two

I AWOKE WITH A START. The night before was forgotten, even if only for the briefest moment as I reached across the cold bed to find Eryk gone. An ache settled in my chest, heavy and cold. Sour and nauseating homesickness for Valhalla twisted in my stomach already, or perhaps it was homesickness for Eryk instead. I wasn't sure I could tell the difference. I pulled my knees to my chest, hoping that if I fell back asleep, maybe I would wake to find it was all a nightmare.

After an hour of tossing and turning, I gave up. Sleep would have been merciful, but it didn't come and so I was stuck with this impossible decision. The worst part was that it shouldn't be impossible. I loved Eryk. He was brave and kind. He made me feel like I was the only person in the world when we were together.

I should have had no hesitation about going to the ends of the earth to save him. But Valhalla was my home. It was all I knew now, and I missed it so viscerally that my bones ached with it. For all I had wanted to escape, it was the one place I truly belonged. What would I do if I were never allowed to return? I had only known Eryk for a few months. He was less my home than Valhalla.

I battled the conflicting loyalties between Eryk and Valhalla as if it were a bloody war raging within my heart. I didn't want to betray either. I had already betrayed Hel and paid dearly for it. Had she known the choice would be so difficult? And what might Freyja have to say if she found out?

My head throbbed, like someone was using a dull knife to scrape the insides of my skull out bit by bit. Combined with my already sour stomach, which twisted and turned on itself, I ended up running to the nearest vessel to vomit. I retched until there was nothing left but bile. I had to make a choice. But it was one or the other. I had condemned one of us to an eternity of misery. Either Eryk would be there forever, and I would be in Valhalla, or I would be exiled and stuck in Midgard forever while he was in Valhalla. In no variation of this story would we ever have a future together.

Unable to stand the walls of Eryk's home for a moment longer, I hurried into my rumpled clothing and slipped the torc he had given me around my neck, then stepped out into the icy air. Snow fell heavily from leaden clouds that shifted quickly with the wind, but I ignored it as I strode aimlessly through town. Women jerked their children from my path when they saw the determination in my expression—or not determination, but simply desperation. Whatever it was, it etched itself in the dark circles beneath my eyes and the scowl that furrowed my brow.

My heavy footsteps left deep prints in the knee-high snow, which led me to the edge of the towering fjords, where the frothy waves bashed themselves violently against the jagged rocks. I wished to obliterate myself into sea foam like those waves. The gods couldn't manipulate me and love couldn't break my heart if I was nothing but mist.

The dark sea held no answers for me. Nor did the icy wind, which howled through the fjord. It buffeted me so hard I thought I might blow away into the sky. That, too, would have been a blessing. But I stayed rooted to the snowy ground, my feet numb now from the chill. I pulled my cloak closer around my shoulders and my hood up over my head, afraid to pray to the gods.

A glimpse of copper at the corner of my eye caught my attention. The girl who had dragged herself from the battlefield stood staring out over the waves. Gunhild was her name, if I recalled correctly from my time wandering the village with Eryk. She turned to me, her bright blue gaze meeting mine. She blinked slowly, as if only just realizing then that she was seeing me, before nodding in acknowledgement. Something told me she was facing a choice of her own, and so I turned back to the sea to leave her to her own deliberations. It was reassuring that I was not the only one making a difficult decision, though I had to wonder if hers was as grave as mine.

The way she held herself made me want to be as brave as she was. Her shoulders were back, her head held high as she stared down the waves like she was challenging them to come and claim her at the top of the cliff. I desperately wanted to be as self-assured. When I turned in her direction again, she was gone, as if she had only been a ghost or a memory. At first, I thought she might have jumped, and so I hurried to the edge to look over, but there was no sign of her below. She must simply have gone back to the village while I was turned away.

I shook my head and bit down hard on my lip, forcing myself to decide. My instinct kept leading my mind and heart back to Eryk, like a solitary light guiding me through the darkest night. The burden on my shoulders, heavy as the snow weighing down on the eaves of the village houses, lifted. My posture straightened and my head rose. Wrong or right, I made my decision.

"I've chosen! I choose Eryk!" I called out to the stormy sky. "Do you hear me, Hel?! I choose Eryk!"

The sky darkened, the gale swirling so strongly around me that I lost my footing and stumbled to my knees. And then, as if it had never happened, the wind stopped completely, and the sky cleared. Hel had heard me, apparently.

I headed back to the market, where I moved with purpose between the stalls, using coins from Eryk's savings to pay for supplies. I would need them for my journey if I were to survive. I would have to be as prepared as possible for many months in the wilderness. With luck, I would find villages along the way to replenish my stores. Eventually I had bought all I was able to carry and returned to Eryk's home.

I packed food, furs, Eryk's sunstone, and any other supplies I could fit in a rucksack and pulled the straps over my shoulders. I strapped Eryk's axe and sword on opposite hips and attached his shield to my pack as if his weapons and shield were my own. Once I was sure I had everything, I wrapped my fur back around myself. It wouldn't be an easy or short journey. How was I even supposed to complete it before midsummer? It didn't matter, I decided. I had to do my best or die in the attempt. Releasing a slow exhale, I forced myself to think only of the next step, rather than the ache in my chest and the frantic spinning of my thoughts.

The sun was as high as it would get in the early days of spring, so I had to leave soon if I wanted to put any distance between myself and the village before nightfall. I found Eryk's silver arm rings and tied them onto my belt. I would need them to pay for supplies later.

But where to go first? This question deflated me entirely, and I sagged onto the bed as I considered. I would never be able to search the entire world bit by bit, or it would take me years. I had to figure out where these pieces of armor might be so hidden that even Freyja did not know where they were. But who could tell me where to find what I was looking for? Oracles were an option, but they were always so cryptic and I didn't have time to figure out yet another puzzle. There was something even better than an oracle, though: the Norns.

The Norns knew better than anyone where hidden things might be, whether they were in Midgard or anywhere else. Their knowledge of past, present, and future would allow them to see with ease where every single piece of the armor was. With any luck, they might tell me where to search. I just had to get to the base of Yggdrasil, where they wove fate, and I could ask for their help. I pushed aside the gnawing in my stomach that warned it would be fruitless. If they didn't give me direction, I'd have no plan.

I set my jaw and closed my eyes to force my thoughts to calm until they were as smooth as the surface of a lake on a windless day. One step at a time was the only way forward. I got to my feet and settled the shield firmly on my back. It was time to leave Eryk's home behind.

Chapter Three

I WALKED until I could walk no more. Hours had passed, and with each step I trudged slower and heavier. My feet ached despite being frozen and I worried about what might lurk in the forest this late at night. Above me, the aurora twisted and swirled in vivid green and blue. It was too cold to stand and watch it, though. I had no choice but to make camp. The night promised to be frigid. The tent I had scavenged from Eryk's belongings would barely protect me, and my furs would be the only other thing to shield me from the night air.

My teeth chattered as I wrapped myself in furs within the tent and tried to settle in for the frozen night. It was easier to plan than to think about what might happen to Eryk in the underworld. Was he afraid? Angry? What might be happening to him there? Torture was the most frightening thought, and I shoved it aside. He would never forgive me if they inflicted that kind of pain. The idea that he might hate me left a painful lump in my throat that I swallowed against as I focused on my plan again.

The surrounding darkness should have pulled me into sleep, but my eyes wouldn't close. Instead, I lay awake, listening to the sound of the wind howling outside and the creaking of the tent poles. The only thing to bring me even a modicum of comfort was the heaviness of the bronze torc around my neck, warmed to my skin. Eventually, I drifted off, but not deeply enough that every little sound didn't wake me.

It seemed like no time at all before the sun was rising again. I couldn't bear to spend another minute stuck with my thoughts inside the tent, and my quest couldn't wait any longer either.

After several miles of walking without a break, I finally had no choice but to rest on a fallen log and drink some melted snow. I should have eaten too, but the newness of my quest and my homesickness for Valhalla made me too queasy to stomach anything just yet.

When I could, I got to my feet again and set off toward my destination. Because of the time I'd spent in Eryk's village, I was fairly familiar with the area. I knew the direction I would need to take to reach my goal, and I refused to let anything get in my way. Determination was all I had left. If I focused on anything else, I would fail. But, for what felt like the first time since I had begun my trip, there was a spark of hope. Yggdrasil called to me deep in my bones. I was headed in the right direction. I kept my eyes on the path as I slogged through the knee-high snow, my boots and breeches soaked with it.

More than once, I stumbled over a tree branch, hidden beneath the drifts, and nearly fell into the deep snow. The last thing I needed was to freeze to death when the sun went down in a few hours.

Only tree limbs occasionally breaking from the weight of the snow and the birds singing high above filled the quiet. Letting my mind drift, I tried only to feel the pull of Yggdrasil, the tree that connected all the realms within its roots and branches. Once I crossed the toll bridge, I would be close to a cave. It should lead to the well beneath Yggdrasil. There I could find the Norns. If I were lucky and they found me worthy, they would read my fate and tell me where to find the armor Hel commanded me to seek.

After a couple of hours of winding in and out of the edge of the woods, I paused and glanced around to make sure of my bearings. I would have to stop soon, and I wanted to get as close to the bridge as possible before it was too dark to walk. I only hoped the bridge was unguarded when I found it.

The root of Yggdrasil tugged harder at me as the sun dipped below the horizon. I fumbled with the lantern attached to my pack and lit it, so I wasn't completely immersed in darkness. Wolves howled in the distance, but I pretended I couldn't hear them. Hopefully, the light would drive them away.

Chapter Four

Snow had started to fall once more in huge clumps of flakes. They landed in my hair and eyelashes, each frozen crystal making me shiver a bit more. The temperature would drop even more deeply tonight than it had the night before. Some tiny part of me whispered about how warm Valhalla would be right now, and how easy it would be to give up and ask Hel to send me home. The rest of me knew that wasn't something I could live with.

As if materializing out of the darkness, a bridge suddenly loomed ahead of me. The inky black beneath it sucked in the meager light from my lantern and devoured it. A shudder ran down my spine, though I was unsure if it was from fear or excitement.

It was the first real sign I'd been traveling in the right direction. I hurried close to the bridge and carefully dropped my pack to the ground where I set up the tent and then lit a fire. I should have thought to hunt for something, anything, so I'd have something fresh to eat for the night. Smoked fish, bread, and rose hip jelly with a few sips of melted snow would have to do.

I had barely settled down before the fire when a whispering from beneath the bridge startled me. My hand immediately went to the axe at my hip, Then the whispering turned into mumbling and moaning.

"This is my home." A vile voice echoed from the darkness under the bridge. "Why do you come here?"

"I'm sorry." I hesitated before speaking further. "I must trespass to find the Norns. Will you let me pass?"

The owner of the voice rumbled out of the darkness. Its stony face and mussed black hair caught the light of the fire. Its eyes were dark, suspicious, and wholly unsettling as it towered over me. There were no irises or pupils, just black abysses that stared menacingly at me. The troll must have been the size of a house. It was barely small enough to fit under the bridge. I stepped back without meaning to and almost tripped into the flames. My stomach lurched as I watched the hulking creature, although it appeared harmless enough as it leaned casually on the railing of the bridge.

"Please," I said. "I must reach them, and this is the only way I know to get there."

After a few moments, the creature tilted its head curiously. "How do you know you have the right bridge? This only leads deeper into the woods, and then you would be trapped."

I knew better than to mock the creature, so I ducked my head and pleaded with it instead.

"I must cross, whatever the cost," I said.

"And the cost will be high, little one." The gentleness in the troll's voice belied how dangerous it was. "Are you certain you're willing to pay?"

"What is the price?" I took a small step forward, despite my trembling knees. I could run and find another way, but I chose to stay, to solve this problem head on.

"Don't come closer until you pay," the troll warned. "Or fight."

The troll grunted and then stood to its full height. It was a veritable mountain, looming over the bridge and me. What would I have to do to prevent a battle with the monster?

"What do you want?" I kept my voice steady, though my knees felt like jelly.

"I want a song," the troll said. "A song I haven't heard before."

The ground quaked beneath its feet as it took another step toward me.

The Valkyrie songs came to mind as I tried to work out what could appease him. I sang every night to the fallen warriors, and yet now my mind was blank. I surely could remember at least one, right? But I had forgotten everything but the troll hulking over me. The troll cleared its throat as it waited impatiently for me to fail in the task it had set out for me.

"Blood flows on the field," I sang in a quavering voice.

"The warriors fallen with their shields,
Valkyries gather like crows,
Lined up together, row by row,
the ravens of Odin, to reap those who fall,
And take them to Valhalla's halls."

The troll closed its eyes as I sang. At least the song seemed to please it. When I paused, it opened one eye and waved its hand for me to continue. I cleared my throat.

"Warriors brave and valiant,
To be honored by the Valkyries
Their fearlessness unsurpassed,
Rewarded by mead, song, and repast."

Nothing more came to mind. I only hoped it was enough for the troll to allow me to pass unscathed. It sighed happily and opened its eyes again to stare at me in silence.

"Is that enough?" I asked, fists clenched at my side as if I could somehow fight him if my song weren't enough. The troll's stony brow rumbled downward at my audacity.

A voice piped up from the nearby woods, its source coming into the light of my fire which glinted off of copper hair and sky-blue eyes. "Surely that's enough."

It was the girl from the fjord—Gunhild.

"It's a song you've never heard before. That was the price you offered." Her voice was defiant and strong, when I felt frightened and weak. I lifted my chin a touch as if her bravery was contagious.

"You're right," the troll replied as he took another step toward me, in my camp now. Gunhild joined my side. With the fire behind us, we couldn't easily retreat. It might simply eat our bones. I shuddered at the thought of the crunching sound between its great teeth. "What if I want another song, though. What then, little girl?"

I placed a hand on Gunhild's arm. Her indignance was palpable through the tautness of her muscles, but she eventually relaxed slightly.

"Will you let us pass, or is there something more you want?" I asked, as calmly as I was able.

"What food and drink do you have?" It glanced at my heavy-laden pack, curiosity raising one of its rocky eyebrows. "Perhaps if you share some of that."

"I have very little of worth." I set my pack on the snow before me. Gunhild had brought her own pack and knelt beside me to do the same. What was she doing out here in the woods with a pack of her own? "Mostly salted meat and bread."

"Butter? Jam? Mead?"

"I have jam, but no butter or mead," I said. "And I only have enough jam for my journey."

"I don't care how long your journey is." The troll laughed. The sound resembled great river rocks tumbling against one another. "It won't matter what your plans are if you can't pass my bridge. There's no way around the river, and it flows too quickly to freeze. You would fall in and be swept downstream to an icy death before you'd have time to drown. Share some mead, and I'll allow you to pass."

"As I said, I don't have any mead," I pointed out with a wince as those dark brows scuttled downward again at the reminder. My gaze flicked to Gunhild, who sighed and pulled a skin of mead from her pack and extended it to the troll. It would barely be a sip for such an enormous creature.

"Will it be enough?" I asked, bowing my head.

The troll took the skin between its fingers and laughed again. The bridge quaked as its laughter echoed around us, a few stones clattering from it and down into the icy river below with a splash. When the laughter finally stopped, the troll gave a brief nod and waved us toward the bridge.

"I can't remember the last time I had good mead," it mused. "Thank you for your contribution. Try not to die on your journey. That would be a waste of a good toll."

I hurried to pack my things and get out of there. As I crossed the bridge, I glanced back to see the troll emptying the skin of mead between its rocky lips. Gunhild hurried with me to the other side before I could stop her. I didn't have time to tell her to go back—it was too important to get as far from the bridge as possible, lest the troll change its mind again.

"What was that song you sang?" Gunhild asked when I stopped half an hour later, well past the bridge, to light a fire to warm my frozen hands and feet. "I've never heard it before."

"You shouldn't have crossed the bridge," I said as I shifted uncomfortably. She didn't respond, but crossed her arms over her chest as she awaited my answer to her question. "I didn't remember any songs, so I made one up."

Gunhild laughed, and the musical sound tinkled through the trees. When she caught her breath, she sat down heavily before the fire that had built itself up into a healthy blaze.

"I suppose that guaranteed that the troll never heard it before." She pulled off her wet boots and extended her feet toward the flames. I worried she would catch her socks on fire, but it wasn't my job to protect her, so I just draped a wolf fur around my shoulders and rubbed my hands together to warm them.

"I suppose it did," I said as I tried to formulate a plan to return Gunhild to her home, or at least to whatever path she had been on before she stumbled across me and the bridge.

"It's too late for me to go back, you know," Gunhild pointed out, as if she had read my mind. "The troll would never let me go back. You should let me come with you. I've been following you and you seem awfully lonely traveling alone."

"Just because it's too late for you to go back, doesn't mean you should come with me," I said with a frown. "Why were you following me?"

"I saw you at the fjord. And then I saw you leaving town with all your things packed—without Eryk," Gunhild admitted. "Have you split up, then? I know you're his consort. More than just his consort."

"Eryk is gone," I managed to bite off before I became too emotional. The last thing I needed was some girl tagging along at my heels asking questions. I couldn't put her in danger like I had done with Eryk, and I didn't really want to tolerate her curiosity. I was already irritable from heartache and lack of sleep.

"Do you know where he went?"

"He. . ." I shoved down the momentary yearning to share the truth with someone. But she would never believe me, and it would only lead to more questions. "He left. That is all you need to know."

"Your name is Yrsa, right?" She smiled, and the sun might as well have risen to its zenith, it was so bright. "I'm Gunhild."

"I know." I tried but failed to return her smile. My face felt frozen in a permanent scowl. "You're a shieldmaiden. You've fought by Eryk's side more than once."

"You noticed me?" Gunhild brightened further at my admission.

"Of course, how could anyone miss that red hair?" I asked. Gunhild's smile only grew.

"I don't know about you," Gunhild said as a change of subject, "but after all that, I'm not hungry."

"We at least need to melt snow and have something to drink. Thirsting to death is much worse than starving. And you should preserve what's left of your mead. You'll need it if you're to go home."

"I'm coming with you," she insisted. "It would be too dangerous for me to go back now, even if I took the long way. That would take two weeks to find the closest bridge."

"Why do you want to go with me? Your place is here with your family and friends."

"My family died long ago, and my friends, as few as they were, have died in battle," she said. I was certain there was more to it than that. "I'm not worried about danger. I had already planned to jump off the cliff when you saw me at the fjord. And I wouldn't have gone to Valhalla if I'd done that. I'm not afraid. If I die, I die. A Valkyrie can simply take me to Valhalla."

I was stunned by her revelation, by the way she said it so nonchalantly, as if it meant nothing that she had been so close to ending her own life. I stared at her for a long time, and somehow, she managed not to squirm under my gaze as I debated how to proceed.

"Not in some of the places I'll be going," I confessed finally. This pricked Gunhild's interest further, but she didn't ask any other questions. It would be easier to offload her at the next village than to sit here and argue with her. "Fine, you can come. For now."

Gunhild nodded decisively and pulled her boots back on before grabbing a pot out of one of the packs. She filled it with snow and set it near the flames to melt.

For a long while we didn't talk, we only stared into the fire pensively. My heart still pounded from our encounter with the troll. Did hers too? I wasn't certain what I would have done if my song and her mead had failed to suffice.

Gunhild must have noticed me breathing heavily, because she reached over and squeezed my knee, a knowing look in her eyes. I offered a brave smile, and she returned it before pulling the pot from the fire.

"I brought some herbs if you would like to have tea," I said. She nodded and rustled through my pack until she found the small tin where I had stored them. I was exhausted, but my eyes were stuck open like a warped door as I stared while she put the herbs into the pot of water and allowed them to steep.

"It's over, Yrsa." Gunhild handed me the pot to drink from. I took a sip, my thoughts jumbled as I considered her words. "At least… that part is over."

"It will only grow more dangerous," I warned her. I absolutely couldn't let her come with me. My habit of putting people in danger had to stop. But how did I convince her not to tag along? Should I wait until she slept and then tie her up and leave without her? No, that would put her in more danger than just letting her come along.

"I'm a shieldmaiden. I've been in more danger than this," Gunhild reminded me. "Whatever your journey is, it's taking you places I've never been. If it's so dangerous, then it will be far more glory than any battle. If I survive, I'll have tales to tell. If I don't, I'm certain one way or another I'll find my way to Valhalla."

"I hope you survive." The last thing I wanted was for her to die simply because I didn't make her go home.

"I'll be fine, I promise," she replied with a determined nod.

There was no way to change what I needed to do, and it seemed there was no way to change her mind. And it was too late to send her home. She would never make it back across the bridge. A strange mix of emotions that I couldn't tease apart tangled in my chest as I considered how to get her back home. Some part of me wanted to keep her with me, not just for safety, but because facing my quest alone seemed less daunting with a companion at my side. It was foolish to consider putting her in danger for my own benefit, but it didn't really matter since sending her home was even more dangerous than keeping her with me.

Chapter Five

THAT NIGHT, the sound of footsteps outside the tent woke us. Both of us sat up in a panic and reached for our weapons. I lifted a hand to tell Gunhild to stay in the tent, but she shook her head and climbed out anyway.

Fortunately, it was only a small red deer eating fungus from a fallen tree at the edge of our camp. Gunhild held her finger to her lips and motioned for me to stay behind as she took tentative steps forward. Raising her axe, she aimed carefully and then let the weapon fly with deadly accuracy into the side of the deer. It made a soft bleating noise and fell to the ground.

I rushed to the deer's side, intending to slit its throat to put it out of its misery, but the axe had flown true and the poor creature was already dead by the time I reached it. Gunhild came to kneel beside me, and we both uttered a soft prayer to Ullr, the god of the hunt, for the gift and for Gunhild's steady hand. It was still dark, and the fire had nearly died, but we quickly field dressed the deer and Gunhild took the entrails deep into the woods to dispose of them away from camp. Thankfully, red deer were relatively small, and the meat wouldn't be too heavy to carry on our journey. There were still a couple of hours before dawn, but no matter how tired we were, sleep was evasive. Instead, we made a quick breakfast of fresh venison and porridge, washed down with a little mead from the second skin of it she had packed, before breaking camp and continuing on our way.

We walked for days, stopping only to rest and eat. Each night we quietly made camp and slept for a few hours. Gunhild seemed to have gotten the idea that I wasn't much in the mood for chatter, and stayed quiet for most of it, though she would occasionally point out something interesting in the woods or tell me about her life.

After hours of walking on the sixth day since the troll bridge, Gunhild's steps grew slower, and she lagged farther behind me, so I paused and waited for her to catch up. Her stamina didn't match mine, but that was understandable. I motioned to a small clearing where we could take a brief break.

"I'm sorry I didn't let you kill the deer the other night; I just wasn't sure you could," Gunhild admitted after taking a drink of water.

"I was a shieldmaiden once as well," I told her, though it seemed like so long ago.

"But you aren't now?" Gunhild asked with a small, confused frown.

"Not exactly." My gut immediately clenched as I realized I had revealed something so significant. Now she would ask too many questions. "We can talk about it later. For now, we should get moving."

Gunhild gave me a skeptical look, but acquiesced and we started on our way again.

The sun seemed to set earlier than the nights before. The shadows stretched out long and seemed to snatch at our feet as we walked, tripping us more with each step.

I didn't want to stop, although it would mean traveling in the dark. The pull of Yggdrasil was stronger, and the cave had to be nearby. As night fell and Gunhild trudged along behind me, I wondered briefly if we should rest. But she was brave and unafraid of the night, no matter how dark.

"We're close," I told her when she startled at the sound of a wolf howling in the distance. Another followed on our opposite side. "The wolves in these woods are known to be aggressive, but I think we can make it before they close in. Are you willing to try, or do you want to stop and start a fire to keep them off us?"

"Keep going." Her breath came in short pants from exertion, I hoped, since she had seemed so unafraid until now. I nodded, invisible in the darkness, and paused long enough to light the lantern hanging at my hip. It wouldn't do much to keep the wolves at bay, but at least we'd see them if they drew nearer.

The snow glowed copper in the light from the lantern. The cave was nearby, but I feared the wolves would get to us first. Their howls grew ever closer as we hurried toward safety. When I realized they were too close for us to get there in time, I motioned to Gunhild to draw her axe and shield, and did the same.

The very thing I had feared—putting her in grave danger—had come to pass, and now I just had to hope she could survive it. I hoped I could survive it, for that matter, as I hadn't fought any sort of battle in the years since becoming a Valkyrie.

One gray wolf, then two more, emerged from the shadows between the tall trees. Their hackles were raised, and their teeth bared. I set my feet and put my back against the shieldmaiden's.

I barely had time to knock the first wolf away before another one snarled and rushed at Gunhild. She smashed into it with her shield with a grunt, but kept her feet under her. By then, four more huge wolves had slipped between the trees and joined the others to surround us completely. The beasts were enormous, standing half our height at the shoulders.

The largest wolf lunged at me and, as Gunhild had, I batted it away with my shield, eliciting a pained yelp. The wolf got back to its feet and let out a low growl that raised the hair on the back of my neck. At least we were in Midgard, where a Valkyrie would take Gunhild to Valhalla if she died fighting.

"We have to get to the cave," Gunhild said breathlessly. She set her feet and leaned forward.

Silence enveloped us as if the world stood still for a moment while the wolves prepared to strike once more. It was long enough for us to catch our breath and prepare for the next onslaught.

When it came, it wasn't one wolf at a time. The beasts forced me to fight off three at once. I slashed at one with my axe and beat the others off with my shield. One grazed my forearm with its teeth, and another bit through my boot and into my ankle. I only hoped Gunhild was having better luck than me.

A gurgling yelp rang out behind me, chased by another, and I grinned as I realized how successful Gunhild had been so far. It gave me strength and courage enough to fight off the next two wolves. I slashed one across its throat and sent it crashing to the ground at my feet before I hooked my axe into the side of another, the razor-sharp blade slicing between its ribs.

Somehow, we killed most of the wolves. The last two ran back into the darkness between the trees. Gunhild fell to her knees, and I feared a wolf had injured her. I quickly turned to check her for wounds, but found none. Only a small smirk was on her full lips as she panted, her hand to her chest, trying to catch her breath.

"I can't believe we survived that," she said. Her smile widened and her eyes sparkled in the light of the abandoned lantern a few feet away.

"I can," I said with a bright smile back at her. "You fought like a bear. The wolves stood no chance against you."

"I can say the same of you." A laugh escaped between her labored breaths. We both sighed and leaned heavily against each other. After a few minutes of rest, I grabbed the fallen lantern and we continued.

We had barely walked a mile when Gunhild suddenly fell to her knees with a pained gasp. Running to her side, I realized I missed something when I examined her after the fight.

Blood seeped through the neck of her tunic. I pulled it aside to reveal two deep bite marks at her collarbone. The white of bone and sinew showed beneath. With a worried grimace, I hurriedly extracted the few bandages I thought to pack and carefully applied pressure to the wound. I didn't know how I missed it, but it bled profusely and weakened Gunhild.

I placed my hands over the wound, as I had done to Eryk's so many times before to heal him. I expected the bright glow to come and my healing magic to do its work, but nothing happened. I closed my eyes and focused harder, determined to heal her, but my hands and body remained as cold as ever. Being exiled from Valhalla apparently meant that I had lost my magic as well.

My heart ached and I felt rather like I might vomit, but there was no time now to react. It didn't matter how the loss of my magic made me feel, or that I wanted to fall to my knees and cry. This was not the time for that. Gunhild was horribly injured, and we were still deep in the woods with the remainder of the pack of wolves.

Drops of blood fell crimson on the snow, steaming as they reached the frosty ground. I helped Gunhild to lie down—whether she froze was unimportant. I needed to stop the bleeding. "Why didn't you tell me one bit you?" I tried to keep the panic from my voice as I pressed hard against the wound. If it became infected, she would die of blood poisoning.

"Because I didn't want you to worry." She pushed me away and pressed against the bites herself. "Get the bleeding stopped, give me a drink of mead, and let's move on. We'll be safer in the cave. There might be bears or more wolves lurking in these woods, and I'm not sure I could fight again."

"Are you sure you can move?"

"Yes," she insisted as she held out her hand. "Now, help me up."

"You can't carry a pack with that injury," I told her as I shouldered both packs. I grabbed the lantern and reached down to help Gunhild to her feet. She winced as she stood, but didn't complain.

"Should you carry both yourself?" She eyed my stooped posture. I nodded and motioned for her to go ahead of me. I didn't want her to fall behind without me knowing.

Chapter Six

It only took half an hour to reach the cave, but it felt like days. I jumped at the slightest sound, and we took frequent, fraught breaks for Gunhild to rest and allow me to check the bites. They had bled heavily, but the flow was starting to slow at least. If she died as a result of my refusal to send her home, I would never forgive myself. Combining that with Eryk's loss would be too great of a burden to bear. I wasn't sure how I could survive something so heavy on my conscience. She had to live.

When we turned a corner of the path, the mouth of the cave suddenly gaped open before us. The pitch blackness inside poured out like spilled ink into the already murky forest. I hesitated, worried about what we might find inside. A bear or other creature could have lurked inside the cave, ready to attack just as ferociously as the wolves had. There was no turning back though, and as Gunhild sagged against me, I knew she desperately needed rest.

Once she was safely seated against the cave wall, I set the lantern down and quickly prepared a fire. The remainder of the wolf pack howled outside the cave again. I was glad our backs were protected while we were vulnerable, but we might not have far to run if they found us.

"I have a poultice we can put on the wound," I said after a little while. "And some salve after that. But I don't know if it will be enough."

"It has to be." Gunhild shifted her shoulder, grimacing at the pain.

"I should find a place to leave you safely, where you can heal. Not be exposed to any more danger." For the moment, she didn't argue. I opened one pack and sorted through its contents for the package of medical supplies. When I found them, I sighed in relief. "This is going to hurt."

Gunhild gingerly removed her furs and stripped off her top so that I could access her injury more easily, though she shivered despite the fire.

As I carefully made the poultice and placed it on Gunhild's shoulder, she squirmed and groaned. I tried to go as quickly as I could to spare her as much as possible from the agony, but I needed to be thorough to be sure she wouldn't end up with a fever from the bites.

"I should never have brought you with me," I muttered, mostly to myself. Gunhild's head shot up, and she shook it vehemently.

"No. I made this decision. I'll be fine." She pulled me to her and pressed her forehead against mine. For a reason I couldn't pinpoint, her reassurance warmed me, or maybe just the physical touch. I didn't know, but it helped me to feel more grounded in the face of what we were up against. "Now, finish up so we can eat something before we sleep."

I stayed like that for a few moments, eyes closed, before hurrying to finish with the poultice, which I bound to her wound with bandages. After an hour or so, I would remove it and work the salve into the wound to help it heal. I wished more than anything that I could use my magic to heal her. Its absence made me want to scream, not just because I was useless to the shieldmaiden, but also because it was a stark reminder of my exile.

She pulled the furs back around her when I was done binding the poultice to her shoulder. While the poultice did its work, I put together a meager meal of what was left of the venison and some bread, with healing tea for Gunhild to drink. We sat in silence as we ate, and when we were done, I put everything but the medical supplies away.

Gunhild dozed as I went back to check the poultice after an hour. It had dried, and the wound looked a little less angry now. I allowed myself to revel in the relief that there was a chance she would survive this. She woke when I gently rubbed the salve into the wound, and hissed between her teeth at the pain.

"I'm sorry. I know it hurts," I told her gently. "But it will help. And hopefully we can avoid a fever from it."

"It's alright, it's not that bad," she lied, offering a small, tired smile. "Will you answer a question though?"

"Depends on the question," I replied with a wary look.

"What did you do back there in the woods? When you pressed on my shoulder and closed your eyes?"

"I… nothing. I was just praying." She raised an eyebrow. She clearly saw right through my lie. But it wasn't a lie I could part from easily. The last mortal who knew what I was had ended up in the underworld as a result. Telling the truth in this case seemed ill-advised at best.

"Look, I know you're more than a shieldmaiden, and I know you weren't always in the village, but there's something special about you. Are you a goddess?"

"No." I didn't respond beyond that, even though I had the strange urge to tell her everything.

Gunhild searched my face for answers. "I know you aren't what everyone says. You're more than Eryk's consort. What in the Nine Realms are you?"

"If I tell you. . ." Something about her set me at ease. I felt myself trusting her despite the knowledge that it was a bad idea to trust anyone with my secrets, if only for her own sake. "You can't tell another soul. It must remain a secret for the rest of your mortal life, and when you eventually travel to the next. Do you understand?"

She nodded and waited for me to gather the courage to tell her what I was. The worry that she might fear me settled uncomfortably in my stomach as if she was something more than a stranger.

"Valkyrie." I was unsure of what else to say. My heart rattled against my ribs, desperate to escape. Her eyebrows raised as she tilted her head to examine me.

"How curious." A slight smile curved her lips. Somehow, it stilled my heart and gave me that calm I sought before. "In all my battles, I'd been afraid to see one, and yet here I am, unafraid."

"You're not surprised?" If my revelation hadn't been shocking to her, her reaction to it definitely astonished me. She didn't appear to be afraid of me.

She shook her head, her smile growing wider.

"Why not?"

"It's not as if I didn't know Valkyries exist. After all, as a shieldmaiden, there's no greater honor than to be taken to Valhalla by a Valkyrie. Why should I be afraid?"

"You're not afraid to die?"

"It's an honor to die in battle." She brushed a lock of hair from her face, the fire glinting rose gold on it. The sentiment was a brave one indeed, and it made me admire her a little more than I already had.

"Yes," I said, "I suppose it is."

"So, what were you doing then, with my wound in the woods?" she asked again.

"I…" I still hesitated even though she now knew what I was. She gave me a reassuring smile, which seemed to warm me like my magic had not when it failed. "I was trying to heal you. But it didn't work."

"Why not?" she asked with a confused tilt of her head. "It has to do with Eryk, doesn't it?"

I didn't answer, but my refusal to meet her eyes still must have told her everything she needed to know.

"I was supposed to take Eryk to Valhalla. And I chose not to." I swallowed hard around a painful lump in my throat, my words momentarily muted.

"Well, I'm certain there's something we can do to right this wrong, no?" Gunhild asked.

Should I tell her what Hel commanded me to do? I hesitated, unsure how to continue. Gunhild scooted a little closer but didn't force me to meet her gaze.

"I…" I paused, my gaze lifting to the tree limbs tangled across the midnight sky outside the cave. Like my first night of travel, the aurora ebbed and flowed in the sky overhead, like waves on the shore. I watched it for a little while this time, musing on what I should say as it twirled and flowed above me. "I must find the lost pieces of Freyja's armor before I can do anything else. And to do that, I must travel to the Yggdrasil to ask the Norns for aid. It will be a harrowing journey. You can still go back home."

"No." Gunhild shook her head. "No, I want to come with you, if you'll have me."

"If you die, in Midgard or otherwise, I can't take you to Valhalla," I told her. She would ask why, and I knew I would be forced to admit the truth, but I had no choice but to trust her if I was going to let her come with me.

"Why?"

"I'm exiled," I explained. "It was part of my punishment for shirking my duties. I can't go back to Valhalla. Ever. And the other Valkyries can't reap souls outside of Midgard."

"I'm willing to take the risk," she decided after several moments.

She'd never be convinced to go back, even if I could stand the idea of facing my quest by myself. The only worry was how much danger I might put her in. But she was an adult, a shieldmaiden who had fought many battles and survived them, and I had to trust that she could make her own decisions and would survive this.

I turned to her with a grim smile. She lifted her chin and let out a long breath as if she'd held it while waiting for me to decide her fate.

"Let's rest and we can move on tomorrow," Gunhild said finally.

"I'm not sure you'll be ready to move on tomorrow." I was doubtful we should even move again that week, much less the next day. "We'll stay as long as we must. I don't want you to fall ill because of me."

"Sleep, Yrsa. Let's sleep. I promise, I'll be alright." She pulled her shirt back on and created a small bed for us on the cave floor in front of the fire. It wasn't as cold as it could be at least, here in the protection of the cave, and the snow had slowly let up.

I laid down beside her and got as close to her as I could so we could share body heat to stay warm. I couldn't sleep, of course, but she quickly drifted off, leaving me with my thoughts and my guilt.

As the sun rose the next morning, Gunhild continued to sleep. She barely stirred when I shifted her to look at her wound. Awful bite marks cut deep into the muscle of her shoulder, but when I sniffed, it didn't smell foul and was less red than it had been before. It was a relief, but I still didn't think we would be ready to move on. I would have to convince her to stay another few days.

When she slept most of the day, that took care of the problem. I eventually woke her long enough to drink some tea, but then she went right back to sleep. I headed out at one point to hunt and managed to bring back a pheasant for us to feast on.

Around sunset, Gunhild awoke fully, and sat up with a wince to quietly eat some of the cooked pheasant with more of the tea. I assessed her wound again, feeling much better this time about the way it looked to be healing.

"I think we should wait three more days, at least, before we move on," I told her as I put more of the salve on her injury and covered it again.

"No way," Gunhild argued with a scowl. "We move on tomorrow. I don't care if it's healed or not. Your quest can't be put on hold. We have to find Yggdrasil and the Norns."

"It *can* wait, and it will," I argued back, scowling as deeply as she did. I didn't want to cause a fight, but she wasn't at all ready to continue. "It's that or I take you home."

"You are absolutely not taking me home," Gunhild said, throwing a pebble at my head. I dodged it and glared at her. "I don't have anyone left to go home to. You'd be abandoning me there."

"I won't take you home if you agree to stay another day at least. Compromise, right?"

"Fine. One more day. But that's all."

"Thank you. I didn't want to have to tie you down," I said. I realized I didn't really want to take her home either. There was something about her that inspired hope.

"Will you answer another question I have?" Gunhild asked, bringing me back to the present.

"Maybe," I said warily.

"You said you were a shieldmaiden once," Gunhild said. "Can you tell me about that?"

"I was the daughter of a king, so they trained me to a higher standard than most." My brow furrowed as I struggled to pull specific memories of my time as a shieldmaiden. There were empty spaces where those memories should be, and it frightened me to realize that being a Valkyrie had made my memories fade more than I thought. I strove to remember details, as I told Gunhild what I knew. "My father didn't want me to become a shieldmaiden but said if I insisted, he wanted me to have the best chance of survival."

"Why didn't he simply deny you the right to fight? I'm sure he could have," she said as she packed the food up. "I never would have guessed the king would allow his daughter into battle."

"I disguised myself as a boy and snuck out one night and hid in the woods, to wait for a battle I knew would come. When Papa found out, he realized he couldn't stop me if he tried. I wanted to be a part of the battles my brothers fought."

"How many brothers do you have?" she asked.

"I had three brothers," I said. "They are all in Valhalla now. The youngest I took myself."

"I'm so sorry." Sadness crept into her blue eyes.

"Don't be," I reassured her. "They were valiant warriors, and I was proud to fight by their side. When they died, it only made me fight harder. And more recklessly."

"And then you died and became a Valkyrie." Gunhild followed my story to its natural conclusion. "But how did you not just travel to Valhalla?"

"Daughters of royalty sometimes become Valkyries when they die," I explained. She didn't seem to know that it was royalty who became Valkyries. What other lore had she failed to learn? I supposed she would learn more as we traveled, meeting gods and monsters on our way. It was exciting, in a way, to know that I would be the one to show her the world and all its facets. "It's the greatest honor to be bestowed upon a woman."

"How old were you?" Gunhild asked. "When you died, I mean."

"Sixteen," I replied, my head spinning a bit the more I revealed to her. The whole conversation felt like it had thrown my balance off. I hadn't thought about my own death in ages. Thinking about it now made me feel cold and alone, despite Gunhild's presence. "I was young and foolish, and died a fool's death, no matter how noble."

"How long ago?"

"I suppose it must be nearly two years now."

We sat in silence after that revelation, and I wondered what Gunhild must think.

Chapter Seven

THAT NIGHT and the next day passed more quickly than I would have liked. At least Gunhild seemed to move around more easily and looked brighter and more herself. By the time the sun set, she was fidgeting and looking repeatedly back into the cave, as if she could see our way to Yggdrasil if she stared hard enough.

We gathered our packs to leave the next morning. There was no telling how long we would have to travel in the darkness before we reached the Norns. It might have been days yet.

"Shall we?" Gunhild waved vaguely toward the cave.

"Are you sure?"

She nodded emphatically and doused the fire so I couldn't say no anymore. Though she may have been eager to head into the darkness, I was less so. The idea of hours or even days in a cave made my skin crawl, but it was necessary, so I shoved those feelings down as deep as I could.

I took the lead as we headed into the cave. I depended only on the tug of Yggdrasil to lead me down the right tunnel. Doubt niggled constantly at the nape of my neck as we traveled. Without the sun, we lost track of time in the darkness. The only light was that of our lanterns bouncing off veins of quartz running through the walls of the cave.

More than once, we nearly stumbled off a cliff and into the impossible depths below us. Clinging to the wall and taking slow, deliberate steps, we continued deeper and deeper into the black before us.

When one lantern flickered before going out, something suspiciously like a whimper came from Gunhild. No, I realized, it came from my own lips. My hands shook and my skin was pimpled with goosebumps, every muscle taut with fear. We had only one lantern left and it wouldn't be far behind the first one. If I had been afraid of the cave before, the idea of traversing it without light terrified me. We didn't know how much farther we would have to travel to get to the Norns, and I wondered if it wouldn't be best to turn back.

"How long do you think we have?" Gunhild's voice was close to my ear, her body heat warming me through our clothes. I appreciated the comfort of knowing I wasn't alone as I thought I would be when I began my journey. If I had to do this by myself, I wasn't sure I would survive with my sanity intact.

"Not long," I replied, when her lantern began to spit and hiss before it went out as well. It plunged us into darkness thicker than the night.

Unsure of how to proceed, I pulled Gunhild against the wall of the cave and held onto her as I slid down to the floor. We were stranded without light to keep us from tumbling to our deaths in an unseen subterranean canyon.

"What now?" Somehow, her voice didn't tremble. I didn't know how she maintained her bravery under the circumstances. I shrugged but then realized it was pointless in the pitch black.

"I don't know," I admitted. Leaning my shoulder against hers, I wondered how long it would be before she died of thirst. We still had our packs and there was enough there to last a few more days, but then she would die in the darkness. Once again, I considered whether we should turn back. Unsure of how long we had been traveling already, and unsure of how far we had left to go, I had to make a decision soon.

I didn't want to think about my eternity spent in the inky blackness. I had bought supplies simply to keep myself from the pain of hunger or thirst, despite them not being fatal to me. The more I thought about it though, the more I wondered if I even was still immortal now that I was exiled. Either way, with Gunhild on this journey, they would be all she had left to keep her alive.

I left Gunhild leaning against the wall and crept forward slowly on hands and knees, afraid of going over an invisible edge. It was important, though, to find some way forward. I wondered if I might somehow eventually crawl my way out of the cave to the Norns.

"Where are you going?" Gunhild asked, voice suddenly brittle with fear. "You aren't leaving me behind, are you?"

"No, of course not," I reassured her. "I was only trying to see if it might be possible to crawl to our destination."

"Do you think that might work?" Her voice was high, the uncertainty echoing through the cave.

"It would be difficult, but we might survive it if we're cautious."

"How will you know where to go?" Curiosity crept into her voice, though the fear didn't entirely seem to dissipate.

"I can still feel the tree," I said. "It's stronger than it was, so we can't be terribly far from it now."

"How far is not terribly far?" She scooted closer to me with a gravelly scuffling sound, as if touching would quash the fear we both felt and chase it away into the darkness. I searched blindly for her knee and laid a hand on it, tapping out a little pattern with my fingertips as if that could comfort her. Four taps, then a long press, then three more taps. She covered it with her own, squeezing slightly as if to reassure us both.

"I'm uncertain." I looked off toward our distant destination as if squinting hard enough would allow me to see it. I couldn't possibly know how far away it was, and with the darkness I was unsure how to tell time anyway, so I lied to Gunhild. "Another few hours."

"Hours?" She shuddered, and I was relieved the darkness hid her face. I tried to think of how to comfort her, how to make her believe that, somehow, we would find our way out of our dilemma. When I didn't immediately answer, she let out a ragged breath. "I suppose there's no other choice, is there?"

"We could try to turn back, but I think going forward is the right path," I said as I pulled away from her once more. "We won't be able to carry our full packs. We must eliminate everything but the absolute necessities."

"But we'll need those things when we get out of the cave!" Her shout echoed, which startled a colony of bats and left us huddling low to prevent any of them from getting tangled in our hair. "Sorry. I'll do whatever you think is best."

"I don't know what's best." Frustration made my throat tighten on a suppressed scream as I leaned my head back against the wall and closed my eyes. "I only know what we can't do, and that is crawling with our packs full of furs and cooking implements. For the time being, we'll have to keep our burdens minimal. It should all fit in one pack that we can drag behind us like a sled."

Gunhild must have nodded in the darkness because other than a slight rustling, I didn't hear a response from her. When she finally moved toward me, it was to pull a pack over to begin sorting through it. I did the same with the other pack to figure out what was dispensable.

It took us nearly half an hour to blindly feel every object, but we finally trimmed down our provisions into one pack and attached it to a pair of ropes that would allow one of us to drag it behind us. Other than a change of clothes for each of us, and two furs each to protect us against the cold, we kept only my sunstone, a pot to cook in, and as much food as would fit in one pack. Our weapons we kept on us, and our shields rested one on top of the other, tied to the pack. The rest would have to be left behind in the cave.

"Are you ready?" I asked, my voice no louder than the sound of water rushing somewhere in the distance. This was not a part of the quest I had anticipated, and I wondered how many other bumps would appear in the journey to prevent us or slow us from going where we needed to go.

"Yes," Gunhild said after a few moments. She shifted, and I pushed at her until she was in front of me, but she pushed back. "I can't go in front. I don't know where I'm going."

"You have to." I sat back on my heels. I wished her face wasn't hidden by the darkness. I reached out to squeeze her hand, and hopefully encourage her. "With that injury, I need to be sure I don't let you trail too far behind. You go in front. I trust you. And I'll tell you if we need to change directions. I'm pretty sure we can just go straight ahead. Be careful of any sudden drops, though. I really don't want you to fall. I couldn't help you if you did."

She swallowed with an audible gulp, but then leaned onto her hands and knees and crept forward. Her breath came in brief gasps. I reached out to grip her ankle whenever she paused as I followed close behind.

The musty smell of the cave had crept into my nostrils by then. The scent of wet stone and the occasional acrid tang of bat feces became overwhelming in the near silent darkness. It was almost a relief when Gunhild hummed a soft song to herself. It was the song I sang to the troll, so I supplied more made-up lyrics, both of us crawling along at a staccato rhythm through the cave. I would have paid a dear price for a fire, not only for warmth but for light and for some other smell and sound that didn't make me feel like we were in the belly of a great beast.

Chapter Eight

"STOP." I tugged at Gunhild's foot until she paused. Something had changed, and I needed a moment to determine what it was. The idea that we had survived the cave and might be close to the end of this arduous part of our journey made my heart leap with hope. "I think we're close. Feel under your hand."

"What is it?" Confusion edged the fear and exhaustion out of her voice.

"Wood." I ran my hand over the gnarled surface. The rough grain of the bark was a relief beneath my raw palms. "We're almost there. Look ahead, is that light, or are my eyes deceiving me?"

After a moment, she cried triumphantly, "Yes! It is light. And I can smell fire."

Our eyes adjusted to the small sliver of golden sunlight creeping into the cave from what seemed to be an exit. The ground at our feet was visible enough to stand and walk toward our destination. The damp smell of the cave was replaced by fresh air with a hint of bonfire spice. It was far warmer here than the outside world should be. My shoulders relaxed immediately, both from the warmth and the relief of being out of the cave. Some part of me had believed we might die in there.

"Hello?" I called out, stepping around Gunhild. The shieldmaiden gave me a frown that could have been worried or insulted, or both, as I passed her. I ignored it and walked cautiously toward the golden light. A shuffling came from the opening of the cave and I paused.

"Yrsa?" The childlike voice was joyous and high. It belonged to a young girl of ten or eleven summers, who peered back at us from outside the cave. "Oh, it is you! And your shieldmaiden, too. We've been waiting for you."

Gunhild pushed me forward, eager to get out of the dark cave and into the light. Stepping from the cave, I found myself speechless as I gazed up into the verdant boughs of Yggdrasil. Its multitude of immense branches expanded in every direction, including into the sky where it disappeared into the clouds above. At our feet were the burled roots, crawling over and under the earth like serpents. I knelt and pressed my hand into the trunk of the enormous tree. It seemed to vibrate, warm under my scraped palms.

"Welcome." Another woman stood over a well nearby, drawing up an overflowing bucket of water and setting it down beside her among the roots. Faint wrinkles lined her face, and a handful of silver strands ran through her raven dark hair. "Why did you take so long to arrive?"

"Their lanterns went out," said a third, wizened, old woman sitting before a loom. Her wry smile was missing several teeth. "I told you that, Verdandi. Why must you always doubt my words? I would wager neither Yrsa nor the shieldmaiden would question me, would you?"

"No, my lady." I bowed low to her and then to the others. The eldest of the three would be Urd, who knew the past. The middle one was Verdandi, who knew the present. The youngest was Skuld, who saw the future.

Gunhild came to my side, watching all three wide-eyed. I stifled a low laugh, which earned me an injured glare from the shieldmaiden. I should probably have been more in awe myself, considering I had never met the Norns either, but instead I was too focused on this part of my quest and the excitement that came with finding out what I needed to know to continue.

"Sit, sit," Verdandi urged us. We slid down Yggdrasil's trunk to sit on one of the larger roots. The bright summer sunlight filtered golden-green down through the verdant leaves, where squirrels and birds hopped about.

It was so warm compared to the cave, and the sun was much higher in the sky than it should have been for spring. Maybe it was always summer here. What a lovely way to spend one's eternity, never burdened by blinding snow and fierce winds, but instead gently warmed by the summer sunlight.

"You brought little with you." Skuld poked through the grimy bag we dragged through the cave behind us.

"Our lantern went out, and we had to crawl," I said. Skuld nodded knowingly, and I wondered what she saw. "We have enough food to last a little while, and we can always drink…"

"Snow?" Urd asked with a crackling laugh. "Don't worry yourself, there will be snow as you travel further from the tree. It's only at her base that it's always temperate. Are you thirsty now? You haven't had a drink since your lanterns went out. You must need to slake your thirst. Have some well-water."

Gunhild accepted the ladle from the child and took a long drink. Her eyes fluttered shut as if the water was the best thing she ever tasted. Skuld returned to the well for more and then brought it back to me.

I glanced at the other two Norns, whose disconcerting gazes settled on us like birds of prey, and took a sip from the water before taking the ladle and drinking the rest. I understood Gunhild's reaction to it then. It was as sweet as mead and nearly as cold as snow.

The crawl through the cave had exhausted me. My neck ached and my hands and knees were scraped raw. All of that faded away with each swallow of water. I felt rejuvenated, as if I never lacked an hour of sleep in my life or fought in any battle. In fact, the scrapes on my hands had healed by the time I thought to check them. I fought the urge to examine Gunhild's wolf bites, but I was sure they had healed as well.

"Are you feeling quite recovered now?" Urd asked from her place behind the loom. She was slight, and her hunched form made her that much smaller.

"Yes." I glanced over at Gunhild, who nodded emphatically. "Thank you."

"She's come for help." Skuld bounced up and down on her toes in anticipation. I couldn't help but smile indulgently at the child and her antics. It would be easy to forget she was an immortal oracle and not simply a little girl.

"Pardon her excitement." Verdandi smiled at the youngest Norn. "We so rarely have visitors who aren't gods. Although, I suppose a Valkyrie is close. Tell us why you've come."

"I suppose you already know."

"It would please us if you said what you were searching for." Urd's gnarled fingers were still nimble as she wove the tapestry that decided every creature's fate.

I suddenly found it difficult to recount my story. Shame settled over me and my words withered on my tongue.

Gunhild watched me carefully before speaking. Slowly, she told what happened to me as best she knew. The Norns ignored her, all three staring at me with curiosity in their eyes. Nothing I could say would surprise them, at least not until Gunhild mentioned what I had been told to find.

"The lost pieces of Freyja's armor," Verdandi murmured as her hands trailed along the trunk of Yggdrasil. "Nobody has known where they disappeared to for longer than you can imagine. No one has had the courage to seek them out, not even the gods."

"Please." I hated to plead. My voice sounded desperate in my ears. "I must find them, and you are the only ones who might help me."

"Of course we'll help." Skuld glanced back and forth between her elders. "But you have to know, the quest will be danger-laden, nothing you want to take on lightly."

"And our help comes at a cost," Verdandi added cryptically.

"I will pay whatever the price is," I replied with a solemn nod. "I must find the armor regardless of the cost."

"Come, then." Urd rose with a put-upon sigh. Pointing the way down a shaded path, she motioned for us to go ahead of her. "At least feed them first."

The Norns followed behind us as we frequently checked over our shoulders to see if they still followed. It wasn't long before we reached a small cottage with a thatched roof and deep-set windows beneath the heavy eaves. It had been decorated with the same blue and amber as people in Midgard used to decorate the homes of seers and vala.

As we grew close, Skuld dashed past us and opened the door to let us in. The interior was cool and dark, lit only by the filtered sunlight creeping in through the small windows. Three small looms stood on one side of the room and a large kitchen was on the other side. In between them were pillows strewn haphazardly across the floor, upon which they directed us to sit.

"I do hope fish is adequate," Verdandi said, fetching a plate from the kitchen. Gunhild nodded and politely smiled as Verdandi handed her the plate, which was heaped high with food. The aroma of freshly baked bread, honeyed parsnips, and roasted fish made my stomach gurgle to remind me how long it had been since we last ate.

We enjoyed the freshly cooked food silently for a long while, the only interruption when Skuld rose to bring bread and mead to us. A fire crackled nearby on the stone hearth, and the smell of smoke wafted lightly through the small room.

"We would offer you apples, but. . ." Skuld trailed off. She glanced at Urd and then down quickly.

"They're the apples of Idunn." I didn't need her explanation to deduce that riddle. They wouldn't give up their ration of apples, which made them immortal, a meal shared only with the gods and Valkyries. Or, at least, Valkyries who weren't in exile. I wondered what would become of me without them. The Norns all frowned sympathetically.

"Thank you for understanding." Urd rose stiffly to take our empty plates. When she returned to sit before us, she let out a small exhale before speaking. "Now, I suppose you'd like your fate."

"Tell me," I begged them, my eyes wide and pleading.

"We won't tell you your fate, but only what you seek from us," Verdandi said. "And you must give us something of value as a fair trade. It is tradition."

My hand went to the bronze torc at my throat. The intricately braided metal with carved dragons at each end had been a comfort since Eryk was stolen from me. Was it something I was willing to part with for the sake of finding Eryk? I had little else to barter with.

Urd gave a soft snort. "Oh yes. That will do nicely. Not only was it his to give, but he gave it as a symbol of love." When my head shot up in horror, she gave a rasping cackle. I shook my head and gripped the torc tightly. Now I doubted whether I could bear to part with it. "Or you can simply leave our home, leave Yggdrasil, and hope you can find your way on your own."

I searched Gunhild's face as if she might offer a solution, or advice, anything really. She grimaced and shrugged helplessly. I had to either relinquish the torc or give up my quest. I would sooner die than give up on my quest to save Eryk.

"You may have it." My voice cracked as I spoke. Skuld extended a small hand and waited patiently for me to turn my treasure over. At first, I couldn't remove it, much less let it go. My hands shook as I slowly took it from my neck and my fingers brushed lovingly over the cool metal.

With a clenched jaw, I passed the necklace to the child, which she gently took and handed to Verdandi. Verdandi passed the torc to Urd who, to my surprise, slipped it around her own neck. I gritted my teeth together against thoughts of what Eryk would say if he knew I gave up such a precious gift for the chance to save him. He might be angry to think I valued information more than his love. Or he could be grateful I was willing to give away something so precious to me just to save him.

"We shall tell you now what you have come to us to ask," Verdandi said, her gaze shifting to Skuld.

My heart raced, beating furiously against my ribs.

Skuld's eyes were distant. Her lips moved without sound. When she finally spoke, it was in a language I didn't understand. A frown creased my brow as I tried to identify it. Unable to translate, I returned my attention to Verdandi. It was Urd, though, who made known what Skuld said.

"The first piece is Fjodfeld, Freyja's falcon cloak, a feathered garment which allows its owner to take flight. You may find it to the east in Alfheim with the elves," Urd said, almost in a chant. "Next is her helm, Gull-hjalm. This object allows the owner to predict the choices of one's opponents. It may be found north from there in Nidavellir, among the dwarves."

"And the other pieces?" Gunhild asked softly. Skuld's blind eyes turned toward Gunhild, but looked right through her. Again, she spoke in that unplaceable language. Urd continued to translate.

"The final piece is Brisingamen, Freyja's prized necklace made those who were exposed to it more impressionable and acquiescent toward its owner. It shall be found among the Jotuns," she revealed. The idea of being among giants frightened me, and I glanced at Gunhild, worried to see her expression. She merely seemed curious. "Travel to Jotunheim and fight for the rights to the necklace. Only then will you take possession of it from the giant Mimir."

"Will I win?" I asked in a small, scared voice.

"You will both fight valiantly in Jotunheim. And Brisingamen will be yours when this is all over," Verdandi told me with a slight smile tugging at her lips. What was it she found so amusing? Although Skuld continued to speak, the elder Norns translated nothing more.

"But will I succeed in my quest for the cloak and the helm as well? The maiden didn't say that I would with those," I said, frustrated beyond words.

"Skuld may see that, but if she told you, it could change your fate," Verdandi warned me. "We can't allow that to happen."

"Yes, mother." I bowed my head. "Thank you. And thank you, maiden. With the help you have offered, we might survive this quest."

"Move beyond the tree now." Urd ignored my last statement. "That's how you'll pass into Alfheim."

"How will we know where to search in each of these realms?" I asked.

Urd frowned, as did the other two.

"I suppose you'll have to figure that out once you get there," Verdandi said in an almost cryptic voice. "Now, leave us. You've taken what you truly needed, and it's time for you to begin your journey."

All three flicked their hands in the door's direction. The youngest smiled as we left, although her eyes were still slightly unfocused.

Gathering our meager pack, Gunhild and I slowly headed out the door. I spared a passing glance back at the cottage, hiked the pack up higher on my shoulder, and departed from the Norns.

Chapter Nine

Summer gradually faded as we traveled away from Yggdrasil. Snow began to fall again, the temperature dropped drastically, and eventually, we were plunged into knee-deep snowdrifts once more. Part of me wished we had been able to stay with the Norns. At least for a good night's rest.

Gunhild chattered at random, her stories of battles and her childhood a welcome respite from the eerie silence of the snow-blanketed forest. The Norns gave us no sign of how long the journey to Alfheim would take. I had to finish this quest by midsummer, so we had to hope it would only take days or weeks instead of months and months.

"I'm going to hunt," I told Gunhild on the fifth day. "Can you find root vegetables and mushrooms?"

"I can try," she replied. Her bright smile lit the late afternoon gloom and warmed me from the inside out.

The woods were a strange combination of comforting and terrifying at that hour. The slanting sunlight left deep shadows among the trees that skulked through the forest as the sun crept toward the horizon. I listened carefully for the sound of movement and scanned the snow to find any sign of tracks.

When I found bear tracks, I realized I'd left Gunhild alone and defenseless other than her axe. But she was a shieldmaiden and could fight it off if necessary, so I let the worry pass. If my hunt was unsuccessful, I would have to lay snares and hope to catch something.

Off to my right, a limb cracked. It was probably a tree giving way to the weight of the snow. Then a brief snort came. I wasn't alone in the woods. A hulking shape hunched beneath the low-hanging branch of a large, leafless oak tree. It stood to its full height as it came face to face with me. I swallowed hard and realized that though I told myself Gunhild could hold her own in a fight against a bear, I was no longer certain of my own ability to do so.

The bear sniffed the air, lowering its head and growling low in its throat as it caught sight of me. I raised my chin and pulled my axe. As I reached behind me for my shield, I cursed. It was still at our campsite.

The bear stomped and prepared to charge me. I planted my feet and took a tighter grip on my axe. It barreled toward me, and I only hoped that I would get in a killing blow before it swiped its massive claws at me. I pushed my fear down and let resolve take its place. I refused to die without finishing my quest to save Eryk.

Moving faster than seemed possible for such a lumbering creature, the bear roared and gnashed its teeth at me. Somehow, despite its speed and ferocity, I hacked gracelessly at its throat and a torrent of blood spilled forth. The bear's dead weight pushed a pained grunt from me as it pinned me to the ground when it fell.

I tried multiple times to push the suffocating weight off me, but it was no use. Until Gunhild came searching for me, I was hopelessly stuck. Sticky, copper-tasting blood covered my face, and I struggled to breathe between it and the bear collapsed on my chest. I tried to shout for Gunhild but didn't have enough breath to make anything more than a groan.

It seemed unlikely that I would die simply from having a bear fall on top of me, but my thoughts still scrambled around what would happen should I die on this quest instead of succeeding. I had worried so much about Gunhild, I had forgotten about myself. Where would I go if I died? Would I go to Valhalla or the underworld?

The time before Gunhild found me slipped by as slowly as the bear's blood that dripped upon me. When she saw me, she cried out, panic painted like a mask upon her face. Her breath came in desperate gasps as she tried to find a way to unpin me. Gunhild's panic gave her more strength than I realized she had in her. With berserker rage, she pushed the bear off my chest so I could sit up.

"Gods! I thought you were dead." Gunhild placed her hand on her heart as if to feel if it was still beating. "What in Odin's name happened?"

"Bear." I huffed the answer because it should be obvious. "Was hunting. Slashed its throat and it fell on me. You have water?"

With a nod, the shieldmaiden quickly passed me a water flask. After I drank, I scrubbed my face and neck with it to clean the blood from my skin. When I'd regained my breath, I stood up slowly with her help. Worry etched her face, her eyes almost haunted with it. I let loose a reassuring laugh, which helped her to relax.

"Don't worry for me," I told her with a rueful smile. "It will be harder to kill me than that. I can't die until I've found the armor and retrieved Eryk from the underworld. I won't leave you behind on my quest, I swear. Not even in death."

Gunhild returned my smile and took my hand. Our fingers laced together as we walked back to camp and silence settled comfortably between us. As much of a panic as she had been in from seeing me trapped under the bear, she seemed to have relaxed with my oath.

I regretted not finding any prey for us to make a meal of, other than the bear. It would take too long to field dress the beast, even if we only took a portion of the meat. Hopefully, Gunhild had found something edible for us in the meantime. Later, I would put out snares. It would force us to remain there, but it wasn't wise to move on without proper food in our bellies.

"Are you truly recovered?" Gunhild gave me a sidelong glance as we walked back to camp. "Unwounded?"

"Indeed. I'm well." I smiled for her benefit. "After your attack by the wolf, I wouldn't hide such an injury from you."

She nodded skeptically, but let the topic go. Instead, she opened the small bag she'd brought with her to collect food for our supper. Inside were two large turnips, a couple of mushrooms, and a handful of berries on top, which were mostly unblemished. I gave an appreciative nod and pulled a small pot from our pack. The mushrooms and turnips would make a decent stew and the berries would be good as they were, or made into tea.

While Gunhild prepared our meal, I found a bit of twine and began making snares to place around our camp hoping to catch rabbits or other small game. It was guesswork for me, as I was never taught how. After several attempts, I was satisfied. I left Gunhild by the fire to wander back into the woods to lay my traps.

I worried there might be other dangerous beasts in these woods who would hunt me, but my luck held, and I made it back to camp with no further dangers. We sat quietly over our meal, deep in our own thoughts. I didn't know what Gunhild was thinking, but for myself, thoughts of Eryk twisted through my mind as they often did. I ran over the places where the Norns directed me to seek the pieces Freyja's armor and repeated them over and over in my mind, so I wouldn't forget them. My heart stuttered to a stop when I thought of Eryk in the underworld, tormented in Hel's realm.

I had heard stories of Nastrond, where the dishonorable dead spent eternity surrounded by the bones of long dead creatures. Whispers of the torture they may face had been kept from children, but I had heard enough to imagine the types of eternal torment he might be subjected to.

"Yrsa?" Gunhild saying my name brought me back to the present. She frowned deeply in concern. "Are you feeling well?"

"Yes, of course," I replied, although I wasn't certain it was entirely true. "Don't worry about me, shieldmaiden. I'm planning our trip."

"Do you hear something in one of your snares? Or is my belly simply inventing it?"

I perked up and listened carefully for the sounds of a struggle. And yes, there it was, the squealing of a rabbit or weasel. My stomach rumbled loudly and urged me to retrieve my prey and return to the fire. The realization that I had been successful, even at something so seemingly trivial, buoyed my spirits and gave me hope that this journey wouldn't be quite as difficult as I feared.

It didn't take long at all for the large hare to cook over the fire, and we ate ravenously as if we hadn't had food in days. When we sat back, Gunhild stared at me over the fire before coming to sit beside me.

"You're quite worried about him, aren't you?" she asked softly, her eyes focused on the fire at first before moving to my face.

"Yes, I am." I smiled ruefully as I met her gaze and nodded.

"We'll free him." She held her hand over her heart. "I vow to help you in any way I can, no matter where this journey takes us."

"Why?" I tilted my head and stared at her as if the answers were in her face. I still didn't understand why she had decided she must fight by my side through this quest. Some small part of me wondered if fate had sent her to me so I wouldn't have to face this impossible path alone. But that was silly. Fate had already dealt me enough blows, surely it wouldn't turn around and help me now. "You don't know me, and yet you stand by my side as if we've fought together for a lifetime. I don't get it."

"You're a valiant Valkyrie in a dangerous position, and I admire what you've sworn to do. We've faced frightening situations and even death together now. I can't put my finger on exactly why I feel so loyal to you, but whatever it is, you have my oath, my axe, and, if need be, my life."

"You're too dedicated," I warned her. The idea that this whole thing very well could cost Gunhild her life frightened me. We hadn't known each other long, but I knew, in my heart, that if something happened to her, I would feel more than just guilt. "I don't require your life and wish you wouldn't offer it. It makes me worry for you, and I can't do that, not if I'm to succeed in my quest."

"Well, you have it whether you like it or not. I would be dead anyway, were it not for you. You'll have to live with the fact that I'm by your side until the end." She lifted her chin and a broad smile spread across her face. She truly was a welcome brightness in an otherwise impossibly black midnight of doubt.

It was early enough in the day by the time we finished, so we moved on. Our single pack was light. Too light. And it had only been a few days since we left Yggdrasil. I was hyper-aware that we had nowhere near the provisions we would need for our journey, but there was little to be done for it until we found a village or town in which to purchase more. I only hoped Eryk's silver cuffs would be enough.

Chapter Ten

THREE WEEKS of travel had passed since we left the Norns, with no telling how much lay ahead of us. We'd been forced to hunt and forage for our meals and to drink melted snow since we were out of all of our supplies.

A meager path crept out of the snowy woods and as we continued, it widened. Someone had purposely cleared the hard packed dirt beneath our feet. Ahead of us, the trees opened up, revealing a large village. I breathed a small sigh of relief and my spirits rose at the sight. We would be able to purchase provisions and rest for a while. As we walked into the outskirts of the village, we received curious smiles and nods of the head from the residents.

The town was small, and the houses were cramped together as if for warmth against the brutal winds of winter. Large trees protected them from the worst of the snow.

"Hello," a little girl said to us from seemingly out of nowhere. She bounced in front of us until her mother pulled her back.

"Hello," I replied to her, with an almost wary smile. One never knew what to expect in a new place, and I still wasn't entirely used to being mortal yet. Gunhild, however, reacted with a smile that matched the child's.

Her mother bowed her head to me. "You're not from here."

"No, we're not. We…" I trailed off, unsure how to say where we were from or how we needed their help. I hoped they wouldn't ask too many questions about us, because I wouldn't know how to answer them if I tried.

"You both look tired," the woman said. Her face was kind, and she waved us toward a small cottage near the edge of the town. "You can rest here."

"Oh, no, we can't stay in your home. We're strangers." My surprise at her hospitality had to be evident on my face. Gunhild's eyes had widened as well, and she glanced between the pair and myself.

The woman laughed and the skin around her pale gray eyes crinkled. "We often have travelers here. This is merely a guest house for those who pass through. For a few hours or days, you may rest here. And when you've rested, you can meet our jarl if you like. He always likes to meet new people."

"Thank you," I replied hesitantly. The door she opened led into a small, warm home, filled to the brim with well-loved furniture and threadbare tapestries along the walls to keep in the heat of the fire. We followed her inside, and I set our pack down near the door.

The girl, who must have been around seven or eight summers old, went to kindle a fire on the hearth. She gave us a shy smile, which I did my best to return. Gunhild wiggled her fingers at the girl, who brightened at the attention.

"What are your names?" the girl asked, her voice and expression filled with curiosity as she watched me wander the tiny space.

"Yrsa, and this is Gunhild," I replied. The time for patronyms would come later, if they asked at all. "What is yours?"

"Hjordis! It means sword goddess." She was obviously proud of her name, and my smile in response was genuine. Her shyness came and went in such a charming way. "And Mama's name is Signy."

"We are honored to meet both of you," Gunhild said with a polite bow of her head to each of them.

"As are we to meet you," Signy said as she turned back to me from arranging some cushions on the floor before the fire. "I hope you will both be comfortable here. We try to make it nice. There is food in the cupboards and a well is in the center of the village. I'll have someone bring you some water in a little while."

"You are too kind," I said, unsure how to behave in polite company anymore. I defaulted back to my Valhalla manners in the absence of any other way to act. "We'll take our things into the bed chamber so they aren't lying out here in the way. I wouldn't want to clutter up this nice place."

Nodding, Signy led Hjordis to the door. "Then we will let you be. Make yourself comfortable. I am in the first house across the road from this one. My door is lilac purple. You cannot miss it. If you need anything at all, you must let us know so we can accommodate you."

Hjordis waved to us after we thanked them for their generosity and then she and her mother closed the door behind them. I sagged onto the nearby cushions. Dropping my face into my hands, I sighed. Weeks of travel, combined with Gunhild's injury and my worry for Eryk, were catching up with me, and I hardly knew how to surmount it all.

"They seemed very kind," Gunhild said as she plopped onto the cushions beside me. "I don't know about you, but I could use a rest. I can sleep here on the floor if you want to sleep in the bed."

"You take the bed," I suggested. "I want to get some fresh air."

"If you're sure," Gunhild said with a squint of her eyes. "Don't be gone long."

The marketplace I visited that afternoon was small and cozy, with the sellers gathered for warmth around their stalls. I walked through, making note of the supplies that were available here that we would need to purchase before we left. It was a relief to see that there were so many options.

When I neared one table, its owner, who sold fur and wool cloaks, rushed over to see what I might buy. I gave my apologies and moved on to the next, where a woman cooked fresh venison over an open fire. Fresh bread sat on the side as well, steaming in the cold. She offered me some of each, and when I told her I couldn't afford it, she made me take a little bit anyway.

As I walked between the various stalls, I noticed a dark-eyed man watching me. His hair was a darker red than Gunhild's, and his gaze was unsettling. It never left me, even when I met it. Was he curious, or something worse? Finally, fed up with being stared at, I approached the man.

"Can I help you?" I asked, a little more sarcasm in my voice than was entirely necessary. I didn't enjoy being the center of attention on the best of days, and today my patience was thin. Besides, I felt like he was stalking me somehow, and it left a nasty feeling in the pit of my stomach.

"I don't know, can you?" the man said with a laugh. It was the old response, but it irked me, and I glowered at him. "You're new here."

"Yes. And?" My hackles were up; annoyed by the gall he had to stare at me as if he owned me.

He raked his fingers through his hair and shrugged. "I'm new too, though not as new as you are. Nice to see another visitor and how they treat one, is all." He spoke with relaxed ease, as if nothing in the world bothered him. "At least they're the same with everyone. It was making me suspicious."

"Suspicious?" I asked as my eyebrows rose. Their hospitality had felt strange, but not enough to make me suspect anything was truly awry. "You think they aren't what they seem?"

"Nah, they probably are, I'm just the suspicious type," he replied with another loud laugh, which garnered attention from the shopkeepers. He smiled at one before waving me away from the market. I followed hesitantly, unsure if he was the real danger here. Once we reached a more private area, away from the nosy villagers, he leaned in with a conspiratorial whisper. "I think they know who I am."

I gave him a blank stare. Was I supposed to know who he was? I searched his face to see if I recognized him, which made him laugh again.

"You don't have a clue who I am, do you? I would have figured someone like you would recognize me." He tilted his head, as if waiting for recognition to hit me. It didn't.

"No, not an inkling," I said with a shrug. Honestly, I couldn't care less if he was Odin unless he could get me to Eryk somehow. More than anything, his amusement at my expense annoyed me. And what in the world did he mean by *someone like you*? I hoped it wasn't a jab at how dirty and tired I probably looked. "Who are you?"

"It should insult me that you don't know who I am. You play among the gods. Surely you should know." He pretended to be hurt, but it was nothing more than teasing. My lips parted in surprise. Surely, he couldn't know that I wasn't just any traveler. "Oh yes, Valkyrie, I would know you anywhere. Your kind always has a certain..." He waved a hand, as if unable to come up with the right word.

"I do not play with the gods like you say. I know Hel and Freyja. I see Odin at the nightly feast, but we have never spoken. Few come to Valhalla." It was frustrating that he knew what I was, but I had no idea who he might be. I gave him a sideways glance as I tried to figure out why I should know him. Red hair... good humor. It came together.

"Ah, there it is. You've figured me out, Valkyrie." He chuckled and tugged at one of my curls as if teasing a child. I batted his hand away with a scowl.

"I think so. But why would Loki be in a tiny village in the middle of nowhere?" If this really was Loki, I couldn't figure out why he would be here, of all places. Nor did I understand if he was here specifically for me, or if it was just a coincidence. I wasn't sure I believed in coincidences anymore.

"Boredom, curiosity. You know how it is. Asgard can be so dull." He did a cheerful twirl, and when I didn't laugh, he huffed in frustration. "You're boring too. Too much time doing your job and not enough playing."

"It was failing to do my job that put me in this position to begin with. Have you noticed there's no battle nearby for me to reap the dead from?" My jaw clenched in annoyance and I looked away.

"Oh yes, I noticed that." He paused as if to examine me closer. "Didn't do your job, you say? Tell me more. You've made me curious."

"No."

"Did you really refuse a *god*?" He put a hand to his chest as if I'd injured him and stumbled back a step. But the laughter still twinkled in his eyes. "Come now, Valkyrie, I've revealed myself to you. The least you can do is tell me your story. Or do I have to guess? I'm quite a wonderful storyteller of my own, you know. I bet I could make up something better than reality."

"Then make up your own story. I'm not handing mine out to anyone for entertainment." I turned to walk away, but he put a firm hand on my shoulder. I shrugged it off angrily and took another few steps away, not willing to tolerate his playfulness. I was already tired and irritable, and now I was furious as well.

"Is it so awful, then?" His voice took on a gentleness I wouldn't have expected possible from a trickster god. I eyed him warily. His expression shifted and became sympathetic. "It is. By Odin, what have they put you through for their amusement?"

"As if you wouldn't have done the same, given the chance." My voice came out sharper than I meant for it to, and I winced. Hopefully, he wouldn't strike me down or turn me into a rat. I crossed my arms over my chest defensively and stared at him, as if challenging him to smite me.

"I toy with the gods, who always deserve it. I rarely toy with anyone else, unless they also deserve it. And by the look on your face, I doubt you do." He leaned against the wall, folding his arms in a mirror of my posture. "Come now, what can it hurt to tell me your story? Maybe I can help."

"Why would you want to help me?" I asked, more suspicious of his kindness than I had ever been of the villagers. Loki was known for his misdeeds, and I didn't want to fall for one of them if I could help it. I was already in enough trouble.

"Because I'm bored, and you seem sad. I don't like it when people are sad. Especially not pretty little Valkyries. Talk to me, lovely. Tell me what's happened."

"*Don't* call me lovely," I growled. "I don't want to talk about it."

"That bad?" His voice took on a gentle quality, the laughter gone from his eyes. My frustration must have been written on my face, because he approached me again and put his hand on my upper arm, squeezing lightly. "I'll tell you what. Come with me, and you can tell me all about it over a drink."

Against my better judgment, I nodded and allowed him to take me by the arm and lead me further from the marketplace. I probably shouldn't even be alone in a room with him, lest he toy with me like one of the gods. I had heard stories of his tricks and mischief and I didn't want to end up on the wrong side of one of them. It would be safer to just get Gunhild and get out of town. But we needed to stock up on supplies. And something whispered in the back of my mind that I should trust him. At least for now.

His house was closer to the center of town, practically next door to the mead hall where the jarl must have lived. He silently opened the door and held it for me to go inside.

"Have a seat. I'll find mead." He directed me to a chair while he searched for a jug and cups. My gaze flitted over the space as I did what I was told. It was much more spacious than the home the townsfolk had lent me, but he must have been there longer. He was quite at home. There were piles of clutter everywhere, and dishes scattered throughout the space where he had eaten and not cleaned up after himself.

"How long have you been in—" I realized I didn't know the name of the village, and flushed deeply.

"Armvind," he supplied. I leaned back in my chair and tried to seem more relaxed even if I was wound as tightly as a snare waiting to be tripped. "Six months now? I think? Time is strange in Midgard, is it not?"

"Yes, I suppose it is." I had quite lost track of how much time had already passed on my quest, like I lost track of how long Eryk and I were together before Hel took him from me. This lack of awareness could be my downfall, considering the midsummer deadline Hel had given.

"What are you doing away from Valhalla, Valk—What is your name? I can't keep calling you Valkyrie." He came over with cups of mead and handed me one before slouching down across from me in a patchwork orange chair.

"Yrsa, and… I'm…" I hesitated, the truth sparking on my tongue. He leaned forward in his chair to wait for me to reveal it. I shouldn't tell him, but my whole body ached to share my story with someone who actually had the power—and maybe the desire—to help me. "I'm exiled."

"What have you been doing since then?" He was more curious about my time in Midgard than he was about why Hel exiled me, which made me more nervous than I already was, though I tried not to show it. If I told him my plight and then he used it to hurt me, or worse, Gunhild, I would never be able to forgive myself.

"Searching," I said simply and took a sip of the mead. I hoped if I stayed vague enough, he would quit asking questions.

"For… a way back?"

"No, that's never going to happen," I said.

That wasn't enough of an explanation for him, because he leaned forward, a curious glint in his eyes. I gave in to the urge to talk, and let more of the truth slip out.

I sighed. "Hel exiled me because I let someone live. She cursed him to Nastrond."

"Unless you what?" Of course he would know there was always a catch, always a way out. It was the way of the gods.

"Find the lost pieces of Freyja's armor."

"Why in the world would Hel want that?" Loki asked, though I thought it was more to himself than to me. He tapped his fingers on the rim of his cup as he stared at me thoughtfully. "You didn't ask?"

"Well, no, I wouldn't question my mistress. It would be wrong." Why hadn't I? Was I afraid? It would be hard for Hel to do anything worse than she already had.

"And so, you've been seeking the armor since then. That must have been…well, a while if you've lost track of time." He searched my expression, as if the clues might lie in it. "Have you found any of it yet?"

"Maybe," I hedged. If Hel wanted it so badly, how did I know he didn't want it too? But here he was, not poking fun at me or twisting my words for his own purposes. He just wanted to know what happened.

"Come now, if you can't trust a trickster god when he is being earnest, who can you trust?" he asked, and raised his hands to show he was innocent. I didn't respond, but raised an eyebrow. "Valkyrie…talk to me. I swear I won't trick you or tease you. Just tell me the truth. Sate my curiosity."

"I'm not your entertainment. Just because you're bored, doesn't mean I'm going to give you everything you ask for. Why should I trust you?" I asked with a frown. If I told him, though, I might be able to convince him to help me.

"Because it's something I can annoy Hel about. I like to annoy her. She's always so serious."

"Sorry, that's not good enough for me," I said, though a plan was formulating in my mind. "What if I told you, in exchange for your help?"

"What kind of help?" Loki asked, his head tilting curiously as his eyes widened a little.

"The kind of help that gets me through this quest and lets me find what I'm looking for," I said. If I spun this right, if I teased the truth well enough, he would agree to assist us.

"What do you think I can do to help?" he asked, watching me interestedly as I tried to come up with a way to convince him. I honestly wasn't even sure how to answer his question. What might he be able to do to help?

"Well, you're a god. I'm sure there's plenty," I pointed out, avoiding a straight answer. If Loki could be evasive, so could I.

"Fine," he said, all too easily. "I'll help however I can, if you let me come with you."

"Right. As if you would ever do anything if there wasn't something in it for you." It was too simple, he had agreed with very little fight and I didn't trust that he meant it.

"That's not very kind to say," Loki said with a deep frown, as if I had truly upset him. "No, Valkyrie. You asked for help. I want to help. For once in my existence, I want to do some good. And besides, Hel is the worst of us, and yet I'm the one with that reputation. Why shouldn't she have to pay for it?"

"The worst?" I asked, my brow knitting in confusion. I knew plenty about Hel, but I had always just thought of her as an inevitable force. She wasn't evil, I didn't think, though now he had me questioning everything I thought I knew.

"You have no idea," Loki said. "Why do you think she wants

Freyja's armor? And here you're willing to simply give it to her. Everyone sees her as inevitable, but nothing is inevitable."

"I don't have a choice. There is no other way to get Eryk back." My frustration grew, and with it my anger crept back in. I wasn't here to be judged by someone like Loki.

"Then let me help you like you asked," he said, pushing harder. He was becoming exasperated with me. I had to tread carefully if I really wanted his help. If a god was offering assistance, even if he was the trickster, it would be stupid not to take him up on it. Though I had to wonder what the cost would be.

"I don't know… I'm not sure I trust you."

"I never said you had to. You're the one who asked for help, though. You should trust someone who probably hates Hel as much as you must." His expression was almost hopeful, which gave me pause. If he truly did want to help me, whether he had ulterior motives or not, it seemed stupid to pass up the opportunity. And he was right, I had asked. I had just expected him to refuse, or at least to require some convincing.

"Why do you hate Hel so much?" I asked, trying to buy more time to think about whether I really meant it when I asked for help.

"She's haughty, overconfident. She thinks she is better than all of us because she controls life and death, or so she thinks."

"So she thinks?"

"Well, the Norns decide really, and humans. They have choices they make, which the Norns use to determine their lifeline. It's very complicated, of course." He shrugged and smiled at me. "Trust me, she deserves to be knocked down a peg or two."

"And you would help me if it means you get to knock her down?"

"Sure, why not? I get some amusement. And of course, you get to seek out the armor—do you know where it is?"

"The armor? Sort of. Do you?" If Loki knew, why would he not have told Freyja?

"Not exactly, but I have heard rumors aplenty. The helm is likely with the dwarves and the falcon cloak seems like something the elves would like. They like pretty things. Not Brisingamen pretty, but pretty enough."

"Yes, that's what the Norns told us," I said, before I realized what I was revealing. I flushed deeply when he sat up in response.

"Ah, so you were smart enough to go to Yggdrasil, were you?" Loki noted curiously. "And on top of that, you're not on this quest alone. Who would you risk bringing with you on something so dangerous?"

I felt guiltier than before about bringing Gunhild with me, now that he'd reiterated how dangerous it would be. My expression must have reflected my guilt, because his eyebrow shot up in response.

"She's a shieldmaiden, and probably a better fighter than I am. And she insisted I bring her, so even if I had tried to get rid of her, it probably would have been impossible." I realized I wouldn't even have made it this far without her. Her attitude and demeanor kept me from despairing in the darkest moments.

"Interesting," Loki said as he tipped his head to one side. "Can I meet her?"

"Why would you want to meet her?"

"Because it takes a very brave person to take on someone else's dangerous quest," Loki replied. "I like brave people. Come on, what could it hurt? Maybe talking to her will give me more ideas for how you can succeed. Besides, aren't you curious how a mortal will react to meeting a god?"

"I never said she was mortal!" I protested.

"Pfft, of course she's mortal, or you would have said otherwise when I called her brave." Loki hopped up from his chair and went to the door.

"I'll introduce you, but only because we need your help," I conceded, and pushed past him to lead the way to the cottage where Gunhild waited.

Chapter Eleven

When we reached the door to the cottage, Loki looked at me expectantly until I opened the door and stepped inside. Gunhild sat in a chair, sharpening her axe. Her entire world was about to be flipped upside down, but I wasn't sure how to warn her.

Loki bounded over to her and flopped on the chair beside hers. His elbows on the armrest, he rested his chin in his hands to inspect her.

"Gunhild, this is Loki," I introduced him. It was rather awkward, considering he wasn't just any random person. This was the God of Mischief himself.

Gunhild's eyes widened, and she stared at me for several seconds before turning to Loki in disbelief.

"It's the red hair, isn't it?" Loki tugged at one of her braids. "Red hair always inspires trust."

Gunhild slapped his hand away before she remembered that he was a god. Her gaze quickly dropped to the floor in obeisance, which caused Loki to laugh. I almost laughed myself, but stopped before I embarrassed her. She couldn't help her natural reaction to being teased, but she also couldn't help the way she immediately cowered before him in fear. Gods were unpredictable at best, and unlike me, she had never met one.

"Don't worry, little shieldmaiden, I won't smite you for striking me. Any friend of a Valkyrie is a friend of mine."

"Thank you," Gunhild murmured, which earned her a wider grin. I nodded at her encouragingly, hoping she would relax at least a little now that she knew he wasn't a danger to her. "Um… how? That is, how did you come to be here? Where we are?"

"Oh, it's a pure coincidence, I assure you," Loki said. "But when I saw a Valkyrie in the market, I just had to introduce myself. And now that I know about her quest. She asked me to help and I agreed to."

"Why?"

"Does it matter?" Loki asked with a slight cock of his head.

"I'd like to know the cost of your help," Gunhild replied, glancing sideways at me. She was wiser than me in some ways, despite being younger and more innocent. She was asking questions I should have.

"Why must there be a cost? Can a god not help someone out of an awful place now and then? I doubt you asked the Norns what their cost was," Loki said in a wounded tone.

"The Norns aren't tricksters," Gunhild pointed out. "And besides, there *was* a cost."

"Interesting," Loki admitted before turning to me. "What do you think the cost is? Or, more interestingly, what do you think it should be?"

"I don't know. I have nothing left to give," I said. What in the world could I possibly offer a god that he didn't already have access to? I wondered if I should offer him an oath of allegiance or my soul or some other intangible but invaluable token.

"That does put a damper on things, but I don't think I mind," Loki said with an appreciative nod. There was no telling what he might ask for instead. I prepared for some impossible task to surmount on top of the existing impossible quest. I was surprised when he didn't ask for anything special. "Perhaps I am searching for adventure myself. I've been in this little village for far too long. I'll go with you and help you find the armor and you can entertain me."

"We're not here for your entertainment," Gunhild said.

Loki pouted and crossed his arms over his chest like a petulant child. "I'm not asking for much, not even a piece of the armor." I laughed loudly, which earned me a scathing glare from him. His scowl quickly bubbled up into a laugh instead.

"It will mostly be a boring journey," I said, as if trying to dissuade him. But internally, I was elated that I had somehow convinced him to help us. "There will be times of danger too, though I suppose those wouldn't bother you a bit. Most of it will be traveling from one place to the next, nothing exciting. Only hunting and walking."

"You need horses, is what you need." Loki lit up a little at the idea. "That would speed up your entire journey."

"We can't afford horses, Loki," I told him. "I have very little silver left and that will have to go toward supplies."

"Oh, I bet the jarl would give you some if you promised to return with some sort of compensation," Loki suggested. "He's my friend, after all. Seriously, just stay for a while, until we can get you horses. There's no rush, is there?"

"Well, there is, but… we probably do need to rest." I doubted it was a wise choice. Eryk waited for me in the underworld, and I only had until midsummer to find all the armor.

"Then you'll both remain here until you're well-rested, and in the meantime, we'll convince the jarl to provide you with free horses." Loki bounced on his toes with excitement.

"No," Gunhild spoke up. "We need to do what we set out to do. I don't need rest."

"You've got a long way to go, and have already traveled quite a long way to begin with by my guess," Loki said with a chuckle. "Trust me, you need rest. A few days added to your quest won't hurt anyone. Time doesn't pass normally in the underworld, anyway. This warrior you want to save won't know the difference. And you'll be better equipped to save him."

"It doesn't matter how time passes there. Hel has given me a deadline of midsummer, and I can't delay that long. But if you're sure it won't waste too much time…"

"I have no reason to lead you astray," Loki assured us. "You've asked me for help, and now I'm trying to provide it."

I considered just how much time we could spare. Between the knowledge that Eryk might be being tortured in the underworld, and that Hel's deadline was growing ever closer, I felt anxious at the idea of waiting, but rest was imperative as well or we'd burn ourselves out like an overused candle before long.

"We'll prepare to leave in a day or two, once we have horses, of course. I'm going to go find something to eat. See you later?" Loki stood and stretched.

"You said you'd help, so I suppose we have no choice now," Gunhild reminded him. He simply laughed and headed out the door, presumably to prepare for joining us on our quest.

Once he was gone, Gunhild pulled me down onto the chair beside hers and set her axe aside. "Was that really *the* Loki?" she asked. Her awe from when she first met him had settled from shock into a doubtful scowl.

"It really was. I'm very glad he's agreed to help us. He'll make this quest so much easier, I think," I said, though my goal was to convince myself at least as much as it was to convince her.

"Why do you trust him?" she asked tentatively, her gaze averted. I opened my mouth to explain, but she held her hand up to stop me. "Loki is a trickster, no? Surely you are wiser about who you trust than that. There must be some reason you trusted him. I want to hear it."

"He doesn't like Hel, at all," I said as if that was reason enough. I hoped it was. Not just for Gunhild but for myself. I didn't want to think of what might happen if Loki betrayed us. But he could get us into places we might not otherwise have access to, and would know things we didn't know. "After what she's done, I'm inclined to trust anyone who doesn't trust her."

"Are you sure that's enough?" Gunhild asked with a raised eyebrow.

"No, but my gut says it has to be," I admitted. "Just like my gut said to let you come with me."

She obviously couldn't argue with that unless she wanted to turn around and go home. I offered a reassuring smile and patted her hand. She turned hers over to take mine reflexively and tap out a little pattern on the back with her thumb like I had done to her knee when we were trapped in the darkness in the cave. Four taps, then a long press, then three more taps.

Even if I wasn't sure about Loki's help, one thing I was sure of was that it had been the right decision to allow Gunhild to come along. She made things seem so much less impossible. So much less dire. With her fighting at my side, I felt like I could do anything.

"I guess that's good enough reason," she said, sighing. "I just hope your gut's not wrong."

"I hope so too."

Chapter Twelve

"Buy your own tent, Loki," I said, for at least the fifth time. "I am not sharing with you. Your own horse too, since you're insisting we get horses."

"You are no fun at all, Valkyrie," Loki huffed. "I was only teasing. I don't want to share a tent with you."

I ignored him and walked on to see what else could bolster our supplies. We had used up most of Eryk's silver in Armvind's market, but we would need more as our journey continued. All I had left of Eryk now was his sword. I feared the day I might have to sell it too.

Thankfully, Loki was willing to purchase anything in excess of what we could afford, though I was unsure where he came up with his coin. He seemed happy enough to pay if it meant joining us on an adventure.

"Oh, don't be like that, Yrsa," Loki said as he came to tug at my sleeve.

"You are such a child!" I chastised him, which only sent him into a fit of laughter.

"You sound like Freyja," he said. "Always so serious. All about duty and fate instead of enjoying life. Relax. We'll find your warrior and then you'll go back to Valhalla and...well, good things will happen, I'm sure of it."

"I'm glad you have a bright outlook," I told him with an

exasperated sigh. His lofty visions for me were all well and good, but they were more than I dared to hope for. "I can't go back to Valhalla, and I don't know that we'll be able to rescue Eryk, much less anything else. We only know the realms that hold the pieces of armor. Not where in each realm, or how to secure them once we've found them."

"I'll know what to do when we get there," Loki promised, though his tone was a bit cryptic. Did he really know or was he just saying so to seem confident?

"I suppose a god *would* know better than anyone else," Gunhild said. "It might not be so bad after all to have you along on our quest."

"Now you say so?" Loki huffed a laugh. "My eternal gratitude for your acceptance, shieldmaiden. Whatever would I do without it?"

"No need to be sarcastic. Now, go get yourself a tent while I see about horses," I told him.

"Make sure to get my favorite. The horse master will know which one." Loki stuck his tongue out at us and headed off into the market. He would be infuriating to travel with, but if it meant this journey would be easier, then I was willing to tolerate his antics. I led Gunhild toward the paddock at the edge of the village. Several fine horses pranced around there, along with two or three less exuberant beasts who were probably more our speed. Assuming they were available for purchase at all.

"Yrsa! Gunhild!" The little girl that we had met the day before, ran up to us with her mother close behind.

"Hello, Hjordis, Signy," I greeted them.

"Are you leaving us so soon? I hear you're taking Luka with you as well?"

"Yes, in a couple of days," I confirmed. The village must have only known Loki as Luka, a disguise that allowed him to move about without any suspicion that he was a god. I was glad he was good at pretending to be human when he needed to. That could come in useful later.

"Aww, why is Luka leaving? He's such fun!" Hjordis complained.

"He is, but that fun is why he's coming with us," Gunhild said. "He misses going on adventures."

"An adventure?" Hjordis stared up at us with wide gray eyes and bounced a little on her toes. Her childlike wonder and exuberance made me ache for the days when I had been so innocent and carefree. The days when an adventure was exciting instead of harrowing. "Can I come? What sort of adventure? Will it be dangerous? Are you going to fight a dragon?"

We all laughed, which made Hjordis give us an injured frown. It was quickly soothed away with a smile from Gunhild.

"There might be dragons," the shieldmaiden told Hjordis. "But either way, I think your mother would miss you too much if you came with us. Wait until you are a big shieldmaiden before you go on adventures of your own."

It impressed me how Gunhild sidestepped the question of what sort of adventure we were on. Neither Hjordis nor Signy pushed for details. Not that we could have really predicted entirely where our quest would lead, other than the vague locations of Alfheim, Nidavellir, and Jotunheim. There was no telling what dangers might await us in each of those places. Not to mention when we eventually descended to the underworld to deliver the armor. A shiver went through me at the reminder that we would have to brave that after everything else.

"Will you promise to come back with stories of your adventure?" the little girl begged, clasping her hands before her chest.

"We'll try," I said. "It depends on where our adventure takes us. It may be a very long way from here and it would be difficult to come back."

"Oh. Good luck!" Hjordis said, as if the underworld itself wasn't our destination.

"Thank you, I will happily take your well-wishes," I said. Hopefully, the well-wishes of a bright-eyed little girl were lucky. I could only hope so. I could use all the luck that might come my way. Especially with the Goddess of Death against me. "But we should finish up our shopping so we can go pack."

We continued to the horse pasture where an older gentleman with eyebrows like bottle brushes and a perpetual frown came over to us. It took me a moment to realize it was the brows that gave him the appearance of a scowl.

"What can I help you shieldmaidens with?" he asked.

"We need horses," I told him. "Three if possible. Sturdy, able to take long trips, not easily spooked."

"Three like that? My, you ask for a lot." The old man chuckled and waved a hand for us to follow him. "Come with me, then. Let's see what we can find for you."

Over the next half hour, he showed us a variety of horses. We saw everything from warhorses to plow horses. I wasn't sure which would be best for where we were going, I just knew they had to be strong and hardy.

"This one has steady feet, and isn't afraid of anything," the old man told us as he pointed to a beautiful gray horse.

"Alright, and for Gunhild?" I asked after giving it a look over.

"Let's see." He surveyed the various beasts and then led us to a bay with a white star on his forehead. "This one is smart as a whip, and strong. A little frisky at times, but there's nothing wrong with that, is there shieldmaiden?"

"Not at all, sir," Gunhild said. "And he doesn't mind being ridden?"

"He loves a solid rider, but if you're at all afraid of horses, he won't do for you."

"I'm a very accomplished rider," Gunhild said. Her ability to ride was news to me, but I was relieved to hear it. It would make this journey easier and safer in the long run. "My old horse back home was as frisky as this one, I bet."

"Then he'll be perfect for you. You said you needed three? Who is your final rider?"

"Luka," I said. "He requested that we secure his favorite for our trip."

"Ah, yes, I know which horse that is," the old man said. He gave a shrill whistle and a larger black horse trotted over, stomping its feet in the snow. This was not going to be an inexpensive purchase and I prayed Loki was able to come up with a way to pay since the horses were his idea.

"She's gorgeous," Gunhild said, running a hand over the horse's neck.

"This one is his favorite," the stable master told us. "She's spirited, hardy, unbothered by much. Though she's not a fan of rabbits. Wolves don't bother her though, nor much of anything else. And she can go for days."

"Well, if it's Luka's favorite, I think we have little choice but to take her, as well as the other two you showed us," I said. "How much?"

The stable master smiled and gave us the price, an amount that almost caused me to choke on thin air. Loki had better have ideas for how to pay.

"I'll have them ready for you whenever you decide to leave," the old man told us.

He nodded, and we wandered off to find Loki and a way to buy the horses. Loki stood in the doorway of a cottage, leaning against the frame and grinning at a pretty young lady with pale blonde hair and dark eyes. They laughed about something together, so I didn't want to interrupt. Gunhild waved, though, which caught his attention. He bid the lady goodbye and came over to join us.

"Find horses?" he asked. "I hope you got my favorite. I wouldn't want to go anywhere without her."

"We did," I assured him, tilting my head to regard him carefully when I continued. His reaction to my request for help had been positive, but asking him to purchase horses for us, even though it had been his idea, would be too much to ask. "Though I don't know how we'll afford them. I have nothing left."

"Don't worry, I'm sure I can convince the jarl to help us. Just the right favors will do the trick," he said with a sly grin.

"Favors?" Gunhild cast a suspicious glance at him. My thoughts likely echoed hers: if he was going to run around causing havoc with miraculous feats, then we might have to leave sooner than expected.

"Sure, a little exchange, some promises, that sort of thing," Loki said, then laughed. "What, did you think I was performing miracles to ingratiate myself? That would give away who I am!"

"We wouldn't want that," I said. At least he was circumspect in who he revealed himself to.

"Come, I think the jarl is expecting us at the mead hall for supper." Loki slung his arms around both mine and Gunhild's shoulders.

Gunhild tried to shrug him off but failed and scowled instead. "I think he may give them to us for free if we speak wisely enough."

"I would have no idea what to say," I admitted. "Promise to come back? Offer collateral?"

"Follow my lead," Loki said . "And don't take yourself so seriously."

"But our quest is serious," Gunhild pointed out in a huff.

"Indeed, it is, but the jarl shouldn't know that," Loki said.

Chapter Thirteen

WE JOINED the villagers at the mead hall as the sun set. It cast deep shadows across the village and slanted blinding gold between the houses. My thoughts were, as always, on what needed to happen next for our journey. We had to have the horses, and we had to find Alfheim, Nidavellir, and Jotunheim. I hoped Loki knew the way to each of those realms, because I had no clue which direction to even start in, much less how to leave Midgard for each of them. Without Loki's help, we would never finish this quest by midsummer, but now there was hope. He couldn't be allowed to know how grateful I was though, or I'd never hear the end of it.

The jarl greeted us as we entered and led us over to a table off to one side. He looked curiously between Gunhild and I and then to Loki, presumably so he would introduce us. I smiled warmly at him, and nudged Gunhild to do the same. She looked up at me for a moment and then smiled to the jarl as well.

"Leif, thank you for joining us," Loki greeted him. "This is Yrsa and Gunhild—they are shieldmaidens adventuring through Midgard. Would you join us for a while?"

"A pleasure to meet you both." Leif sat down with us and helped himself to a plate of smoked salmon and carrots roasted with sage and rosemary. "Is Luka regaling you with impossible stories? He's a very good spinner of tales, I've found."

"Oh, yes, he is very good at it," Gunhild replied, her voice a little too high.

"I heard you needed horses. Did you find them?" Leif asked. "I hate that you're all leaving us. But I know adventure calls, and when it does, one must answer."

"We did, thank you," I said with a smile. "They'll do perfectly."

"The problem," Loki said around a mouthful of carrot, "is that the horse master wants a handsome payment for them. I'm not sure we can afford it. How can we earn our keep and strike a deal for them?"

"Bring us something in the future? Little Hjordis told me you promised to come back," Leif said, tapping his fingers on the table as he considered. My face fell with his response, which dashed my hopes of an easy way out. It would have been easier if Loki had just come up with the silver to pay for them. Surely he could create some out of thin air. "Where exactly do you intend to go?"

"Oh, we aren't sure yet," I said, perhaps a little too quickly, because Leif gave me a dubious frown. "We plan to go north, and east, but where we will end up is anyone's guess. You know how adventures are."

"I'll tell you what," Loki said with a glance that told me to stop talking immediately. "I know where to find some elven artifacts. I would be happy to acquire one and bring it back to you."

This meant Loki would probably have to steal said artifact directly from Alfheim. If it was possible for anyone to manage such a thing, it would be Loki. The idea of angering the elves was an awful idea, but it might be unavoidable.

"Elven artifacts, you say?" Leif asked, eyes widening incredulously. If he doubted Loki's ability to bring back what he promised, then the jarl might not give us the horses to begin with. It was clear he was doubtful about the prospect, but I just had to hope Loki could convince him. "Those must be pricy to come by. If you can't afford horses, how will you afford those?"

"I have connections to someone with access to them," Loki said breezily. "It won't be a bit of trouble to get them, I promise. And we'll bring them back to you afterwards."

"And you swear that you *will* be returning?" Leif was clearly doubtful.

"You have my oath," I told him, holding out my hand to shake. I wasn't sure *how* we would manage to get back here, but I wasn't about to break my oath. "We wouldn't lie to you after how kind you and your people have been to us."

Leif took my hand and shook it, satisfied with my promise. "A shieldmaiden's oath is good enough for me. We'll look forward to your return. I'll pay the horse master for your horses personally."

"I'm very grateful for your help," I said with an earnest smile.

"No need. It's not as if I'm giving them to you. In any case, please take my prayers and good wishes with you. We hope to see you again soon." He stood and bowed to us, before heading off to speak to a man beckoning to him from across the mead hall.

"So, we have horses, we have supplies, everyone is well rested, does that mean we can leave tomorrow morning?" Gunhild asked.

"I would think so," I agreed, already making plans for our next steps. I felt lighter than I had in a while as things started coming together in a positive way for once. We knew where we needed to go, and we had a way to get there more quickly than walking. I could finally breathe more easily. "The sooner we leave, the sooner we can find the armor."

"Are you sure there's time? We shouldn't have stayed so long here," Gunhild said with a worried frown.

"I wouldn't worry. It's only been an extra day. We'll cross Bifrost to get to Alfheim more quickly and with my help, it won't take as long as you think," Loki assured us. I wasn't sure how long it might have taken otherwise, since we would have had to find some other way across Bifrost without him. I didn't want to think about that now, though. We had a solution, and that was what mattered.

"Then let's all finish our meal and get a good night's rest," I said with a nod. "The journey has really only just begun, and we've a long way to go."

Chapter Fourteen

THE ROAD from Armvind was well-maintained for the first few days, but the neatly trod path soon turned rocky and ultimately disappeared. I was glad we had horses, so that there would be no turned ankles to slow us down. We rode in silence most of the time. Only the clopping of hooves and the birds chirping around us accompanied our steps.

On the sixth day, the woods rose before us. They did not seem intimidating or dreadful like so many of the forests we'd traveled through on our journey thus far. Instead, they promised something. Something hopeful and important. The snow was freshly fallen, pristine among the tall trees that reached up to brush the sky in watercolor blues. The cardinals and robins hopped from branch to branch, watching us with their interested black eyes. Our next steps took us that much closer to our goal.

Gunhild glanced over from where she rode abreast of me and smiled. We could both feel it, then. I wondered if Loki did as well, but he rode ahead of us and seemed to have forgotten we were there altogether.

"Loki, tell us about these woods." I called up to him. He slowed his horse and turned to look over his shoulder, before stopping to allow us to catch up.

"Ah, the Frostbend Forest," he said authoritatively, waving a hand around the woods with a flourish and a grin. Gunhild raised an eyebrow and shot a look at me. "Alright, alright, I'll be honest. This forest has no name. It's a good forest for hunting and gathering. Lots of game to hunt, and plenty of berries and nuts to be found if you know where to look. There's a river that runs through it as well."

"Will we have to cross it?" Gunhild asked. The last time we'd crossed a river had almost been disastrous. Loki's teasing charm would definitely not help us survive another troll.

"No, but we could ride alongside it, and keep our path truer," Loki said. "It should lead us to where we need to go."

"And where exactly is that?" I asked with a frustrated frown. He was still reticent about where we were going. Obviously, we were headed to Bifrost and from there, Alfheim, but not knowing our exact path to them was maddening. Loki was a trickster, after all. He could be leading us anywhere, rather than to our requested destination. I never could be sure whether or not to trust him. Following my gut seemed stupid sometimes, but I knew of no other way to get where we needed to go in time to rescue Eryk without trusting the trickster. My mind twisted around the possible consequences of trusting him should he lead us astray.

"There's a way onto Bifrost at the outskirts of the forest, a little south of where we'll end up if we stay on this path. The river will lead us straight to it," Loki said.

"So, we need to go south and find the river," Gunhild said, looking up at the sky through the branches that stretched across the sun. It rose higher in the sky today than at the beginning of our quest. Dappled light fell on her features, setting her eyes aglow and making her skin shine like porcelain. The delicate freckles that dotted across her cheeks mixed with the light, weaving over her features like a fine lace veil. She was easily the most beautiful sight I'd ever laid eyes on.

"Right, Yrsa?" she asked.

I snapped out of my reverie with a gasp. "Oh, yes, right. South. That way."

"Can you feel the pull of Bifrost like I can, Valkyrie?" asked Loki as he looked over at me. He looked at me with his brown eyes, curious as the birds that watched us from the trees. I had felt Yggdrasil so strongly, but I had been expecting that. Bifrost seemed impossibly far away, so I hadn't even paid attention. Now that he mentioned it though, I did feel *something*.

"I think so, yes," I said. Gunhild brightened noticeably, her vivid blue gaze locked onto my face as if it was the only thing keeping her sane.

"What does it feel like?" she asked.

"Like… like a hunger," I said as I considered the sensation. Hunger wasn't exactly the right word, but it was close enough. It was completely different to the sensation of Yggdrasil tugging at me like a rope attached to my heart. "Like when you are hungry and can smell dinner cooking in the distance. You're drawn there because you cannot stand to wait," I said.

"That's accurate," Loki said with a grin. "Now you know why most of us don't come to Midgard often. I'm surprised you didn't feel it sooner. For the gods it is more like starving. Utterly famished. And the food is in the next room."

"Interesting," Gunhild murmured, looking around inquisitively.

"Come on then," I told them, turning my horse's head southward.

They brought their horses around as well and we picked our way south through the trees. Although there was still snow on the ground, the signs of spring were everywhere around us: the gold haze of budding leaves surrounding the trees and the cautious eyes of the fawn who scurried away from us, followed by his wary mother. We kept still as she tiptoed across our path and then continued on our way. The coming of spring reminded me just how quickly time was slipping past. Before we knew it, it would be summer and my time would be up. I urged my horse a little faster, as if the extra few minutes I might gain would make a difference.

Loki had not told us how far away this river would be. It was almost sundown by the time we saw it. The last remains of the sun twinkled through the trees to reflect off its ruffled surface. We allowed the horses to drink their fill before we led them a little ways away to where we would make camp, and dismounted.

Loki started haphazardly removing packs from the horses, tossing them here and there in various, scattered locations. Gunhild and I exchanged a glance and watched him as he tried to set up camp. As he began to dig through the bags, I grimaced. I should have really helped him, but I was amused at how poorly this whole endeavor was going for him.

At some point, Loki found one of the tents and started *trying* to erect it. Unfortunately for him, he ended up tangled inside of it, unable to find his way out. Gunhild laughed loudly, and I did everything I could not to join her.

"That's not very kind," he told us in a muffled shout, still trying to untangle himself from the tent. "You could help me instead of laughing."

I did laugh then. Laughter felt good after so long without it, even if it was at Loki's expense. He was used to laughter though, so surely he wouldn't be too offended by it. Gunhild and I went and unfurled the tent from around Loki.

"There now," I said with a chuckle. "That wasn't so hard, was it? You've never set up a camp before, have you?"

"No," Loki muttered with a sullen pout.

"Well then, you can't be expected to know what you're doing, can you?" I said.

"Yes! I make a mess all the time when I do something I've never done before," Gunhild added. I offered her a smile and reached over to squeeze her hand gratefully. This journey would certainly be easier if we could all see eye-to-eye.

"Well, you could have helped *before* I made a mess, you know," Loki huffed.

I resisted the urge to tell him not to be a baby about it. Instead, Gunhild and I began to quietly set up the tent. Loki stood back and watched, eyes wide as if in awe of our ability to do it so efficiently.

The journey down the river the next day was easy enough. It seemed there would be no troubles other than the dreary sleet-rain that drizzled down the backs of our necks and hissed through the trees like an angry cat. But there were much worse problems than being soaked through and we were about to find that out the hard way.

On the tenth day of travel through the woods, beside the burbling river, the cloud cover lifted, and the sky turned blue once more. The sun streamed through the tree branches in rays that made me expect to see one of the gods standing in the footprint of the light.

"Halt!" A stony voice said. It was not a god standing in a ray of light, but a little old man standing in the shadows of a yew tree that was at least as wizened as him. Loki laughed as we were shouted at, so hard that he nearly fell off his horse. I hissed at him to sit up and act right, and looked to the old man with a tilted head and raised eyebrows. The last thing I needed right now was another delay in our journey. I just wanted to get to Bifrost so we could cross and enter Alfheim and find the first piece of armor.

"I said halt!" The little old man stamped the foot of his staff—which was taller than him—on the ground. It barely made a sound, thanks to the thick layer of pine needles and leaf litter on the forest floor.

"Why are we halting?" I didn't bother to get off my horse yet. The old man was barely taller than a child, his eyes clouded with cataracts, and his face so carved with wrinkles that his features were almost obscured. I doubted he could do much damage, but it wasn't as if we could just run him over with our horses. And there was no point in being rude.

"Because you are in *my* forest!" His voice cracked as he shouted at us and stomped his foot instead of his staff this time, like a sullen toddler.

"Darling," Loki said breezily, "trust me, this forest belongs to anyone *but* you."

The old man's eyes widened at being denied and he had another little tantrum of foot stamping and screaming and pumping his arms in the air as he shook his staff at us angrily. He reminded me of a squirrel defending its acorn stash. I ended up laughing with Loki. Apparently, Gunhild was the only one of us with any sense of decorum this time.

"It is *my* forest!" the man insisted at the top of his lungs, his voice squeaking as it cracked like a teenage boy's. "Mine! Mine!"

"Is he a dwarf?" I asked Loki under my breath with an uninvited giggle.

The god of mischief shook his head. "No, only a hermit. A mad one, apparently."

A crow flew down from the yew tree to land on the old man's staff, which gave him a little more gravitas than before. The tantrum had passed and now the old man glared at us as if he could make us go away with his look alone. Something about this felt wrong, but I couldn't put my finger on why. I glanced at the crow, or was it a raven? It glared at me just as balefully as the old man.

"I am *not* a madman," the man insisted. "I am Ingi Stonebreaker and I will cast you out of my home!"

"When was the last time you broke a stone, old man?" Loki asked with an irreverent grin. I flicked my fingers at him, hoping he would stop taunting the poor old man. He was obviously quite insane and didn't need anyone to make it worse.

"Fine," Loki conceded. "When was the last time you ate? We could feed you if it means you would let us pass."

"Feed me? As if I cannot take proper care of myself? Humph," Ingi scoffed. "Unless you've something unique to share with me, I've no interest in you and you can go back the way you came."

"What sort of something unique?" Gunhild asked. She was so gentle and kind about it, it softened my heart a little. "I have some jewelry, or we could sing you a song, or tell you a story?"

"Ooooh, I do like a good story," Ingi admitted, looking between the three of us. "But I doubt you've a story I've not heard yet."

"I bet we do. Did you know that Yrsa here knows the story of an exiled Valkyrie?" Gunhild said. I shook my head vehemently at her. The last thing I wanted was to recount my story to another stranger.

Ingi deliberated the offer for a few moments. "No, I want something better. Something I can say nobody else in the world has. Give me that and I will let you go."

"Old man, how are you going to stop us?" Loki asked wearily. "Why should we care if you don't want us to pass? You're one small, elderly man. You couldn't stop us if you tried."

"Except I can," Ingi told him with a gap-toothed grin. All his teeth were gone but two. "You see, there are a thousand traps in these woods. All set by me, and all to be unset by me if I feel like it."

I looked over at Loki and Gunhild with a raised eyebrow. Did they believe the story of the traps? Could this old man really have set so many?

Gunhild and Loki seemed to have no more answers than I did, though, and the old man was growing angry again. "Go then, go, and see whether you survive. You'll lose a horse, or a leg, or your head. Try it and see if I'm right."

Loki seemed the least likely to die in the event these traps were real, so I jerked my chin at him. "Go check."

Loki opened his mouth to protest but muttered something inaudible and dismounted his horse to go look for traps. It wasn't long before he found one, a yelp escaping him as a bear trap closed on his ankle, neatly snapping it. Thankfully, he wiggled his fingers, and the trap let go of his foot, his ankle healed. A nice little trick, which seemed to impress Ingi.

"Well, well, seems we've got ourselves a magician here," said Ingi with a little hoot. At least he didn't put together that Loki was a god. "What will you do now?"

"I suppose we'll have to think of something that you don't have and can't get anywhere," Gunhild said with a small smile to him, which was, miraculously, returned. It seemed he liked her. I glanced at Loki to tell him, silently, to let her do the talking.

"Indeed, you will, little lass, so what shall you give me?" Ingi asked with a toothless grin.

"I could give you a braid made of god and Valkyrie hair, twined together," she offered. "Do you have anything like that?"

The hermit scoffed. "There's nobody in Midgard who could get me that. Not even a Valkyrie or a god."

"Want to bet?" Gunhild offered a toothier grin than Ingi's. I hated to give away that Loki was a god, and I was a Valkyrie, but it was the best choice we had. "Here's the catch, though. You have to turn around so you cannot see where I get it from."

Ingi might think Gunhild was a vala or a god herself. He did as was asked of him and turned around, covering his eyes. Not that he could really see anyway, with those cataracts blurring his vision.

Loki had rejoined us by then, and Gunhild held her knife up to her hair to show us that we should each cut a lock. Once we gave her the hair, Gunhild bound them together at the top with a bit of twine. She quickly twisted the hair into a copper and gold braid and then tied the other end off. "There. You may turn around now, Ingi Stonebreaker."

Ingi did as asked and held out his hand for the hair to be given to him. Gunhild dismounted her own horse and walked over to gently lay the hair in his outstretched palm, which I noticed was remarkably smooth considering he lived and worked in the woods for survival. His palm should have been as wizened as his face and covered in scars and callouses.

Ingi snatched his hand back and inspected the hair before he laughed loudly. The laugh grew from a cackle into a roar, something that didn't seem like it could come out of such a small body. My stomach clenched suddenly, and my heart clattered against my ribs.

"Oh, you really *are* a god and a Valkyrie." Ingi's voice changed from the creak of an old door opening to the boom of a new one slamming shut. I found myself trembling more than I would have liked to admit. He was obviously not who he seemed, and the aura of danger that roiled off of him made me cringe. "Of course, I already knew, but now…now I have proof you are here where you shouldn't be. What would Hel say, dearest Valkyrie?"

Was it worth it to give him more fodder? Or should we try to leave and risk the traps? Loki had barely gotten a dozen yards before he was caught in one though. Who knew how many more there could be?

"Hel knows. Hel is the reason I am here, in fact," I said, barely louder than a whisper. "She exiled me, when I disobeyed and shirked my duties."

"Ah, an exile *and* a traitor. I love it. I love a good plot twist. And you…" He pointed at Loki and crooked his finger. "Come here, my boy."

Loki looked absolutely taken aback by being called *my boy* but did not argue. He scowled and headed over as demanded by Ingi, who seemed stranger by the second. The old man lifted a hand to Loki's face, and as he made contact, Loki leapt back and gaped at him.

"You aren't Ingi Stonebreaker," Loki said finally, voice shaking.

"No, Loki, I'm not," Ingi told him with a wider grin. He now had a full set of white teeth. And he seemed taller, as though between one glance and another he had surreptitiously grown. "Who am I, Loki?"

"Your Grace, you are…well, you are Odin, the Allfather," Loki managed to get out through stumbled words and a great deal of genuflection. This time when I looked from Loki to the man, I recognized him. It was the Odin I spent every night of my life entertaining until the last weeks. The Odin who ruled Asgard and wandered Midgard testing mortals. I let out a shaky breath and prayed Loki wouldn't ruin this for us.

"Oh stop, you aren't in trouble this time, and we both know you don't really mean it," Odin said, flicking a hand at Loki. "But you, Valkyrie, and you, shieldmaiden, I know the trouble you are in, and I hope you are able to find your way out."

"How do you know?" I asked, which earned me a withering look. It was a truly stupid question. Of course, the Allfather knew the trouble I was in. Though why he should call it Gunhild's trouble too, I didn't know. "Why did you trick us?"

"Why not? I knew who Loki was the moment I laid eyes on him, of course, and I knew you weren't a mere mortal. Your shieldmaiden is, though. Do you realize the gravity of traveling with a god and a Valkyrie, little shieldmaiden? And yet you were the only respectful one, which is something to be proud of." Odin nodded to Gunhild. "I think you've earned a reward for that, in fact."

Gunhild's eyes went wide, flicking to me questioningly and then back to Odin. All I could do was shrug. She couldn't expect me to tell her to refuse, surely. It would be foolish not to take any bit of help Odin offered, though it might have been a trick now I thought about it. Either way, there was no getting around it. And in the end, it might even help.

Loki's eyes narrowed on Odin suspiciously, his head cocking to one side like a puppy trying to hear something better. But there was no questioning Odin's motives. And it wasn't as if he was Loki, with a penchant for tricks and traps. Though the wood was filled with them, apparently.

"I don't think I've earned anything, Allfather," Gunhild said. Her flushed cheeks gave away how surprised she was to be offered a reward from the king of the gods.

"All the more reason you shall have something, then. You showed me respect even before you knew who I was. Before I proved to be more than a mad hermit," Odin told her. "What is it you would like to have?"

Gunhild's eyebrows raised minutely and her gaze found the leafy ground at her feet. The toe of her boot dug into the bed of pine needles as she considered. What did one ask of the king of the gods? Definitely not some trinket or minor favor, not when he was offering literally anything she could think of.

"I think…what I want might require…a brief preface. So, you understand better what I need," Gunhild said very slowly, after several moments of thought. Odin searched her expression with a single eye instead of the two he had before, one no longer clouded by cataracts. He might already know what she was going to tell him or what she might ask for, but nothing in his stoic expression or the relaxed way he carried himself hinted that he did.

He regarded her for almost as long as it had taken her to think of what to say. "Well, go on, then."

"Alright…" Gunhild hesitated and looked over at me apologetically. "As you know, Yrsa here is a Valkyrie, exiled because she fell in love with a mortal and allowed him to live past his allotted time."

Odin's expression did not shift even a hair as he listened to Gunhild, though his gaze did slowly move to me. His pale green eyes bore into me, but I couldn't tell if he was curious, disappointed, or angry. Odin was a blank stone, or one with its runes defaced, the actual meaning obscured beneath the scratches.

"And what happened to her after she fell in love?" Odin asked, not taking his eyes off me, even though the question was directed to Gunhild. Loki watched all this in horror from where he stood some yards away. My stomach twisted on itself and I thought I might vomit from fear of what might happen when he knew the truth.

"The goddess of death came to make her pay for it," Gunhild said with all the finality and softness of a lock being turned in a door.

"Unless?" Odin asked the most obvious question. "Come now, shieldmaiden, of course a god would want something in exchange for the punishment. Some impossible way to pretend that they gave a chance for redemption. What was Hel's offer?"

Gunhild's mouth opened several times without finding her voice.

"I must find Freyja's lost armor," I said instead of her. I climbed down from my horse and took Gunhild's hand since she seemed overwrought. "I don't know why Hel wants it. Only that if I want to rescue Eryk from Nastrond, that is the price."

"But it is not impossible!" Gunhild argued, her face turning a bright pink. We all looked at her; Loki with amusement, myself with shock, and Odin with that same inscrutable expression. "It's not! We just need help. Now that we have Loki it will be easier. And if you give us permission to cross Bifrost into Alfheim, then we can get the first piece."

"Well, I did offer you a gift. I thought you would want riches, or power. That is usually what people want, though I suppose they are usually men," Odin said, stroking his beard.

"I mean, if you really want to give me what I want, you would give me all the remaining pieces of Freyja's armor..." Gunhild said. I couldn't help the helpless little laugh that escaped me. The chances of it being that easy were zero, and I didn't even bother to hope that he might do what she asked.

"No, I can't completely eliminate a task set out by a god as punishment," Odin said with an apologetic smile. "I wish I could. Those fall under the heading of oaths. How about this: I will give you a token which will give you free passage over Bifrost to wherever you need to go. Does that suffice?"

"Yes, Your Grace," Loki said, almost too quickly. He shifted this way and that, as if he had a flea infestation, and every time he looked my way it was with pleading in his eyes, though I wasn't sure why. "Thank you."

"Behave yourself, Loki, and you can be of help to this pair," Odin told the god of mischief. "But if you get too involved in your tricks, you will be the reason Yrsa fails in her quest."

Loki's eyes widened, and he looked ready to argue, but I moved closer to put a hand on his arm reassuringly. My voice wasn't quite loud enough for the others to hear when I spoke. "It's alright. He's not accusing you of anything that's not in your nature, and I trust you."

Odin produced a shiny little bauble from the air: a small golden marble that made a little chime when shaken. The surface was iridescent and caught the afternoon light slanting through the trees to create a myriad of colors that reflected from it.

That was when I realized how much time had passed, here in this clearing with the Allfather. I frowned deeply as I assessed the angle of the sun and realized it was now late afternoon. How had time flown so quickly?

"Now," said Odin, breaking my reverie. "Why don't you stay here tonight? It has gotten late, hasn't it Yrsa?" There was my explanation, which should have been obvious.

"We would be honored to, Allfather," I said. I tried to keep my voice calm and respectful, but my heart was screaming that I was running out of time to find the armor and save Eryk. I couldn't say no to the king of the gods, though.

"Good, then you can tell me all of your good stories," Odin said, heading off into the woods without waiting for us to follow. We scrambled to mount and hurried off after him. I thought of turning back to our route now that we had the token, but it would be foolish to lie to a god *again*.

Chapter Fifteen

Eventually, we came upon a small cottage hidden deep in a wooded glade. Even the path looked forbidden. Gnarled branches twisted down into the shadows we walked through, which probably helped discourage visitors. That was assuming the cottage was even visible or on this plane when Odin did not wish it to be. Bluish smoke crept from the chimney and wheedled its way up through the trees and into the afternoon sky. The sweet and spicy scent tinged the fresh spring air.

I wondered how often Odin spent time in this cottage, or if he just used it as a trap. I honestly didn't know what he might have planned for us, only that we had to tread carefully if we didn't want to end up on the wrong end of the Allfather. For now, he seemed harmless enough, but even thinking that was probably a bad decision. I decided to stay alert and keep myself ready to run and take Gunhild and Loki with me, should the need arise.

"Come in, come in," Odin said, his pale green eye bright and grin cheerful. "I don't have visitors often, though that is my own fault. But I am glad to have you now."

The cottage was, not unexpectedly, larger within. As soon as we walked in, we were hit with the aroma of baking bread and stewing meat. My stomach complained loudly that I hadn't eaten since breakfast. Odin pushed me gently toward a den-like area in the center of the cottage, where a pair of ancient-looking wooden chairs decorated with moose antlers sat facing each other.

Two young women bustled about cleaning and cooking and otherwise making the space homey and livable. One stood in the roomy kitchen, stirring a large cauldron of bubbling stew. When she looked up and met my gaze, a shocked gasp fell from her lips.

"Yrsa?" She called my name, and I paled at seeing the Valkyrie I had shared a room in Valhalla for two years. Eir. She brushed her bronze hair behind her ear and stared at me with wide storm-blue eyes.

"Yrsa! Where have you been? We haven't seen you for weeks!" the other cried. She had silvery-blonde hair and gray eyes. "Nobody could, or at least *would*, tell us where you went! Where have you been?"

"Eir, Astrid...I am glad to see you. But...it is a very long story," I said faintly, feeling suddenly off balance and dizzy.

"I'm sure the Allfather will want to hear the story too," Astrid, the younger one with the silver hair said, glancing at Odin hopefully.

"Of course he will. He loves a good story, don't you, Your Grace?" Eir insisted. I gritted my teeth and looked to Odin with a silent plea that he might not make me recount what had led me to his cottage.

"Do you mind telling us your story, Yrsa? I think your sisters would appreciate an explanation, even if it is a very short one," Odin said, in a gentler voice than I could ever have expected him to have. The Odin I knew from Valhalla had a booming voice and was a veritable mountain. This Odin was smaller, kinder, wiser. I liked him much better. No matter how much I liked him though, I still didn't want to share my story. My whole body was rigid with reluctance.

"Please?" Astrid begged. She was the youngest and newest of us, barely sixteen when she died and only a Valkyrie for a few months.

"Fine," I said, unable to deny her sweet expression. I kept most of the details to myself. All they needed to know were the very basics. I fell in love, I didn't take him to Valhalla, Hel sent him to Nastrond and exiled me from Valhalla, and I had to find Freyja's lost armor to save him. I did not tell them I had yet to find any pieces.

The Valkyries sat in awe as I told the story. I was embarrassed, but they had asked, and Odin was right. Finally, Eir spoke up.

"We missed you, truly. We thought…well, we were honestly not sure what to think. It's not as if you could have died. But we knew it couldn't be right that you had just…left. You can't leave."

"I would have, though," I admitted. It wasn't something I had even realized until just now. But it was true; had I been brave enough, I would have stayed with Eryk. Even if it meant losing the only home I had. "If it had been possible? I would have stayed with Eryk instead of going back to Valhalla. But now…now I cannot do either."

"You will save Eryk, at least, and can stay in Midgard with him," Astrid said brightly.

"Yes, perhaps that will be the case," I admitted. I stood a little straighter. "Regardless, you can't tell anyone else. Not the gods, not the other Valkyries, nobody. Not a soul. Do you understand?"

Astrid and Eir both looked immediately to Odin. He nodded. "Yes, of course. It must remain a secret. You were never meant to know, and it is her story to keep or tell."

"Thank you," I told him, my voice weak and wavering. If he hadn't given the command, they would likely have told everyone, and even if I wanted to go back, I would never be able to. Not that it mattered now. Still, I offered Odin a grateful smile. He waved a hand dismissively, so I changed the subject. "So, Astrid, Eir, how did two Valkyries end up in Midgard serving the Allfather? There must be a story there as well."

"Oh, well, I suppose there is a little one, but nothing as exciting as yours," Eir demurred, ducking her head as she always did when she was trying to get out of doing something.

"Well, I think a story for a story is only fair," I said with a too-sweet smile.

"We served in Valhalla so well that the Allfather chose us to serve him here," Astrid said, as bright as before. "It gives a bit of variety to all of us."

"Eir has been one of my favorites for a long while. And, of course, Astrid here is just as sweet as mead. We all deserve some time away from the daily repetitiveness here and there. But I think we should skip the stories and enjoy some dinner," Odin suggested.

He crossed to a modest burled walnut table in a room of its own and beckoned all of us to follow him. We each took seats in comfortable chairs around it while Odin looked to the Valkyries. "Astrid, Eir, what have you prepared for us for our nightly meal?"

"Well, we didn't know you would have guests…" Eir admitted, her cheeks a little pink. "But there is enough elk stew for the four of you and then Astrid and I can eat something else later."

"That will do," Odin cut me off before I could protest that we shouldn't take their dinner from them. One did not argue with the Allfather. After the Valkyries scurried off to do Odin's bidding, he turned to us with another proclamation. "It's gotten late, will you stay here tonight?"

I wasn't sure if we were really being given an option, but I wasn't just going to cave in to Odin's wishes if he was giving me the illusion of choice. I looked to Gunhild and Loki, noting how tired they both looked. Once we ate, it would indeed be late and we wouldn't be able to travel on in the dark anyway.

"We would be happy to stay," I said with a bow of my head. Gunhild looked ready to fight me, but I shook my head to her. Loki seemed uncomfortable with the idea, but crossed his arms over his chest and glanced away.

"Good. I think that's the right decision. With the elk stew, we shall have buttered pumpkin and squash, and some fresh mushrooms that Astrid found growing nearby," Odin said. "Thank goodness spring is finally here, no? Oh, and we'll have apples." He looked between us as he said this, and I raised an eyebrow to Loki. It seemed that Odin was offering us the apples of Idunn. Mortals were forbidden from eating them, but Odin *was* the Allfather, and therefore was the one who made the rules, wasn't he? If he was offering, it would be rude to refuse.

"I'm sure it will all be excellent, thank you," Gunhild said, blissfully unaware of what she might be about to eat.

"Such a well-mannered young lady you are," said Odin, eyeing her up and down. "Are you royalty yourself? Possibly a Valkyrie one day?"

"Oh, no Your Grace, I'm an orphan. My mother died in childbirth and my father died in battle during my seventh winter," she told him. I reached under the table to squeeze her hand and she turned to give me a soft smile, tapping out our little pattern on the back of my hand with her thumb. Four taps, then a long press, then three more taps. "I've relied on the kindness of others for most of my life. I have been very fortunate."

"Most would not consider themselves fortunate to have been orphaned so young," Odin said quietly, continuing to appraise her.

Loki must have noticed because he offered up, "I think Yrsa might fight you if you try to steal away her shieldmaiden, Allfather. They are rather attached at the hip. But I'm glad to be on their adventure with them and help as much as I can."

"I wonder why, hmm?" Odin nudged. "Your dislike of Hel? Plenty of reason even without an impressive Valkyrie to catch your attention. It's a perfect little mix of ingredients to catch the attention of the God of Mischief. Or perhaps… there is something more."

"We are lucky that he has been kind to us," was all I could manage to murmur as Loki and Odin stared each other down. The table settings rattled, and the candles on the table flickered as the pair faced off over the dinner table. What did 'something more' mean? I wasn't sure I wanted to know just yet, and so instead I asked weakly, "What is happening?"

"A bit of fun," Loki assured us. The Valkyries had disappeared into another room, as if they sensed the storm on the horizon. Gunhild and I should probably make ourselves scarce as well.

"Before we eat, we should make sure the horses have water and food," I suggested to Gunhild, my voice a little shriller than intended.

"Oh tosh, we'll stop. It was just a little fun, as Loki said," Odin told us. "No harm done. Nobody was hurt or will be. Astrid, Eir, is the food ready yet?"

"Yes, Your Grace," Astrid said. She and Eir brought the plates to the table, which had stopped rattling. "Would you have wine to drink? Or mead?"

"Mead of course, love," Odin said. The term of endearment surprised me. He was never so familiar with the Valkyries in Valhalla.

When he saw my confusion, he said, "We are much more relaxed here, as you can see. It's only the three of us, most of the time. I rarely have guests, and never as illustrious as a god, a Valkyrie, and a shieldmaiden. Typically, it is only the occasional unknowing traveler through the woods."

"No warriors to impress, I suppose," I noted with a nod as a bowl of stew and a plate of squash and mushrooms was set before me. It smelled delicious, with a hint of thyme and rosemary.

"None of the sort," Odin agreed, settling back in his chair as the food was placed before him. He raised his glass of mead. "To finishing quests and rescuing lost warriors."

"Hear, hear," said Loki, raising his antler cup and smashing it against Odin's hard enough that the mead sloshed within.

"To finding things you did not expect to find," Gunhild said in a low enough voice that only I could hear. Odin sulked at her a little, and Loki pouted, but neither insisted she say it louder. I ignored both of them. I was glad she had found things on this quest she hadn't expected, beyond just death and danger. I had found my own surprises.

We all settled in and ate silently. When we were done, the table was a mess of empty plates and cups, and we were all pleasantly full and slightly drunk.

"Well, I don't think I can eat for another month," Odin said, happily downing another cup of mead. I wondered if this mead was from Asgard. It must have been, considering that even the gods were feeling its effects.

Gunhild hadn't drunk much, and I leaned over to whisper in her ear to be careful how much she had. The last thing we needed was for her to be so intoxicated she said or did something she would regret. I didn't want that for her. She nodded and pushed her cup away, which caught Loki's attention.

"Are you too good for drinking with us, shieldmaiden?" Loki asked, slurring the slightest bit.

"Er, of course not," Gunhild said, looking to me for assistance. I just smiled tensely and hoped she could manage an answer on her own. It would be more suspicious if I answered for her. "I just…don't want my senses to be dulled. I like to stay sharp."

"Oh, she's worried we'll attack her in her sleep," Odin said with a loud laugh, which physically shook the cottage. "No worries, shieldmaiden, it's harmless and so are we."

"No offense, Your Grace, but I think the two of you are anything but harmless, even if you mean me no harm at the moment," Gunhild said, lifting her chin a little. "I'd be foolish to get drunk in the presence of even the kindest of gods, and you two are known for your tricks and manipulations."

"Ooh, I think she called us out, Allfather," Loki said with a raucous burst of laughter. His cup sloshed mead onto the table and his gaze bore into Gunhild. "Are you calling me namipul– no. Manipulative? Are you calling me manipulative?"

"Well, you *are* the trickster god, are you not? That rather requires manipulation, I would think," Gunhild argued. I was so glad now that she was sober. "And you, Allfather, you already showed that you like to trick and trap people. As you did to us when we arrived. What is the difference?"

"None at all, I suppose," Odin said. "I did not mean to be manipulative, though. I am supposed to be wise and all-knowing."

"Can you not be both?" I asked. "Can you not be anything you wish to be? You are the Allfather. The Wise One. But you are also the Bane-Worker, are you not? You can be many things at once. Trust me, mortals are a collection of broken pieces pasted together to make one person. I can't imagine a reason why the gods wouldn't be the same."

"And they call *me* the Wise One," Odin said, leaning back so far in his chair that I thought he might fall over. "Look at this little Valkyrie being all full of wisdom. I feel like I should take credit somehow."

"I'm sure all wisdom ultimately comes from you," I said, trying to be reverent.

"Don't turn into a boot licker now," Odin snapped, the spell broken. He hooted a laugh though, much more like the crazy old hermit in the woods than the Odin we had found inside the cottage. I found myself on edge again, though Gunhild taking my hand under the table helped to ease the tension I felt.

"We still have the apple crisp for dessert, Your Grace," Eir pointed out. "Unless you are all too full."

"Never too full for apple crisp," said Odin with a wink to Gunhild, who frowned slightly. His wink all but confirmed this wouldn't be normal apple crisp, but instead made from Idunn's orchard.

I leaned over to Gunhild to explain this in a nearly inaudible whisper. She gasped and looked wide eyed at Odin.

"Consider it a parting gift, in anticipation of you returning to your journey tomorrow," he said. As a Valkyrie, I was quite familiar with the rules of Idunn's apples. Immortals had to eat them daily to maintain their eternal youth and health. Eating only one, on a single day, wouldn't grant Gunhild immortality, but it would offer her strength and healing for the time being.

As we ate, Gunhild sat up straighter in her chair, the dark circles under her eyes fading within moments. I felt rejuvenated myself. The bone-tired of travel slipped away with each bite, though I was still drowsy from so much food and drink.

"You look tired, shieldmaiden," Astrid pointed out gently as she cleared away the plates. "Allfather, you should allow them to go to bed."

"Yes, yes, of course," Odin said, sitting up straight now. "Eir, will you take our guests to their rooms?"

"Yes, Your Grace," Eir said.

Loki, Gunhild, and I followed her across the cottage to our chambers, and once Loki and Gunhild had closed their doors, Eir pulled me into a hug.

She whispered in my ear, "You must be careful with Hel… She has not mentioned you, but I have seen her. You know she rarely shows emotion, but she is *always* angry lately. She nearly killed Skadi for some minor offense. I honestly don't even know what she did, but Hel's rage is palpable. We all have been trying to avoid her."

"I'll be fine," I assured her. "I've come this far, haven't I?"

"Don't be prideful, Yrsa. We both know if she wanted to stop you, she could," Eir warned, but after a moment she softened and hugged me tighter. I held on as firmly as she did. I didn't think Hel would try to stop me. If she did, she wouldn't get the armor she wanted so badly. "I am glad to know you are still alive and well,"

"Of course, I'm alive and well," I teased as I pulled away. "I'm a Valkyrie after all. And a shieldmaiden before that. I am not so easily stopped."

"Keep believing that," Eir told me. "And you might succeed. I will pray that you do. Good night." She hugged me one last time and pushed me gently into the bedroom. I offered a grim smile and shut the door.

Chapter Sixteen

AROUND MIDNIGHT, a short, quiet knock came at my door. At first, I thought I might have dreamed it, but then I heard it again. I got out of bed and padded over to the door to open it partway. Gunhild stood outside with a sheepish expression. I pulled her into the room and closed the door behind us.

"What's wrong?" I gently pulled her over to sit on the bed.

"They're gone," she said cryptically. I tilted my head, waiting for her to explain. "Odin and the Valkyries. They aren't here. I heard them leave and looked for them and they're not here anymore."

"When did they leave? I didn't hear them go."

"A couple of hours ago, I think," Gunhild said. "Why would they leave after all that?"

"I imagine they all went back to Valhalla, as they do every night," I said. Time had obviously moved strangely here, and Asgard would be on its own schedule. There was no telling what time it actually was outside the cottage.

"Yes, I suppose so," said Gunhild with an uncertain nod. "I can't believe the things I've seen on this quest."

"It is rather hard to believe for a mortal, I guess," I agreed. "Gods and monsters. It is quite a bit to take in. But you will have stories to tell your grandchildren one day."

"You think I would marry myself off to a man and have children, when I know what adventures there are to be had in this life?" She leaned away to look up at me. "I don't want that life. I never really did, but now I could never even imagine it for myself."

"You wouldn't want a normal, average life?"

"After all of this? After meeting gods and Valkyries? I couldn't even fathom having a normal life, whatever that might entail," she admitted. "Do you think you will settle down with Eryk, have babies and grandbabies, and live a quiet life as a warrior's wife?"

"I don't think I could imagine myself with that life either, if I am honest," I said, tilting her chin up with my index finger. "I don't know what exactly I want."

"We all make messes, I think," she said, sighing heavily. "It's the way life is. It's never easy or straightforward, and when the gods get involved, it gets even messier. It's not all on you."

"It all started with my decisions," I said with a frown. "I suppose I shouldn't blame the gods for my mistakes."

"You can't blame them for your mistakes, but they have certainly affected the outcomes of those mistakes," Gunhild said. "I think you have every right to be angry at that if you want to be."

"The only one I am truly angry at is Hel," I admitted, lowering my voice as if Hel might step out of the shadows upon hearing her name. "Everyone else did what they were born to do."

"Either way, dwelling on it won't help you succeed."

"I know, I know, but it's hard not to wonder what would have happened if I had done my duties," I said with a sigh. Gunhild pulled my face down and looked me deep in the eyes.

"You wouldn't have met me," she pointed out with a playful smirk. I couldn't help but laugh, despite how worried I always felt for her every second of the day. Her presence really did make things less dire. She was part of why I hadn't given up yet.

"I don't regret that for a second, even if it does put you in danger."

"I am here now, and I will be by your side until you have succeeded in your quest. I swear it again as I have sworn before."

"I appreciate that, though I wish you were not so dedicated to me," I said. "I'm worried something awful will happen to you and it will be my fault."

"Let's not think of that for now. Can I sleep in here with you?" she asked, though she was already climbing under the covers. I laughed and shifted to lay down under the blankets as well.

"Go to sleep," I told her. "We should enjoy a warm bed while we can."

Chapter Seventeen

The cottage was still empty when we woke the next morning and stepped out of our rooms. I half-expected Loki to be gone too, but he was there to side-eye Gunhild and me as we came out of the same room.

"I see how it is, poor old Loki, left to fend for himself," he teased. I found the closest unbreakable thing—an antler cup—and threw it at his head. It bounced off and tumbled to the floor. I hadn't thrown it hard, but he stumbled back onto a chair and flopped into it, hand to his head as if gravely injured. "Am I bleeding? Oh, I'm seeing stars. Valkyrie, you have wounded me!"

"Quiet or I'll throw another, harder this time," I warned him, though a smile tugged at my lips as Gunhild giggled. Loki gave a beleaguered sigh and rolled his eyes.

"Oh, the indignity. I am abused, assaulted, disrespected! I, a god, treated so horribly! Watch out, shieldmaiden, or you'll be next," he groaned pitifully.

"Get up, we need to eat and be going," I told him with a scowl that was difficult to maintain. "How far is it to Bifrost?"

"You are absolutely no fun at all, Yrsa." Loki threw the fallen cup back at me. I caught it midair and set it on a table rather than letting it bounce off me as Loki had. He sobered a little. "About four days' ride.

Shouldn't take long. And now we've got the token, things will be much easier."

"You didn't think they'd be easy before?" Gunhild asked, her eyes narrowing on Loki's face. Of course, things wouldn't have been easy. Nothing on this journey had been thus far, and we hadn't even gotten to the hard parts. We had barely begun.

Loki gulped dramatically, his gaze darting away to the window. I wasn't sure if he was trying to be funny or if he was genuinely scared of Gunhild's reaction. "Erm…maybe not?"

"Did you really expect it to be?" I asked Gunhild with a raised eyebrow. "It won't be as difficult as it would have been without Loki, but it definitely was never going to be easy. It still might not be."

"I know," Gunhild muttered, ducking her head. She scrounged the cabinets for food. "We should eat."

Loki and I both nodded and went to help her. We had a bit of fruit and some honey cakes before gathering our things and heading out.

"Should we lock the door?" I asked as I pulled it shut behind me.

"No point," Loki said with a shrug. "I have a feeling this place moves around at Odin's whim, so it can't be stumbled upon easily."

We tacked up our horses and brought them around to ride away from the cottage. When I looked back over my shoulder, the cottage was gone and even the glade it had been in had disappeared, leaving only budding trees.

"Be careful of traps," I called to Loki as he rode out ahead of us. The last thing we needed was for one of our priceless horses to be wounded or killed. Or one of us.

"I'm sure Odin took those with him when the cottage disappeared," Loki assured us, though when I gave him a death glare, he sighed and added, "I'll be careful."

We continued onward, picking our way through the trees. Birds flitted about above our heads, singing merrily to accompany us. With Loki in the lead, and assuming he knew the way, I could let my mind wander.

"Is everything well?" Gunhild asked as she pulled her horse up next to mine. Her voice was soft enough that Loki would be unlikely to hear us. I nodded, but she continued to stare at me until I sighed and shook my head.

"No, but it would be difficult to explain. I'm caught up in my thoughts, is all."

"Eryk?" she asked, and I nodded. It was easy to be honest with her. Easier than it had even been with Eryk, who I sometimes lied to just to coddle his feelings. "We'll find him. Didn't Loki say time doesn't pass in Nastrond like it does here? Maybe he hasn't even noticed."

"Even if Loki is right, it seems likely that time would pass in a way that made every torturous moment seem longer," I pointed out with a frown. "Either way, we only have until midsummer to get the armor to Hel. We need to hurry."

"We're hurrying as fast as we safely can," she told me, giving me a sympathetic smile, which certainly helped the tension in my stomach settle a little. How had I thought I could survive this quest without her? "We'll get there. Bifrost is only a few days away, Loki said, and then we'll be able to cross quickly to Alfheim to get the falcon cloak."

"Yes, but we don't know how to get it from them once we get there," I said.

"There will be a riddle or trick!" Loki called back to us.

"You're obnoxious," I told him, but nudged my horse into a trot to catch up to him.

"I know. But you love it," Loki teased.

"When you say a trick or riddle, what do you mean?" asked Gunhild as she pulled her horse alongside mine.

"Just that. Some sort of test, to see if we're clever enough to earn what they don't want to give us," Loki said with a shrug. "Obviously it will be impossible to solve, because they wouldn't *actually* give up the cloak, but that's what you've got me for. I'm a trickster. I can solve any riddle."

"Well, if you think you can answer an impossible riddle, then we'll be grateful for your help," I told Loki. He looked back over at me and grinned. "Don't let it go to your head."

"Too late. We're friends and I'm indispensable. It's all I've ever wanted," he said with a laugh loud enough to spook the horses. Mine shook its head and stamped its feet, and Gunhild's threatened to rear.

Loki's horse seemed not to care, but it must have been used to his antics. "Aren't you glad you brought me with you now? Who knows where you'd be without me."

"Well, I imagine we'd still have the Bifrost token, since that was Gunhild's doing," I said. "And I'm sure we're plenty clever enough to figure out a riddle without you."

"Are you, though?" he asked, squinting at me as if trying to determine my worthiness. "I kid, I kid, of course you are. But I'm still helpful, I hope. Enough to make my presence worth your while?"

"Don't get too desperate for praise," I chastised him. "Let's get where we're going and get this quest over with. We can praise each other later."

"Fiiiine," said Loki with a pout. "But I would rather have the praise now."

"You are such a child," Gunhild huffed. Loki merely grinned at her and pulled his horse in a circle around ours before coming back to the front of the line.

"I've never been a child in my life," he said with wide, serious eyes. He wasn't wrong—gods didn't really have childhoods. "How could I be a child now?"

"You certainly act like one," Gunhild muttered under her breath. Loki stuck his tongue out at her over his shoulder—like a child—and kept going.

Chapter Eighteen

Four days of riding later, we reached a small rise overlooking a little valley that revealed a waterfall I hadn't expected. The sound of rushing water filled the area, mist billowing up from where the falls reached the river below. The cliffs they fell from seemed impassible, but I hoped that Loki had another secret up his sleeve.

"We have to go through the falls," he said. I raised an eyebrow, impatient for more information. "There's a path that leads into a cave behind them."

"Ugh, not another cave. Can we take the horses?" Gunhild asked, a small crease appearing between her brows as she eyed up the waterfall and the path leading to it. I understood her concerns. Neither of us had enjoyed our experience in the cave on the way to Yggdrasil. I could only hope this one was much smaller and easier to traverse.

"We can," Loki confirmed. "The path is wide enough, though slippery. Horses might balk at going under a waterfall though. It gets loud."

"Will we not have issues taking them onto Bifrost?" I asked, my gaze also focused on the falls.

"Well… maybe?" Loki admitted. I scowled at him. Could he not give a straight answer for once? "Look, I haven't ever tried, so I don't know the answer. I usually go alone, without a horse or anything. This is new to me, too."

I huffed and nudged my horse forward, hoping it wouldn't resist going into the cave beneath the falls. But I was determined, and the horse seemed to sense that. It only hesitated for a few moments before hurrying behind them. The water roared, blocking out the sound of anything else, even my own heart pounding in my ears. I looked over my shoulder to see if the others followed.

Loki's horse would follow him anywhere, of course, and headed into the cave without so much as a skipped step. Gunhild's, on the other hand, tossed its head wildly and backed up when she tried to lead it through.

"Come on, stubborn, you have to go," she fussed and nudged its sides until it rushed forward into the cave and clattered past us to the exit at the other end.

I hurried to join her, and Loki followed more slowly. When I reached the mouth of the cave, my eyes widened.

The valley leading to Bifrost on the other side of the waterfall was like a painting, with vivid green grass, blue skies, and wildflowers of every color dotting the landscape. A few deer nibbled at the wildflowers near us, completely oblivious to our presence. At the opposite end of the valley rose Bifrost, a rainbow that stretched out before us.

Loki and I pulled up on either side of Gunhild, looking out across the valley at the bridge. Gunhild pulled the token Odin had given her from the pouch at her hip and looked down at it.

"What do I do with it?" she asked, frowning as she glanced from Bifrost to Loki. The token rolled back and forth in her palm as she shifted it. It glinted brightly in the rainbow light, its iridescence more pronounced now.

"Should anyone question us, we show them that little bauble and they'll let us pass." Loki instructed. "Specifically, Heimdall. He'll have lots of questions, but that token *should* silence them."

"Heimdall is the guardian of Bifrost, yes?" Gunhild asked. "I didn't pay attention to all the elders' stories as a child, but I do remember that."

"Yes, Heimdall is the one who keeps the bridge between realms safe, and free of people who don't belong there. But this token will tell him we belong, so there's nothing to worry about," Loki said. I eyed him up and down, to see if he looked like he was worried, but he seemed relaxed, almost excited, to be there.

"We'll let you lead," Gunhild promised, bouncing eagerly in her saddle, which upset her horse a little. It stomped its feet and backed up.

"Good plan," Loki agreed, and nudged his horse forward.

As we crossed the valley to the rainbow bridge, a warm breeze kicked up. The bridge's multicolored surface flickered slightly, as if on fire. The horse's hooves sounded like they were walking on glass. I worried it would crack under our weight, but Loki seemed unbothered as his horse stepped onto the bridge, followed by Gunhild's. When I looked down to be sure it wasn't going to crack, all I saw was my face reflected softly back at me from the shiny surface.

We moved forward slowly at first, but as our horses grew more confident, our pace picked up. As we made our way across, I wondered how long it was. I couldn't see the end and wondered if we might have been smarter to camp in the valley and start over the bridge the next morning. It was too late now, though.

"HALT." I was jerked out of my reverie by a man on a golden horse, staring us down from the peak of the bridge. He was pale skinned, with golden blonde hair, and teeth which seemed to be made of solid gold as well.

"Gullintanni!" Loki called brightly.

"Just because my teeth are gold doesn't mean you should call me Gold-Teeth, God of Mischief," Heimdall replied with a small scowl. He relaxed after a moment though, and he and Loki both dismounted and hugged each other tightly. "I thought you'd abandoned us to Midgard, Loki. It has been too long. And you've brought friends? A Valkyrie, I see. And...a mortal?"

I flushed as he noted what I was with ease, but he seemed not to care about me. It was Gunhild his blue-eyed gaze was intently focused on. I had a feeling this was not at all a good thing. Mortals certainly weren't permitted on Bifrost. My heart raced as I tried to think of how we would cross should the bauble not buy us passage.

"Yes," Loki said, leaving it at that. "Well, not just any mortal. A shieldmaiden. But yes."

"You know mortals are not allowed across Bifrost..." Heimdall pointed out. He seemed almost hesitant, as if he was afraid to upset Loki. "I can't really make exceptions because she's your friend."

"I know," said Loki. "But she's special. Show him, Gunhild."

Gunhild looked about as frightened as a rabbit cornered by a wolf, and it took her a few moments of shock to realize that Loki was speaking to her, and what he wanted her to do. She gulped and took the token out of her pouch to show the guardian of Bifrost.

"I see." Heimdall raised his eyebrows appreciatively. "Your shieldmaiden apparently has friends in very high places. Who gave that to you?"

"Er, well, Odin," Gunhild stammered.

"Why would Odin give you a Bifrost token?" Heimdall asked, a skeptical look in his eyes, which were just as golden as the rest of him.

"I was polite to him?" Gunhild replied, to which Heimdall snorted in disbelief.

"There's more to it than that," he said, a small muscle ticking in his jaw as he watched us carefully.

"There's really not. We ran into him in the woods, disguised as a hermit, and because Gunhild here was polite, and didn't mock him like I did, he rewarded her with this token," Loki explained.

Heimdall still looked doubtful, but he turned to me after a moment. "And what has brought you here, Valkyrie? Why are you with Loki and this shieldmaiden, with a token from the king of the gods?"

"We're only passing through," I said. It wouldn't be enough of an explanation, but I was hesitant to give more.

"To where?" Heimdall asked, his eyes narrowing on my face as he tried to figure out what we were up to. I swallowed hard and opened my mouth to answer, but Loki just had to get a word in first.

"Does it matter? We have the token. That should be enough," Loki replied flippantly.

"Yes, it matters, it is my duty to prevent people from crossing to places they aren't meant to be, and I have a feeling you aren't meant to be here," Heimdall grumbled.

"We're going to Alfheim," I said with a wince, afraid of what might happen should Heimdall ask why. I couldn't bear to tell another soul of my failures and their consequences.

Heimdall stared hard at me for several long moments that seemed to stretch out for hours. He seemed to finally decide that it was safe enough for us to go to Aflheim.

"As long as you aren't taking a mortal to Asgard, I suppose. But why are you with them?" he asked, brow furrowed accusingly.

"I wanted an adventure. Can you fault me for that?" Loki shrugged, obviously not so worried about Heimdall's opinion.

"I would think going about making mischief would be adventure enough," Heimdall grumbled under his breath. "I suppose if you've got the Allfather's permission, it doesn't matter what I think, does it?"

"While you are entitled to your opinion, you're right, it doesn't really matter in the grand scheme." Loki's tone was that of a toddler sticking out his tongue in defiance. I shot him a glare. I didn't want to antagonize anyone who might hinder our quest. He didn't seem to care much, though, and instead swaggered forward.

"Is there anything else you require of us? Or can we be on our way?" I asked.

"I should not let you pass," Heimdall said reluctantly. "But you do have the token. I guess you can be on your way."

"Come on." Loki bounced on his toes excitedly as Heimdall stepped aside and grudgingly returned to his post. "We've got time to make up."

We rode our horses for another mile or two until Bifrost ended in a bright meadow.

"How do we get to Alfheim from here?" I asked.

"Right this way, ladies," Loki said, bowing with a flourish. He turned his horse toward where the sun hung low in the sky. I hadn't realized so much time had passed.

Gunhild and I looked at each other, then headed off behind Loki. He urged his horse into a canter across the wide field to make up the time we had lost talking to Heimdall. I didn't even have to urge my horse on, as she was eager to keep up with Loki's and took off before I could truly get my seat under me. Gunhild laughed as I wobbled for a moment and took off past me, red hair streaming behind her in the wind like a pennant.

I caught up quickly, and soon enough we had crossed the meadow into an emerald wood. The trees here were tall, but slender, with vines climbing up them toward the sky and birds lost in their branches. Squirrels and chipmunks skittered this way and that among the undergrowth, barely stopping to look up at us as we slowed and passed through the trees. This forest felt almost like a holy place. We had to be close to Alfheim.

"We're about a day out," Loki told us.

"We should stop for the night before the sun sets completely. It will be safer to travel in the morning," I decided. Gunhild looked ready to argue, but I held up a hand to stop her. "We don't want to travel in foreign woods in the darkness. At the very least the horses could get hurt. At worst, we could run into something unpredictable and *we* could get hurt. We need to camp here and move on in the morning."

Gunhild sighed, but argued no further. We all dismounted and quickly made camp and a simple supper so that we could be well-rested and fed before moving on the next day.

"Don't fall behind, ladies, still many miles to go before we reach Alfheim," Loki told us the next morning as we started back on our trek through the woods. His voice was hushed as if afraid to disturb the forest air. I nodded and nudged my horse to walk a little faster, picking my way through the trees. I wished our whole journey had been this easy. Having a god on our side had its upsides.

It took us nearly the whole day to make it through the woods. Once again, the sun sank toward the horizon. The shadows beneath the trees lengthened, though not the way they had in Midgard, like claws reaching to grip at our feet. No, these shadows were like the arms of a drowsy child, stretching out before settling into a deep sleep. There was nothing to fear here. I felt at peace, for once, as if the forest had cast a spell over me.

It was nearly dark when we arrived at the gate to Alfheim. White marble arches swept up into the sky between the trees, their pinnacles hidden among the branches. A pair of slender women stood on either side of the gate, armed with long bows and a quiver full of arrows at each of their backs. They raised their bows as we approached.

"Hail and well met, my friends," said Loki in a soft voice as we came closer.

"Well met," one of the elves echoed warily. "State your names and reason for coming to Alfheim." Her skin was like alabaster, her hair similarly pale, and the other looked almost like her twin, with the same facial features. The one who had greeted us was a little taller and had eyes that matched the deep green of the twilight forest. Her hair was braided intricately atop her head. The shorter one's eyes were so blue they made Gunhild's look dull and colorless. Her hair curled lightly in ringlets that fell around her shoulders. In the dim sunset light that reached through the trees, their eyes seemed to glow.

I pushed my horse past Loki's, partially because I was afraid he would tease these women, and partially I felt I should be the one to speak, this being my quest.

"I am Yrsa of Valhalla, this is Gunhild Torstensdottir, and this is Loki of Asgard." I couldn't really claim to be of Valhalla anymore, but it was easier than explaining my whole situation outright.

The shorter elf's sapphire gaze shifted from me to Loki, narrowing on his face as she determined whether I told the truth. Or whether this was all part of a ruse by the God of Mischief. He preened a little under her gaze, tucking an auburn curl behind his ear with a charming grin. I gestured quickly to him to keep quiet, which he did for once.

"What brings you here?" she asked, looking back at me.

"We come on a quest." I decided the truth might serve me better here.

"A quest for what?" asked the other elf, the last of the sun glinting in her gaze.

"Freyja's falcon cloak," I said simply. This earned me a skeptical look, but the women glanced at each other for a moment before nodding and motioning us to come closer.

"Even if it is here, you will be sorely disappointed if you think our Queen will give it to you," the taller elf said.

"We would be grateful for the opportunity to at least speak to her about it," I said. If we could just get to the Queen, we might be able to convince her to turn the cloak over. It seemed unlikely, but if Loki was right, maybe she would give us a task or riddle to solve and we could get it that way.

"You may enter Alfheim," the elf with blue eyes told us. She pulled a horn from her belt and blew it, which caused a fury of movement from beyond the gate. Soon enough, another elf appeared, again with a similar face. Her eyes were a soft shade of violet, her hair cropped short, but still that same silvery color.

The guardians of the gate whispered to her for a moment, before she turned to us and gestured for us to dismount and follow her. We did as we were directed and kept quiet for now as she led us past the gate. The other two elves returned to their post.

"I am Brynja," she told us softly as she hurried along through the woods on the other side of the gate. She looked at me curiously. "The Queen will be surprised to have guests. Eydis said your name is Yrsa? You're a Valkyrie?"

"Yes, well… it's a long story, but yes."

"A long story," Brynja echoed. "Your story is yours to keep. It is nice to meet all of you. Even you, Loki."

Loki seemed surprised to be acknowledged and flushed as the elf said his name. I raised an eyebrow at him, but he simply shrugged sheepishly and kept his eyes on the ground. Brynja led us down a long, winding path through the woods.

As the last of the sun slipped far enough below the horizon that we could no longer see easily, lights began to glow atop poles on either side of the path. They did not flicker like flames, but instead emanated a soft, bluish glow, which lit the path easily. At my surprise, Brynja smiled and led me over to one.

"They are elf-lights. Have you never seen one before? They are lit by the juice of a type of mushroom only found in Alfheim." She pulled one off the top of its pole and offered it to me. I took it in my hands to find that the blown glass globe was filled with liquid. "When it grows dark enough, the mushrooms glow. Our ancestors discovered that one could take an extract from them and create lamps. They last for centuries. These have been here since before I was born."

Elves lived exceptionally long lives—well over two hundred years in many cases—so there was no telling just how long the lights had been here. I marveled over the lamp and then let Gunhild have a look. She smiled shyly at Brynja as she took it from me. The soft blue glow lit her features so that she was almost as ethereal as the elves. I couldn't help but admire her for a moment as she focused on the lamp.

After a minute or two, Gunhild handed the lamp back to Brynja who replaced it on the post before she motioned for us to follow her. Loki hung back a little and fell further and further behind until I turned around and went back to him.

"What is your problem?" I whispered harshly. "We need to see the Queen, convince her to let us have the cloak. I need *your* help for that. Come on."

"Ermmm…. Well…"

"What are you not telling me?" I narrowed my eyes at him. "Tell me before I find out the hard way. Have you stolen something from them before?"

"No…" Loki replied slowly, avoiding my gaze.

"Then what?" I glanced back over my shoulder to where Gunhild and Brynja were discussing the elf-lights, before returning my gaze to Loki.

"I might-have-bedded-the-Queen-once-or-twice…" he mumbled quickly. My eyebrows shot up and my eyes widened as I looked around myself. He couldn't possibly be serious. And he hadn't bothered to tell me before leading us to Alfheim. It wasn't as if he could have thought we wouldn't find out.

"Are you kidding me? Please say this is some trick or game!"

"No, I'm afraid not," he said with a sigh. "I kind of had a fling with her for a little while. Then I kind of left and never came back."

"*Kind of?*" I tried not to shriek at him for his carelessness. "And you're just now telling me? Please tell me she doesn't hate you, Loki."

"I honestly don't know," he admitted with an awkward grimace. "I didn't realize we'd be going straight to the Queen when we got here. I thought we'd look for the cloak elsewhere first."

"For the sake of the gods, Loki, if you ruin this for me, I will never forgive you," I told him, turning on my heel to return to Brynja and Gunhild, who both paused and looked at me with concern.

"Is everything well?" Gunhild asked. I put on a false smile and nodded.

"Of course, everything is fine," I lied. There was nothing to be done for it now, but to hope the Queen had forgotten. That seemed unlikely, but I hoped it had been long enough that she had at least forgiven the trickster god's antics. "Loki's horse has a stone in its hoof so he's being careful. That's all."

"We have an excellent farrier at the palace," Brynja assured me. "We'll just take it slow until we reach it. There is no rush, is there?"

"No, there's no rush," I confirmed, because now I was dreading the moment the Queen laid eyes on Loki again.

Chapter Nineteen

WE CAME to a path paved with neatly-fit stones. The elf-lights grew larger and closer together. From ahead of us, the sounds of horse hooves on stone, voices and hammering and all manner of other indistinguishable noises came. The aroma of spiced meats and roasted vegetables filled the air, as we found a city rising up out of the forest. White buildings twisted up in beautiful edifices through the trees that peppered the city. It was dazzling, even in the darkness. Everything was lit to a misty blue by the elf-lights scattered throughout the streets. They were busy even at this late hour.

In the middle of the city rose the palace, its white marble facade glowing like the moon. Brynja smiled and nudged me forward. After what Loki had told me, I was beyond nervous, but there wasn't much I could do about that. I wished Loki had been right and that we could have searched elsewhere, but the elves at the gate had made it seem like the Queen might have the cloak and I had to have it, so we would just have to brave her wrath.

"Come on, it will take us twenty minutes to cross the city and we have to leave the horses at the stables. We don't want to keep the Queen waiting."

"You mean she's expecting us?" I asked, my hands growing clammy and my stomach tightening.

"Of course. You don't think anything happens here without the

Queen knowing, do you?" Brynja looked at me with amusement dancing in her eyes. "As soon as Eydis sounded her horn, the news was sent to the Queen that you were coming."

"I suppose we had better hurry then," I said, glancing back at Loki, who was still dragging his feet. He seemed very concerned with what few weeds had managed to grow between the stones of the street and kept pausing to look at random things that couldn't possibly have been of any interest to him.

Brynja led us through the city, down perfectly laid streets that were bustling with elves, all of whom looked so much alike I thought I must be imagining the similarity. They were varied in height, eye color, hair style, but not in hair color or facial features unless one looked very closely. One's eyes might be a little more slanted, while another might have a wider mouth, but otherwise they could all have been twins to each other.

"They're all women," Gunhild whispered to me, and I nodded. I had noticed that too, but I wasn't about to ask where the men were.

"There aren't men here. They live in the countryside and only come together certain times of year to bed the women so there are children," Loki murmured as he caught up to us, careful not to let Brynja hear him.

Gunhild's mouth opened as if to ask more questions, but Brynja turned around, so Gunhild closed her mouth again. The elves were such an insular race, so far removed from everyone else, that I knew very little about them. Of course, Loki being Loki, he knew more than he probably should.

Once we had deposited our horses at the stables, we headed for the palace. We were much nearer to it now, and its size and sheer grandeur intimidated me. I didn't know how the Queen or her staff might react to our presence. I didn't know what I would do if she refused to see us, or saw us but refused to even entertain giving us the cloak. The idea that we might leave empty-handed was daunting and I tried to push it down and be hopeful instead. If we had to, surely Loki could steal it for us. Thievery was part of being a trickster, I hoped.

As the palace gates loomed before us, Brynja called out something in elvish, and someone responded from the gatehouse in the same language. The massive silver gates opened before us without so much as a creak, and we were permitted into the courtyard.

"This is where I leave you," Brynja told us as another elf rushed over, eyeing us suspiciously. "Aina will take you to the Queen. It was very nice to meet you all. Aina, this is Yrsa of Valhalla, Gunhild Torstensdottir, and Loki of Asgard."

Aina seemed unimpressed but nodded as Brynja left us with her. She did not say much, but turned and walked silently toward the large palace doors, which opened slowly as we approached. They were made of solid oak, burnished until they shone in the blue elf-lights, with runes and spirals carved into them. I stared up at them as they opened, but had no time to try to read the runes because Aina was hurrying us into the palace faster than we could keep up.

The various identical palace guards stared at us in shock as we passed. How long had it been since non-elves had passed through these halls? How long had it been since Loki had passed through these halls, even? For all I knew, it could have been a hundred years since he was here last.

We were led through the marble-floored halls, and up a winding staircase, before we stopped before the throne room doors, which were almost as grand as the palace doors themselves. Gunhild stared around at everything wide-eyed, lips parted as if she wanted to ask a million questions. Aina looked each of us up and down with a frown.

"You're hardly dressed for seeing the Queen, but I suppose there is no helping it, is there?" she said dismissively. I looked down at my grimy, tattered clothing. Laundering it in the river before Bifrost hadn't made much difference after weeks of travel. I had no time to think of what to replace them with though, because Aina pushed the heavy doors open and announced us. "Yrsa of Valhalla, Gunhild Torstensdottir and…"

"Loki of Asgard," said a resonant voice. The face it came from was exquisitely beautiful, not one of the many multiples outside of these doors. Her cheekbones were so high and so sharp they seemed like they must have been cut from glass, and her eyes were wider and farther apart than the other elves as well. "What in the world brings you back here? And after so long?"

At least she didn't seem angry. I glanced at Loki, who offered a low bow to the Queen of the elves. When he rose, it was with a self-deprecating smile.

"Queen Asa, what an honor it is to see you again," Loki greeted her. He was far more cheerful than his demeanor had been as we approached the palace. "I come with friends this time. Yrsa is on a quest to find Freyja's falcon cloak."

Normally, I would have protested at Loki sharing our story, but the elves were wise enough to see through any tale even he might have told. It was best to be honest with the Queen, as we had been with the gatekeepers.

The Queen's eyes drifted to me with a curious golden gaze.

"Ah, a Valkyrie on a quest," she said almost disinterestedly, as she tilted her head to look at me more closely. She stepped off her throne after a moment to walk down the steps of the marble dais and stand in front of me. "How curious. I have never met a Valkyrie before. Are you not a pretty little thing?"

"Erm, thank you, your majesty," I mumbled, suddenly quite unsure of myself. She was by far the most striking woman I had ever seen, in a sort of frightening, unapproachable way.

"And you have brought the God of Mischief with you, though I assume you did not know our... history... when you decided to bring him on your quest?"

"No, your majesty, I only found out today, once we were already in Alfheim on the way into the capital," I admitted, looking down at my feet with embarrassment. The last thing I needed was for her to decide to throw us out. "I hope I haven't offended you by bringing him here with me."

"Not at all, Yrsa. I am pleased to see him again," she said, her gaze sliding to Loki with a certain heat in it. "It has been far too long. Come, let us sit and talk."

I thought she meant just Loki, but then she was looping her arm through mine. She smelled vaguely of lavender and rose. Her pace was leisurely as she led me over to an area behind the dais where a heavy table made of twisting silver vines and matching chairs were arranged, for dining during the day. Gunhild followed behind timidly, while Loki, looking utterly confused, stalked along behind her. Queen Asa let go of my arm and gestured to the other chairs before taking the finest one for herself.

"Yrsa, tell me more about yourself."

Gunhild squirmed like she felt quite out of place as she took a seat next to me, so I reached over under the table to grab her hand and squeeze it, out of sight of the Queen. She squeezed back, tapping that familiar pattern, and returned her focus to Queen Asa with a little more confidence than before. I honestly felt out of place myself, even if I was used to entertaining the gods in Valhalla. Normally I was dressed in much finer garb than what I was wearing now.

"There's quite a lot to tell, and I've told it so many times now, it hardly feels real," I admitted quietly.

"Maybe it isn't," she suggested with a cryptic smile. "It could all be a fever dream. Perhaps all of life is, and you will wake up one day as a child and realize you imagined all of this, from the moment you became a Valkyrie."

I glanced at Loki and then back at her. The Queen was odd, to say the least, and it left me feeling out of sorts and off-kilter. "Yes, perhaps so. It would be quite strange, if that is the case."

"Is that not every dream?" she asked. "Tell me why you are looking for Fjodfeld. It is a treasure of mine that I am loath to part with, unless Freyja herself comes looking for it. Did she send you?"

"No, your majesty." I considered lying, but I had a feeling she would see right through it. "Hel did. I failed her, and this is the quest she sent me on. To redeem myself, I suppose."

"And what might your reward be if you deliver it to her?" the Queen asked, spreading her delicate hands on the table before her.

"I get to save the warrior she condemned to Nastrond for my disobedience," I said

Why did you disobey her? I assume you kept the warrior from Valhalla, but why?" asked the Queen,

"I love him. I chose to keep him in Midgard, against his fate, and Hel punished him for it."

"And did she punish you as well?" The Queen raised an eyebrow at me. "Or have you decided to give up Valhalla because you love him so much?"

"I was banished, and I had to choose between saving him or going back." My voice was hushed with this admission. It felt as if the Queen and I were alone in the throne-room.

"And you chose to save him, how interesting," the Queen said, her eyes flicking downward to where my hand tucked into Gunhild's under the table. She tilted her head to look back up at me, as if she saw something I did not.

Loki cleared his throat as he danced his fingertips over the Queen's hand. This caught her attention. I raised an eyebrow at Loki, grateful that he had managed to draw her attention away so that my stomach could unclench.

"About that falcon cloak," Loki said. The Queen's eyes narrowed on him. "Would you be willing to part with it? For such a good cause, surely you must be moved to do so."

"You think I would easily give up my most prized possession for a sad story?" Queen Asa asked. Her brow lowered, not quite angrily, and she shook her head. "Not even for the favor of the gods. It is mine. I have no intention of parting with it."

"Technically it is Freyja's," Loki pointed out before I could respond.

"And how do you think I got it? At a market?" Queen Asa countered. "It was a gift from her to my ancestors. One she probably forgot she gave after long enough. Did she really tell you it was lost? I wonder if she says the same about the rest of the armor."

"Hel told me the various pieces were lost, and that I had to bring them to her. It's not even really armor, is it? Just a few random items that hold significant value to her, but which she didn't even care enough about not to misplace." I tried to seem nonchalant about the whole thing, though inside my whole being quaked.

"Brave little Valkyrie," the Queen purred. "If only Freyja could hear you now. What do you think she would say?"

"It doesn't matter," I admitted as I kept my voice cold. "I need the cloak, the helm, and the necklace."

"That old helm? It is dented and dirty by now, in the hands of the dwarves." Queen Asa looked me over with an appraising glance. "I tell you what. We will come up with a way for you to earn the cloak. If you can rise to the challenge, then I will give it to you."

"What is the challenge?" I asked warily.

"A simple thing really. Go to the marketplace and purchase something for me," Queen Asa said, examining her fingernails.

"What's the catch?" I asked.

"Take the evening to sleep," the Queen said, rather than answering. "I will tell you in the morning what I require you to purchase. No point in setting you on a quest this late in the evening."

I turned away to hide my scowl. There was no arguing with the Queen of the elves. She would likely change her mind about giving us this chance at all, which would undo the effort we had made so far.

Chapter Twenty

GUNHILD and I were given a room to share, with only one bed, but it wasn't a big deal considering we'd been sharing a tent for weeks now. Nothing shocking was bound to happen between two friends who had been as physically close as two people could be in such a small tent.

Morning told a different story. A blinding ray of sun sliced through the window and across the room into my eyes. I cringed away from it and buried my face into Gunhild's neck without thinking. We were tangled together in such a way that most would have assumed something untoward had happened the night before.

And in a way, it had. Sometime before dawn, I had awakened just enough to cuddle further into Gunhild's arms without realizing we had become entwined to begin with. She had pressed her lips to the back of my neck in her sleep. This sent a shiver down my spine and caused me to wriggle slightly against her, enough to wake both of us.

She panicked for a moment, going completely stiff, before I turned in her arms to face her, our noses just touching. Rather than speak, I gave a soft shake of my head and then leaned my brow against hers. My heart pounded heavily against my ribs, matching hers beat for beat. I could feel it through our clothes. She put her palm against my chest, as if to still my pulse at least a little. I bit my lip and smiled into the darkness at the tender gesture. Nothing was ever said, no words ever spoken, just silence and the soft sounds of our breath as we relaxed against each other.

We would be exhausted come morning, but these moments in the darkness felt too precious to shatter or let disappear into sleep just yet. Her lips were so close to mine, but I couldn't quite bring myself to kiss her. What if she pulled away? What if it offended her? No, I couldn't risk it. This was perfect exactly as it was, and I refused to ruin it by pushing too hard. Eventually, an hour or two later, I finally succumbed to sleep, drifting into a comfortable and blissful slumber in Gunhild's arms.

When morning came all too soon, I sat up with a curse and shook Gunhild awake as well.

"What?" She rubbed her eyes and groaned before struggling upright. Her hair was a mess, and I was sure mine was as well. "Are we late for something?"

"Yes, well no, but we've got to figure out the Queen's task still. I'm not sure how late it is," I told her as I slipped out of bed. I hurried into a change of clothes and smoothed my hair. "Come on!"

Gunhild still sat bleary-eyed in bed. I wondered if she even remembered what had happened in the middle of the night. When she rubbed the sleep from her eyes and made eye contact with me, her concerned expression told me it wasn't forgotten. When I offered a reassuring smile, she merely bit her lip and ducked her head with a pleased little smile of her own as she stretched like a cat.

"It can't be that late, can it? We can't just have a few more minutes?" she begged.

"No. Get up! I need to figure this out so we can get Loki and move on," I urged her as I pulled on my boots. I would have loved to stay and re-enact those moments in the middle of the night, just to see what they meant, but there wasn't time now. We were already late. I crossed back to the bed and tugged on her arm. "Get up, sunshine. Get up."

The use of an endearment was enough to brighten her, and she rushed out of bed as someone knocked on the door, calling that breakfast awaited us. I told them that we would be out shortly and went to sit on the window seat. It seemed to be sometime before noon, but I couldn't tell how much before.

Gunhild dressed and gestured for me to come with her. The handmaiden who awaited us looked us both up and down with a bit of distaste.

"The Queen awaits your presence in the dining room," the handmaiden said in a disdainful tone.

"Please lead the way," I said, trying not to respond in the same tone.

We followed the handmaid down the marble corridor until we reached another set of large wooden doors. They opened onto a room with a long, polished marble table. Loki and the Queen sat at one end, already eating.

"Good morning," Loki greeted us cheerfully. "We're almost done. You slept late."

"Late indeed," the Queen agreed. "The day wears on quickly. You must be wondering about your task."

"Apologies, we did not realize how late it was," I told her, hoping our tardiness didn't hurt our already tiny chance of getting the cloak.

"Regardless, you are here now, I suppose," the Queen said with a sigh. She stood gracefully and slipped away from the table. We stumbled to follow her as she stalked out of the throne room and down a long corridor. Her shoes echoed on the marble floor and rang out from the high ceiling above us, which was painted with intricate murals depicting various histories of the elven people.

At the end of the hallway, which seemed to go on forever, was a small, out-of-place blue door. Queen Asa produced a key from a chain around her neck and unlocked it, leaving it open for us to step inside without her. I half expected her to lock us in the pitch-black room without another word and leave us there to rot.

She merely smiled cryptically and motioned into the room. "You must buy, with one copper coin, something which will fill this entire room. Loki, you will stay here with me while the Valkyrie and her shieldmaiden shop. We have much to catch up on."

Gunhild and I looked at each other in confusion, before glancing to Loki. He looked rather pleased with himself. My confusion turned to anger as I realized that despite his promise to help us with any riddle the Queen might offer, he was now abandoning us to figure it out on our own so that he could spend more time with the Queen.

"You'll be fine, Valkyrie," Loki told me. He dug in his pocket and found a handful of copper coins, which he pressed into my palm. "You'll figure it out."

"Now, go," the Queen said. "You have until sunset to pass the test."

She flicked her hand dismissively at us and turned as Loki put an arm around her shoulders to lead her away. He winked over her shoulder at us before they disappeared around a corner together.

"Do you think Loki knows the answer?" Gunhild asked. Music floated through the walls from somewhere outside, but it was more of an annoyance than a comfort. "I can't even think of something that could fill a whole room, much less for only a single copper coin."

"I don't know," I said as I rubbed a weary hand over my face.

"Can we buy enough feathers to fill the room? Or is it a bed or something?"

"Feathers sound more like the answer to a riddle than an answer to the Queen's test." I rubbed my eyes until I saw stars behind my eyelids. "And a bed isn't going to cost a copper. Neither would a room full of feathers, if we're being honest. Feathers are expensive too."

"It could be a trick," Gunhild said as she continued to pace. Her movement was almost hypnotic.

"Oh, it certainly is, but that doesn't lead us any closer to an answer," I said with a sigh. "What could the trick be? A riddle? A trap? We could fill it with nothing. That seems like the answer to a riddle."

"You can't buy nothing," Gunhild pointed out. "It has to be something we can buy at the market."

"Ugh, I know. I just don't know where to start." I had to stop myself from snapping at her. It wasn't her fault we didn't know the answer. If anything, the blame fell on Loki. His attachment to the Queen meant that she wanted him with her instead of letting him help us with the problem. "We have to get to the market. Come on."

Chapter Twenty One

THE WORLD outside the quiet of the palace was bustling and loud. We carefully wove through the courtyard, past a bevy of hard-working gardeners. The marble exterior of the palace blazed a brilliant white in the sun. Its soaring arches and parapets glinted brightly and made me squint as I gazed up at them.

Gunhild gently took my arm and tugged me onward to the market, which was a good hour's walk from the palace. We took the winding path down the hill, and into the city proper. Alfheim's capital city of Gimlé was even more beautiful in the day than it had been by elf-light. As we walked, I tried to think of what the answer to the riddle could be.

Eventually, we reached the market and started looking into shop windows and stalls for possible solutions. The market was a long street lined with a marble building that housed a variety of different shops. Out front of all the shops were brightly colored stalls and booths which sold various wares as well. Gently swaying oak trees rose over the street and shaded it from the sun, which climbed toward its zenith. Willows stood on the corners of the market square, with musicians playing quiet tunes beneath them. It was warmer here than in Midgard as well, so our furs were almost stifling without freezing air to protect us from.

The aroma of spiced food wafted through the market, leaving my stomach growling. It might have been better to stay for breakfast with the Queen, but our mission was urgent. Unlike the market in Armvind, this one was not filled with the shouts of fishwives selling their wares, but music and conversation instead.

"Do you think it could be music?" Gunhild asked suddenly as we passed by a music shop. She stopped with so little warning that a woman behind her ran into us. The elf glared as she went around us with a huff.

"Music? I suppose that could fill a room, yes, but are there any instruments that cost only a single copper?" I took her arm and looked through the shop window at the instruments inside.

"We could ask."

We pushed the door open and stepped inside with a jingle from the bells over the door. The shopkeeper greeted us with a dubious hello and watched as we looked around to see what might cost a copper coin.

"Everything here is so expensive," Gunhild whispered to me. "Dozens of gold coins, rather than a single copper. This can't be the answer."

My heart sank. She was right. This couldn't be the answer unless the shopkeeper had something stashed somewhere that was shoddily made or used until it wore out and barely worked anymore.

"Do you happen to have a flute of any sort?" I turned to the shopkeeper with a hopeful smile. She nodded and pointed toward a shelf where a delicate silver flute with various keys and stoppers sat on a stand glistening in the sun that slanted through the window. "Er... maybe something a little less... costly?"

The woman gave a sour look and shook her head. "We don't sell cheap or poorly made instruments here. This is Alfheim, not Midgard." She spit the word Midgard out like it tasted bitter. I had to put a hand on Gunhild's arm to keep her from doing or saying something she shouldn't to the woman.

"I didn't mean that you did," I said apologetically. "I only wondered if you might have something used? That would suit a beginner? Maybe a child's instrument?"

"I do, but even that will not be cheap, as a child needs to learn on a quality instrument," the woman scoffed, going behind the counter to open a box and show us a simple clay flute. "I have this. It is five silvers."

I sighed and turned to Gunhild with a shrug. There was our answer to that question. Gunhild still seemed livid about Midgard being slandered, but the elf wasn't wrong about the differences in quality of such luxury items.

"Thank you anyway, but this doesn't suit our needs." I bowed my head to her and pulled Gunhild out of the shop with me. The elf muttered something behind our back about useless humans.

We stepped back out into the street and paused beneath a tree to collect our thoughts. "If not music," I said, "then what else could it be?"

"Perhaps we should find something to eat while we think," Gunhild suggested as a girl walked by with a tray full of sugared buns, dripping with cinnamon icing. "I think hunger is an impediment to thinking clearly."

"Oh, is it?" I teased, my mood lightening a little at her hopeful expression. She nodded and bounced on her heels, her gaze following the tray of buns. "I suppose we'd better get them while they're hot. We can discuss our other options while we eat."

I pushed Gunhild gently toward the tray, and she called out to the baker who gestured for us to follow her. She was headed toward a small tavern with outside seating under a willow tree. We followed her inside, where she set the tray down on a table and looked to us with a smile.

"You wanted some sweet buns?" she asked. Gunhild nodded eagerly, and the girl smiled and went to get plates. "These are a copper each."

Gunhild's eyes lit up, and she looked over at me as I paid. I wasn't sure why she looked like she wanted to drag me outside.

"What if it's the aroma of delicious food? That could fill a room, right? And these are only a copper each," she pointed out as she sat down at a table outside and tore a piece off to shove in her mouth.

"I think it would take more than the scent of one sweet bun to fill that entire room. Probably a whole tray. And that's a dozen coppers." I hated to disappoint her, and the way her expression faltered made me wish I would have just gone with the idea. But it was too important for us to succeed.

"Oh. Well. It was worth a try," Gunhild said.

"It certainly was. And a good idea. I wish it were enough." I patted her hand reassuringly and then settled to eat my own sweet bun. After a few bites, I said, "So, it's not music, it's not food, it's not nothing, what could it be? What else is left?"

Gunhild couldn't answer because her mouth was full of pastry, but she shook her head and shrugged, which was answer enough. I was stumped. What in the world would fill a room but only cost a copper?

We ate the cinnamon buns in silence for a while. Sunlight dappled through the willow and left lacy patterns across the table and on our faces. If I had not been so desperately disappointed in myself for not being able to figure out this riddle, I might have thought it beautiful, even if it was a reminder of how quickly the day was passing.

Something about the light twisted in my thoughts, though. I had a niggling feeling that the answer was right there if I was intelligent enough to figure it out. What was I missing? What about this situation made me feel like I had the answer in my hands when I knew I didn't?

"Yrsa?" Gunhild said my name like it was the third or fourth time she had done so, and I looked up with a quizzical expression. "You were a million miles away. What are you thinking?"

"The sunlight." I tapped the little lacy patterns on the table. "It has me thinking. I feel like there's something to it telling me the answer to the Queen's task, but I can't seem to place what it is."

"Sunlight?" Gunhild asked, tilting her head, and squinting up through the tree branches. The sunlight dappled her face and lit her hair to molten copper where it touched. And that was when I realized.

"Light! That will fill a room! Come on!"

I dragged her to her feet before she could ask any further questions and pulled her from the table and our sweet buns to dash off into the street.

"Where are we going?" she asked as I strode down the street, looking in shop windows and into stalls and booths along our path.

"We have to find a candle. A big candle." It was almost the end of the street before we came upon a shabby booth with a young girl sitting inside, tossing a coin between her hands. On the table in front of her were a variety of candles. Some had been carved so that the wax arched from the body of the candle in winglike or waterfall shapes. Some were molded into the shapes of different animals. But the one I wanted was a massive, cream-colored pillar candle that sat on a shelf behind her.

"Good day," I greeted her, and she looked up at me curiously. Her expression morphed into one of disbelief as she realized I wasn't another elf.

"You're—I mean that is—I'm sorry but you aren't—" the girl stammered, trying to find what she wanted to say.

"Elf? No, we're not. But the Queen has given us a task which requires that candle behind you." I gestured to the one I wanted and she turned to pull it from the shelf and make space on the table to set it down.

"Why would you want a candle? Nobody wants candles. They want elf-lights. When they do want candles, it's the pretty ones or the scented ones."

"No, that one right there is absolutely perfect. Its light could fill a whole room, don't you think?" I took the candle in both my hands and twisted it between them to get a better look.

"I suppose it would," said the girl, who looked at me now like I was slightly mad.

"Can I offer you one copper for it?" I held my breath to see if she would say yes, or if she would also have exorbitant prices for her wares.

"A copper is probably more than it's worth, but yes, I'll accept a copper." She held her hand out for the coin, which I promptly deposited. "Thank you. Would you like me to wrap it for you?"

"No, there's no time," I told her. She eyed me suspiciously as she handed the candle over. My heart leapt anxiously as I prayed to whatever gods might be listening that this was the answer to the Queen's task.

Chapter Twenty Two

We hastened back up through the city and made our way to the palace. It took longer than expected to get there. There was a grand commotion in the streets halfway to the palace. A cart had overturned and made it impossible to walk.

"This way! It will get us there faster." Gunhild grabbed me by the wrist and tugged me down a back alley. Thankfully, she had the sense of direction to lead us back up the hill to the palace without getting hopelessly lost.

As the sun lowered on the horizon, blazing copper like Gunhild's hair, we made it to the front gates of the palace, where they let us in and led us to the throne room before the sun set completely.

We were out of breath and sweating as we were presented to the Queen. Loki sat on the arm of her throne and chatted quietly to her as she listened with an amused smirk twisting her full lips. After a moment, they finally seemed to realize we were there and sat up straighter, separating from each other reluctantly.

"Have you managed to figure out my task?" Queen Asa raised an eyebrow and looked down at us with an imperious gaze. "A candle? How quaint. I have not seen one of those in… well, I cannot recall how long."

"There is a girl in the market who sells them. Candles of all shapes, sizes, colors, and scents," Gunhild told her.

"Your majesty, does this fulfill your request?" I held up the candle, unsure what to do with it. "It cost us one copper."

"It looks quite small to fill a room," Loki teased. The Queen laughed with delight. "Why don't we take it to the room and find out?"

"An excellent idea, dearest." Queen Asa stood up, ignoring the shocked expression on all our faces at her pet name for Loki. Loki looked the most surprised of all of us. "Come with me."

She stood and held her hand out to Loki for him to assist her down the dais without tripping on her ornate violet gown. One would have thought she was hosting foreign dignitaries by how she was dressed. Instead, it was just us, and I felt terribly underdressed. Not that I had fineries such as hers even in Valhalla. And even if I did, I couldn't have kept them safe and clean for weeks on end as we traveled. I merely had to push aside the sickly feeling in my stomach standing next to her.

"I hope you have thought this through." The Queen flicked her hand for us to go inside the room she and Loki led us to.

"I have, thank you." I pulled a flint box from a small pouch slung over my shoulder, and had Gunhild hold the candle at the center of the room so I could light it. The candle had three wicks, and I carefully lit each of them. The room glowed a little brighter with each new flame that flared to life. "Care to close the door?"

The Queen's mouth changed from an amused smirk to a flat line as Loki closed the door. We had fulfilled the Queen's impossible task. The room was filled with flickering light, a golden glow that bounced from the marble floor and plaster walls.

"Is this what you had in mind?" I motioned for Gunhild to hold the candle a little higher. There was no denying that we had filled the room for a single copper.

"I knew you'd figure it out in no time, Valkyrie." Loki clapped me on the shoulder. "I told you, my Queen. Never underestimate this pair. A little riddle is nothing to them."

Queen Asa looked ready to light the whole palace on fire. I'd assumed it was a riddle all along, but it turned out she thought she was giving us an impossible task. She clearly never intended to give us the cloak. Would she now? Or would she renege on her deal? I held my breath as she decided.

"I suppose you leave me no choice," the Queen said in a deadly quiet voice. "An elf does not go back on her word. We pride ourselves on our honesty. At any cost."

The Queen opened the door and stalked out into the corridor. Loki pushed me forward to follow her.

"Go get your prize, Yrsa. Now's your only chance. I'll be right behind you." Loki's voice carried a note of concern. His expression had shifted too, but instead of anger like the Queen, he now looked worried.

I blew out the candle and motioned for Gunhild to leave it on a table along the corridor. We hurried behind the Queen as she stormed away from us. When I called out to her to wait, she simply lifted a hand to hush me and kept up her pace down the hallway. We practically had to run to catch up.

She turned down another corridor, and then another, then up two flights of stairs and down another corridor. This one led to a dead-end passageway, at the end of which was an ornate set of double doors locked with a padlock and chain. The Queen pulled a golden necklace from around her neck and looked over her shoulder at us for a moment. She lifted a pendant hanging from it to her lips and then put it into an opening in the padlock, which clicked and came free in her hand.

"Do not dally, then," the Queen told us as she pulled the chain free and pushed one of the doors open. Gunhild and I hurried inside and looked for the Queen to follow us, but she shoved Loki hard into the room and then slammed the door shut without coming in herself. The muffled rattle of the chain made its way through the wooden door and left me with a hollow feeling in my chest.

Loki turned back to the door as it thudded shut and pounded his fists against it. "Asa! Let us out! This is ridiculous! You shouldn't have given them the task if you didn't want them to solve it!"

His protests were met with silence.

Gunhild took my hand as we stared at Loki, who slid down to the floor with his back against the door. My heart gave a panicked flutter as reality set in. The Queen had imprisoned us, all because we had beaten her.

"What do we do?" My voice trembled more than I liked. I forced myself to breathe deeply to maintain a sense of calm. This would not be the end of our journey. I would make sure of it. Even if I had to knock down a door and kill the Queen with my bare hands, I wasn't leaving without the cloak. Although at this rate, I might not be able to leave at all, cloak or not. I looked to Loki. "Can you get out of here and unlock the door to free us?"

"I could get out of here, yes, but that door only unlocks with the Queen's pendant."

"She can't just keep us in here," Gunhild said, voice rising with her own fears. The room was quite large and finely decorated. It contained a giant canopy bed with purple and gold linens, a small seating area with matching furniture, barred windows, and a large wardrobe against one wall. There were no other doors to escape through.

"What is this room, Loki?" I forced myself to breathe as I went to one of the windows to inspect the bars. Maybe they could be manipulated so that we could escape. A glance out the window showed that we were too high above the courtyard below to escape unscathed, even if we could get through the bars.

"It's the old Queen's bedroom. Asa's mother. She died here and Asa sealed it up after." He cursed under his breath and closed his eyes. "I should have known this would happen. She must have planned this all along in the event you solved her task."

"It wasn't that hard," Gunhild said. "You probably knew the answer before we even left to look for it."

"Well, yes, of course I did. It's one I've used on any number of people. I probably taught it to her at some point." Loki rubbed his temples and groaned. "That's probably what upset her so much."

"She probably feels like you played her, if you're the one who came up with the task to begin with," Gunhild said with a huff. She went to one of the windows and pulled hard on the bars, as if she could pry them open somehow. "Ugh! There's got to be another way out! Loki, this is your fault!"

"Yes, yes, of course it is. Always blame the Trickster. That's the easy way out." Loki growled furiously and then, between one blink and the next, he disappeared.

"Loki!" I screamed. Surely, he hadn't just left us and gone back to Asgard. "He's looking for a way out for us, right?"

"You're the one who asked him to come along," snapped Gunhild. "He's probably gone to do something more enjoyable. No more adventure to be had here."

"He wouldn't just abandon us. He promised to help. He's probably trying to find us some way out." My voice was strained with the effort not to snap back at her. "He probably left because you upset him with your accusation. If we're lucky, he's just sweet-talking the Queen into letting us go."

Gunhild scowled at me and sat down heavily on the large bed. She crossed her arms over her chest and refused to look at me. Her anger was the least of my worries, though. We had to escape from this room, with the cloak, and move on to find the helm, one way or another.

Instead of focusing on the solidly chained and locked door, or the barred windows, I made my way around the room to inspect every nook and cranny, hoping I might find some clue which could give us a way out. This could just be another riddle, though that seemed unlikely.

"What are you doing?" Gunhild asked, looking over at me with a scowl. "Looking for dust isn't going to help us."

"This was the old queen's bedroom, right?" I pointed out. "There's no way she stayed here with only one way in and one way out. There's got to be another exit. Even if it's just some tiny little tunnel. I'm trying to figure out where it is."

"If you say so," said Gunhild.

"Was trying to pry the bars off the windows working?"

"Well... no. But searching for imaginary doors isn't going to work either."

"Look, Valkyries are made from the daughters of royalty. That means I grew up in a royal household. Every single one of our bedrooms had multiple ways in and out. Just in case." Gunhild's eyes widened at this revelation, but I didn't give her the opportunity to question it. I just continued my circuit of the room, pressing on moldings and cornices, pulling on shelves and frames, and looking underneath rugs for trap doors.

"Where would a hidden doorway or tunnel be?" she asked once she got over her shock.

"Somewhere you wouldn't think to look. But still easily accessible."

"So hidden behind a curtain or bookshelf or something?"

"Exactly. I had a trap door under a rug, under a chair in my bedroom at home. Help me move this table." I pushed from one side and Gunhild pulled on the other until we could move the rug beneath it. I knelt on the floor and pushed at various tiles on the marble flooring, trying to find one that might click or give way to a trap door.

"Looking for this?" Loki stood in front of the bed. The headboard was folded down, and a tunnel was visible behind where it had been.

"Loki, you prat! Where did you go?" I huffed. As annoyed as I probably sounded, I was flooded with relief at the sight of him and the exit to the room.

"Well first, I went to get this," he said, shoving what seemed at first like a pile of feathers into my hands. "Then I had to sneak into the tunnel. Now come on, let's leave before Asa realizes I've stolen the cloak and come to steal you as well."

"You did *not* steal the cloak." There was no denying that the cloak I held was Fjodfeld though. Its iridescent feathers glittered in the elf-lights that lit the room now that the sun was setting. I could almost feel the magic emanating from it. "Gods, Loki, you're going to get us killed."

"Then let's get out of here before she realizes." He grabbed Gunhild and shoved her toward the bed as I tried to figure out what to do with the cloak until we got back to our horses and packs. "We've got to get the horses and our gear, and leave Alfheim as soon as we can."

"Can't you just vanish all of us like you did yourself?" I asked as Loki gestured for Gunhild to climb through the hole.

Loki looked thoughtful for a minute as he considered whether he could do that. "I don't know. I've never tried. I guess we could attempt it."

"Then what are we waiting for?" I asked, the cloak a little more tightly. "Get us to the stables, then vanish us and the horses somewhere outside of Alfheim."

"I can't take two people and three horses along with myself, I don't think," Loki said with a doubtful frown.

"You don't *think*? What can you do? You're a god, you should be able to do anything you want," I huffed impatiently as Gunhild came to stand at my side. "The whole reason you came with us was to help. So help us!"

"We're standing here arguing about what I can do instead of taking the certain escape. Why not move and figure out the rest once we're out of the palace?" Loki suggested.

Gunhild made a disgruntled noise and climbed into the space behind the bed. I handed over the cloak to her and followed behind, while Loki climbed in after us and pulled the headboard back into place.

"Why cover our tracks here? She's going to know we escaped," I said as we crawled in near darkness. Someone had thought to put elf-lights along the passage at some point, but they had nearly all gone out by now from the passage of time.

"Because I'm not sure if Asa knows about this tunnel, and it's better if she has to search for it like you did," Loki whispered harshly. Considering how many of the elf-lights had faded to darkness, it seemed likely she didn't know at all. "Also, keep your voice down. We don't want to be found."

"Fine. Now, can you vanish us or not?" I whispered back. Gunhild struggled to keep from dragging the cloak as we crawled.

"Let me try," Loki said with a sigh and grabbed my ankle and Gunhild's. "Grab that cloak."

Gunhild hugged the cloak to her chest, and I took her hand. The next thing I knew, we were all three crouched on the floor of the stables. Thankfully our horses didn't startle too much from our appearance, except for Loki's, which gave a low whicker. Gunhild turned away to vomit in the corner. Even I was a little dizzy. It had been a while since I traveled that way.

"I guess mortals don't handle that kind of travel well." A bit of guilt crept into Loki's voice.

"You could have warned me," Gunhild said miserably. She wiped her mouth. "Come on, let's get moving."

"Can you shift all of us elsewhere?" I asked in a low voice so that the grooms wouldn't hear us. As I awaited Loki's answer, I carefully tucked the feather cloak into my pack where it sat with the rest of our gear and weapons near the horses. Gunhild took the hint and helped me get all of our belongings strapped back to the horses so they wouldn't be lost when Loki transported us away from Alfheim. Assuming he was actually able to do so.

"Maybe. Can't hurt to try." Loki linked arms with us and then put a hand on two of the horses. He frowned though and looked perplexed. "I think I need to be touching everything, but I don't know how to touch three horses at once."

"Maybe as long as one of us is touching the other it will be fine?" Gunhild wondered. She reached over to take the mane of her horse. "Try now?"

"Worst that can happen is we end up with only two horses and two-thirds of our supplies. As long as I have the cloak, that's all I care about. We need to get out of here. That's what's most important." I tried to keep the urgency out of my voice so it wouldn't make Loki nervous.

"Worst that can happen is none of us poof and Asa catches us." Loki let out a slow breath, closed his eyes as if about to vanish us, and then opened them again.

"It didn't work?" I asked, voice trembling.

"No, I didn't try yet. Where do we want to go?" Loki asked.

"I don't know. Can you get us to Nidavellir, or at least close?" I asked impatiently.

Loki made a frustrated face at me and muttered something under his breath. "Brace yourself, shieldmaiden, this will be much worse than last time. Longer distances are more dizzying."

Gunhild nodded and gripped the mane of her horse a little tighter until her knuckles went white. I gave her a grim smile and closed my eyes as well, gesturing for her to do the same. It would help with the disorientation of a longer trip.

Chapter Twenty Three

WE STARTLED a flock of seagulls as we appeared near a dock at the edge of a fjord. They shrieked and flew up around us like a tsunami wave as we ducked and tried not to take any claws or wings to the face.

Loki gave me a concerned glance as the horses reared and tried to pull away. I offered him a brief smile to let him know that I was fine despite feeling like my stomach might rebel. Gunhild was a sickly green, clearly nauseated from the journey. After a moment, though, she nodded that she was alright too.

"Where are we?" I asked after I had gained control of my stomach.

"About two days by boat from Nidavellir," Loki said, looking around the fjord to determine our exact whereabouts. It was hard to tell now that the sun had mostly set. "I couldn't transport us directly there—it's on another plane and only the dwarves and their boats can get in."

"Thank you, that works well," I replied. Why couldn't we have traveled this way all along? The dark circles under Loki's eyes, and his sagging shoulders told me all I needed to know. God or not, traveling that way with passengers was clearly not easy. Even Odin might have felt the effects if he'd tried it.

I turned to my horse to remove the cloak from within my pack and let it unfurl. Now that I was able to properly look at it, I realized just how beautiful it was. The cloak was crafted of gorgeous iridescent feathers from some mythical bird. It would have been long enough to graze the ground, even on my tall figure. I wasn't about to wear it though.

"What exactly does it do?" Gunhild asked as she watched me wrap it and carefully put it back in my pack.

"It lets its wearer take flight," Loki said vaguely before turning to me. "Just keep it safe for when you're ready to turn it over,"

"I hate the idea of turning it over to Hel." The idea of giving it to the Goddess of Death, even if it was her price for freeing Eryk, seemed ill-advised when we didn't even know why she wanted any of the armor so badly. "What if she uses it for ill?"

"Oh, she will," Loki said with a confident nod. "But your only choice is to give it to her if you want to free your warrior. Let's just get the helm and then Brisingamen and worry about who to give everything to once we've got it. One step at a time, right, Valkyrie?"

"One step at a time," I echoed. "The problem is, we don't have a boat to get to Nidavellir now."

"Give it some time. I've called in a favor," Loki said, shielding his eyes as he looked out across the water.

"How long is 'some time'?" asked Gunhild impatiently. "And when did you have time to call in a favor? And what will this favor cost us, for that matter?"

"Do you ever *not* ask questions? The favor won't cost *you* anything, just me. And I'll worry about the cost, if there is any, later," Loki said, which made me raise a curious eyebrow at him. He waved his hands about in a vaguely magical way. "I called it in when I was busy shifting us all about to get here. Godly stuff. You wouldn't understand. They should be here within the hour."

The wind blew frigid off the fjord. The ice along the edges cracked and groaned as the breeze pushed it against the shore. At least it wasn't snowing. I tucked an arm around Gunhild when I saw her shivering, and she cuddled closer for warmth.

"I'm betting we can't take the horses on this boat you've summoned," I said, looking over to Loki.

He thought for a moment and then shook his head. "No, but there will be people who are planning to stay on land when this boat gets here, so we can sell the horses to them. Probably a good idea to have silver in hand when we go to Nidavellir, anyway."

"Is there anywhere warm that we can wait for the boat?" My teeth had started to chatter from the chill. I looked around us for signs of civilization, but the only thing there was the dock. It stretched out into the narrow fjord, whose cliff faces careened into the sky.

"There's a town half a mile inland, but then we won't be here when the boat comes. Maybe they'll be early. You never know," Loki said with a shrug.

That carelessness enraged me. I shot a glare at his back as he turned away to face the water. Between the cold and our near miss with the elven queen, it was as if a thundercloud was rumbling over me despite the sunny skies.

"So, we get on this mystery boat, sail for two days, then we just float into Nidavellir?" Gunhild asked. She sounded more doubtful than curious.

"Well, Nidavellir is a cave system, so the boat will take us into the caves before... Oh look! There's the boat," Loki said, waving his hands excitedly in the air to get the sailors' attention. That left Gunhild and me with a sour expression. He hadn't told us what would happen after the boat took us into the cave.

The boat slipped up beside the dock on the smooth-as-glass sea, and the sailors threw lines out to tie the vessel to the dock. Several of the passengers disembarked with their bags and trunks. I pulled one aside and gestured to the horses.

"Would you be interested in purchasing three sturdy horses? We won't be able to take them on the ship, and I hate to just set them loose or anything," I said.

"How much do you want for them?" he asked after turning and murmuring something to one of his colleagues about the horses.

"How much are you willing to offer?" I countered, because I had no idea whether what the old man in Armvind had wanted to charge for them was how much they'd be worth here at the edge of the world.

The man pulled out a handful of silver coins and counted out several before offering them to me. It was more silver than I'd seen in quite some time and I had to stop myself from snatching it from his hand. I pretended to consider his offer for a moment and then nodded. We exchanged silver and I called to Loki and Gunhild.

"Remove your belongings from the horses," I told them. "They're going to take them. Even offered to sell them back if we returned."

I busied myself by removing all my things from the back of my horse, and patted its rump when I was done. "Good girl. Thank you for helping us on our journey."

Gunhild did the same, while Loki took what little he had brought with him as well before turning back to the boat as the others left with our horses. I supposed we wouldn't really need them in the caves, anyway. And who knew what might come after Nidavellir?

"Luka, yes?" the lead sailor asked, pointing to Loki. As I looked the man over, I realized he wasn't entirely human. He was quite short, and had dark hair and eyes. But he couldn't be a full-blooded dwarf, either. I had thought they were smaller yet, and stockier. When he caught me staring, I looked away quickly with a muttered apology, which earned me an amused grin.

"You must be Yrsa and Gunhild, the shieldmaidens," the man said. "I'm Hakon, emissary to Nidavellir from Midgard."

I wondered if he was half-human and half-dwarven. That would explain his appearance and his position. I nodded a greeting to him, and Gunhild did the same, before he motioned for us to join him. We stepped across the dock and into the boat, which swayed dangerously beneath our feet.

It was rather small to be sea-worthy, but I supposed it also had to be small enough to fit inside the caves of Nidavellir. It was long and narrow, crafted of a dark wood made even darker by years of sea water. There were sails which could easily be taken down to fit inside a cave.

"You may shelter in the prow," Hakon told us as he led us to the front of the ship, which boasted a dragon figurehead. "It will prove warmer than out in the elements, especially when we take up speed. The wind will cut right through you out in the open."

"Thank you," I said with a warm smile.

We bobbed quietly against the dock as Gunhild and I took seats with our packs in the sheltered area under the dragon. Loki didn't join us right away but instead murmured back and forth with Hakon for several minutes as we cast off from the dock.

The boat shuddered for a moment, before the sailors took up their places at the oars and suddenly propelled us forward into the fjord. Loki managed to keep his feet, which surprised me. How often had he been on a boat like this that he was so sure-footed?

Finally, Loki came to join us, while Hakon set about unfurling the sails so that the wind could propel us to our destination. Once it had taken hold and we were far enough from shore, the sailors left their oars and set about making sure the sails were trimmed to take us in the right direction. Many of them were human, but there were a good number that were clearly either like Hakon, or were full-blooded dwarf. The dwarves' arms were bigger than my waist, and their necks were as big as my thighs. Clearly, they were used to manual labor. I watched them curiously until Loki caught my attention.

"You've never seen one before, have you?" He gestured to the dwarf closest to us, who I was fairly sure was a woman. It was hard to tell, though.

"No, they are entirely new to me. How do you know which is male or female?" I asked, unable to help my curiosity.

"Oh, nobody really knows but them," Loki said with a shrug. "That one you were watching is Goldbringer, and that one up there, up the mast, is Windhorn. Their names are traditional to the dwarves, rather than to the rest of the realms."

"I wish I had an interesting dwarf name," mumbled Gunhild as she looked back to us.

"They might give you one while you're with them," Loki said, only halfway teasing it seemed. "What about Copperlocks?"

Gunhild perked up at that, visibly pleased at the idea of having a special name given to her by the dwarves. "Do you really think they will?"

"I hope they do," I said warmly as Loki was called away again by Hakon. "I wonder how fast this thing will go. I hope the winds are on our side."

"Me, too," said Gunhild. "Two days is a long time to huddle here.

Though I suppose we could lie down if it came to it. Where would Loki sleep though? I'd rather not have him cuddling with us."

"He probably does need to sleep after transporting us from Alfheim." We were all in need of rest, but he had to be most of all. "We should encourage him to rest. We can see if the sailors need any help. Though, we're more likely to get in their way."

"Probably, but it would be nice to offer anyway," Gunhild said, getting to her feet.

I crossed to the prow, where Loki stood glowering at the lead gray waves that were quickly turning black as the sun finished setting. Dwarves lit lanterns across the deck to illuminate it. Hakon had left him there alone with his thoughts, and from the looks of it, that wasn't a good thing. I wondered if he regretted joining us on this quest. I hoped not.

"Go to sleep," I said as I approached him. He glanced over to me with a scowl. "You need rest. You have bags under your eyes that could carry hordes of gold."

He seemed about to argue but sighed and pulled his furs around him to curl up in a corner of the prow. Once I was sure he was taken care of and that the falcon cloak was safely tucked beside him, I went to find Gunhild. She had struck up a conversation with Goldbringer, who was explaining the process of properly coiling rope to her. They smiled at me as I passed and went to find someone else to help.

I ran smack into the back of one of the shorter sailors with an apologetic yelp. They turned to look up at me. "My, you're a tall one, aren't you? Even for a human. Especially for a girl."

"Yes, I suppose I am," I said with a laugh. "Is there any way I can be of use? I don't suppose you have a kitchen that needs cleaning or blades that need sharpening."

"No, none of that. You don't look like one who cleans kitchens much, anyway," they said, laughing as well. "You want to climb that mast and tie off a line for me?"

I looked upward and felt dizzy just thinking about it. It apparently showed on my face because they laughed again and shook their head. "I was only teasing. Beastfall's my name. You're.... Oh, Hakon told us.... Yrsa?"

"Yes, I'm Yrsa, and that," I pointed at Gunhild, "Is Gunhild. And I think you know Luka already. Are you sure there's nothing—on deck —that I can help with?"

"No, miss, make yourself comfortable. The seas will get rough once we get out of this bay, and you'll want to be somewhere safe," Beastfall said.

"I'm surefooted enough to manage," I argued. "I'd like to earn my passage if I can. I hate to just be a pretty face."

"Who said you were pretty?" Beastfall teased. I laughed and ducked my head. I supposed to dwarves I might not be pretty at all. They probably had their own beauty standards that had nothing to do with soft curves or smooth complexions. "Tell you what, Prettyface, you can go stack those coils of rope for me in the stern, so they aren't in the way when we start slip sliding around, aye?"

"Aye," I said with a grin. "Consider it done."

"They're heavier than they look," they warned me with a bushy raised eyebrow.

"I'm stronger than I look," I countered.

"I'll bet you are," they replied with a hearty laugh. "Well go on, then, all those ropes over there to the stern. You'll see how the others are stacked. When it gets too rough for you, don't hesitate to get to safety, yeah?"

"Of course," I promised. Beastfall grinned and patted me on the back—almost the rump, they were so short—before sending me on my way to get to work. I hurried about the job I had been given as I considered what the dwarves might want in exchange for Freyja's helm.

Chapter Twenty Four

Near midnight, the seas began to swell. We had exited the large bay an hour or two earlier and now the vast sea opened up before us. Gunhild had been forced to find a seat in the prow with Loki, as she learned the hard way that she got seasick. Thankfully, I managed to keep my feet as we sloshed along in the waves. I had stacked over a dozen heavy coils of rope before I ran out and went to sit in the prow with the others.

A storm was brewing, and I was exhausted from all the hauling. I could easily fall asleep, regardless of the weather. By now, Gunhild was out cold. It started to rain as I joined her and Loki there, and a jag of lightning struck off in the distance with a slow-to-follow rumble of thunder.

Loki grumbled himself awake as thunder thudded closer and the sea grew more violent. He sat up to look at me with an accusing scowl, though I wasn't sure how this could be my fault. I widened my eyes innocently at him and shrugged. He grumbled again and crossed his arms over his chest.

"What is your problem?" I frowned and scooted closer to him so we wouldn't wake Gunhild with our talking. I couldn't figure out what I might have done to upset him. Surely helping the dwarves wasn't a bad thing, and I couldn't have anything to do with the storm.

"Nothing is ever easy when you're around. This was supposed to be a clear night. But here we are with storms. I hate storms at sea. They always bring sea serpents to the surface," Loki complained.

"Sea what now?" I asked, raising my eyebrows.

"Sea serpents. Like dragons almost, but without the fire or the wings. Long enough to encircle a ship and bring it to the bottom of the sea," Loki explained. This sent a chill down my spine, and I looked over the side of the boat instinctively.

"Pray that doesn't happen, because if it does, there's nothing to save us," Loki said darkly.

"You couldn't transport us away again before that happened?" I asked.

"All the people on this boat? Or would you have me leave them to their fate when we're the ones who put them in danger? By Odin, Yrsa, I thought better of you than that." Loki shook his head, and I felt shame for the first time in a while.

"No, I suppose not," I said, lowering my gaze. "But how in the world did *we* put them in danger? I have no control over sea serpents."

"Because sea serpents are attracted to magic," Loki pointed out with a frustrated huff. "Valkyries and gods? That's about as magical as you can get. If there's a sea serpent, it's because of us."

"Oh. Well. Are sea serpents sentient?" I asked, changing the subject a little. If we were going to be attacked by a monster potentially, I wanted to know everything I could about the monster who might be out there.

"Not a clue. I've never met one," Loki admitted.

"So, you've only *heard* of them sinking ships, then. You've never experienced it. It could all be a myth." I crossed my arms over my chest and looked back up at him with a raised eyebrow.

"Trust me, it's not a myth. I've met sailors who've survived. Barely."

"Survived what?" Gunhild asked, sitting up and rubbing her eyes.

"Nothing, sunshine. Go back to sleep." I pushed her to lay back down. She didn't fight me and was soon sleeping again. Once she was out, I turned back to Loki and said, "We'll just have to hope there are no sea serpents."

"Hoping won't do much. Try praying. Seriously." Loki glanced up to the glowering sky, which split with lightning so bright it turned the night to day for a second. I had never seen him afraid like this. My hackles rose with the idea of a danger so profound that it even frightened Loki. "I don't like this."

"I don't either."

The sailors hurried to take the sails and mast down so they wouldn't topple in the rapidly building winds. I was afraid the mast would be struck by lightning and set the ship on fire before they could get it down, but they were successful in dismantling it before that happened.

The storm raged for hours with the sailors hunkered beneath the canvas sails they had pulled down. I met Beastfall's gaze from under the canvas and they looked terrified, which surprised me. It wasn't until they looked from me to the side of the ship again that I saw why.

What looked like a blue-scaled tentacle, or the end of a giant snake's tail, had curled up over the rail, and was feeling its way across the deck. It didn't seem to find whatever it searched for and eventually slithered off the deck again. Everyone breathed a collective sigh of relief.

Then a tremendous, reptilian head of the same blue scales reared over the ship.

The beast eyed everything on the deck with slitted golden eyes that glowed red every time the lightning flashed. Its scales shimmered rainbow-like with each strike. The beast was as big around as an oak tree, and just as tall. And that was only what was above the waves. No matter how brave I might try to be, I couldn't deny the way my whole body trembled or how my stomach churned with fear as the sea serpent gnashed sharp teeth at where the mast had once been.

Struck with some maddening inspiration, or possibly pure foolishness, I grabbed my battle axe and slid out onto the deck. Whatever fear I may have felt, I couldn't let it get these people killed just because I was too afraid to act. I lost my footing more than once as I changed position and had to be held up by the dwarves who still hid under their sail. I might be able to kill the beast if I got a blow in at its throat.

"Valkyrie! What in Nastrond are you doing?" Loki shouted, which distracted the beast from me long enough that I could leap into the air and slash at its exposed throat.

This only infuriated the creature. It let out an ear-piercing screech and snapped its teeth at me. I barely managed to jump out of the way and slashed again now that it was closer. Its teeth clamped down on my axe and wrested it free. The handle broke and the poor weapon spun into the waves.

"Eryk's sword!" I shouted to Loki. He dug out the sword and slid it across the deck to me. I caught it and lifted it instead. "Begone, foul beast! You will not have this boat!"

The beast seemed to pause and blink, as a membrane briefly covered its slitted eyes. It leaned its head very close to focus on me, but I hesitated to take a killing blow.

"OR WHAT?" Its voice was a shrill hiss. I had not expected it to be able to speak. I gave a few stunned blinks instead of responding immediately. "WHAT WILL YOU GIVE ME IN EXCHANGE, VALKYRIE? I HEARD WHAT THE GOD CALLED YOU."

"What do you want?" I managed to squeak out. I felt less brave now that I knew it could speak.

"PERHAPS I WANT TO EAT A VALKYRIE, TASTE HER BLOOD, SEE IF IT IS AS SWEET AS A GOD'S," the serpent shrieked.

"Have you even tasted a god's blood?" I surprised myself by asking.

The beast paused again, and then let out a grating, metallic noise that might have been laughter. It slithered back from the boat a little way, twisting this way and that in the wind.

"I HAVE NOT. BUT YOU HAVE ONE JUST THERE. I COULD HAVE BOTH, ONE AFTER THE OTHER, AND YOU COULD NOT STOP ME."

"Come close again and I will sever your head from your body," I warned, waving my blade.

"LIKE YOU DID WITH THAT AXE? LET ME EAT YOU AND I WILL SPARE THE CREW, YES?"

"You're not eating me, beast. You'll tell me what you want, and we will bargain like civilized…" I paused.

"CIVILIZED PEOPLE? YOU ARE AMUSING, LITTLE VALKYRIE. I BET YOU TASTE AS SWEET AS HONEYED APPLES."

"No, I am bitter and gristly, and I am very painful going down. Now, tell me what you want." I stood my ground on deck even as waves washed over the sides and the beast rose up to tower over me again. I could almost reach its throat if it just came a little lower.

"I WANT TO DRAG THIS BOAT TO THE BOTTOM OF THE SEA WITH THE OTHERS AND TAKE ITS TREASURES FOR MY OWN."

The shrieks awakened Gunhild, and she joined me then with her axe. The sea serpent barely spared her a glance, though. Its golden eyes focused only on me. Its interest in me had spared the boat a few minutes.

"That's not an option," I yelled. "If you come close enough to do so, we will chop off your head. Think of something else you want. Is it gold? Is it furs? What is it?" Gunhild's shoulder bumped against mine as the boat rocked violently.

"FURS AREN'T VERY WARM WHEN DRENCHED WITH SALTWATER..."

"Gold, then? I have a whole trunk full of it from my last raid," Hakon called from across the ship. He had a sword in his hands and looked ready to take the sea serpent out himself if I failed. "Goldbringer, grab the trunk and show the serpent what we can offer in exchange for our lives."

Goldbringer did as they were told, dragging over a large trunk which opened to reveal dozens of ingots of gold, which shone each time the lightning flashed. This got the sea serpent's attention, and it looked away from me finally, to loom over the gold instead.

Without warning, it snapped up the trunk in its razor-sharp teeth and then disappeared over the side of the ship, back into the waves with a hiss. We waited for it to return for us. My sword arm trembled and Gunhild's axe seemed to sag, though I told myself it was because we were growing weary, and not because we were afraid. Goldbringer scuttled back under the sail, and Gunhild looked over to me questioningly.

"Is it gone? Has it been satisfied?" My voice shook as I asked, walking closer to the railing to see if the beast lurked just below. There was a swirling whirlpool in the waves where the beast had once been, but I saw no sign of the serpent itself. I half expected it to shoot up out of the water and eat me in one bite. Would I taste like honeyed apples?

Sure enough, the beast lurched out of the waves again. It startled me enough that I fell back onto the deck on my back and slid until my head slammed against the rail on the other side of the boat.

When I sat up, I saw stars for a moment, then saw the serpent looming over me again. I had lost my sword when I fell, and Gunhild had scurried out of the way as the serpent shot over the deck to get to me. Hakon called my name and slid me his sword, which was almost too large for me.

"YOU THOUGHT THAT WAS ENOUGH, DIDN'T YOU? I *WILL* HAVE BLOOD. AND IT WILL BE YOURS."

"Not if I have yours first," I growled, launching myself upwards with Hakon's gigantic sword. It pierced the scales at the beast's throat and emerged into its head. The serpent gave a horrible hissing scream that was painful to our ears, and then collapsed into the ocean, taking the sword with it.

There was no whirlpool this time. The sea serpent's body floated at the surface for a minute or two. Its blood turned the sea foam pink, before the creature slowly sank beneath the surface with a disturbing gurgle. Gunhild, Hakon, and I rushed to the railing, watching to see if the creature would rise yet again, but this time, it seemed to have been vanquished for good. With the defeat of the sea serpent, the storm died as well. A soft rain was all that remained, pattering down on the sail and the deck.

"Your ears are bleeding," Gunhild said. She reached up with her free hand to touch my face, pulling away a blood spotted finger. "We all have bleeding ears."

"The sea serpent's scream must have done it," Hakon said. Everyone's voices sounded muffled. "Doesn't matter now. It's gone for good. Thanks to Yrsa. Who apparently is more than Luka led us to believe."

"Yes, yes, she's a Valkyrie," Loki said, waving a hand dismissively. Hakon raised an eyebrow at Loki. "And yes, I'm a god. So what? Does that really change anything?"

"It means we have guests of extreme honor who we carry to your destination with quite a bit more care." Hakon folded his arms over his chest and looked us over with a stern gaze. "Is the ginger anything special? A Valkyrie as well? Or a vala?"

"No. I'm just a shieldmaiden. You could throw me over the side and nobody would notice," Gunhild said with a shrug.

"That is not at all true!" I dragged her to me by the wrist and frowned at her. I hated that she thought so little of herself, especially after what we had just been through together. Turning to face her, I cupped her cheek. "You are my friend, and you are important to this quest. We have made oaths to each other. How many other shieldmaidens can say that they have the oath of a Valkyrie?"

"Probably none," Hakon admitted. "I suppose we can put the sail back up and get moving. We've a way to go still to get to Nidavellir."

A shimmer at the horizon hinted that the sun had begun to rise. It was a relief after the stormy, serpent-filled night.

Chapter Twenty Five

THE LAST DAY of our journey went smoothly. The sun was back out and shining. The seas were a little choppy, but that only meant there was a strong wind to blow us to Nidavellir. I dozed off and on for most of it, exhausted still from the battle the first night. Gunhild curled against me and slept as well, taking refuge from seasickness in sleep as I gently stroked her hair to comfort her. Loki made himself a nuisance by chatting up various sailors while they were trying to work, but most of them were unimpressed by the trickster god.

Eventually, Loki shook me awake in time to see the cliffs of another fjord rise above us. At the base of this one was the entrance to a cave which would lead us into Nidavellir. Runestones stood in the sea on either side of the cave, wound with looping designs and carved with runes that warned those who might consider traveling inside.

The dwarves had already begun to take down the sail and mast so that the boat could fit into the cave. Before long, we left the choppy waters outside for the smooth water inside the cave. As the sun disappeared, the cave grew so dark I thought we would run into something without some light to guide us. But there was light after all. Stars flickered above us in every direction. No, not stars, but something else that glowed in the darkness with a beautiful turquoise glimmer that illuminated the cave.

"It's beautiful," I breathed, mostly to myself.

The deeper we went into the cave, the more of these lights there were. The cave formations were not like the ones we had traveled through to get to Yggdrasil months ago. Instead, the stones were hexagonal stair steps leading upwards, like they had been crafted rather than merely created by natural forces. I looked over to one of the dwarves to ask about it and noticed that their pupils were so wide they swallowed up the gold irises entirely. The dwarf caught my glance and smiled.

"The rock formations are natural, believe it or not, from ancient volcanoes," the dwarf, Stormfeet, said.

"I didn't know there had been volcanoes in Midgard. I thought that was in Muspelheim?"

"There were volcanoes in a lot of places once. That's how the Nine Realms formed. From fire. And to fire they'll return, if the prophecies are right," Stormfeet said with a grin, as if an apocalypse was something to joke about.

"Let's hope that's a long way off." Gunhild shuddered.

"I'm sure it will be, don't worry," Stormfeet assured us. "That shudder isn't due to the end of the world, is it?"

"We had a bad cave experience earlier on our journey," I explained in a low voice. Gunhild shivered again at the memory. "Our torches went out and there weren't… Lights? Like there are here."

"Oh, you mean the luminosa? Yes, they're useful and ethereal," the dwarf agreed. "I can't imagine a cave without them. The deeper caves sometimes have none, but they are rarely used, anyway. They are the larvae of a beetle which glow in the darkness."

I nodded and looked up at the roof of the cave as it slid past us. It was similar, in a way, to the elf-lights, though those had been crafted and the luminosa were simply native to Nidavellir and glowed without aid. The luminosa cascaded from the cave ceiling, adding such a lovely ambiance that it was hard to believe they were luminescent larvae. Stormfeet wandered off to work and left Gunhild and I alone. Loki was in the stern talking to Hakon.

"You fought so bravely," I said quietly to Gunhild, and reached down to squeeze her hand and tap out our familiar little pattern.

"I'm a shieldmaiden, and you needed help," she said, as if her bravery meant nothing. "Besides, we *did* swear oaths to each other, as you said."

There was something unspoken in her blue eyes as she gazed at me. Something that made my stomach flip flop in a strangely familiar way. I pushed that feeling down, because whatever it might be, I didn't have the time to think about it. There were bigger things to worry about than my emotions and whatever it was that made my stomach fill with butterflies.

"You're right, we did, but you were still brave, and I'm proud of you for it. Proud to be at your side," I told her, squeezing her hand again. She lifted the other and hesitated for a moment in the air before placing it on my cheek.

"You were braver than me. You are the bravest person I have ever met," she said. I wondered if her cheeks were as flushed as mine felt, but it was impossible to tell in the turquoise light.

"You are a warrior. I'm sure you've met many braver than me," I said, trying to brush off the compliment, though I couldn't help but lean into her hand. She smiled and then dropped her hand back to her side with a bashful duck of her head. I let the conversation drop for the time being and gestured to get Loki's attention.

"Hakon knows where to find the helm?" I asked. "What will we have to do to get it?"

"He knows who to ask about it," Loki said. I scowled, because this was less than helpful. "Just trust me for once, will you? I haven't gotten you killed yet."

"Not yet, but there's still time. After the helm, I need the necklace," I said. "Do you know the way to Jotunheim from here?"

"North," Loki said, in that familiar teasing tone. I huffed, but I didn't have time to scold him.

A shouting echoed from up ahead and we pulled up to an underground dock outside of another cavern. This one we'd have to walk into.

"If you would be so kind as to follow me," Hakon told us. We grabbed our packs and he led the way down a slick pathway along the water into another set of caverns. The lights on the ceilings and walls grew brighter the further into the caves we traveled. After a few yards, we left the underground river behind and were on solid ground.

"Is there a king or queen we are meant to see?" I asked. "Some leader of some sort?"

"The council of elders? Yes, you will meet them eventually, but let's get you comfortable first," Hakon told us with a chuckle as he led us down another corridor. "We're very careful about how things are governed here. No kings or queens, no one person or family with all the power. Everyone has a say, everyone is equal. We trust our council of elders for guidance, but every adult has a vote."

"That is very progressive of you," I said. "Is everyone happier that way?"

"Not always, but if they don't like something, they can try to get others to change their minds and vote with them. Nothing is set in stone." Hakon knocked on a wall playfully, though it gave a mere thud as it was, in fact, made of stone. "Just this way, if you will."

We were eventually led to a carefully carved-out chamber where two beds had been wrought from solid iron into flowing, floral designs. The room was lit with oil lamps as well, which made the luminosa hide. I gasped, and Hakon looked mightily proud. Gunhild stepped further into the room and went to set her things on the floor at the foot of a bed with a canopy made of gossamer. I set mine down as well and looked to Hakon for further instruction.

"We have another cavern for Loki, of course. We know men and women in Midgardian culture tend not to sleep in the same quarters unless they are mated. I'll come back once you've washed up and are ready to meet the council. There's a wash basin and some towels in that cabinet for you."

"Thank you, Hakon." I bowed my head to him.

"Loki, if you'll come with me." Hakon bowed his head in return and then led Loki out. The forged iron door closed behind him with a clang.

As soon as Hakon and Loki were gone, Gunhild flopped back on the bed she had claimed. I came to sit beside her, tousling her hair.

"Glad to be off the boat? You're no sailor, are you?" I grinned at her and laid down as well.

"So glad. I hate sailing. I'll stick to battles on land, thank you very much," Gunhild said. "I suppose we shouldn't lie around if we're to meet this council of elders. Do you want to wash up first or should I? We should probably change too. Our clothes smell of saltwater and yours are all bloody from the sea serpent."

I sat up and looked down at my clothing. Both the furs and tunic beneath were coated in blackened, dried blood. "I suppose I should wash up first. There's probably blood all over my face too, isn't there? I bet I look a fright."

"You look like any shieldmaiden after battle," Gunhild said with a shrug. "I think it's beautiful."

"You obviously have poor taste." I went to the cabinet to pull out a towel and then found some fresh clothing in one of my bags.

I stripped off my furs, tunic, and breeches, and began to wash up with the water in the basin, which was surprisingly warm. By the time I was done cleaning up, and dressed in cleaner clothes, the water was murky and not suitable for anyone else's use. Fortunately, there was a second basin in the cabinet where I'd gotten the towels, and still some water in the ewer for Gunhild to use.

"Go on then," I encouraged her as I went to sit on the other bed. It was just as ornate as the one she had chosen. "You're not as filthy as I was, but you could still use a wash and clean clothes."

"Oh thanks," she said, but laughed and washed up. My gaze lingered on her as she changed, noting the curves of her hips, the smoothness of her belly, the swell of her breasts. She was beautiful, and such a different creature from Eryk, who was all hard lines and sharp edges. She flushed to her toes as she realized I was staring at her.

"Sorry." I flushed as well. "I should keep my gaze to myself. You're lovely to look at though, for what it's worth."

"Nobody's ever really looked before," she admitted as she quickly finished washing off and began to pull on fresh clothing.

"I'll be sure to keep my eyes to myself from now on." Guilt and possibly a little hurt gnawed at me for making her uncomfortable.

"No, I don't mean that." Gunhild shook her head as she pulled up her breeches. "I mean… I'm not used to people *wanting* to look. I'm not that pretty, I know that. But I do like the way you in particular look at me. As if I really am lovely to you."

"Because you are, sunshine," I told her, grabbing her by the wrist to pull her over to me now that she was dressed. "You are the loveliest person I've ever met. Sheer perfection, down to each battle scar."

I traced one of the scars at her throat, then followed it under the collar of her tunic. I startled as a heavy knock came at the iron door. Gunhild quickly scrambled away from me and went to her own bed to put on her boots.

"Come in." I got to my feet to open the door.

"Hakon said the council is ready to see you now, my lady," a young dwarf told us. "Are you ready?"

"As ready as we can be." I looked to Gunhild who finished with the last strap around her boot and stood as well. She didn't quite meet my gaze, and I hoped I hadn't said or done the wrong thing before. I looked back to the dwarf with a smile. "Do we look presentable enough?"

"You look beautiful to me. But that doesn't really matter. They like cleverness and kindness more than beauty," the dwarf said. "I'm Lightshaper. And you're Yrsa and Gunhild right?"

"Yes, we are. It's an honor to meet you, Lightshaper. You have a wonderfully evocative name. Are you particularly skilled at something involving light or was that just a name chosen at your birth?" I asked as Lightshaper led us out into the corridor.

"When I was born, they said the luminosa changed colors for a few minutes, or at least my birth giver did," the young dwarf told us. "I think they were merely delirious."

"Deliriously happy, I'm sure. But perhaps the luminosa really did change, and it portends something important in your future. You never know," I told Lightshaper. They laughed and ducked their head bashfully.

"Come this way," they told us instead of responding to my prediction. Gunhild and I followed them down the path leading deeper into the caves.

My attention was drawn, as before, to the strange hexagonal formations of the rock columns on either side of us. They stretched up to the ceiling in stair steps too small for anyone to climb. In the strange turquoise light from the luminosa, they gleamed iridescent.

Eventually, we found ourselves outside a pair of great bronze doors carved with stylized dragons and runes. Lightshaper paused and reached up to ring a large bell to announce our presence. The doors opened without so much as a creak. Their hinges were so perfectly crafted that they barely made a whisper.

Inside, the luminosa were even brighter. There were more of them in this chamber than in the others. At the center of the chamber was a forged table of silver and gold filigree, so finely crafted that I couldn't imagine how much it would be worth outside of Nidavellir. We stood in an auditorium, filled with seats carved from the rocks themselves, though they were currently empty.

Seated at the table were ten elderly dwarves, their hair gone white and their faces carved with the years they had experienced. Loki waited for us in front of the table, and Gunhild and I were led to join him. He fretted as he stood there, nibbling at his cuticle nervously. Both Gunhild and I crossed our arms over our chests and bowed in deference to their power, rising only when the one at the center gestured for us to do so.

"Welcome to Nidavellir, Valkyrie, shieldmaiden," said the elderly dwarf at the center of the table.

"Thank you for the warm welcome. We are grateful to be allowed into your realm." I kept my voice soft but firm. I couldn't deny my nerves, but I had to be confident yet deferent to them so that I could hopefully get what I came for.

"I am Emberthane, the chair of the council," the dwarf explained, and then identified the others by name. "I am told you come seeking a specific item from us."

"Yrsa, we are told you wish to take possession of Freyja's helm, which we crafted for her millennia ago," said a dwarf, Hillspine, with a long silver beard that nearly touched the ground.

"Yes, that is correct, though I know that it is much to ask." My voice had begun to tremble, just a little. Did I fear denial, or was I just excited for the opportunity to come another step closer to finishing my quest?

"It is much, yes," said a third dwarf, named Snowguard. "Possibly too much."

"The Valkyries are considered sacred by Freyja, who chooses them personally for their task," said Emberthane gently. "Giving Gjull-halm to one of her chosen might please her."

"Did we not already please her by crafting Brisingamen and Gjull-halm?" Snowguard said, a little bitterly.

"Do you know the details of my quest?" I asked. "I need the armor to free a warrior from Hel's grasp. She has condemned him to Nastrond for my transgressions and has set me this task to free him."

"Yes," Hillspine said. "Loki has told us. He told us as well that you already have Fjodfeld. Now you want Gull-hjalm as well."

"I am trying to save someone I am responsible for bringing to harm," I explained, hoping it would be enough. It was exhausting telling my story over and over, reliving my mistakes each time.

"But what does Hel want with it?" another dwarf elder named Thunderback asked sharply.

"How is that our business?" Emberthane snapped.

"It is our business because she wishes to give the helm to a goddess to whom it does not belong," Thunderback grumbled.

At this point, the remainder of the council were murmuring amongst themselves. I could catch snatches of their conversations, the name Hel coming up frequently. My stomach knotted as they argued, but thankfully Gunhild was there to take my hand and tap out our little pattern.

"Find out what Hel plans to do with it, and we will consider turning it over to you," another dwarf, this one with curly silver hair, told me. "We wouldn't want something that led to Ragnarok, for example."

"No, of course not," I agreed quickly. But how in the world was I supposed to discover what Hel wanted the armor for? Once more I felt as if I was in a quagmire of my own making.

"Return to us with this information and we will discuss further," Emberthane said after getting the rest of the council to quiet. "You are dismissed."

"As you wish," I said with a bowed head. Hakon stood from his seat and led us out of the council chamber with a frown.

"I'll take you back to your chambers," Hakon told us, glancing at Loki, who looked utterly unimpressed with this turn of events.

"I'll go with the Valkyrie and shieldmaiden to their chamber," Loki insisted. My brows drew together in confusion. He leaned and spoke in a more hushed tone. "I'm not letting you face Hel alone. And I might be able to help get answers out of her, as a fellow god."

Chapter Twenty Six

ALL THE WAY back to our chamber, I considered how best to gain an audience with Hel. Of course, we could go to Helheim, but showing up without the armor would ensure that none of us would ever leave. So instead, we would have to summon her to us. That would not guarantee a straight answer from her, but at least we would be on our own ground.

"Hakon, how do the dwarves do away with their dead?" I asked when we reached the chamber Gunhild and I shared.

"We sink them in the lake deep in Nidavellir. Why?" Hakon tilted his head as he tried to understand my need.

"I need to do a ritual to summon Hel," I explained.

"Not that she'll tell us the answers we seek," Gunhild muttered. She didn't even know the Goddess of Death, but she wasn't wrong that Hel would be unlikely to divulge her motives.

"We have Loki's help, so maybe he can wheedle it out of her," I reminded her.

"I would have to ask permission to take you to Hraesaevar," Hakon said with a frown.

"We have permission. The council told us to speak to Hel. Surely, they would allow it under those conditions. I'd rather not delay." I opened the door to our chamber, and went inside, to search through my belongings for anything that could be helpful in a ritual. Unfortunately, nothing in my pack seemed like it would be useful.

"I'll have to ask," Hakon repeated.

"Fine, ask. But I also need some supplies, while you're out asking them," I said, my patience running thin. "I'll need a veil of some sort; bones—animal bones will be fine; incense—preferably of myrrh or apple blossom; and any kind of black stone. Agate, jet, onyx, whatever your people might have on hand. Oh, and apples."

"Please," Gunhild added gently. "It is urgent. That is the only reason Yrsa speaks so sharply. I apologize."

I flushed as I remembered that I was being quite demanding as a guest. That wouldn't earn me any favors, and I needed all of the favors I could get right now. I bowed my head to Hakon as an apology. "Yes, I'm sorry. I would appreciate any help you can offer. This is important to me. I must save the man I lost."

"You loved him?" Hakon said dubiously, with a glance at Gunhild.

"Yes, I did," I admitted. I swallowed hard as I realized I used past tense. Why did I say it that way? Guilt crept in, but I tried to edge it out with bravery. I was still trying to save him, after all. "Er… it's complicated."

"Complicated is not even close to the word for it," Loki scoffed. My gaze snapped over to him with a glare. What did he know about any of it? "I tell you what, I'll owe you a favor. A favor from a god is something, right?"

Hakon mused on this for longer than I would have liked. His gaze moved over each of us in turn. I shifted impatiently from foot to foot but let him have his silence to think. Gunhild chewed at her lip as Hakon considered, and Loki polished his nails on his chest as if it didn't matter to him. Maybe it didn't.

"Alright, I'll help. After I ask the council for permission." Hakon held up his hands as I began to protest. "I won't help otherwise. I'm not a full dwarf; I won't risk losing my status here for strangers. Even for a god and a Valkyrie."

"Thank you," I said with a long sigh. I could only hope that the council would give their permission. It would just depend on how badly they wanted to keep the helm. If they didn't really want to give it away, they would deny my request and I would be stuck. Unless I was willing to go to Helheim itself to find the goddess.

"Don't thank me yet," Hakon said, before turning on his heel and heading off to find the council again.

I went to sit on one of the beds with sagging shoulders and covered my face with my hands. I was exhausted and on the verge of tears. This quest would be the death of me. Was it even worth it anymore?

That thought took me by surprise. How could I think something so awful when Eryk's salvation was on the line? A sob ripped from my throat at the realization of how selfish I had become.

Gunhild was kneeling at my feet before I knew it. She placed her hands on my knees, gently squeezing. For a little while, she said nothing. Loki cleared his throat and the other bed creaked lightly as he sat on it to stay out of the way.

"Tell me what made you cry," Gunhild said gently. "What changed?"

"I-I wondered what the point was. Why I-why I was doing this. If-if it was worth it. But I sh-should know very well that Eryk is worth it." Sobs hiccupped their way through my words.

"Oh, honeybee, you haven't forgotten. You've just been trying so hard and you are so weary and broken down. It's hard to focus on anything but the goal, even at the risk of forgetting the reason for the goal." Gunhild pulled my hands from my face and kissed my palms before wiping away my tears with her sleeve.

"But how could I forget the reason? I love him. Don't I?" I asked, uncertain of everything now.

It had been months since this journey began. The seasons had turned while we traversed the Nine Realms in search of the armor. So much had happened in the interim, and now I felt lost and unsure of myself. All I knew anymore was this quest, and the unwavering compulsion to reach its conclusion. But I was exhausted, both physically and emotionally. I just wanted to lay in a soft bed and sleep for a week. I wanted to be somewhere warm and comforting and eat real food with people who didn't fight me at every turn.

"Of course you do. You wouldn't still be trying so hard to get the armor if you didn't, right?" Gunhild said as she cupped my cheek.

"Maybe it's just my purpose now. Maybe it replaced my purpose as a Valkyrie, and that's all I know," I suggested.

"I suppose you won't know until you see him again, and you won't see him again unless you get this armor, so either way, you have to get it," Loki pointed out from across the room. "Let's just get this over with. I'm not looking forward to a conversation with Hel."

"So sensitive." Gunhild glared at Loki, who shrugged carelessly. "He's right, though. You won't know until you see him again. We can do this. No matter what, I've got your back."

"Thank you," I said with a sniffle. "I'm not sure what to do until Hakon returns."

"Tell me your plan for getting this information out of Hel," Loki said, raising an eyebrow. "Surely you have one."

"I don't. I'm just going to feel her out, figure it out when I see her mood," I admitted. The tears had dried up now, and I felt dried up too, like an autumn leaf, ready to crumble at the slightest breeze.

"I suppose that's one way to go about it," Loki said dryly.

Someone knocked on the door and then opened it without waiting for a response. Hakon stepped inside, looking a little perplexed. He carried two baskets, one in each hand.

"They gave permission," he told us. "I'm to lead you to Hraesaevar and let you do your ritual."

"Thank you," I said. "Are those the tools I asked for?"

"Everything but the apples," Hakon said. "Were they especially important?"

"I suppose not," I said with a shrug. While they apples may have helped, I hoped Hel would appear without them. "I guess we'll see. Let's go."

Chapter Twenty Seven

THE LAKE where the dwarves put their dead to rest was deep within Nidavellir. Hakon led us silently into the caverns. He was not pleased to show us to this sacred place, but it was necessary for us and I was grateful the council had given its approval. The further we descended, the fewer dwarves we saw in passing, until eventually we saw almost none at all.

Hraesaevar appeared before us as we stepped into a massive chamber. Its ceiling was so high that the light from the luminosa was barely enough to make things visible. Their glow reflected dimly from the glasslike surface of the subterranean lake. Below was only darkness. Around the edges of the lake were various little altars and shrines built up for the dead, though some had all but deteriorated with age. Everyone who died was eventually forgotten.

I tried not to think about what might become of me when I died. Being exiled from Valhalla likely meant I was no longer immortal, but I also knew that because of that exile, I was unlikely to be allowed to rest there for eternity even if I did die in battle. Pushing that thought aside, I tried to focus on what I needed to do, and that was to summon the Goddess of Death and question her motives. Definitely not the simplest or safest task in the world.

"Where do you wish to do your ritual?" Hakon paused at the edge of the water to look back at us in the dim light of the chamber.

"Right where you are standing, I think," I said after a moment of thought. The closer to the water, the closer to where Hel would likely appear. I needed to be as close to her as possible so I could see her facial expressions and hear the inflection in her voice as she spoke. Assuming she came at all when I summoned her. "At the lake's edge. I wouldn't want to disturb any of the existing shrines."

"At least you have that much respect," Hakon said with a huff.

"Can I please have the baskets?" I asked gently. I understood his discomfort. To be honest, I wasn't much more comfortable with the situation than he was. It wasn't best practice to summon a death goddess, especially one whom I had been warned was infuriated with me last time I spoke to a fellow Valkyrie. "You probably shouldn't stay. Hel will be very angry to be summoned."

"I'm happy to make myself scarce, but you must promise not to disturb anything." Hakon handed me the baskets, which were heavy with all the tools necessary for my ritual.

"I promise, we will not touch anything aside from the lakeshore itself." I put my hand to my heart to seal my oath. That seemed to satisfy Hakon, who nodded and headed back out of the chamber to wait elsewhere for us.

"This is it, Valkyrie," said Loki. "Are you sure this will work?"

"I've never summoned her before, but I know someone who has, and this is what they used." I emptied the baskets, item by item, onto the shore. The someone who had done it before just happened to be my grandmother, who had been a seer and had called upon Hel to bring back a murdered child. The summoning had been successful according to my grandmother, though Hel had not restored the child to life. It didn't matter now. Hel didn't need to resurrect anyone this time; she just needed to answer my questions.

I put the veil over my hair and face and handed one to Gunhild to do the same. There was no point in giving one to Loki. He wouldn't take it seriously, and Hel wouldn't care. Next, I set out the bones Hakon had provided in a circle. They belonged to small creatures, perhaps rabbits or foxes, and were perfect for this task. After that, I set the incense alight in its stand. The chamber was so large that the incense dissipated quickly, making it hard to tell that it was myrrh.

Inside the circle of bones, I set the onyx and jet that Hakon had put in the basket, but only after passing them through the incense smoke with a soft prayer.

The last step of the ritual was to offer my blood as I sang the song to summon Hel.

I pulled a knife from my belt and passed it across my palm. Gunhild winced as the skin split deeply and blood pooled there. I was so focused on my task, that I barely noticed the sharp pain it caused.

Once there was enough blood, I dropped it into the waters of the lake and began to chant the words that would summon her.

"Hel, the inevitable, the bringer of order, the harbinger of fate,
Come now to me, a humble living soul, awaiting death,
The time grows short, the minutes go quick, the hour grows late,
Visit now, oh dark goddess, so I may pay my debts..."

Seconds, then minutes passed by, and nothing happened for a long while. Gunhild held her breath until she couldn't any longer and let it out in a huff. Loki raised an eyebrow and looked over at me expectantly, but I just held up a finger, indicating for him to wait.

After a quarter of an hour or so, a rippling came from the surface of the lake, disturbing the reflections of the luminosa far above. The ripples grew more violent, sending water sloshing onto the shore and over my altar. A wave rose, and I quickly stood so it wouldn't overtake me and drown me in the depths with the dwarven dead.

Finally, from the midnight waters, rose Hel, her expression as empty as usual. At least she wasn't furious. Yet. Water dripped from her bare feet and dark hair as she hovered over the lake. Gunhild took a knee, but Loki remained on his feet, looking utterly unimpressed by Hel's dramatic entrance.

"Why in the world have you summoned me? And to here of all places?" Hel hissed, her voice as sibilant as dead leaves brushing across dry ground. As always, it sent a shudder through me. Her gaze shifted to Loki, and something in her expression shifted. Was that fear I saw? It was certainly more than simple recognition.

"Hello, Hel," Loki said casually before I could answer Hel's question. "Good to see you as always."

"Father."

"Wait…" I said, blinking in confusion as I looked between Loki and Hel, who were locked in a staring contest. "*Father*?"

"Yes, I am Loki's daughter." Hel barely glanced at me before looking back at Loki with hatred in her gaze. I honestly couldn't have cared less if she hated him or why she might hate him. All I wanted to know was how Loki had failed to mention that he was Hel's father. "What in the Nine Realms are you doing here? And with this traitorous Valkyrie?"

"I wanted an adventure, and she told me you had set her on this quest. I figured I'd find out what you were up to." Loki shrugged. I was so angry now that I was practically trembling with fury. He made it sound so simple and unimportant when there was literally a life at stake.

"I see you forgot to tell her how we were connected." Hel gave a husky, dark laugh, which contorted her face.

"I forget a lot of things," Loki said with a grin.

"Loki, you need to explain this. How is this something we didn't know? Why didn't you tell us?" I hesitated to remove my attention from the goddess, but Loki was more important now. I had to be sure he wasn't going to suddenly betray us.

"He's a trickster," Hel hissed. "What did you expect?"

"What would you have done had I told you?" he asked. I opened my mouth to answer, but nothing came out at first. It took everything in me not to strangle him half to death. If talking to Hel hadn't been quite so important, and if strangling him might not have ended with me being the one who died, I might have gone for it. "You wouldn't have had me along with you. But I knew I could be useful, and I needed to know what Hel was up to. So that I could stop her if you couldn't, if it was something awful."

"*Is* it something awful?" I asked as I turned back to Hel. "Is the reason you want the armor so you can start Ragnarok?"

"Is that what the dwarves fear? Is that what Loki has told you?" Hel asked with an uncharacteristic, amused smirk. "No. I just want back what was mine."

"What was yours?" Gunhild asked.

"Yes, little shieldmaiden, mine. I once ruled Valhalla. I once made sure the valiant warriors were cared for, that the Valkyries kept to their tasks. That they did not disobey like Yrsa here has. And then Odin cast me out." I winced as she mentioned my disobedience. Surely, *I* wasn't the reason she had decided she needed to overthrow the rightful order of things in Asgard.

"Why?" I asked, though I was honestly afraid to know the truth.

"Because she tried to seduce him, to steal Freyja's place as his wife." Loki's voice was as dark as the depths of the lake. I couldn't help but look from Hel over to him, stunned by Loki's revelation.

"Oh dear, is that what you think happened, Father?" Hel asked, striding forward across the lake to step onto the shore. Gunhild and I stepped back, sheerly out of instinct, but Loki stayed where he was so that they were practically breathing one another's breath.

"I know it's what happened. I watched you try," Loki said.

"I suppose we all see what we wish to," Hel replied. "It's not as if Odin is monogamous. He has Freyja and Frigga. Why should he not have me as well? I would be suitable, especially as the ruler of Valhalla. We could have watched over the warriors, side-by-side."

"And yet...?" I watched her carefully, unsure where this story was going.

"And yet, he wanted nothing to do with me. Freyja asked him to cast me out, and so he did," Hel's expression shifted to anger. "As if she was so much better than me. As if she had more power than me. I am the goddess of death. She is merely a pretty face."

"She is the goddess of war and love, I think that is fairly powerful," Loki pointed out. I made a quick line of my finger across my throat to urge him silently not to tease Hel, but he ignored me. "Regardless, that leaves the question of why you require her armor."

"So that I can take my place back. Freyja can have the underworld if she wants it, so long as I'm back in Valhalla where I belong." She gave Loki a pleading look. "Father, you know that's what is right."

"The dwarves will never give us the helm if this is her reasoning," I murmured to Gunhild, who gave me a questioning look. The dwarven council was unlikely to entertain Hel's plans for revenge, but at least it wasn't Ragnarok. "I could lie to them, tell them it is merely greed for riches that others do not possess, I suppose."

Hel's head snapped toward us as she heard me whispering. "Don't keep secrets from me, child. Loki is teaching you bad habits."

"We were merely trying to devise a way to take possession of the helm, my lady," I told her. "The dwarves refuse to give it to us without knowing why you wish to have the armor."

"Then you will have to go find it," Hel said, as if the labyrinthine tunnels of Nidavellir were so easy to navigate. As if we knew where the helm was hidden within them. "Or you may tell them what I have told you and see what they say. They might not care what my plans are."

"Maybe not," I echoed.

"Until you bring me the armor then," said Hel, stepping back out over the water. She glanced to Loki. "Father. Seeing you was a... treat... as always."

"Oh yes, I always look forward to it," Loki said with a sarcastic grimace.

This earned a quiet scoff from the goddess, who sank back beneath the surface of the lake with a ripple, leaving us alone again. The altar had been all but washed away, but I gathered what was left of it and put it in the baskets as I considered what to do.

Chapter Twenty Eight

RATHER THAN GO STRAIGHT to the council, we returned to our chamber. I needed to devise a plan, because I wasn't sure how to get the helm. Should I even still try? Eryk awaited my rescue of course, but how could I betray Freyja and Odin for one man?

When I stood on the cliff and shouted my choice into the sky to rescue him, Hel had responded with gale winds that had nearly knocked me from the edge. Did that count as an oath too? I wouldn't wish to offend the gods by not keeping it and then end up in Nastrond myself when I died—if I died.

"What else have you been keeping from us? What else do we need to know? And how can it help us to convince the dwarven council to give us the helm?" I asked Loki as we got back to the chamber. If we were going to deliver the armor to Hel despite what we had learned, then I needed the entirety of the truth from Loki for once.

"I can give you the exact layout of Helheim," Loki admitted. Gunhild and I raised our eyebrows. "I've been there a handful of times. To check in on her. Especially right after she was cast out."

"Another secret," I said.

"Look, I didn't realize she had her eyes on Odin. I really didn't. At least not to be his wife. I figured she was just angry at Freyja and wanted her belongings to spite her." He paused and then added, "Or that she was planning Ragnarok. You know. Whichever came easier."

"You really thought she might be planning Ragnarok?" I asked.

"It was always a possibility, just an unlikely one. Ragnarok wouldn't help her any more than it would help any of the rest of the gods," Loki said with a shrug. He looked up at us with those dark eyes of his, wide and childlike in their pleading. "Are you going to send me away?"

"I should." I flopped down on the other bed. "For all I know, you're more loyal to her as your daughter than you are to us. I shouldn't be stupid enough to trust you anymore."

"And yet?" He looked between me and Gunhild with a hopeful smile.

"And yet, I think we may still have need of you. I did ask you to come with us to help on our quest, even if I didn't realize you'd be lying to us every step of the way." I rubbed my temples as a headache formed behind my eyes. "Why don't we all get some sleep and I'll decide for sure in the morning? It's been a rough few days."

"That it has." Loki hopped up from the bed with a liveliness to his step. "I'll come find you in the morning and we'll go to the council to convince them to give us the helm, if you decide you still want to give it to Hel."

"Fine, just don't go making trouble," I told him. This elicited a tiny, snorted laugh from Gunhild, who tried to hide it behind her hand. I elbowed her, which only caused the laughter to bubble up further. "You go to sleep too, shieldmaiden, before I send you with Loki."

"Yes, my lady," Gunhild said with a salute, before shifting around to climb under the covers instead of going to the other bed.

"Good niiiight," Loki told us in a sing-song voice. He slipped out the door with a little wave.

Chapter Twenty Nine

LATE THE NEXT MORNING, we met Loki outside the council chamber. I was not nervous; I was whatever was beyond nervous. Gunhild noticed my hands trembling and fidgeting endlessly with the hem of my tunic. She took my hands in hers and squeezed. That settled the turmoil in my chest, even if only slightly.

"It will be alright. One way or another we'll get the helm. We must," Gunhild reassured me.

"I'm not even sure if we should." I pulled my hands away but quit fidgeting.

"Leave it up to the dwarven council—and the Norns. If it's meant to be that you end up with the helm, then you'll get it. If it's not, then you won't," Loki said with a shrug. He had a good point. The whole quest could be doomed to failure and we wouldn't know it until the very end. If the Norns had seen Ragnarok, or even anything else terribly dark, they wouldn't have helped me to find the armor to begin with. I kept this in mind as I looked up at the massive door to the council chamber.

"What do I even say to them?" I huffed out a frustrated breath.

"The good news is, Hel doesn't intend to bring on Ragnarok. The bad news is, she's jealous of Freya and wants to take over Valhalla and be Odin's wife?" Loki suggested with a playful grin. I wanted to punch him.

"This isn't funny," I told him with a scowl. "This is someone's eternity at stake. Or worse, an entire pantheon's structure."

"Oh, even if Hel tries something, I doubt she'd be successful." Loki waved a hand dismissively. I had a million questions about how he knew and why she'd fail, but now was not the time to ask them.

"I hope you're right," I said as the doors opened to the council chamber. I took a deep breath before stepping inside, Gunhild at my side and Loki just behind us. Hakon greeted us from within and led us over to where the council had gathered once more.

"Were you able to summon the goddess of death?" asked Emberthane.

"Yes, I was. She was… cooperative." It was a start, and not untrue at least.

"What did you learn? Are we to fear Ragnarok if she gains control of the armor?" asked another of the dwarves, this one with curled white hair and crow's feet around their eyes.

"No, Ragnarok is not her goal," I assured them with a shake of my head.

"Then what is?" Emberthane asked, bristly eyebrows raising in curiosity.

"She…" I paused. This was the moment that I had to choose between truth and lie. There was no delaying further. "She wants it to take what she sees as her rightful place in Valhalla as one of Odin's wives."

The council had no reaction to my news. It was as if I had merely told them the state of the weather rather than the potential fate of the Asgardian hierarchy. One of the dwarves leaned to whisper to another but didn't seem overly concerned.

"The whims of the gods do not concern us, so long as they do not affect us," that dwarf told us. "We do not fight battles in Midgard; therefore, Valhalla means little to us. And who Odin marries is of little consequence either."

The rapid beating of my heart slowed. "Will you give us the helm then?" I asked.

"It does us little good here, and you are not the first to come looking for it." Emberthane said. "The difference between you and the others though, is that you have a noble cause, rather than greed to motivate you. As long as the dwarves can keep their neutrality, I am not sure any of us care who takes possession of it, as long as they aren't using it to enrich themselves at our expense. Or to end the world, of course."

"She could be lying," one of the other dwarven elders pointed out. "And we have not posed it to Nidavellir as a whole. We are collaborative, let us not forget."

My internal rejoicing at Emberthane's words turned bitter as I was accused of being a liar.

"It has literally been gathering dust for hundreds of years now," Emberthane said with a roll of their eyes. But the elder who had accused me of lying simply looked even more angry at the idea than before. Emberthane's gaze shifted to me, and they nodded decisively. "Then let Nidavellir vote on it. We will circulate what the Valkyrie has told us, both of her motivations and of Hel's, and let the people decide whether to give her the helm."

"How long will that take?" Gunhild asked.

"Give us a day and we should have every vote in," Emberthane said.

"Thank you." I bowed my head.

"Don't thank us yet," said one of the dwarves. Their skeptical expression gave away their thoughts about our mission and our motives.

"Thank you for even considering," I offered a reassuring smile, which seemed to placate them and earned me some small smiles in return.

"Go now, and we will call for you when the vote has been counted," Emberthane waved their gnarled hand to dismiss us.

The three of us headed back towards the chamber Gunhild and I shared. Hakon joined us on the walk back, and I looked over to him with a hopeful but anxious smile.

"Do you think there's a chance they'll let us take the helm?" I asked, my hands twisting nervously in front of me. As we arrived at my chamber, a bell rang.

"What's that for?" Gunhild asked, distracting from my question.

"That is the midday meal bell." Hakon opened the door to the chamber. He seemed all too glad not to have to answer what I had asked.

"Then it will be midday tomorrow before we hear of the results." Gunhild said with a sigh. "That seems like such a long time to wait."

"It will seem longer without anything to do," Loki pointed out. "Is there any form of entertainment we could take part in? Or is everyone working when they aren't eating or sleeping?"

"Most entertainment tends to take place between evening meal and the final bell of the day," Hakon said. "The elders and children have their own entertainment, but I don't think you would be welcome at either of those."

"So, we just… wait?" I grimaced at the thought of losing an entire day.

"Yrsa is not so good at patiently waiting," Loki teased. Both Gunhild and I glared at him. "What? It's true, isn't it?"

"We'll manage just fine," I assured Hakon. "Though you may have to show Loki to his own chamber. I am not sure I can tolerate him for a whole day."

Loki lifted a hand to his chest and gasped. I let out an annoyed huff and flopped down on the bed. I could have asked for a tour of the caves, or a demonstration of their crafting prowess, but it seemed intrusive. I didn't want to push our luck among the dwarves when we needed their kindness and generosity to complete our quest.

"I suppose we will wait here, then. Will any food be brought to us or will we need to go to a dining hall?" I asked. How exactly did one pass an entire day and night in this place? I had been on the move constantly for so long, but now I had to simply wait patiently. The idea seemed like torture.

"I'll make sure food is brought. You'd probably best leave the dwarves to their devices for now, since they'll be discussing the vote and wouldn't be able to do it as freely with you around," Hakon advised. "I'll bring some games for you to play as well. Something to pass the time."

"Do you have Hnefatafl?" Gunhild asked.

"You know how to play Hnefatafl?" Loki asked skeptically.

"Of course, I am a shieldmaiden—what did you think warriors played between battles?" Her raised eyebrow earned her a low whistle from the trickster god.

"Of course, I should have guessed, you are just one of the boys, aren't you?" Loki shrugged and sat down on the other bed in the chamber, kicking off his boots and putting his feet up.

"Hey! That's my bed!" Gunhild protested. Hakon slipped out as she and Loki began to quarrel. Loki threw a pillow at Gunhild, who growled angrily and threw it back, much harder than necessary. Fortunately, it was just a pillow, and it also narrowly missed the lamp beside the bed.

"Alright children," I said in a commanding voice. "That's quite enough bickering."

"I'm not a child." Loki poked his lower lip out in a childish pout, which caused Gunhild to giggle.

"You're both acting like children," I pointed out. "Come, let's figure out what we have to do next, assuming we are given the helm."

"Next, we go to Jotunheim, right? To get the necklace from the giants?" Gunhild sat on the bed beside me with the pillow in her lap.

"Right, but how do we get there? What will we have to surmount to achieve that goal? More tricks? More rituals?" I asked.

"I believe there is another entrance to Nidavellir through the caves, and outward to the North. There is a forest a couple of weeks' travel from there. You just have to hope the giants are as kind as the dwarves," Loki said, though he looked terribly unconvinced.

"You don't think they will be?" Gunhild asked.

"No, I don't," Loki admitted. "They are a fearsome and merciless people, who rarely give up anything once they have taken possession of it."

I narrowed my eyes at him as he seemed to be leaving something out. Something important, if my intuition was right. I glowered as he gritted his teeth instead of telling us the rest immediately.

Finally, he opened his mouth to do so, but a knock came at the door, followed by Lightshaper opening it, hands full of with a tray of food. Behind them was another dwarf we had yet to meet, with an armful of boxes.

"Oh dear." Lightshaper looked between us and noted that Loki had been about to speak. "I didn't mean to interrupt. Only, it's midday meal, and I thought you might be hungry. Hakon said you hadn't broken your fast yet today."

"Not to worry," I told Lightshaper, pretending to be easy going and uncaring about it even though I wanted nothing more than to throw something at Loki's head to get him to say what he'd been about to say. I was tired of his tricks and secrets, but I supposed that was the price of asking a trickster for help. I managed a soft smile to Lightshaper though, keeping focused on the young dwarf rather than on my anger at Loki. "We're grateful you share your food with us. And Nidavellir is your home; you can hardly be an interloper in your own home. You're welcome to come and go as you please."

Both dwarves seemed to relax at that, and the other dwarf came into the room to set the boxes on the foot of a bed. Once that was done, they hurried off.

Chapter Thirty

We spent the subsequent hours distractedly playing games and trying not to bicker. I tried to get Loki to tell me what he had been about to say before, but he brushed it off as nothing and seemed more irritated every time I asked. I probably should have continued pushing, but I always worried he would simply vanish like he had done in Alfheim when the Queen trapped us, but not come back this time. It wasn't a risk I was willing to take when we still had only one piece of armor.

When it grew too late, Loki returned to his chamber so that all of us could sleep. I tossed and turned the entire night, unable to rest even for a moment. Poor Gunhild finally got up and went to sleep in her own bed.

The morning bell eventually rang, and shortly after a dwarf came to bring us food to break our fast. They weren't one I recognized, but I called out to them before they left.

"Sorry but… Do you know the status of the vote?" I assumed the dwarf would know what I meant since every dwarf was meant to vote.

"I believe a final count is taking place now. You should know by midday," the dwarf told me. I offered a grateful nod, and the dwarf slipped out back into the corridor.

"Any time now, eh?" Loki slipped in after the dwarf left. He seemed a little more grave than usual as he took a seat on the bed across from me.

"I'm not sure what to do if the vote goes bad." It wasn't a thought I wanted to entertain, but it was a possibility whether I liked it or not.

"Let's pray they vote in our favor then, instead of borrowing trouble," Gunhild suggested, her voice sweet but confident. It settled my stomach, which until then had been roiling like a stormy sea.

"Gunhild is right," he said. "It won't hurt to stay positive. There is every chance they'll give it to us. What else are they going to do with it? Most of them probably didn't even know it was here. And you've given them a good story. They like stories."

"That's true, I guess. It is certainly a tale to be told." I wasn't sure I wanted to have the story of my quest go down in dwarven history, but if that was the price of retrieving Eryk, then I supposed it would just have to be worth it. As long as I didn't fail in the attempt, it couldn't be too terribly embarrassing.

The rest of the morning passed dreadfully slowly. By the time the midday bell finally rang, Gunhild and Loki were at odds over their current game of Hnefatafl. I thought she might reach across the game board to strangle him, or that he might vanish from the room if she angered him any further.

I was just about to force them to make peace with each other, when someone knocked at the door. I called for them to enter, and Hakon came in. I couldn't decipher the expression on his face, which was grim but almost looked as if it hid something. Was it a grin trying to break free? Or was it disappointment? Whatever it was, we all got to our feet quickly, the game forgotten.

"The vote has been counted, and Emberthane wants you to come to the elder council."

"Is it good news?" Gunhild asked.

"The elders wish to tell you themselves," Hakon said. "Come with me, please."

We followed Hakon through the glowing tunnels, back to the chamber of elders, where the members sat at their table, awaiting our arrival. They looked just as grave and indecipherable as Hakon. Gunhild's hand slipped into mine, her fingers tapping out our little pattern on the back of my hand to reassure me.

My stomach twisted itself in knots as we waited for Emberthane to speak. If we were refused, we would have to find some other way to acquire the helm or else leave Eryk in Hel's grasp and give up. I could never give up, but what would I do if they refused us? Hel had said we would have to search the tunnels bit by bit to find the helm. I couldn't begin to imagine how long that would take, even assuming the dwarves let us stay long enough to do so.

I was so tangled in my own thoughts that I had to be drawn out of my reverie by Emberthane clearing their throat. I looked up, flushed and bashful and put my hands behind my back to stand at attention.

"We have completed our vote, and the choice has been made," Emberthane said in a commanding tone. This felt more official than I had expected, though I supposed a vote of this nature would have to be more ceremonial than we had experienced thus far. Outside a different door leading into the council chamber, dwarves swarmed outside, listening to see how the vote turned out.

"Well, go on and tell them, then," said an elder named Brewminer. "No need to keep the poor Valkyrie waiting in suspense. I'm sure she's got better places to be than here."

"I assure you," I said gently, "We are more than willing to be patient while you make your decision."

The council murmured to each other, and then they all turned back to face us.

"The vote was close. Our people were torn by the question of whether to allow you to take possession of Gull-hjalm," Emberthane explained. I took a deep breath and held it. "It has been decided to give you the helm. But…"

Of course, there was a "but". Of course, it couldn't be as easy as just handing over the helm and letting us go on our way. That wouldn't be fair anyway, I told myself. They deserved something in return. I only hoped it wouldn't be another impossible task.

"Yes?" I prompted them softly.

"You must bring us something back from Helheim," said an elder named Gravelflayer.

"One of our ancestors was buried with a treasure they should not have been buried with. We wish to have it back," explained yet another elder, this one named Leadbuckle. "When they went to the bottom of the lake, the item went with them to the underworld. You should be able to find it with them."

"What is the item and who has it?" Loki asked before I could.

"Merrymaul was their name," Emberthane said. "They were a revered vala and the reason we vote on everything. They brought justice and peace to Nidavellir centuries ago. Their staff was sunk with them to the bottom of Hraesaevar. We wish to have it returned to us."

"But if it was their staff, surely it belongs with them?" I asked hesitantly. It seemed rude to question them, but I also didn't want to disrespect their dead either. It could be a test in itself.

"The staff was not originally Merrymaul's. It was passed down through their ancestors and should have gone to their children, and their children's children," Emberthane explained. "The former ruler sank it with Merrymaul because they thought it was a curse to have everyone's voice represented in Nidavellir. We know better now. Their family deserves to have the staff back."

"If it is possible to get it back, then I assure you I will." I put my hand over my heart to seal my oath. Hopefully, that was good enough for them. It wasn't as if I could swear to get the staff when I wasn't even sure that Merrymaul was in Helheim.

"Then, our vote says the helm is to be yours," Gravelflayer said, pulling an intricately made metal box from beneath the table. Through the filigreed gold, I could see the helm inside, gleaming silver in the low light of the luminosa. "I'm told you have the cloak already."

"Yes, we will only lack Brisingamen now." I stepped forward hesitantly.

My fingers itched to take possession of the helm. To finally be only one step away from saving Eryk. It seemed unreal that I should have made it this far. Though looking back, I wasn't sure how I ever thought I could make it so far alone. Gunhild and Loki had been instrumental in getting me to this point alive.

"Then come and take it. We wish you luck on your journey. I am told you need to travel North to Jotunheim?" Gravelflayer asked. When I nodded, he smiled gently. "We will have Hakon lead you to the Northern entrance, so that you may continue your journey."

There was a lump in my throat as I crossed the chamber and

climbed the dais to the table of elders. Emberthane pulled the helm from its box and handed it to me. I half expected something magnificent to happen as I took it, but other than a warm glow that seemed to emanate from the helm, nothing else happened.

"Thank you, truly." I bowed low over the helm, and when I rose it was to smiles from the elders. They all patted my hand or squeezed my arm in congratulations and good luck, and I murmured my thanks again to each of them.

Chapter Thirty One

THE TREK through the caves of Nidavellir took longer than I expected. I should have predicted it would take the days it did. After all, an entire realm was situated within the luminosa-lit walls. It was remarkable that they could manage to gather all the votes in one day, but it was a testament to how efficient and procedural things were in Nidavellir.

I wished now that our horses could have come with us into the caves, because we had been forced to pare down our packs again so that we could carry them on our backs. My pack was mostly filled with just the feather cloak and the helm; the only other things that would fit were medical supplies and a couple of changes of clothing. Gunhild and Loki carried the rest.

If it hadn't been for the regular ringing of the bells throughout the day, it would have been impossible to tell how much time had passed. We stopped along the way each night to sleep in chambers offered up by different clans of dwarves within the caves. We thanked them each morning, but I felt we should be offering more than just thanks. Even Merrymaul's staff wouldn't be enough to pay back their kindness.

Eventually, we reached a staircase that led upward toward a great iron door which must lead back out into Midgard. We climbed to the top, struggling with our packs as we tried to keep up with Hakon's quick pace.

"Shield your eyes," he said as he paused at the door. "The sun will blind you after so long in the darkness."

I put my hands over my eyes, though I felt unsteady on the stairs as I did. Gunhild put one hand over her eyes and took hold of my elbow with her free hand to keep her feet under her. Loki crossed his arms over his chest defiantly as if he had no need of such precautions, but then closed his eyes tightly, just as Hakon pushed the door open.

Light flooded into the cavern, blinding us even through our hands and I shuddered away from it after so long in the darkness of Nidavellir.

"Take a few moments to let your eyes adjust," Hakon advised, though he seemed unaffected by the sudden change in brightness. His pupils had gone from saucers to pinpricks by the time I pulled my hands from my face. "There. Now you may take the path northward and be on your way to Jotunheim. I wish you all the luck of the gods in finishing your quest. May you be successful and see Valhalla again one day."

"Thank you." I offered a solemn bow of my head to the half-dwarf.

"I look forward to seeing you when you return with Merrymaul's staff," Hakon said with a smile.

"I look forward to seeing you again too," I said. "I suppose this is where we leave you. Thank you again. For leading us here and for everything else."

Hakon bowed and then gently gave me a shove out into a sunlit meadow. We were far enough north now that despite it being late spring, it was still covered by shallow snow. Part of me was glad to see the dregs of winter still sticking around because it gave me more time to find the rest of the armor, but another part of me was so very tired of winter and wanted it to be warm again.

Gunhild followed me away from the door, with Loki trudging dutifully behind, though he fell further and further back until he was no longer with us and I had to stop to turn around and look at him. There was clearly something wrong and I wasn't about to let him keep any more secrets from me.

"What is it?" I asked, searching his face for answers.

"I, um… I can't go with you," Loki admitted. He refused to look at me and instead sought out the tree line in the distance.

"So, that's what you wouldn't tell me before," I said with a heavy sigh. "Why not?"

"Because the giants… have a sort of grudge against me. And I swore never to set foot in Jotunheim again, in exchange for not being tortured for a century," Loki admitted.

"Should we even bother asking what you did to anger them so much?" Gunhild raised an eyebrow at him and crossed her arms over her chest.

"Probably not," Loki said with a grimace. "Let's just say I insulted them gravely by stealing something I shouldn't have. I should just go back to Armvind and let you finish your quest without me. Maybe you can come find me again after you get Brisingamen."

"We're going to be stealing something too, so surely it couldn't be so bad to have you with us when we do it," I pointed out, but Loki's expression grew even stonier. "You'd rather go to the underworld than to Jotunheim?"

"Absolutely." He gave a vehement nod.

"Fine. Go back to Armvind. If we need you after we get Brisingamen—on our own—then we'll…" I trailed off.

"Do you know how to summon me if you need me when you get out of Jotunheim?" Loki asked.

"No, I only know how to summon Hel and Freyja."

"Well, you're going to think it silly, so you have to promise not to laugh," he said, cringing a little.

"Go on," Gunhild said, promising nothing. I only tilted my head.

"Well, there's a prayer you have to say, of course, and then you will need some items that are associated with me," he explained, his toe creating small circles in the snow at our feet as he hesitated. "Spiced liquor, peppers, salmon, anything resembling a snake. And… well… toys."

"As in, children's toys?" Gunhild asked.

"Um. Yes." Loki again couldn't meet our gaze.

A bubble of laughter escaped me, which set Gunhild to laughing too. This only made Loki flush and turn around to stomp off a few yards away from us until we gathered ourselves and stopped laughing long enough to follow after him. I only felt a little bad for laughing at him. It was a bit of payback for the times he had kept secrets from me.

"Alright, sorry, but toys *are* funny. You have to admit," I told him when he turned around to look at me with a hurt expression. "They are! But you still have to tell us the prayer."

"Can you memorize something longer?" he asked, still looking a bit put out with our laughter.

"Of course she can," said Gunhild. "She has memorized dozens, probably hundreds of Valkyrie songs, haven't you, Yrsa?"

"Maybe not hundreds, but quite a lot of them, yes," I admitted.

"Fine. Then this is what you say," Loki said. "Loki, flame-haired wordsmith, mischief-maker, discord-weaver, lover of chaos, come now and bless us with tongues clothed in deception, as you are the deceiver. *Bjoda heim.*"

He made a face as he called himself deceiver, a name he obviously had not chosen. I sympathized. Though he had hidden much from us, I couldn't remember a time he had ever lied to us maliciously with the intent to deceive or manipulate. He had just chosen not to tell us things like the fact he had bedded the elven queen, or that he happened to be Hel's father. Neither had been with ill will or out of malice, as far as I could tell.

I repeated the words a few times, with him correcting any mistakes I made, until I knew it by heart. He nodded when I said it over and over a dozen times without any errors. I wished he could just come with us, so that we didn't need to know how to summon him. The journey wouldn't just be more difficult without him; it would also be a lot less entertaining in his absence.

"That will do," he said with a grim smile. "Now, go. The way to Jotunheim from here is hard, to say the least. But I have faith you will succeed. When you finish, I'll be happy to join you again, if you'll still have me."

"I'm sure we'll see you again," I assured him. "Goodbye, then?"

"I hate goodbyes," Loki huffed. "Just say we'll see each other later. Or until next time we are together. Anything but goodbye."

"See you later, then," Gunhild said, pulling at my arm. She was right, we couldn't drag this goodbye out for too long. There were commitments I had to keep, which meant getting to Jotunheim as quickly as possible.

"Until next time, Loki," I told him, reaching out to grip his hand and give it a squeeze. "We'll see you soon. Wish us luck."

"I bless you with all the luck I have," he said as he pulled me into a hug. I wasn't sure how much luck that was, all things considered. It was a sweet offering, though.

"Off we go then," I said with one last glance over my shoulder at Loki, who looked quite glum. Perhaps he was sad to be separated from us after so long traveling together. I would miss him as well, that was for sure. His presence had buoyed our spirits thus far, and his knowledge of the world around us, the different peoples outside of Midgard, had been indispensable. Some small part of me wondered if I could even finish the quest without him at my side.

Gunhild and I took the path that led through the fields from the door to Nidavellir. The cliff face rose behind us as we trudged onward. Low snow clouds began to block the sun and would likely shed their burden upon us before the day ended. No trees grew there, only acre upon acre of empty fields, well past harvest and blanketed with snow. When the path soon disappeared, we walked with the remains of the crops crunching beneath our feet. The snow above them came up well past our ankles, making us both shiver.

When we came to a fork in a dwindling path, I paused, unsure which way to take. Gunhild gave me a questioning look, her eyebrows raised as if I might immediately know the answer. I would have given away my sunstone for the same pull I felt to Yggdrasil. Instead, all that remained was an empty aching that never passed. But while I felt no internal tugging, my gut did somehow whisper to me that I should take the path on the left.

The path was too narrow to walk side-by-side. We trudged, single file, still mostly northward. I forced myself to hurry, though I dreaded what I would find when we reached our destination. Behind me, Gunhild hummed a low tune that seemed to be a variation on the song I had sung to the troll. I hummed a descant harmony to it.

The fields stretched off on either side of us, devoid of all life but for the two travelers trekking across it. I could only guess the creatures here were still deep in hibernation even though it was late spring in the rest of Midgard, but there were no snow hares or foxes either. It was rather disconcerting to be the only living things around. I felt colder from the knowledge that we were alone than I did from the wind and snow itself.

The further we walked, the more nervous we became. Something was off about the path, which was still barren of both wildlife and trees. The brown fields that had once held crops had long since passed and now we walked across a barren plain. I wondered if it was simply a meadow in spring, bright and cheerful with lovely green grass, wildflowers, and birds singing. Somehow, I knew it would be just as dead when the snow melted. The realization made my stomach turn over dangerously.

We kept walking, for days and days, stopping only to eat and sleep, curled together in our tent against the cold. The only sound we ever heard on our path was our breath and the soft crunch of our feet in the snow. I wanted to scream, just to make some other type of noise than the dead silence around us. The only reason I didn't give in to the urge was the strange feeling I had that making any noise louder than we had already might wake something that shouldn't be awakened.

As the sun set on the tenth day and the snow started to fall much harder, I met Gunhild's gaze and she nodded silently. We needed to make camp soon, though there was still no shelter nearby. Instead, we would have to spend another vulnerable night on that dead land. She looked terrified, but I was too afraid of breaking the silence to say anything to comfort or reassure her.

We dropped our packs to the ground as the wind picked up into a fitful gale. We needed to hurry if we wanted to have our tent set up before the blizzard and the coming darkness blinded us both. Strangely, thunder rumbled in the distance, which only caused us to unpack faster. We quickly pounded our tent stakes into the frozen ground and threw our furs inside. The wind buffeted the tent, nearly blowing it down as we crawled into it and pulled our packs in with us.

We found ourselves huddled together as if our closeness would fight off anything that might lurk outside the tent. I was afraid to light a lantern lest something malicious see us, so we sat in total darkness. Neither of us spoke, though Gunhild breathed heavily beside me. Or was it me whose breath came in shallow gasps? I put my arms around Gunhild and held her as tightly as I could manage, though whether it was to help with her fear or mine, I wasn't entirely sure.

The roaring of the wind that tried to uproot our tent was enough to stave off any drowsiness we should feel after days of constant walking. We would be exhausted tomorrow, but we had to keep moving, if only to escape that strange territory. I couldn't bear the thought of staying her any longer than we were forced to.

When the sun finally crept over the horizon, silvering the inside of our tent, Gunhild's eyes were still wide, though there were dark circles under them from lack of sleep. I was quite sure mine were no better.

Our breath fogged the air around us and filled the tent to show how hard we gasped, as if an invisible fist had squeezed our lungs. At least it was finally light enough to see it and each other. Gunhild shifted beside me and moved away. The lack of her warmth chilled me to my core, until she reached out and squeezed my hand, tapping a small pattern on the back as she always did to reassure me.

"Do you think it's safe to continue?" Gunhild breathed the words, and I was glad she wasn't louder because a whisper felt too loud.

"I think so. Something tells me it's far too dangerous to stay here." A rumble of thunder in the distance answered my fear, and I shuddered. "We should pack and strike camp. I don't wish to stay here any longer than we must."

"But the wind is still raging. And it may still be snowing. We could quickly become lost." Worry and fear pinched Gunhild's features.

"We are no better than lost as it is," I pointed out. I helped her pack in silence, though we glanced at each other often to seek reassurance in one another's eyes. I couldn't imagine how I would have faced this alone. The idea that I once thought I could face this journey without her seemed like a dream now. A silly fantasy that could never have been true.

Despite my fears of what might lurk outside, I pushed aside the flap of the tent and stumbled outside into the knee-deep snow, which still fell heavily, blown sideways by the wind. Gunhild was right; we would easily lose our way in a blizzard like this. Without the sun to guide us, I would have to hope the sunstone I had filched from Eryk's home would lead us northward. When held up to the sky, regardless of any clouds, light through the crystal would line up with lines carved in it to tell us which way was north.

We quickly struck camp, blinking away the snow as it blinded our vision. It was hard to see each other, much less any path. When we needed to speak, we had to shout to be heard over the wind. Instead, we used hand signals when we could. It still felt forbidden to make much noise.

The longer we walked, the more constant the rumble of thunder grew. It was no longer the wind or the snow creeping through our clothes that left us shivering. The air was heavy and wrong.

We had no sense of time as we walked. It might have been minutes or hours since we began. If it weren't for the sullen gray glow of the clouds through the driving snow, I would have thought it had been days. Still, we kept moving. We had to escape the blizzard and the eerie thunder that plagued us.

"How long can we continue like this?" Gunhild shouted over the wind. "We'll freeze if the weather doesn't break soon."

I shrugged helplessly, unsure of the answer. It had to give way before long. Surely a blizzard wouldn't last forever, though it felt as if this one would. The constant rumble of thunder reverberated around us as we trudged through the snow. It would be another sleepless night, but we had to keep going until it got closer to dark.

Thunder still rumbled, though the wind had died down. The snow slowly ended, leaving us in eerie stillness broken only by the rumble of thunder. It had been odd enough while it snowed, but that was stranger.

I scanned our surroundings with a frown and looked at the sunstone to get my bearings. The thunder had grown quieter, but instinct told me we should move toward it, not away from it. I paused long enough to glance at Gunhild, whose eyes were clouded with concern.

"What is it?" she asked, obviously confused.

"I think... I think we should go toward the thunder." It would certainly seem to her as if I'd lost my mind, but this was the surest I'd been about what to do in quite some time.

"But why?" She stared in the thunder's direction for a few seconds, as if my reasoning would become clear if she squinted hard enough.

"I can't say exactly. Something in me says that's where we need to go."

"Like the pull you felt from Yggdrasil?" Her expression turned to one of curiosity.

"No, not exactly." I shook my head and readjusted my fur around my shoulders. "Please, trust me. I feel this more strongly than the tree. Will you go with me?"

"Of course, I will." She huffed, stomping back to my side. "Where you go, I go. I told you that. Even if I disagree with you."

I nodded and hiked my pack higher on my shoulder. The last thing I truly wanted was to find out why the thunder existed. Something told me Jotunheim was the source, and that was our destination. As much as I dreaded what might come next, what we might find among the giants, I was still eager to delve into that realm and find the last piece of armor.

Sure enough, as we turned and walked toward the thunder, it grew ever louder. We both shivered and our teeth chattered, more from anxiety than from the biting cold, at least for me. The sky grew imperceptibly darker, though we only noticed it after a mile or two. Both of us turned to each other with a frightened grimace. The last thing we wanted was to spend another night huddling together on the tundra, so we hurried our steps.

The barren field turned suddenly into a pine forest, with trees so massive that two people wouldn't be able to put their arms all the way around one. I peered up into the canopy, half expecting to see stars clinging to the branches there, but only the gray of a stormy sky was up there.

Two stones stood strangely ahead, straight and proud, and nearly as large as the trees. As we grew closer, we discovered that they were carved with intricate swirls and knots, interrupted now and again by foreign runes. Ahead of us, the trees stretched even higher. A chill went down my spine.

"You were right," she whispered, as if afraid whatever was beyond the stones might hear us. If only it were possible to disappear into the shadows and go unnoticed within the realm of the giants.

"Let's stay quiet and tread as lightly as we can. The last thing we want is for someone to hear or see us." My voice was almost too low to be audible.

Lifting my chin, as if to defy my fear, I took a deep breath and stepped through the stones. I paused long enough to wait for Gunhild, who appeared unsure until our eyes met and I smiled encouragingly.

We dashed among the gnarled roots of the trees. The thunder was so loud it drowned out anything we might have to say to one another. I stopped and hid between the roots under a tree with Gunhild as I tried to decide what to do next. We would keep moving deeper into Jotunheim, looking for the nearest village—assuming the giants lived that way—until we absolutely had to stop for sleep. I pushed Gunhild to move while I considered how best to stay concealed as we rested.

Settling into a pattern, we moved furtively from one tree to the next. We kept our footsteps light and communicated by hand signals. When night fell, Gunhild's eyes grew wide with uncertainty. We had to make camp. Going much longer without sleep would cause us to make stupid mistakes. And I was already exhausted from the poor sleep of the last few days of blizzard.

I sought a solution in the surrounding woods. The nearest tree had a hollow among its roots that we could hide in, so long as there was something to cover us from prying eyes while we slept there. It was also the largest tree in sight. I considered how best to manage a hiding place, my gaze flitting over the forest floor. After a few moments, I walked away, though it elicited a shocked yelp from the shieldmaiden. It took some time, but eventually I found fallen evergreen boughs that were small enough for me to carry and dragged them back to the hollow of the tree I had chosen.

When Gunhild realized what I was doing, she hurried to help. We carefully laid the branches against the trunk. It didn't take as long as I would have expected, and we soon huddled within our shelter, our belongings—including the helm and falcon cloak tucked into my bag —taking up most of the space among the roots of the tree.

"Do you think this tree hides us enough?" asked Gunhild.

I shook my head and sighed. I didn't know what to say, but she stared at me long enough that I felt the need to answer. "I suppose it will have to do. We can't continue in the dark. It's far too dangerous. And we desperately need rest."

"True. I only wish it weren't too dangerous for a fire." Gunhild exhaled loudly and dragged a fur out of one of our bags. It would have to be enough for us to sleep under. Another one wouldn't fit in our small shelter. At least it was warmer here than on that desolate plain outside Jotunheim.

We huddled together beneath the evergreen boughs, our backs against the trunk of the tree, and prayed to the gods the giants wouldn't find us. If they did, it was likely they would eat us in one bite, barely noticing as our bones crunched between their teeth.

I would have given anything for a fire. The cold seeped into my bones and left me frozen from the inside out. The only warmth came from Gunhild, so I moved closer to her. It would keep her warmer too, I told myself. It wasn't only the feeling of safety that I sought.

The unmistakable sound of heavy breathing jerked me into wakefulness. I nudged Gunhild, who slowly stirred, only to sit bolt upright a moment later. I put a gentle hand on her shoulder and placed my finger on my lips. It was impossible to tell if the source of the breathing sought us or only happened to be nearby. If it found us, we stood no chance of survival.

Thudding footsteps approached as we held our breath, terrified that the giant would find us. Parents used tales of the horrors of Jotunheim as a cautionary tale to every Midgardian child. The idea of being found by one sent uncontrollable shivers down my spine. Gunhild sat tall, her jaw clenched as if ready to fight should something discover us.

Slowly, the footsteps moved away, and we both quietly released our breath. Gunhild's face still showed determination. Pride swelled in my heart. I was a coward compared to this brave shieldmaiden.

"Do you think it's safe to sleep again?" she asked.

"It would be wise to take watches. Though I'm unsure what we would do if we were found. At least nothing would surprise us, and we would have the chance to run if need be." I risked sticking my head out of our shelter to find that we were truly alone.

"You're right," Gunhild said with a decisive nod. "Shall I take the first watch?"

I hesitated. It was my quest, my journey to collect the armor, and my gut twisted with the thought that I'd dragged Gunhild so far from safety. I nodded and Gunhild smiled. She motioned for me to sit closer to her again and wrapped an arm around me as I tentatively sat back against the tree again.

Chapter Thirty Two

I EVENTUALLY FELL ASLEEP, but it was far too brief before Gunhild shook me awake and whispered that it was my turn to keep watch. It wasn't long after that before footsteps came closer once more. I quickly nudged at Gunhild until she woke up. Her eyes grew wide at the sound of stomping so close and loud it shook the ground.

"Do we run?" Gunhild breathed.

I shook my head. It was too late to run. They were so close; they would surely see us. Instead, we huddled together. I wished we had dug our shelter further into the hollow to hide us better.

"Little ones…" the voice outside boomed in a sing-song tone. It echoed from the trees. My breath caught in my throat, and I put my hand to my mouth to keep from making a sound. We were surely dead. I had led Gunhild to her demise, and even the Valkyries could not save her here, no matter how bravely she might put up a fight against the Jotun that had found us. My heart broke at the idea of her soul going to the underworld instead. I had not condemned just one soul there, but now two. "I see your shelter. Would you like to come out and face me?"

Gunhild's blue eyes were wide and frightened, and sought me out as if I had an answer. Neither of us had any chance to make a choice though, as a large hand reached down and pushed the evergreen boughs protecting us aside to reveal us huddling together. A kind face peered down at us with a genuine smile.

"There you are. Why do you hide?" The voice belonged to a giantess, who towered over us by several feet, though the trees dwarfed her. Her hair was raven-dark, a little matted as if she didn't care for it very well, and her eyes were black as well. "Come out and let me see you."

We hesitated, but got to our feet and came to stand before her. Gunhild raised her chin defiantly, but I tugged at her arm until she lowered it. I forced a neutral expression and Gunhild mirrored it. The Jotun examined us with a tilted head. I couldn't understand her seeming kindness. She could have been a cat playing with the mice she was about to eat.

"Shieldmaidens," the Jotun said, as if amazed at what she had found. "How curious. What brings you here, little ones?"

"We… we got lost," I lied. Hopefully I was convincing. The giantess frowned but accepted my answer, motioning us to come closer before kneeling before us. "Forgive us for trespassing."

"Oh, it's no matter. You little ones are always so afraid to come here. Not all of us are monsters." She shook her head sadly. "I'm Arnbjorg. Will you come out of your hidey-hole and follow me? I promise, I don't bite." The last part she said with a toothy grin and a hand to her heart.

Gunhild and I sought each other's gaze. I tried to impress on the shieldmaiden with my eyes alone that I thought we might trust this giantess, at least for now. Gunhild's brow twitched lower as she somehow interpreted the way I looked at her, and she shook her head minutely in disagreement. I tilted my head just slightly to tell her that we had no choice but to go with the giantess at this point. She sighed imperceptibly as she gave in to my wishes.

Eventually we both turned back to Arnbjorg and nodded. The giantess's smile grew wider as we shoved the tree limbs aside and prepared our furs and packs to follow her. When she started off into the deep woods, we chased behind her as quickly as our much shorter legs would carry us. Her strides were long, and it was hard to keep up.

The house we came to was larger than I would have imagined.

Gunhild nudged me gently in the ribs, so I glanced over at her. A frightened frown creased her brow. I shook my head and gestured toward the giantess to acknowledge that we had no choice but to follow her. Our only other choice was to leave Jotunheim empty-handed.

"You can't really expect me to go in a giant's home, can you?" Gunhild whispered.

"I think we can trust her, for now anyway," I replied just as quietly, urging her forward.

The door opened upon a brightly lit home. The warmth and light of the fire were a welcome relief to the relentless cold and dark outside. In fact, it was almost too hot. The fireplace was so enormous that the flames reached as high as a bonfire. The massive furniture and high ceilings left me speechless.

"Please, make yourselves comfortable," Arnbjorg told us as she motioned to a bench near the fire. I looked up at it, and then back at her, and she laughed. "Oh. I did not think of how small you are. Give me a few moments."

She rushed about, finding soft cushions to pile on the wooden floor far enough from the fire that its heat wouldn't burn us. We both stared at her until her face lit in a wide grin and she motioned to the cushions. Gunhild's hands trembled as she dropped her pack and unclasped the pin holding the fur around her shoulders. I gave her an encouraging smile as I did the same. We both begrudgingly set aside our weapons as well, though we kept them close in case we ended up needing them.

With a brief glance at the giantess, I clambered onto one of the massive cushions. It had been almost two weeks since the last time I sat or laid on something soft. Gunhild climbed up onto the cushion beside me and gave my shoulder a squeeze. Her expression had relaxed now that she was warmer and more comfortable.

"Now, little ones," Arnbjorg said. "Tell me what in the world you're doing in Jotunheim. And how long you've been here."

I sat in silence while the giantess stared at me with one bristling eyebrow raised. I was still hesitant to trust her. And for good reason. The Jotun appetite for humans made them infamous. But what if those stories were wrong, told to make children behave? I decided that whether I told her what she wanted to know or not, the outcome would likely be the same, with an infinitesimal chance she may help us instead of consuming us. I wished Loki were here to weave an effortless story that she might believe.

"We've come seeking…" I paused. I wasn't ready to reveal what we searched for. Arnbjorg frowned when I didn't say what it was but didn't push. I couldn't just leave it there, regardless, or she would grow too suspicious. What could we be seeking that was mostly harmless? "Adventure. We've come seeking adventure. We've only been here for a brief time. Not even one day."

"Then you haven't had time to eat or sleep, and you little ones need both so frequently." Arnbjorg watched us for a moment before moving to the fire and extracting a massive pot. Her eyebrows raised with realization. "I have no bowls small enough for you."

"We have bowls." Gunhild's voice was barely loud enough to be heard over the roar of the fire. Arnbjorg's face lit up with a wide grin. Gunhild left a trail of our supplies in her wake as she searched for our bowls in the pack that didn't contain the cloak and helm. I quickly put our scattered belongings away.

The Jotun carefully spooned out a savory stew. She made a bit of a mess because her ladle was much too large for the task at hand. When she handed us the steaming bowls, my stomach growled loudly. We had run out of food three days before, and the path to Jotunheim had been devoid of any life we might have hunted. I smiled up at her gratefully. If she ate us, at least we'd be warm and full when it happened.

"You know," Arnbjorg said, staring at me, "I believe you are the first shieldmaidens that have ever wandered into Jotunheim. Whatever you seek must be quite important if you are brave enough to venture here. And lucky I happened across you. I cannot say what might have happened had any of my fellow Jotuns found you."

"I thank you for your graciousness," I bowed my head in thanks. "But as I said, it is merely adventure that we seek. We just got a little lost in our search for it and ended up here."

"Oh, it's no matter. Eat, warm yourselves. I have mead if you have cups." Arnbjorg moved to a cabinet on one side of the room and pulled a flagon as big as me from it.

Gunhild set her bowl down to find our cups. She replaced whatever else she removed with a small glance at me. I nodded minutely and offered an encouraging smile. The giantess took the cups in between her fingers and filled them with mead which splashed over the sides onto the floor.

When we finished and set aside our bowls, I smiled. "We're indebted to you for your kindness."

"It's my pleasure." Arnbjorg ducked her head as if modesty prevented her from saying more. For all the fear I felt, I also found myself relaxing around her. Which was probably terribly dangerous, but I couldn't help but slowly start to trust her. Gunhild clearly didn't feel the same as her jaw was still set. I reached over to tap out our pattern on the back of her hand, hoping it would relax her a little. She barely spared me a glance.

"What is it we hear?" Gunhild skipped any small talk. The thunder the shieldmaiden spoke of still rumbled loudly outside.

"Oh, that?" Arnbjorg laughed, a strange barking sound that echoed from the rafters of the enormous room. "It's only thunder."

Gunhild tilted her head to one side like a confused bird and I nearly laughed. The Jotun's mouth turned up in an amused smile.

"Well. Thunder and Jotun footsteps. But mostly thunder," Arnbjorg explained. "The weather here is different from Midgard. There you have seasons and varying weather. Here it nearly always storms. In fact, you're very fortunate that it wasn't raining when you arrived. Was the weather more terrible the closer you got to Jotunheim?"

I thought back to the blizzard we nearly failed to escape. The freezing, non-stop winds and blowing snow, accompanied by the constant roar of thunder, that plagued us for days. It was a miracle we survived it at all. Even just the memory of it set a chill through me that made me shudder.

"Yes," I replied, "the worst of winter. I have seen nothing of the sort."

"The weather does get nasty around Jotunheim. I imagine the gods made it that way to keep little ones like you out of our realm, and to keep you safe. But I'm glad you made it here." Arnbjorg smiled and turned away to open another cabinet and pulled out massive blankets. When she returned her attention to us, she grimaced. "These won't work, will they? I always forget how small you are. Why, I could squish you between my fingers."

My heart stumbled sluggishly over her words, my eyes widening. This seemed like the part where she showed that her kindness was all a display meant to earn our trust so she could eat us. Gunhild's hand in mine tightened painfully. Arnbjorg was silent for a moment before she realized what she said and shook her head vigorously.

"Oh, no, I didn't mean that I intend to do such a thing. I assure you, you're quite safe with me," the giantess said before returning the blankets to the cabinet. "You must be tired. It's time to sleep now. Will you be comfortable on the cushions?"

Gunhild and I nodded, glancing at each other sideways as the giantess left us to sleep. We were unlikely to fall asleep. For all we knew, Arnbjorg only waited until we were asleep to do whatever it was Jotuns did to humans.

As soon as she left, we faced one another. Gunhild's eyes were still wide with fear, and I tapped our little pattern on the back of her hand again. We had landed in deeper trouble than expected, regardless of whether the giantess was as kind as she seemed.

"Do you think she'll let us go?" Gunhild asked in a low whisper. She glanced once at the door through which Arnbjorg had disappeared. "If she doesn't, we'll be here until we die. And we're so close to you being able to free Eryk."

"I know," I whispered back. "I think she may be what she seems. If she is, then we have nothing to worry about other than keeping our mission secret. No matter how harmless she may be, she won't take kindly to learning that we intend to steal from her fellow Jotun."

"How do we escape?" Gunhild muddled over how we might get free. "Do you think we might sneak out now?"

"No, I think we need to gain her trust, so she lets us go on her own. Otherwise, she will chase after us and probably alert the others to our presence. If we can convince her to let us go, then we'll be able to hide from the others I hope," I told Gunhild after a few moments of thought.

"But that could take days!" I tightened my grip on Gunhild's hand as her voice rose loud enough to be heard by the Jotun. She grimaced and clamped her jaw shut, biting her lip hard. "You're right. I'll follow what you think is the correct path. This is your quest, not mine."

"The quest belongs to both of us now," I told her as I let loose her hand. "You've stood by my side. There's no reason to think you've changed your mind."

Gunhild's smile lit the room brighter than the fire that blazed on the hearth. Her eyelids drooped, reminding me we had not truly slept in days.

"I think it would be wise for you to sleep, at least for a little while. We're both exhausted and will make poor decisions if we don't rest soon. The blizzard kept us awake for too long," I said as I brushed a lock of hair from her face.

"No, I can't leave you awake to defend from the giantess on your own," Gunhild whispered. I scowled at her and she crossed her arms over her chest defiantly.

"With or without you, we're not defeating a giantess if she turns against us," I pointed out. "You might as well get some rest in the meantime and pray that she is what she seems."

Gunhild relaxed a little and nodded. She laid down among the cushions and furs and closed her eyes. We spoke no further as I waited for her to sleep. When I was sure she had drifted off, I turned my face to Arnbjorg's bedroom door. I hoped the giantess went to sleep as well and would leave us in peace. No noise came from that room, which gave me hope. It was still too dangerous for me to fall asleep.

If I hadn't been so terribly weary, I might have made plans for the next step in our quest. But I could barely think straight, and my thoughts twisted and turned on themselves like the aurora. Planning would have to wait until later when I could make more solid decisions.

I allowed Gunhild to sleep for a couple of hours before my eyes became too gritty from lack of sleep to keep them open. Shaking her awake, I continued to watch the door until she opened her eyes with a sleepy smile.

"You wish to sleep now?" Drowsiness slightly slurred her words, but she quickly grew less sedated as she saw how tired I was. I nodded and laid down, falling asleep quickly.

Memories of Eryk flooded my dreams. I saw him for the first time, fighting valiantly among his compatriots against invaders from the south. The very existence of Eryk's people depended upon his army winning. And he was the fiercest of them all.

As hard as he fought, he still lost his life. But it was impossible to take him to Valhalla, regardless of my oaths to the gods. He was too brave, too skilled, to waste there. Instead, I watched to be sure my sisters hadn't noticed him and dragged him from the battlefield. We hid in the woods until the other Valkyries were gone. When he finally awoke, confusion flooded his expression. Realization eventually dawned on him. His brow went up in shock and he moved as quickly as he could with such grave injuries to genuflect. I laughed and helped him sit up properly.

"Don't do that," I told him. "I'm obviously not a proper Valkyrie if I spare every brave warrior from death."

"But why?" He was yet again confused, his eyes searching my face for answers.

"I simply couldn't take you," I said. Then I hesitated, nibbling at my lower lip while I tried to plumb the depths of my own motivations. "Do you hate me for it? I can still take you to Valhalla, if that's what you prefer."

"Don't take me," he said, reaching out for a moment as if to touch my face, though he pulled his hand back to his chest before he did. "Let me stay with you."

Chapter Thirty Three

GUNHILD PUSHED at me until I stirred. Tears slid down my cheeks as I woke up. She sighed and brushed them away. I didn't need to say what had brought them on. She'd been with me long enough not to have to ask why I cried. Even if she had wanted to, she couldn't, since Arnbjorg emerged through the doorway at that moment. As silently as someone her size might, she crossed to stir the fire back to life. When she finished, she turned to us with a crooked smile.

"Have you slept, little ones?" she asked. It seemed like she was attempting to remain quiet but the house still rumbled a little with her voice.

"Thank you," I said with a tentative smile. "Yes, we did. The cushions were very comfortable, and the fire warmed us."

Arnbjorg gave me a skeptical look, those dark eyes reminding me of a robin's when it wasn't sure whether a perch was safe enough to land on. My smile might not have been as convincing as I'd hoped. She moved toward her kitchen, where she began pulling things from shelves and setting them on a table in the center. She left us inside by ourselves for a moment as she disappeared out the front door without a word.

"We can't stay, Yrsa. You can't think we can stay," Gunhild whispered harshly. "This is madness. She'll crush our bones to make flour."

"She will not. I think we can trust her." I quickly clamped my mouth shut as the giantess returned. Whether or not she was trustworthy, I wouldn't like her to hear us speaking about her. If nothing else, it would be rude. Gunhild made a small, unhappy sound but said nothing else. As Arnbjorg cooked a much-too-large breakfast for us, she looked over her shoulder.

"What brings you to Jotunheim?" she asked again. I wasn't sure if she had forgotten that I had already answered, or if she was trying to catch us in a lie. Either way, I had to stick with the story I had started with.

Unspoken yet understood words passed between Gunhild and I in a glance. No matter how kind Arnbjorg appeared to be, it was impossible to share what brought us to her world.

"Well, technically we got lost, but we're seeking adventure and did hope to come here eventually anyway. It's simply something we've always wished to do," I lied. I tucked my hands beneath my thighs to keep them from shaking. Was I a good enough liar to rival Loki? "We hope to at least attempt to visit each of the Nine Realms. We might even become famous for it. Wouldn't that be something?"

"It's quite a foolish task you've set yourself, little ones. And dangerous beyond belief. Why, pray tell, would you want to do such a thing?" Arnbjorg squinted at us as she tried to understand our lie.

"I suppose the danger is the very reason behind it," I said, earning me a skeptical raised eyebrow from Arnbjorg. "What kind of shieldmaidens would we be if we refused to face down danger and survive? It's for the glory of it that we do it. Is that not reason enough?"

"I'll never understand you little ones," Arnbjorg laughed. "Always diving into danger headfirst, simply to impress the gods. Well, I suppose if you're determined, I can't fault you for it, nor try to stop you. Why, if you're as fierce as you think, then I would be foolish to try."

Gunhild and I laughed nervously. I glanced at the shieldmaiden sideways. She widened her eyes slightly and shrugged as if to accept what I said. I was still trying to figure out how we would get away from Arnbjorg long enough to find the piece of Freyja's armor in her realm.

"It wouldn't be wise of me to let you wander Jotunheim alone, my wee ones. They would snatch you up and crush you before I could say a thing to stop it. Will you accept my guardianship while you're here?" Arnbjorg asked. She was simply being a generous host, but it certainly limited how easily we might seek what we came to find.

"If you think it best." I nodded and offered an earnest smile, though inside I was desperately trying to find a way around it. If we were quiet enough, it might be possible to sneak out while she slept and go find what we came for. It had been Gunhild's idea to do so originally, and it seemed she was right. I was sure I would hear a resounding 'I told you so' when all was said and done.

"You're far too kind," Gunhild told her. I elbowed her in the ribs. The gleam in her eye was enough to tell me that what she was about to say wouldn't help our cause. "Surely a pair of shieldmaidens can venture out alone without risking our lives too dreadfully. Don't you agree, Yrsa?"

"While it's truly a greater adventure to set out alone, I see our host's point of view as well, especially since she knows Jotunheim far better than we ever will. Still, if we were most careful, certainly it couldn't hurt." I smiled at Arnbjorg hopefully. "Do you think you might allow it?"

Arnbjorg narrowed her eyes at me as if suspicious of our protests. She was right to be, but I had hoped she wasn't clever enough to be wary of our motives. I was always told the Jotuns weren't a race known for their intelligence. I hoped I had been told right.

Instead of answering us, the giantess turned away and began straightening items around her kitchen. If she didn't allow us our freedom, our quest would be for naught. And I worried if she would let us leave Jotunheim at all, or even her home.

"I suppose..." the giantess began. "If you're truly as brave as you seem, it can't hurt. Though I refuse to be held responsible for your actions, or for anything my kinfolk may do to you if they find you. Behave yourselves."

Gunhild glanced at me with a triumphant grin that I met with a smile in return. Our quest was not over yet. Arnbjorg looked at us suspiciously but seemed resigned to our choice.

"You'll wait until darkness falls," she warned us. "We have poor eyesight in the dark, so no one will see you. I've been told humans can see much better in the dark than we can. You'll be safer that way. And leave your packs here so they don't slow you down should you need to run."

"But won't we need them if we are to explore?" I asked, because I really didn't want to leave the rest of the armor with Arnbjorg, even if she would likely have no idea what it was. If we had to run, like she said, I didn't know whether we would be able to stop to retrieve our packs while we escaped. But she was right, we also wouldn't be able to run if we had them with us.

"No. You can't explore that deep, little ones. You must only go to the nearest village and then return when you have seen what you came to see," Arnbjorg told us.

We would have to be cautious in our search for Freyja's priceless necklace. We knew where it was, or at least who had it. We only needed to find his home to extract it and run.

Chapter Thirty Four

It was hard to tell when it grew dark enough to leave. The constant rain and thunder kept the house dim except for the firelight. Eventually, though, Arnbjorg rose from the chair she dozed in to usher us out the door.

"Be safe, little ones. Don't let your curiosity be the death of you." It was a warning that I took very seriously. She meant it, and I knew it was for good reason. Jotunheim was just as dangerous as Midgardian children had been warned. Arnbjorg was simply an exception to the rule.

"Thank you for your hospitality," I said with a nervous smile. Gunhild nodded in agreement, her smile a little warier than mine.

We slipped out the door into the night, though I looked back at the house as the door shut, leaving Freyja's feather cloak and helm within my pack inside Arnbjorg's home. It might be foolish, but what choice did I have if I also wanted to acquire the necklace? The cloak and helm would do me little good without Brisingamen.

Thunder still grumbled angrily around us, with flashes of lightning interspersed. Rain cascaded through the towering trees drenching us until we were waterlogged. Whether it was the rain or the darkness that made us shiver, I was unsure. Regardless, we stayed close together and crept on near-silent feet through the forest.

Arnbjorg lived a two-hour walk from the village that loomed ahead of us. Keeping to the shadows beneath the eaves of the massive houses, Gunhild and I peeked into windows that were within our reach and through darkened doorways to barns filled with animals more impressive than anything we'd seen before. Colossal cattle, enormous horses, even the chickens were nearly as large as one of us. We paused at each only long enough to marvel at their size, before moving on to the next building.

In the center of the Jotuns' village, a raging bonfire blazed higher than any tree I had seen outside of Jotunheim, despite the storm. Around it, the giants danced. The rumble of their feet blended seamlessly with the rumble of the persistent thunder. Gunhild and I hung back and watched for a long while in awe and horror.

"This is our chance." My voice was hardly a whisper, barely audible over the thundering feet and sky. Gunhild frowned and gave me a doubtful look. As she shook her head, I pointed to the giants. "They're occupied. It's unlikely Mimir is in his home if there are so many Jotuns here."

Gunhild nodded after a moment to consider and got to her feet carefully. We kept to the shadows as we crept together toward the nearest house. I was unsure how we might know which house was the correct one, though Gunhild pointed out the runes high on the door of one. The markings were nearly too high to see in the darkness, lit only by the leaping light of the bonfire and the occasional flash of lightning. It was too much of a risk to stay too long.

"This one says Folki," Gunhild whispered as she peered up at the door. I nodded and quickly pulled her back to the shadows. We moved from one door to the next, taking turns reading the plaques and keeping an eye out for the giants to return. By some luck, we found the house that belonged to Mimir after only a dozen or so doors. It seemed like Loki's blessing had been worth something after all.

Sneaking around to the back of the house, we located a window low enough to the ground that I could wrap some cloth around my hand to break the glass and climb inside. It made more noise than I liked as it shattered, but it was the only way in unless we wanted to risk attempting to open the massive front door right under the noses of the Jotuns.

The house was pitch black, aside from the flashes of lightning and the firelight that crept through the windows. Mimir might return at any moment. Already the thundering of the Jotuns' feet had quieted, leaving only the thunder of the sky to rumble outside. The realization of how little time we might have left set my heart to racing out of control.

We barely reached the giant's bedroom in time to dart beneath the bed as the door of the house slammed open. There came a sniffing, as if the owner of the sound smelled something foul in the air. Or us. The thought sent a shudder through me, and Gunhild put a hand on my arm to steady me.

As Mimir lit candles in the main room of his home and stoked the fire back into a blaze, I noticed something glinting in the candlelight that flickered past the bedroom door and under the bed where we hid. My eyes fell upon a delicately wrought necklace made of woven golden chain with amber beads cascading from it like raindrops. It was too dangerous to move. I held my breath and stared at it. The movement it would take to point it out to Gunhild was too much of a risk.

Forever passed as we waited for the giant to go to bed. Both of us trembled with fear of what would happen if he came into the room and smelled us. I clenched my teeth against the fear that rose like bile in my throat, the regret that I had led her to the most terrible of endings.

Mimir never entered the room. I risked sticking my head out to see where he was and found that he had passed out in a chair in front of the fire in the other room. It made me breathe slightly easier, though I still moved carefully so my movements didn't wake him. I lifted my hand and took Gunhild's chin to turn it toward Brisingamen, where the necklace sat in a box of random, forgotten items. I hoped Mimir didn't care enough about the necklace or its origins to worry about what happened to it. Not that he would simply give it to us if we asked nicely.

"Do you think we can steal it?" Gunhild mouthed the words. I glanced back toward the door, relieved to hear a snort from the other room that quickly devolved into deafening snores. We were so close to having the last piece of this puzzle. That relief gave me the freedom to beam at Gunhild with a nod.

The bed was high enough off the ground that I didn't need to crawl on my belly to reach Brisingamen, but I did anyway, to avoid the sound of boots on the tile floor beneath the bed. Before I reached for the necklace, I glanced back and saw Gunhild watching me wide-eyed. Ever so carefully, I pulled the necklace from the box, timing it so that I took it right as Mimir snored. Unsure what else to do with it, I made quick work of putting it around my neck and hiding it under my tunic. The amber and gold quickly warmed against my skin.

Jerking my head toward the window, I pulled Gunhild from beneath the bed. We clambered through the broken glass. The crunch beneath our boots was impossibly loud, but it was too dangerous to freeze. The snoring stopped suddenly. Our eyes widened as something moved inside the house.

Chapter Thirty Five

I SHOVED Gunhild until she ran. Close on her heels, I kept one ear out for movement behind us. A massive door slammed. My heart plummeted into my belly at the unmistakable thud of Jotun footsteps. Unable to take a breath, I pushed Gunhild to run faster. There was no way we could outrun the giant. He didn't hurry, but he was gaining on us quickly. Gunhild tripped, and I tried to catch her. It barely kept her on her feet.

"Keep going!" I didn't bother to keep my voice lower than a harsh whisper. Behind us, Mimir snorted as he sniffed the air. He must have smelled us on the wind that picked up. The rain that might have washed away our scent had stopped. I wished I had known that Jotun's had such a sharp sense of smell. We might have smeared dirt and pine sap on ourselves to hide better had we been informed better.

"I can smell you, humans. You won't outrun me." Mimir's voice boomed through the trees and echoed in my chest.

"What do we do? There's nowhere to hide!" Panic laced Gunhild's voice and her body was taut with fear. I had never heard her sound quite so scared in all the time we had traveled together.

"There's nothing to do but keep running. Maybe Arnbjorg will protect us." I knew better than that, of course. She said as much herself. No matter how kind she had been to us, she wouldn't betray her own people on behalf of two humans she barely knew.

It wasn't long at all before Mimir caught up to us and plucked us up off the ground by our collars. He turned us before his face to appraise us with strangely pale eyes. The troll we had faced at the beginning of our journey seemed tiny by comparison to this mammoth creature.

"What exactly were you doing in my house?" Mimir raised a heavy brow as flashes of lightning lit our faces. I fought the strong urge to lift my hand to my chest where Brisingamen lay under my clothes.

I opened my mouth to answer the Jotun's question, but no words came out. Gunhild stared wide-eyed at me, as speechless as I was.

"No answer at all?" Mimir's brow beetled downward. His dark eyebrows nearly obscured his oddly light blue eyes. "You are intruders not only in Jotunheim but also into my home. You've nothing to say for yourselves?"

His voice was alarmingly loud. My blood froze in my veins. Every giant in Jotunheim, or at least that community, must be able to hear him shouting at us.

"We…" A choked noise came from Gunhild when she spoke, but it was still better than I'd managed. "We were only curious. It's our goal to visit all Nine Realms."

Mimir's sudden laugh shocked both Gunhild and myself. I could only hope Brisingamen would make him amused and curious about us rather than enraged. My eyes met hers in shared horror. Why was he laughing?

"That explains why you're foolish enough to risk traveling to Jotunheim, but not why you were in my home." He tilted his head and eyed us more closely. "If you're travelers, where are your packs?"

"We… wished to see inside the house of a Jotun. We thought we had chosen one which was unoccupied. You must forgive us. Truly, we meant no harm. Our packs are near the gate. We left them there so we wouldn't have to carry them throughout Jotunheim." I somehow got the words out before my throat closed off again.

"I don't believe you," Mimir grumbled. He continued to inspect us, squinting as if it might help him see what we were up to better. I gasped like a fish on dry land. I had a feeling the only reason he hadn't already killed us was because of the magic of Brisingamen hanging around my neck.

"You must…" Gunhild's voice sounded edged with tears. I wanted to reach over and take her hand, but the Jotun held us too far apart.

"WHY IN THE NINE REALMS WERE YOU IN MY HOUSE?" Mimir's voice overwhelmed the persistent thunder. Brisingamen must not have been powerful enough to overcome a Jotun's wrath. In the distance, doors slammed, and footsteps approached. We were surely as good as dead.

"I told you," I whispered, my voice almost inaudible, "we were curious what the inside of a Jotun home was like, so we snuck into yours, thinking it was unoccupied. We beg your forgiveness."

"What do you have there, Mimir? Why are you shouting at this time of night?" a young giantess asked angrily. Her eyes widened as she saw what Mimir held in each hand. "Humans? In Jotunheim? What are they doing here?"

Others soon gathered, all of them staring at us in varying degrees of surprise. Without thinking, my left hand grasped at the priceless necklace I hid beneath my shirt, which drew Mimir's attention.

"What have you got hiding there, human?" Mimir's voice grew dangerously quiet and his face settled past curiosity into determination.

"I… am unsure what you mean…" How could I lie convincingly? My mind raced over all the things I might say. Leaving there without Brisingamen wasn't an option, but I had now placed Gunhild in terrible danger. "I simply… I'm so… afraid, I'm having trouble… breathing…" I made sure the words came out in terrified gasps. It wasn't hard to do, as frightened as I was.

Mimir gave a doubtful frown but did not respond immediately. Gunhild and I held our breath as we awaited the reaction of the giants. Finally, after ages, they all laughed. Mimir loudest of all. They laughed and laughed until they were all breathless. The entire time, Mimir continued to hold us out in front of him. We bounced up and down as he quaked with laughter. It felt as if I was having my spine wrung out like wet laundry.

"Why do you laugh?" Gunhild spit out. I shot a warning glance at her and she paled so visibly I saw it in the darkness.

Mimir raised an eyebrow, his gaze snapping to the shieldmaiden. "I laugh because you thought you were brave enough to risk not only entering Jotunheim but breaking into my house and yet here you are, trembling in terror. Isn't that humorous?"

"What will you do with us?" I asked. I decided to try to bargain our way out of this. I tried to think of what I might say or do to gain our freedom. "Might you simply banish us?"

The giants laughed again, albeit briefly, and then fell terribly silent as they all focused on Mimir. For a long while, only the building storm made any noise as Mimir let us squirm. The giants didn't seem to care, or even notice, that it had started pouring rain again, but I was hyper-aware of every frigid drop that slid down my face and neck.

"Oh no, little human. We can't banish you. I'm not that forgiving." His brow furrowed once more. "And I still think there is something you're hiding from us. I am determined to know what it is."

Mimir's eyes fell once more to my throat, and then my chest. After a moment, he turned to hand Gunhild off to another giant. She looked terrified as she changed hands and was taken by a giantess who looked much less friendly than Arnbjorg. I swallowed hard as Mimir reached out a huge finger to push aside my furs and rip my tunic. As they fell away, Brisingamen flashed brightly in the lightning that lit the surrounding forest.

Chapter Thirty Six

THE EYES of every giant around us widened with surprise to see Mimir's treasure at my throat. If I hadn't been trembling before, I certainly was then. He held his free hand out to me. Did he expect me to give him the necklace? If I didn't, he could certainly kill both myself and Gunhild without a moment of hesitation. The only thing that kept him from doing so was the one thing he was about to take from me.

But how could I just let it go? It was the last piece of armor that was missing, the one final piece that would free Eryk from Nastrond. If I left Jotunheim without it, it would mean I failed. I would be stuck in Midgard forever and Eryk would be tortured in the underworld for the rest of eternity. Neither was something I could fathom surviving, but more than that, I didn't have any choice in the matter if I wanted to keep Gunhild alive. She was more important now than my own safety or Eryk's well-being.

I fumbled with the necklace until it came undone and placed it into Mimir's outstretched hand. If I gave it back, I might convince him to let us go. We could find some other way to steal the necklace—this time without getting caught.

"You thought you could steal from me? And not only steal from me, but steal *this*? You're bolder than I would have expected." Mimir's laughter faded into a tone of disbelief. "But what might you want with such a treasure? Is it merely a trophy to show off to your fellow humans? Or something more? Who are you trying to impress with your theft?"

I forced myself to take a breath, to think of what to say that wouldn't end with our deaths. I had to keep Gunhild from dying in Jotunheim, out of the reach of the Valkyries. Mimir watched me impatiently while I considered my next words. What would happen if I told him the truth? Attempting to elicit sympathy from Mimir might be our only chance.

"I need it to free a warrior who Hel wrongly condemned to the underworld. She commanded me to find the lost pieces of Freyja's armor to save him from his fate."

Gunhild's eyes found mine. I held her gaze for a few moments before turning back to Mimir to see his reaction. The other giants had fallen into an eerie silence, as if they held their breaths and waited to see what might happen next.

The storm grew more violent as Mimir stared at me. Rain lashed against the trees, flattening our hair to our heads and across our faces. He didn't speak or betray any emotion. Was he still angry, or amused? Or did he respect and sympathize with me? If the gods blessed us, it would be the latter. If he let us go out of sympathy, it would certainly not be with Brisingamen. My attempt to save Eryk had truly failed.

"I can't decide if you're lying to me or not." Mimir's attention turned to Gunhild. "Perhaps you'll answer truthfully, shieldmaiden?"

"I will," Gunhild replied with a nod, somehow maintaining a calm facade. "My friend is a Valkyrie. She broke her vows and kept a mortal warrior in Midgard instead of taking him to Valhalla. Hel has punished her by sending the warrior to Nastrond and exiling her from Valhalla. Yrsa must find all the missing pieces of Freyja's armor to free him."

The giants all murmured among themselves. They were too quiet for us to hear what they were saying over the sound of the thunder, which had only grown louder. Mimir searched my face again to see what my expression might have to say about Gunhild's story. There was no need to school my face—it would hold the same guilt, shame, and determination it had during my entire quest, I was quite sure.

"I see. It's an interesting and sad story, to be sure. But how do I know it's the truth? Do you expect me to trust a pair of thieves?" A small smile twitched at the corner of the giant's mouth. Was he mocking us?

"You can ask the Norns if you know how to reach them. Or Hel herself, though I am sure she's much more difficult to contact than the Norns." Was I really being so defiant in my answer? I darted a glance at Gunhild, who only nodded emphatically.

"What do you think, Kori?" Mimir asked an ancient-looking Jotun, who shrugged.

"They seek to save their own skins. It might be an elaborate lie." Kori studied us for a few moments, his catlike green eyes glinting from the ever more frequent bolts of lightning. "Somehow, though, I think it's the truth. And a sad tale if it is."

"Thank you, Kori. As ever, we appreciate your wise counsel." Mimir's expression shifted into a curious smile. "You're fortunate that our elder believes you. Though that doesn't mean my sympathy will allow you to take what you've stolen from me."

"What can we do to earn the necklace from you?" Gunhild asked in a voice edged with insolence. I shot her a warning glare as Mimir's grip on me tightened. The giant lowered me to the ground and allowed me to stand on my feet instead of being dangled in the air. The giant holding Gunhild did the same.

"What about challenge of sorts? A trial?" Mimir suggested, more to Kori than to us. Kori shrugged. That answer surprised me, as I thought there was no chance at all. It could be an impossible trial. A trick designed to kill us or at least earn us derision and laughter from the Jotuns. But we had to try. I raised my chin slightly.

"Whatever it takes, I'm willing to at least attempt it." If I sounded nearly as defiant as I was trying to feel, then I might be in trouble. They probably wouldn't be fans of a trespasser standing up to them, but I couldn't just lay down and let them do as they wished with us.

"What should their trial be?" Mimir turned to the other giants. This elicited an excited multitude of whispered conversations between the Jotuns as they tried to come up with a challenge for us. One of the Jotuns stepped forward, giving Gunhild and me an amused smile. That smile, so wide yet devoid of warmth, made the hairs on my neck prickle. It meant nothing good. Gunhild would be in more danger now than we would have been had we just fled without the necklace. And it was my fault.

"They must fight each other to the death. Or we shall kill them both. Whichever one survives may have the necklace." The giant chuckled loudly and Mimir laughed too.

"I think that sounds as if it may be quite fun to watch. And all too fair a trial for a pair of thieves. Are you willing, Valkyrie?" Mimir raised an eyebrow, his eyes dancing.

Fear twisted in my belly as I met Gunhild's gaze. We were both experienced shieldmaidens, and it was anyone's guess who might win. I didn't want to imagine killing her, no matter if it was to win Brisingamen. The cost was too high. But surely if I didn't do it, she would die anyway.

"We'll do it," I said as I broke away from Gundhild's gaze to focus on Mimir. My voice had gone from fragile porcelain to unbreakable iron. I was surprised by my own bravery, but when I looked over to Gunhild, her chin was raised proudly.

"Are you sure?" she asked me quietly. She didn't seem to be trying to talk me out of it. It seemed more like she wanted to be sure we were on the same page and this wasn't some sort of trick of my own.

"We'll both die if we don't. This is the only way." I hated that I was putting her in danger, and for a moment, I considered changing my mind. Maybe we should just run and forget the necklace and the quest.

Gunhild stepped closer to me and placed a firm hand on my rain-soaked shoulder. She must have seen the internal debate raging in my expression. "This is your quest. It's important that you succeed. We'll get the armor and save Eryk. I'll take over your burden for you if I need to. I promise you that much."

I searched her face, wishing we didn't have to do this. Surely, there must be some other way. I could allow her to kill me and then go to the underworld to attempt to save Eryk while I was there and Gunhild would come to no harm. Mimir tilted his head questioningly.

"Well, Valkyrie? Will you do it?" It wasn't Mimir who spoke, but Kori, with an almost sympathetic tone. His eyes were gentle as he watched us, filled with curiosity rather than wrath; nothing like the others.

I glanced one last time at Gunhild, then turned back with a nod. "Yes. We'll do it. And you'll give the necklace to whichever of us survives."

"We will," Kori confirmed, shooting a warning glare at Mimir, whose grin quickly faded. "We'll do as we have promised. Whichever of the two of you wins, you will have the necklace. I'll make sure of it."

"You little humans are so strange. Death is death. I don't know why you care so much about saving this man you love. Let him be dead." Mimir shrugged, as if he didn't understand any of it, but didn't care either. "Do you need a bit of time before you begin? Any last requests?"

Gunhild shook her head as her eyes found mine to tell me she was ready. "You must promise to fight as hard as I do. I don't want you to sacrifice yourself. Not like this."

"Gunhild… I…" The words that I meant to say wouldn't come out, so I sighed and nodded instead of continuing. "We're ready now."

Chapter Thirty Seven

GUNHILD and I searched each other's expressions. I studied hers, wondering if I would see the light fade from her eyes, or whether those eyes would watch as I fell lifeless to the ground in defeat. Gunhild closed the few steps between us and brought up a hand to the back of my neck to pull me close and press her forehead against mine. We were still thoroughly drenched, our clothes clinging to our bodies, but I barely noticed it now that we had promised to take on the Jotuns' trial.

"Let's give them a proper show of how fierce we are," Gunhild told me, her voice filled with determination.

Her words elicited a strangled laugh from me, and I nodded. "Yes, of course. We wouldn't want to disappoint them."

If only it were possible to summon Loki now to save us from the mess we had found ourselves in. But I had no liquor, no pepper, no toys to make an altar with. And I could barely remember the prayer he had made me memorize in the face of this fight.

Giving me a proud smile, Gunhild closed her eyes for a moment and then stepped away. Settling into a battle stance, she pulled her axe from her belt. I darted a glance to the giants who watched us eagerly, then pulled my sword—Eryk's sword. It felt so dreadfully wrong.

For a few moments, we circled one another, poised to strike but afraid to do so. Or at least, I was afraid. The idea of my blade slicing into the shieldmaiden and her lifeblood spilling out at my feet left me hollow and shaken. Unlike me, Gunhild appeared to be strategizing rather than fearful of what must come next.

"Strike, Valkyrie! Here is your chance to show us your prowess!" one giant shouted at me, his voice booming through the trees. I kept my focus on Gunhild instead of turning to look.

When she leapt forward, axe raised to attack, I lifted my sword barely in time to block her blow. Lightning flashed as if to punctuate the beginning of our battle. Everything after that was a blur as I focused only on fighting her. She was the last person in the world I thought I would ever fight.

We dodged and parried, but fear kept us from fighting to our full strength. The giants shouted louder for us to do more than just spar. Mimir especially seemed enraged that we weren't actually attacking each other. If we angered them too much, they would kill both of us and then this whole quest would be for nothing.

Setting my jaw, I struck in earnest despite everything in me screaming to lower my blade. My stomach lurched at the unmistakable sound and feel of my sword slicing into Gunhild's side. She fell to the ground with a gasp. When she tried to rise again, pushing herself to her knees, she only fell flat again.

"Finish her, Valkyrie!" It came out as nearly a chant from the Jotuns as they watched, enraptured by our battle. Only Kori quietly urged Gunhild to stand.

I gave Gunhild the opportunity to rise again, and eventually she did. When she made it to her feet, she swayed for a moment before lifting her axe again. She stumbled toward me with blood flowing at a frightening rate from her side. With my eyes affixed on her wound, I nearly missed her axe as it lunged downward. I spun away in the nick of time, the blade only catching my shoulder and slicing into the flesh.

She would die either way now. I could see in her expression that she was in terrible pain, and that she was quickly growing weak. Rather than draw out her torture, I brought my blade around, quick and heavy, as I spun back toward her. The sword drove into her abdomen as our eyes met. The sickening tug of her falling body ripped the sword from my grasp, and I choked on a scream, but she made no sound as she fell. Her body fell into a puddle with a splash as lightning struck close enough to raise the hairs on my arms and neck.

As she lay on the sodden ground, her summer sky-blue eyes stared up at the lightning lit sky, unseeing already. It was a deadly blow, and she bled out quickly. Knowing I saved her from pain offered a hollow comfort, but it didn't lessen the agony of losing her. I gripped my hand to my chest as if I was the one gravely wounded.

My heart splintered.

It was worse than losing my brothers, worse than my own agonizing death before I became a Valkyrie, worse than when Hel took Eryk from me. A strangled sob left my throat as I pulled Gunhild into my arms. If I held her close enough, maybe it would bring her back to life. Her blood was hot and sticky on my hands, and it was my fault that it was there. How could I have ever let this happen? Why did I allow her to come with me on my quest?

As I always did when Eryk would die, I put my hand to the center of her chest, focusing on the magic that flowed within me as a Valkyrie to bring her back. She did not move. She did not breathe. The magic was dead.

"No… no, please, Odin. Loki, I summon you! Wordsmith—deceiver —flame-haired…" I cursed as I struggled to remember the prayer. "Gods, please, take me instead. Send her home but do not let her die. Please." The words came out in gasps, the wound to my shoulder forgotten because it didn't hurt as badly as my heart did. But no god came to have mercy on Gunhild for what I had done.

The giants kept their distance for a long while, though eventually Kori stepped forward with Brisingamen in hand. He knelt beside me, though he still towered over me. He gently took my hand between his fingers and pressed the necklace into it as I wrested my gaze away from Gunhild's lifeless eyes.

"I don't want it anymore. Keep it, keep it, and help me bring her back. Please. Please." My tears made Kori's face blurry, but his hand was suddenly heavy on my back.

"Little Valkyrie, don't make her death in vain. She knowingly gave her life for you to do what you promised. Don't let her down now. Take this and find this warrior you need to save." the giant elder said in a gentle voice, lower than the cracks of thunder that still shook Jotunheim. "Just be careful with it. This necklace has a way of making people bend to your will and fall at your feet in adoration. If you're to finish your quest, it will come in handy."

I stared at him, but I didn't push away the necklace as he placed it in my palm and gently closed my hand around it. It was the last thing I wanted, but he was right. I promised Gunhild that if I won, I would finish our quest. A part of me cursed ever having met Eryk. If I hadn't, then Gunhild would have been alive.

Chapter Thirty Eight

Mimir carefully lifted Gunhild's body from the ground and took her to where the fire had been at the center of the Jotun village, and where the Jotuns now gathered to bring the fire back to life. If they burned her, there would be no way to bring her back, but what chance was there of that, anyway? She was dead, and who knew where her spirit had gone? What good would a body do for her? And did she not deserve a proper send off?

As we reached the circle surrounding the bonfire, Mimir put Gunhild into the flames. If only I could abandon my quest, walk into the fire with her and go wherever she went, so she was not alone there. It was a better choice than going to Nastrond to free Eryk. I reminded myself I had not known Gunhild so very long, that I had a loyalty to Eryk, to Hel, to my sisters, but that only made it sting that much worse.

Sparks flew up into the night sky in a fountain of stars and reflected from the clouds and the treetops far above me. I stared at the sparks as if I might see her spirit rise with them, but all I saw were the echoes of them behind my eyelids whenever I blinked. She was gone.

It took a moment before I realized the raw noise I heard came from me. It was not quite crying, nor screaming. No, it was closer to the sound of a feral animal in pain. And that might be what I would become. I tried to run forward, as if to throw myself on the bonfire with her, but Mimir kept me from doing so and before long, flames engulfed Gunhild's body.

"She's gone. And now you must leave here," Kori said, kneeling before me. "Mimir will not forget his anger for long. Go. Do not look back."

And so I ran.

Chapter Thirty Nine

ON THE WAY out of Jotunheim, I stopped by Arnbjorg's home to get our packs. I couldn't forget the cloak and helm, especially now that I had Brisingamen as well. If I abandoned my quest or failed to risk the danger in stopping on my flight out of Jotunheim, I would only betray Gunhild and her sacrifice.

Pausing outside the house, I stared up at the massive purple door with my heart in my throat before knocking solidly. It was a moment before loud shuffling came from inside, and then the door opened. Arnbjorg peered around for who might be there until I cleared my throat to catch her attention.

"Oh! Little shieldmaiden! There you are. I wondered when you might return." She paused and then sought Gunhild in the forest behind me. I flushed and shook my head. "Dead?" she asked quietly. I nodded, not meeting her gaze.

"We... I... We upset Mimir and I paid for it with her life. I have been —" My voice cracked, and I collapsed to my knees.

"Oh! No, no, no! Do not fret, my dear. Here, let me help you inside." Without allowing for protest, Arnbjorg reached down to pull me to my feet and lead me inside. She sat me down before the fire and handed me a thimble, which she filled with mead. I sipped it gratefully as I watched her putter around the cabin.

"I failed her," I said, unable to hold the cup steady in my hands.

"How so?" Arnbjorg asked gently.

"I brought her on my... quest..." I hadn't intended to tell her the truth, but it poured out of me. I babbled on about what happened, and Arnbjorg listened without interrupting. I kept having to stop and breathe so I didn't break down. My entire body ached as if I had lost a limb. When I finally finished explaining what happened, Arnbjorg crossed the room to refill my thimble.

"Well... it sounds as if you found yourself quite a lot of mischief. I am sorry to hear it cost Gunhild her life. She was a bright little thing. It must hurt." Arnbjorg's eyes were full of sorrow for me.

I nodded miserably as I kept my eyes on my cup. "It does."

"Does it make you feel guilty?" Arnbjorg asked gently.

My gaze shot up to meet hers in surprise at the question. Was she trying to cause me more pain than I already felt? Or this could just be part of the universe's punishment for my selfishness. "I... Yes. Of course it does. How could it not? I am the reason she is dead. If I had never allowed her to come with me. If I had never brought her to Jotunheim. If I had never fallen in love with Eryk and kept him in Midgard and angered Hel. If I had not stolen Brisingamen from Mimir. So many ifs."

By the time I finished laying out my guilt, tears threatened again. I felt like an overtired and frightened child. And I had no right to cry. It was my own damned fault. I didn't deserve to be heartbroken. I only deserved to pay, somehow, for all the transgressions I committed. Every bit of my misery was not my own. It resulted from the misery I caused others.

"It is my doing. I should make it right. But how?" I asked, desperate for an answer that Arnbjorg probably didn't have.

The giantess sighed and shook her head. "Little one. I was not saying you *should* feel guilty, only that I understood if you do. Gunhild chose her own path. It happened to follow yours. She is an adult—or was—and had to be allowed to make her own choices, regardless of whether they led to her death."

"But *I* am the one who killed her!" My voice cracked at the admission. "I am the one to put the sword through her. Not anyone else. Me. I murdered her because finding the armor was more important than her life. How do I live with that?"

"You live in such a way that she did not die for nothing," Arnbjorg said. For a little while, she let me sit with that idea before continuing. "You continue on your quest. Go to Helheim and rescue your warrior. Make sure you honor her memory, *her* quest to help you find it. Her path was with yours, but they have parted now, and you must continue in the way she would want you to. Do not let her down."

I looked down at the thimble in my hands, feeling as small as a beetle. "How do I go on? I feel... broken. First Eryk, now her. And always the fault lies at my feet. The blood is always on my hands. When will I stop putting the people I love in harm's way?"

"You love her?" Arnbjorg asked quietly. I sighed and nodded as it was all I was able to manage. My heart wrenched with the realization of just how much I had sacrificed. Had I been aware of my feelings for Gunhild, I might have made entirely different choices. It was too late now though. "Then you must make it worth it. Whatever your quest might have been, you must complete it."

"You're right," I agreed. I took a deep breath and held it for a moment, the tension building in me as I decided what I must do. Finally, I let it out in a rush. There was only one thing to do. I had to finish this quest. I would find my way to Nastrond and free Eryk, and while I was in the underworld, I might find Gunhild and free her as well. I wasn't sure what I would do with both of them once they were saved, but that was a problem I could deal with when I got to it.

"You're leaving then?" Arnbjorg asked.

"I have to. Goodbye, Arnbjorg. Thank you for your hospitality." I offered a fragile smile and received a sympathetic one in return.

"Go safely, little one. I will send prayers to the gods for you." Arnbjorg followed me to the door and opened it for me after I gathered what I could carry—including the armor—and stepped out into the chilly, rainy night of Jotunheim. Arnbjorg nodded encouragingly when my focus returned to her. She shook her head and gave me a gentle nudge to my back with her large index finger. "Go, go."

I watched as the door closed behind me and left me in the dark, utterly alone. With a deep breath to fortify myself, I took off toward the gate. Who knew what I might find in Midgard? Possibly another blizzard. I didn't know how I would face that alone again, but I didn't have much choice. I lifted my chin as bravely as I could and began the short walk out of Jotunheim. The gate, which towered over me, nearly as tall as the endless trees, stood abandoned. If I had known what would happen in Jotunheim, I might never have passed. As I stepped through, the thunder echoed behind me still.

Chapter Forty

THE WORLD outside of Jotunheim had warmed in my absence. The sun was high in the bright blue sky when I emerged. The blue made me ache for Gunhild. It was the same color as her eyes. The snow had melted and tiny blades of grass had started to peek out of the soil.

The trek across the dead land from Jotunheim still took nearly two weeks just as it had before, though it was easier now that the blizzard had passed. I crunched my way through the snow toward a road in the distance, trying to let the sound of birds chirping around me buoy my spirits. Their song felt empty though, like it was a mere echo of the real thing even though the birds hopped around right in front of me as they sang. My fingers strayed to the warm amber of Brisingamen at my throat. I probably shouldn't have been wearing it, but it was the safest way to carry it. If it was around my neck, it would be much harder to steal or lose. The cloak and helm were in my pack, weighing me down.

My feet dragged without Gunhild at my side. The birds did no good at cheering me. I was empty and broken. Only shattered fragments of myself remained. I tried to remind myself that I had planned to face my quest alone when it began. Surely, I still had it in me to do so. Gunhild would want me to.

I reached the road and then traveled until I came to a crossroads. I didn't know which way to go. There was nowhere I could think of to go that would take me to Helheim, or back to Gunhild, or somewhere that I could go back in time and start over. Grief and fear overwhelmed me, and I crumpled to my knees at the center of the crossroads with a feral scream. I screamed until there was no breath left in me to do so. Once I was spent, I pulled my knees up to my chest and sat there for a few minutes, trying to determine what in the world I could do or which way I should go. Then I remembered that I didn't have to be entirely alone, not that anyone could replace Gunhild's warmth at my side.

I didn't have much to summon Loki with, but Arnbjorg had sent me onward with mead and some food, and I thought I remembered the prayer he told me. Surely if I was in enough need, he would come regardless. He had to be expecting me to summon him. I pulled out the mead and a little smoked salmon, and placed it in front of me, before turning my face to the sky and shouting the prayer Loki had made me memorize.

"Loki... flame-haired wordsmith, mischief.... mischief-maker, discord-weaver, lover of chaos, come now and bless *me* with... with a tongue clothed in lies—no, deception... as you... you are the deceiver. *Bjoda heim!*" I screamed the last words into the sky, hoping my desperation would make it to him, wherever he had gone.

There was only silence at the crossroads. No gust of wind, no darkening of the sky, no sign of anything that might resemble an answer from the god of mischief. I growled in frustration and called out the prayer again, correctly this time. And again, when Loki still didn't appear.

Something caught my eye at the edge of my vision, and I looked up to see a fox slinking across the road ahead of me. It was beautiful, and it looked over to me furtively, its dark eyes curious. After a moment, instead of continuing on its way, it took a couple of steps toward me and then paused as it stared at me.

"Hello," I whispered, picking up the smoked salmon I had used in my attempt to summon Loki. "Do you want this? I know you must be able to smell it. Come and I'll give it to you."

Almost as if it understood me and my offer, the fox looked at me doubtfully before scurrying a little closer. It darted toward me to grab a piece of the salmon and then darted away again to eat it some distance from me.

"There's more, if you want it," I said, momentarily distracted from my grief, though I still felt scraped raw.

The fox crept over again, and this time took the salmon directly from my palm. Instead of darting away, it sat in front of me and ate it, then looked up with an almost familiar expression. Those dark eyes held something I recognized somehow, but I couldn't figure out what it was until the fox shimmered in the air and became a red-haired man sitting in the snow before me.

"Hello, Valkyrie," Loki greeted me with an appraising glance. Then he looked around with a frown for Gunhild.

"Hello," I said, my throat closing around a relieved sob as I threw my arms around his neck. He chuckled and hugged me to him.

"Where is she?" he asked against my hair, before he released me to pull away and meet my gaze. "The giants killed her then?"

I shook my head, unable to admit that it was myself who had ended her life, not the giants. Loki pulled me to him again, the most affectionate I had ever experienced him being. I buried my face in his neck with a shuddering exhale.

"I killed her," I finally admitted in a trembling voice.

"Why did you kill her?" Loki asked, his voice gentle but curious.

"It was… sort of an accident." I paused, because that was not quite true. I had agreed to the battle, and I had chosen to take her life instead of standing there and letting her take mine. I shuddered with the effort to keep my story in, but I ended up babbling out what happened. His eyes widened as my words poured out like a geyser.

"That's some accident, Valkyrie. But you did not go in intending to kill her. I am sure her spirit forgives yours," he assured me.

"I don't know where her spirit is! We were in Jotunheim. I couldn't take her to Valhalla and my sisters wouldn't have been able to take her either and if she is in the underworld too, then I will—"

"Shhh… stop that," he interrupted. "She's not in the underworld unless Hel was feeling particularly cruel. She's probably in the in-between place until they determine what to do with her." Loki squeezed me to him again, hushing me. It only made my throat tighten and my stomach ache.

"Who determines that? How long does it take?" Panic clawed its way up my chest. It dragged at my lungs and made it hard to breathe.

"I think the important question that you are completely forgetting to ask is what you can do to get her back," Loki pointed out.

"The Jotuns burned her body. I can't get her back. Even if I went to the in-between place." I trembled with the effort not to rage at him for suggesting the impossible.

"Well, that's entirely untrue. A body is nothing. You simply need the right magic to get her back, and I know a friend who can help."

"How do I get Gunhild back, then? How can your friend help? Where are they?"

"Lucky for you, she lives in Armvind. You'll have to see if the jarl will let you meet her. He claims she is his aunt." Loki leaned in with a wicked grin. "He claims this, but she's not at all."

"Then who is she?" I asked with a frown.

"Well, she's not his aunt," he said simply. "He just thinks calling a vala his aunt brings him prestige."

"So, she's just a vala then?" I asked, which earned me a few moments of silence. "You won't tell me?"

He grinned instead of answering. "All you need to know is that she is a powerful vala. That's what matters, right? Her bringing Gunhild back to you?"

"Of course," I replied, a little harshly. I was too eager to find Gunhild to put up with his teasing. "Can we go now?"

"Well, erm, yes." He shifted a little uncomfortably.

"But?" I raised an eyebrow. Of course, there would be a catch. I was so very weary of everything to do with Loki coming with a catch. I stared at him with a frustrated glare until he responded.

"She may not want to see me. I stole a pie from her window before we left for Alfheim."

"I thought she was your friend!" I shouted at him, which caused him to sit back in shock.

"She is. Sort of. Let's get you to Armvind so we can go talk to Leif.

Say you heard of his aunt and would like to speak to her. Say you want her to tell your future or something."

"What if I can't see her? Then what?" A sting of panic burned in my chest.

"Calm down," he said, which only made my hackles rise. "Sorry. Just… don't worry. I think she'll see you."

I nodded and took a deep breath. It was the only choice I had if I didn't want to leave Gunhild at Hel's mercy. I got to my feet and stared at Loki for a long moment before straightening my shoulders.

"Take me there, then."

Chapter Forty One

ONCE LOKI SPIRITED us back to Armvind, it didn't take long to find the young jarl. He sat on a small, ordinary-looking throne in his mead hall. As we approached, I recited in my head what I might need to say to convince him to let me see his so-called aunt. If he didn't allow it, I would have to sneak a visit with her. I had no choice but to see her if I wanted to bring Gunhild back.

"Your grace," Loki greeted the jarl with more deference than I would have expected. Though I was grateful he was being circumspect so that we could get what I needed. "You remember my friend, Yrsa. She wished to say hello again now that she's returned and to pay her respects."

"Ah, how nice to see you again, Yrsa. Luka told us you had traveled on without him." Leif got to his feet with a broad smile.

"Yrsa came to ask you something, your grace," Loki said as he nudged me with an elbow to the ribs.

"Did she? Go ahead then, Yrsa, you are welcome to ask anything," Leif said quietly. Perhaps he could sense my grief. He seemed like the type who could. His gentle blue eyes watched me curiously; his head tilted to one side as I gathered the courage to speak.

"Oh. Yes. Luka told me of your aunt…" I trailed off, realizing Loki hadn't told me her name. My heart raced with panic as I feared that something so simple could stop me from meeting her and asking her to bring Gunhild back. Thankfully, Loki was right there and placed a hand on the small of my back to steady me.

"Solveig," Loki said, as if reminding me.

"Yes. The vala. I was wondering if I might pay my respects to her."

"You told her of Aunt Solveig?" Leif glanced to Loki—or Luka as he knew him—as if he might explain why he would have anything to do with the vala Leif claimed was his aunt. Loki didn't do much to answer that question, so Leif looked back to me with a raised eyebrow.

"He did, in passing," I said, with an earnest smile. "I was glad to hear she was here."

"Well, I suppose she would quite appreciate that. She *does* often complain about not getting the respect she deserves."

"I would very much like to offer her that respect, if I may." I tried to keep my tone light and eager. "We didn't have a vala where I come from. She died when I was a child, and we never were fortunate enough to have another." It wasn't a lie, though the place where I came from was a distant memory.

"Alright, then. I'll take you to her. Did you want to go now, or might you eat first? The others should join us for a meal soon." Leif gave me a warm smile that reminded me of Gunhild.

"Thank you. I'd like to join you for a meal, but I'd prefer to meet her first. Dinner tomorrow?"

"Of course, of course," Leif agreed. I glanced at Loki to silently rejoice that I had gotten what I wanted and didn't have to do anything special to get it. "Come, then. She is on the outskirts of the village. She likes her privacy, but I am sure she will be glad to see someone who honors her."

I offered a bright smile, brighter than it should be for such a simple request, but the hope of retrieving Gunhild burned within me. We bid Loki goodbye before Leif led me through the village to a small house bedecked in vala blue, with beads of amber and bone hanging from the eaves.

"Aunt?" Leif called through the door after his knock went unanswered for a few moments. It opened finally to reveal a woman who was nearly as small as a dwarf. Her back was bent with age and her face lined with wrinkles as deep as ravines. Her cornflower blue eyes twinkled though, as if the body were old but the soul inside was quite young. Cataracts clouded them, but she seemed to see me well enough despite that.

"Come in! Come in! Don't let the warmth of the fire out," she chastised us, though she winked at me cheerfully. I followed Leif inside and took a seat when she gestured for me to do so. "Who is your friend, Leif?"

"This is Yrsa. She passed through the village recently but has returned just today."

"Hello, my lady," I said with a respectful bow of my head and folded my hands before my chest. I wanted to pour my heart out to her and beg her for help, but it seemed rude to just jump right into demands, and it would be hard to explain everything with Leif standing there anyway. I reined in my urge and simply said, "I heard you were here and wished to offer my respects."

"Ah, I see," she replied, though her bright eyes seemed to see through me. Her raised eyebrow hinted she knew I was there for more than that. "Leif, why don't you leave us to talk? That's a good boy."

Leif chuckled and left to give us some privacy. Solveig watched him go and then returned her hawk-sharp gaze to me. For a long while, she sat in silence as she determined what I might be up to.

"What do you really want, Valkyrie?" Solveig asked after the minutes stretched out endlessly. "You want more than to pay your respects. Your eyes are haunted with a great sorrow that I think you have come to me to soothe."

My hands gripped the arms of the chair so tightly my knuckles had gone white. I swallowed hard and tried to find words to explain while she waited patiently for me to decide what to say. I wasn't sure if I should tell her everything at once or be more circumspect about it. While I didn't feel the need to hide anything from her, I also didn't want to overwhelm her with too much information.

"I was told you might help," I squeaked out finally.

"Yes, I'm sure you were," Solveig replied with a sigh. "Loki sent you?"

"Yes, my lady," I admitted. I wondered who she was that she knew Loki by his true name and not the name everyone else in the village called him. He had said she was a friend, but I hadn't realized he meant a friend to him as a god. That could change everything. Maybe she really could help.

"Then it must be dire if he sent you. He doesn't feel sympathy for many." Her gaze softened and her hand reached out to grab one of mine ever so gently. "Tell me your story and we'll see if I can help."

Something in her words, the way her gentle gaze settled on me, made my heart crack all over again. All that came out was, "She's dead."

"Who, dear? Tell me who. Tell me what I need to know to help. And how you think I can." She reached out to lift my chin which quivered with emotion.

My story poured forth more easily with her than it had for anyone. She didn't have to yank it out of me or wheedle it away from me. I trusted her with it all in the hope she could somehow fix what I'd broken.

"What is to be done?" I asked.

Solveig gave a solemn smile. Her cloudy eyes studied me before she patted my cheek and sighed.

"You have two choices, Valkyrie."

I bit my lip as I waited for her to say what my choices were. If one of them wasn't a way to bring Gunhild back, I might just scream. For a long while, the vala reverted to silence. There was no urgency in her, only sadness and serenity.

"What are they? I'll do anything it takes to bring her back. Only tell me what I must do." I gripped Solveig's hand tightly, though I relaxed my hold a bit as her frail bones creaked between my fingers.

"You can let her go and get on with this quest you've been sent on. Which is what I recommend." She paused, studying me with something between a sigh and a huff. "Or you can risk going where the shieldmaiden has gone. I can send you there, to the place-between, if we are quick about it. But you might both end up trapped there if you're not careful. Don't take too long to decide. It won't take Hel long to realize she has a soul to collect."

"I'll do it," I said without hesitation. There was no debating this. I had caused Gunhild's death and I would see to it that she was returned to Midgard where she belonged, whatever the cost. "Send me where she is, and I'll find us both a way back. Or go straight to Nastrond from there myself."

"The only way to Nastrond from there is if Hel takes you, which I doubt she would. This will anger her," Solveig advised. "You'll need another way if you plan to go to Nastrond to rescue your warrior."

"Whatever it takes," I said with a nod.

"Well, then Valkyrie. Lie down on the floor before the fire and think of her as clearly as you can. If you had died next to her, it would have helped you find her, but if you can picture her face and hear her voice, it will help nearly as much when you die now."

I didn't have to be told twice. I quickly did as I was directed. It was easy to picture Gunhild and imagine her voice. There was nothing that could keep me from her, not even the Goddess of Death.

"I'm coming for you, Gunhild. Don't be afraid," I promised as I closed my eyes. Solveig pulled a pot of blue liquid from a nearby cabinet, and quickly drew symbols on my forehead, my cheeks, and below my collarbone.

"Close your eyes, Valkyrie. And hold tight to your friend's memory. This will hurt." Before I could ask why, Solveig dragged a knife across my throat. The blade cut deep enough that I choked on my blood. My eyes were wide for the few moments before death took me in its grasp and dragged me to the other side. Most would have been afraid to die, but I was triumphant. Gunhild would soon be resurrected and I could leave my guilt behind in the place-between.

Chapter Forty Two

I HAD NEVER BEEN to the place-between before. Heavy fog shrouded it, and dim light crept through the mists. The sound of distant voices echoed around me, but no matter how long I walked toward them, their source never seemed to reveal itself. After several minutes of aimless walking, I remembered why I was there.

"Gunhild?" I didn't quite shout, and my voice was tentative. Where could she be? How would I find her? I paused and searched the fog for any sign of movement, but it was too thick to detect anything at all. When I spoke her name again, it was with more certainty, and louder. "Gunhild!"

Footsteps shuffled nearby, and I turned to find their source. Was it my shieldmaiden? I ran toward them, searching for who might have moved so near to me. When I reached where I was sure they must be, nobody was there. The place-between couldn't be as empty as it seemed. Gunhild was there somewhere, as were the people who murmured somewhere in the distance.

Unsure where I should go, I stood frozen in place for several minutes, hoping to get my bearings. That was impossible, though. Sighing, I closed my eyes. I tried to sense her the same way I had sensed Yggdrasil with enough concentration. There was a tug at my center as I focused on the sensation of her hand grasped to my chest, her body in my arms as she died, her sky-blue eyes looking up at me. I missed her more than I had ever missed anything in my life.

I clung to the memories of what we shared in our time together and sifted through each one until the tugging sensation grew stronger. It manifested as a golden binding at my throat, similar to Brisingamen. When following it didn't seem to lead me any closer to her, I stepped backward and tugged against that which had been tugging me. There was a gasp, and so I tugged again, eliciting a soft whisper which almost sounded like my name.

"Gunhild?" I tugged again, then traced the binding in the hope it would lead me to her. The voice that came then was slightly louder, but I still wasn't quite sure what it said. Was I only imagining that it was my name?

No matter how I tugged, no matter how I followed, I never reached what I hoped was at the end of my binding. I paused and tried to think of what else I might do to find her or lead her back to me. An idea occurred to me as I felt another tug of the golden thread that connected me to what I hoped was Gunhild.

I cleared my throat of the last feeling of blood clogging my windpipe and lifted my chin to sing the song I sang to the troll near the beginning of our journey. My voice wavered more than it did then, but I didn't stop. There came another, stronger tug at the binding, and I increased my volume, hoping to lead Gunhild to me.

As I sang, I pulled again at the golden thread. It faded into the fog near me, but hope bubbled up in my chest as I caught a movement through the mists. I sang louder, repeating the song again, and my voice became more confident. Suddenly, the unmistakable sunlit copper of Gunhild's hair shone through the fog. I ceased my song and ran in that direction.

Gunhild stumbled into my arms with a sob. Her arms wrapped around my waist, and her forehead came to a rest against mine. I breathed a relieved sigh and closed my eyes as I held her tightly to me.

"Hush, my sunshine, it's done. I found you," I whispered into her hair as relief poured through me like a heavy rain.

"I was so frightened," she replied in a shuddering breath. Her face lifted with a confused frown. "How did you get here? How did you find me?"

I hushed her again and ran a gentle hand over her hair to tangle my fingers in her braids. Holding her in my arms settled the pain in my heart. It was as if it could beat again, now that she was with me once more.

"There was a vala who helped me find you and bring you back. You don't have to stay here. We simply have to find a way out." I pulled away slightly to inspect her more closely. My fingers ran along her cheek, drying the tears that fell in her distress.

"But how?" Her eyes widened, as she realized what my presence in the place-between must mean. "No. No, you shouldn't have done that. You should have left me and gone on with your quest. You should have left me here."

"Gunhild, I would never leave you here, not for anything in the world. Especially not after I was the one who took your life. I couldn't bear losing you, couldn't bear having your blood on my hands instead of your presence by my side." It was as close to a confession of my love for her as I could manage at the moment. The place-between hardly seemed like the right place to pour my heart and soul out at her feet.

Shaking her head, Gunhild closed her eyes and leaned her forehead against mine again. After a moment of silence between us, I tilted her chin upward to see her face better, unable to believe I found her.

"Oh, Yrsa. Now we're both—" Gunhild's words were cut off as a shadowy figure stepped from the fog. My stomach twisted as I recognized the form the mists swirled around.

"You're a difficult one, aren't you, Valkyrie?" The hollow voice caused a familiar shiver to trip down my spine. I pulled Gunhild closer to me to keep the goddess from stealing her away. I wouldn't lose her again.

"Leave us, mistress. I only came to retrieve her, so I might finish the task you gave me." I spoke with more authority than I really felt. Gunhild's shoulders straightened at my words, but she kept quiet.

"You killed her. Therefore, she's mine to have. You shouldn't have taken her from Midgard. If she were there, a Valkyrie could have taken her to Valhalla. How many times must you transgress upon the rightful order of things?" Hel sneered at me and anger flashed in her normally expressionless eyes.

"I broke the rightful order of things when I took her life. The Norns didn't say either of us would die on this quest..." My words caused the goddess's brow to furrow. Her head tilted to one side as if considering what I had said.

"You know that, above all else, maintaining balance is my priority. Not torture, not death, but order." Hel's expression was not sympathetic, but neither was it angry any longer. "Still, she's here now. You can't take her back."

"And what of me?" I raised an eyebrow, almost in defiance. It was the first time I had ever been truly brave enough to stand up to my mistress, and the feeling was like being struck by lightning.

"I don't want you. You may return to Midgard for all I care." Hel shrugged, her gaze turning to Gunhild. She took her by the wrist and wrested her from my arms. "Come with me, child. You are brave and have fought valiantly, so I will see that you aren't sent to Nastrond. You can be my handmaiden."

As Hel attempted to lead Gunhild away, the golden tether that bound the shieldmaiden to me pulled taut and jerked Gunhild backward. I glanced from her to Hel with a surprised laugh. It must have been the magic wrought by Solveig. How well might it stand up to a goddess?

"What is this? How are you entangled?" Hel turned around and reached out to grasp at the golden thread, but it slipped through her fingers like water. She glared at me and then tried again to take hold of the binding but failed.

"You can't separate us. A certain vala named Solveig has bound me to Gunhild. You can't take her without taking me." I darted a glance to Gunhild, whose tears had dried.

"Solveig? *Solveig*?" Hel shrieked the name. Gunhild used the opportunity to struggle out of the goddess's grasp and return to my side. I put a protective arm around her shoulders as I watched Hel.

"You know her?" Curiosity crept into my voice. I had thought Solveig might be more than she said, but Hel's recognition told me she was much more than I could have expected.

"She likes to say her name is Solveig, but she is no simple vala." Hel shook her head, though it was unclear if it was from disbelief or anger.

"Then who is she?" Gunhild asked.

Hel's gaze returned to Gunild, and she let out a heavy exhale. One that always meant anger. We would be wise to tread carefully.

"Var," Hel hissed. I stumbled back a step as she spoke the name of the goddess of oath-keepers. Gunhild glanced my way in confusion. Loki must have known who Solveig really was and knew that she could use our oaths to save Gunhild from Hel's grasp. I owed him more than I had realized and wasn't sure how I could ever repay him for this help.

"Var is a lesser-known goddess who, among other things, protects those who make oaths. She must have known of our oaths to each other and seen them as more sacred than death." I shifted my gaze to Hel with a laugh. "You may be a goddess, but so is she. Can you break these bindings?"

"I can't," Hel replied in a stony voice. "She'll make sure I lose Helheim too if I cause your oath to one another to be broken. Your promises bind you to each other. And those are sacred to her."

"Then I suppose you'll have to let us go," Gunhild said, a defiant smile tugging at her mouth as her courage grew.

"Or perhaps you'll both have to stay in the place-between. Forever." Hel's voice had returned to its normal, hollow nature. It was unfeeling, cold, and irrevocable. I shrugged nonchalantly, as a plan developed in my mind.

"You're a goddess and I'm only a Valkyrie. I suppose I have no choice in this matter," I told her with a sigh that was merely for show. Bowing my head to her, I pulled Gunhild closer to me. "Though I can't understand why you would if you wish to have Freyja's armor so badly."

Hel's brow lowered dangerously as a small, frustrated noise slipped past her lips. Another shiver slithered down my spine at her menacing expression.

"You think you are so clever don't you, Valkyrie? You are right, though. The armor is more important than punishing you for yet another transgression."

"Then will you release us?" I asked in a careful voice. She didn't need to know that we already had gathered the entirety of the missing armor. Letting her think we still had more pieces to find would ensure she restored us to Midgard.

"I suppose I have no other choice unless I wish to take the trouble and the time to find the blasted armor myself."

"Then we will continue to seek the armor."

"Fine. Go."

Chapter Forty Three

I OPENED my mouth to ask when Hel intended to send us back, when suddenly I woke up gasping. The ceiling of Solveig's cottage was above me instead of the endless fog of the place-between. My mouth still tasted like blood, which nearly gagged me, but I managed not to retch and instead turned my head to see Gunhild waking beside me.

I pulled the shieldmaiden into my arms with a joyful cry. Gunhild was as unharmed and perfect as the day I met her. I lifted my hand to my throat to find my wound had disappeared and then turned to drag Gunhild into my arms. It was a miracle that I had managed to bring her back. I would never take her presence for granted again.

"You brought me back!" she said with wide eyes, as if she didn't believe it despite the warmth of the room and that of my arms around her.

"Of course I did." My hands cradled her face as my gaze pored over her again to be sure she was safe. When I was sure she was, I rested my brow against hers and closed my eyes. Her breath was warm against my lips as her eyelashes fluttered closed.

"I didn't know if it was possible."

"Nothing in the Nine Realms could have stopped me from bringing you back," I told her. Without thinking, I lifted my face enough to kiss her. She gasped and her hand clutched at my tunic, but she didn't push me away. I only stopped when Var laughed quietly.

"I had a feeling, you know," the old woman chuckled. Gunhild, breathless and flushed pink, pulled away with a curious tilt of her head as she looked up at Var. "Nobody goes up against death itself unless there is love involved. I hope you love her back, shieldmaiden."

I swallowed hard and watched Gunhild for her reaction. Her sky-blue eyes studied me for several long moments before she let out a joyful burst of laughter.

"How could I not? She is the most wonderful person I have ever met. I…" Her hand hovered over my cheek, then landed feather-light, her touch lingering as if she feared letting go. "I never gave a thought to her loving me back. She has her warrior, and her life as a Valkyrie. Why should she want me?"

"I think I will leave you two alone," Var said, and before any protest might leave my lips, the old woman slipped out the door into the village. My stomach twisted as I turned back to Gunhild.

"How can I love two people? It isn't fair to either of you." I shook my head, but she lifted my face gently to meet her gaze.

"The heart is not so easily convinced, apparently. But I understand if you don't want me." Her voice was barely loud enough to be heard over the fire. "You loved Eryk long before you knew me. You are on this quest for him. I am… a tagalong."

"Gunhild, you are *not* a tagalong. You haven't been for a long time." We laced our fingers together. "I don't know what to do. I love Eryk, but… it is not the same way I love you. They are so very different, but not in a way I know how to put into words. We made oaths to each other, but I haven't gone to the underworld yet to get him back."

She squeezed my hand, tapping out that same pattern on the back as she always did to comfort me. Four taps, then a long press, then three more taps. After a moment, she took a deep breath and let it out slowly and decisively. "Well, if you must choose, choose him. You are loyal to him, and you loved him first."

"Gunhild, it's not that easy. I can't simply push my love for you aside. No more than I can push my love for him aside." I rubbed my curls anxiously, leaving them a mess. Gunhild immediately smoothed them with a gentle hand. "You deserve someone dedicated only to you."

She pulled me to her to kiss me again instead of answering. I melted into it, unable to stop myself. It was something I hadn't known I'd been waiting to do, but when her lips were on mine, everything felt right. Or it would, were it not for Eryk waiting for me in the underworld.

"Push nothing aside, then. We will take things as they happen. You don't have to kiss me ever again if you do not want to. At least not until you decide the best course of action." She patted my hand and smiled so brightly I thought it might blind me.

"And if I want to? Will you think awfully of me for betraying Eryk?" My voice wavered at the question. If I was betraying Eryk by doing so, then why would I do it at all?

"I won't think awfully of you, no. Because I can't know your heart. I can't make your decisions for you. Only you know what is right or wrong for you." Her tone was so gentle, so reassuring, that I had to lean in to kiss her again. When I finally pulled away, she asked, "Where are we, anyway?"

That pulled a laugh from me, and I saw the cottage with fresh eyes. "Back in Armvind. The cottage of the goddess Var, apparently."

"How did you know she was here?"

"Loki told me," I said with another laugh, barely able to believe it myself.

"He actually came when you summoned him?" Gunhild asked with wide eyes.

"He actually did. He's a good person, I think, when it comes down to it," I admitted.

Before either of us said anything else, a streak of red hair and a bright grin darted through the door. Var berated Loki as he barreled in. He obviously didn't care a whit because he inserted himself between Gunhild and I with a curious, exuberant laugh.

"Loki!" I chastised him, with about the same effect that Var had on him. He didn't care. He turned excitedly to inspect Gunhild further.

"You figured it out, finally?" Loki asked with a smirk.

"Figured what out?" I replied with an innocent expression. Of course, I knew what he meant, but I wasn't just going to give it to him so easily.

"Oh, please. That you're in loooooove," Loki teased. "I've known it all along, you know."

"I'm sure you think that." I rolled my eyes, but Gunhild giggled, which told me that she had felt like this longer than I realized as well.

"Oh, I don't think anything, I know it. I'm a god, after all. We know things," Loki said with a careless shrug. "I suppose Gunhild will need to rest awhile before we head to Helheim."

"No, we should go right away," Gunhild argued.

"You just came back from the dead, shieldmaiden," Loki pointed out. "You need at least one good night's sleep before you make a trek to the underworld."

"He's right, sunshine, you need to rest. Eryk can wait a little longer. He probably wouldn't even notice the difference," I assured her. It was nearly midsummer, but there was still time to meet Hel's deadline.

"Fine, fine," Gunhild said with a sigh.

I turned to Var who stood nearby sipping a cup of tea. She smiled as our eyes met.

"How do we repay you?" I asked.

"Keep your oaths to each other," Var said. "That is all I require. I brought you back because of them. Do not break them now."

"We wouldn't dare," Gunhild said solemnly. "Not that I ever would, anyway. And obviously if Yrsa freed me from… whatever that place was… then she wouldn't go back on hers, either."

"That is good enough for me," Var said with a slight smile. "Now get out of my house. Go wash up and find supper. Make plans for the rest of your quest."

"Yes, my lady," Loki said, giving her a brief salute, which earned him an irritated huff from Var. "You heard the goddess. Get out!"

Chapter Forty Four

LOKI LEFT us at the door to the cottage where Gunhild and I had stayed in the last time we were in Armvind. As soon as Gunhild and I closed ourselves inside, she pulled me down onto the cushions beside her and laced her fingers with mine.

"I'm so glad to be here with you again. Only us for a little while, in a nice warm house, with plenty of proper food to eat," Gunhild said, curling against me comfortably.

"You wouldn't want to be with me without a bed and a meal?" I teased and poked her in the side. I was full of good humor for the moment and allowed myself to enjoy it for today. Tomorrow I would worry about Eryk. For now, I was glad to have Gunhild back.

"What? No! That isn't what I meant," Gunhild protested with a squeak. "I meant I am glad we have no other distractions."

"I knew what you meant," I assured her, brushing a stray strand of hair from her cheek. "I'm glad for it too. Though we can't let Loki convince us to stay too long."

"No, we can't," Gunhild agreed. "But I don't want to think about it right now. I know you can't help thinking about it, but I don't want to."

My stomach gave a guilty twist. "Is it bad that I don't want to, either?"

"No, of course not," Gunhild assured me. "You've been thinking of that non-stop for months now. It's time for you to take a break. You've done everything you can."

The urge to argue rose in my throat like bile. I wanted to rant that I hadn't done enough, that Eryk was still in the underworld. But she was right. I had been going without stopping to rest for more than a night or two since Hel took Eryk, and I needed a chance to breathe.

I nodded and rested my head on her shoulder. She leaned her cheek against my hair and sighed. For a long while, we enjoyed the peace that had been so lacking. It was a relief, although there was still so much to be done. For tonight, I wouldn't think about it. One night. One night to appreciate what I still had. One night to be grateful that Gunhild was by my side again.

"Have you ever been to Helheim before?" Gunhild traced the lines of my cheek and jaw as we curled around each other. It was so peaceful, but her question verged on shattering that peace.

"No, I had been nowhere but Midgard and Valhalla before this quest," I admitted.

"Do you know anything about it?"

"Not really, no. Loki will know more about it than I do." My heart thumped a little harder as I thought of why I needed to visit Helheim. I didn't want to think of that now. I wanted our peace to remain intact. "Let's talk about other things. Tell me something good. Something happy."

"I'm happy now," she said, her cheeks flushing a little. "Happier than I have ever been. I don't want to leave this room. If I could make one moment in time last forever, it would be this one."

I nodded, because she was right. I had never felt this kind of peace with Eryk. We always tiptoed around. We argued frequently, our differing views on things always coming to a head. With Gunhild, that almost never happened. Yes, occasionally we disagreed, but never had it turned into a fight.

"I'm happy, too." I pressed my lips to hers. "I wish we could stay here. They would let us."

"They would, yes," Gunhild agreed, pressing sweet kisses to my jaw and cheeks. "But would you be able to live with that?"

The answer was obvious. I wouldn't abandon my quest and leave

Eryk in the underworld, no matter how complicated my feelings about him had become. I had a duty to rescue him. After all, it was my fault he was there. I gave up Valhalla to save him. Hel waited in Helheim for me to make good on our deal. I just had to figure out how to get there from Armvind.

Chapter Forty Five

"Are you sure she will see us?" I asked Loki as we stood outside Var's door. "She has already done so much. I wouldn't want to upset her by asking for more."

After supper at the mead hall, during which Loki sat with us and discussed our options for getting into the underworld, we went to Var's home to ask just one more favor of the goddess. It seemed ill-advised, but our other option—to go back to the roots of Yggdrasil— would take ages. Midsummer would be long gone by the time we reached it, along with Hel's deadline.

"I'm sure," Loki said, though he didn't sound all that sure. "Besides, what else can we do? Helheim is one place I *can't* spirit people to and from."

"Just be kind and respectful, as you always are," Gunhild reminded me. "She liked you, and she wants you to succeed. You made an oath to save him, just like we made an oath to fight at each other's sides. She will be glad to help you fulfill your oath."

"See? The shieldmaiden knows this is the right thing to do," Loki said with a grin.

"Fine," I said with a sigh, and turned to knock at the door, which opened before my knuckles could even touch the wood.

"You're back, I see," Var said, raising an eyebrow to our group. "I suppose I should have guessed you would be. Come in, then."

"Thank you, and I'm sorry for the inconvenience," I told her as I offered a solemn bow. Gunhild did the same, and so did Loki once Gunhild elbowed him in the ribs.

"It's no bother, have a seat and we'll talk about what you need," Var said with a small, knowing smile.

We stepped into her cottage, taking seats wherever they were to be had, and Var came to sit in a threadbare, well-loved chair that was very clearly hers and which we had avoided sitting in for that reason. She steepled her fingers in front of her and looked between us for a moment.

"Well, then, tell me why you're here," she said, though she must already have guessed the reason by the way she looked at us.

"Oh, well, um," I hesitated. She raised an eyebrow and gestured for me to spit it out. "As you know, I need to go to the underworld to rescue Eryk—I told you about him. But the only way back, that we are sure of, is Yggdrasil, which is a long journey away from here."

"Yes, I do know that," she agreed. "And you think I can get you there quicker?"

"Can you?" Loki asked.

"I can, yes," Var said, but left it at that.

"I suppose the more important question is, *will* you?" I said after another moment of hesitation. "I know it is a lot to ask after how much you have helped us—helped me—already. But I don't know how else to accomplish this last task."

"It is not so much to ask," she assured me gently. "I can send you there quite easily. And you do have an oath that you made to the warrior, and to Hel, I suppose. I can't exactly ignore that, all things considered."

"So, you will send us?" Gunhild asked eagerly. This earned her an amused but gentle smile from the goddess.

"Yes, I will," Var conceded. "Come back here at midnight with the armor, and we will do the ritual. You might want to bring Hel-cakes. To appease Nidhogg."

"Who is Nidhogg?" Gunhild asked.

"A great dragon that is wrapped around Nastrond to protect it," Loki told her, his tone dark and foreboding.

"Oh, well, if all it takes is Hel-cakes to get past him, that shouldn't be so hard," Gunhild said with a shrug.

"I didn't say Hel-cakes was all it would take, only that it might help," Var replied.

"We will see you at midnight then," I said. "Thank you."

We spent the afternoon at the cottage, baking Hel-cakes to appease Nidhogg for when we descended to Nastrond. It hadn't been hard to find the necessary ingredients: flour, honey, hazelnuts, apples, currants and poppyseeds. They were simple enough to make. Before long, night had fallen, and midnight came. Gunhild, Loki, and I made our way back to Var's cottage with Freyja's armor, a single pack filled with some essentials, and the Hel-cakes. Var stood in the doorway, awaiting us.

"Come inside, we've little time to do the ritual. I've already prepared everything we need," Var told us. We were ushered into the small house and directed to lie on the floor before the fireplace as I had when I retrieved Gunhild.

"Will you slit my throat again?" I asked warily. That had been an unpleasant experience, to say the least.

"Of course," said Var with an exasperated sigh. "You can't descend into the realm of the dead without being dead yourself. Surely you already knew that from before."

Gunhild winced at the idea but lay down on the floor with the pack of essentials as she was instructed. I did the same, holding the pack with the armor and Hel-cakes in it on my chest so I could take it with me to Helheim, and gestured for Loki to lie on the floor as well. He hesitated of course, though I couldn't blame him. Gods were unused to death in any form.

"Will this even work on me?" he asked Var. "Can a god be killed?"

"It's a ritual, it will work regardless, and gods *can* be killed, so you need not worry," Var said matter-of-factly.

"I'm sure this will be fun," Loki replied in an unimpressed tone.

"Just shut up and lay still," Var said. I grabbed Loki's wrist to tell him to be quiet and then reached down to take Gunhild's hand as well. It seemed right that we should all be connected if we were to descend to the underworld together.

"Good, you've already done the most important part," Var praised us. "Now, close your eyes. This time you need not imagine anything. But hold on to the Hel-cakes and armor for dear life."

As before, she painted each of us with blue markings, then she began to dance and sing around us, throwing things into the fire which made it flare up with flames that seemed almost black.

"Now close your eyes," she sang.

The ritual singing and dancing grew to a fever pitch, until, finally, everything went silent.

Chapter Forty Six

THE DOOR to the underworld slammed behind us with a mighty bang that vibrated my teeth. We stood at the top of a flight of stairs that led so far down I could not see the bottom of them. Their end was cloaked in inky darkness. If I looked out from them, far in the distance, I could almost make out what might be a mountain peak silhouetted against a night sky. There were no moon or stars though, only ominous clouds with occasional lightning that flickered but never struck the ground below.

Gunhild and Loki waited at the top, a few steps above me, for me to take the first steps downward. Their faces were nearly invisible in the darkness of Helheim. It was hard to tell, but I thought Loki looked concerned, or even afraid. I could have sworn Gunhild gave me an encouraging nod with a grim smile, but in the pitch black, I could just have imagined it.

The pack with the armor and Hel-cakes was in my arms, so I slung it over my shoulder and took a deep breath. I stepped onto the first step, glad that at least it was solid under my feet. I'd half-expected it to collapse beneath me so that I fell a million feet down to wherever the bottom of this place might be. If there even was a bottom. The stairs might just go on forever as they appeared to, and we would never reach our destination. Or maybe I just hoped, in some dark part of my heart, for that to be the case so I didn't have to face Hel or Eryk and his questions about why it had taken so long.

I shuddered away those thoughts and took the next step, then the next, until I set a steady rhythm down the stairs. My pack was too light, with only the helm and falcon cloak inside, along with the tin of Hel-cakes. Brisingamen was around my neck, so precious and small I couldn't trust it not to get lost in the pack.

Dozens of steps later, I looked back only to find that we had barely made any progress at all. I could still see the top, and yet below us the stairs stretched onward into the darkness. How many steps could I descend before I went mad? There was only one way to find out, and that was to continue down until I couldn't any longer.

This darkness reminded me of my time in the caves with Gunhild on our way to Yggdrasil and the Norns. It seemed like eons ago now. Our journey had led us across Midgard and through the Nine Realms. It seemed impossible to believe that we were almost at its end now. The fear I had felt in that cave when our lanterns went out had returned and was so pervasive I wasn't sure how to survive it. Was it a fear of the darkness and the journey, or a fear of what came at the end of it?

I paused without realizing it, and Gunhild reached forward to place her hand on my shoulder. She gave it a gentle squeeze, tapping out that same gentle pattern as she met my gaze in the darkness. At first, it settled me. Then I realized that her presence would require an explanation to Eryk, and that was something I dreaded. When I looked quickly away from her to the mountain peak in the distance, she removed her hand from my shoulder.

As I stepped onto the next step, she quietly began to sing. It was the song we had sung in the caves and during the blizzard on the way to Jotunheim, the song I had sung to the troll and to find her in the place-between. It brought a smile to my lips despite everything. It was *our* song now. I joined her as she sang, and we ignored Loki when he cleared his throat. What else were we to do to pass the time and chase away the darkness that seemed to worm its way under our skin?

The darkness ate up our voices. There was no echo to come back to us or give us a sense of the vastness of this realm. Besides the lightning-lit clouds and the mountain peak, there wasn't much to see. It might all be shrouded in darkness like the bottom of the stairs, or maybe there just wasn't anything else. It was deathly silent aside from our singing.

We continued down the stairs, one at a time, for hours. My knees and hips ached, but I couldn't stop. Not now, when I was so close to my goal.

The stairs started to crumble under my feet, giving away a little with each new step. Eventually, the steps became a path into a ravine. The darkness had crowded closer now and smothered the view of the mountain in the distance. It had also gotten quieter, so that it felt like we were being buried alive. I slipped and slithered down into the darkness of the underworld ravine, until, eventually, I lost my grip altogether and slid haphazardly downward with a shriek.

Gunhild and Loki lost their footing almost immediately after I did, and both cried out in turn as they slipped down the remains of the stairs and landed atop me with a huff. My ankle twisted uncomfortably beneath me, and my arm was at an odd angle, trapped between Loki and the rock wall to our side. I managed to get out and looked through the inky darkness.

"Are you both alright?" I asked, my voice hushed as if I might wake something I shouldn't.

"We're fine," Loki assured me. I waited for Gunhild to say the same before I slowly got to my feet and offered them each a hand.

"Where do we go now? I can't see anything," Gunhild asked.

"Toward the mountain, which is away from the stairs. At least I assume so. Loki?" I looked at him or at least tried to. He didn't respond at first, and I reached out in his direction just in time for him to pull an elf-light from his own pack. Trust him to plan ahead.

Unfortunately, the elf-light didn't help much. It only illuminated our faces and no further. But we could see each other now, which would help with morale. Loki looked around to get his bearings.

"You're right, though it's not a mountain." Loki set off in a direction roughly perpendicular to the stairs.

"If it's not a mountain, what is it?" Gunhild asked.

"It's a palace." Loki didn't look back. "Eljudnir, or Misery, as the gods call it. They're dramatic of course. It's not all parties and parades, granted, but it's not as bad as you would think. Most of the dead end up here, so it's not a punishment."

"You've been here before?" I tried to let curiosity buoy my mood.

"Of course." Loki scoffed and finally looked over his shoulder at us. "I do visit my family, you know. I'm not a complete waste of breath."

"I never said you were. But I'm glad you know your way around. Do you think we'll have trouble getting in?" Once again, I was very glad to have Loki on this journey. He knew more about Helheim and its ins and outs than Gunhild or I could ever hope to.

"No. I think she's likely expecting you," Loki said. "It should only take us a couple of hours to get there. As long as we aren't walking in circles. Which we're not. I assure you."

The last part was added so quickly, I worried he wasn't being entirely truthful. I also didn't like the idea of Hel expecting us. It must be better than actively preventing our arrival, though. If she didn't want us there, we'd never get in. Who could say what she might throw in our path to keep us out if we weren't allowed?

We walked on, and on, until it felt like we'd walked for hours. Our stomachs growled with hunger, so we paused long enough for me to pull out some berries from my pack for us to eat while we walked. In the darkness, I still couldn't see the palace, so I had no idea if we were making progress towards it or not. The clouds above us were barely even visible through the darkness, aside from the occasional flicker of lightning.

"I can't see anything. How do we know we're going in the right direction?" Gunhild finally asked as she stopped in her tracks.

"We're headed in the right direction. There's a road beneath our feet. Can you not feel it?" Loki said with a huff.

Gunhild stomped her foot a few times, and it did ring out as if there might be stone beneath it rather than the packed dirt of the ravine at the bottom of the unending stairs. I knelt to feel it under my hand. It was cold to the touch, and individual stones had been laid closely together in a repeating pattern. Loki was right; at some point he had guided us to the road to Helheim. Or stumbled upon it. One might never know with Loki.

I was one step closer to freeing Eryk, and one step closer to telling him about Gunhild. That particular revelation could wait until we were back in Midgard. How would I explain her presence on my quest, or our body language when the other was around? It didn't matter now. All that mattered was fulfilling my duty and getting Eryk out of Nastrond.

"Come on then, let's go." I stood and set off in the direction we'd been heading. I tried to keep my head up and feel confident about the fact that our quest was nearly done. I could return Eryk to Midgard and then the gods could take him to Valhalla where he belonged. I couldn't take him myself anymore, and the pain of that stung like a hornet, but it was better than where I had started this journey.

The road crept onward and onward. After hours that felt like days, the palace suddenly rose up before us, the pinnacle so high that I couldn't see it in the darkness. Gunhild and I looked to Loki for direction. He took a deep breath and nodded toward the palace gates ahead of us.

They loomed over us, foreboding and impossibly strong. Nothing passed in or out of Helheim without Hel's knowledge or permission. Whether Hel had prepared for our presence by locking the gates or by making our beds, there was no way to know other than getting through that gate.

As I reached out a hand to touch its steely surface, cold as ice, it sprang open and silently opened inward into a barren courtyard of paving stones and dead trees. Their miserable limbs stretched toward the flashes of lightning above us. Out of the corner of my eye, I thought I saw movement. When I turned to look, there was a still figure in the shape of an elderly man. It did not move or breathe, at first glance. After a moment, it shifted and moved to ever-so-slowly water one of the dead trees.

"Hello?" I stepped closer to him, and bit by bit he turned his weathered face to look at me with hollow, empty eye sockets. I shivered under the blank gaze and gave a little bow of my head. "We are here to see the goddess. She is likely expecting us. I am Yrsa."

"She... is... expecting... you..." The old man's words came so slowly, so quietly that it seemed more likely that it was simply the groaning of one of the barren trees in the wind, even if there wasn't even a breath of wind here. "You... may... go... in..."

"Thank you, Ganglati," Loki told the stone manservant, before turning to us. "There is a handmaiden inside somewhere, named Ganglot, who serves Hel's bidding within Eljudnir. Let's go find her." Loki gave an awkward nod to the manservant, who had already slowly turned his face away to return to his task.

I took a deep breath, though the too-still air felt like it caught in my throat and choked me. I coughed to clear my airway and looked back up at the gloomy palace.

Gunhild hesitantly took my hand. Mine trembled a little with trepidation, but hers was solid as ever. I turned my face toward hers, and she lifted her chin with an encouraging smile that lit the underworld for a bit. I could face anything with that brightness at my side.

We headed, hand in hand, toward a pair of glossy, black doors that reflected the lightning back at us when it flashed. Loki was behind us, and I looked over my shoulder to make sure he wasn't falling too far back. When I was certain he was still there, I reached out to twist the latch on one of the doors. A sharp pain slashed through my senses and I looked down to see that I was bleeding from a slice in my palm. The doors were made of solid obsidian, sharp and dangerous.

Gunhild gasped and hurried to dig through her pack for something to use as a bandage. She found a piece of cloth, which she wound around my hand and tied it off. With my palm now guarded, I reached out again to open the door. We would have to be more cautious, it seemed.

Chapter Forty Seven

IF THERE HAD BEEN MORE light within the palace, it would have glittered from every black surface. Every furnishing seemed to be crafted from ebony, onyx, or obsidian, all polished to a gleaming shine. It might have been beautiful were it not so forbidding. Even the walls were hewn from basalt.

"You… should hurry…" Came a voice similar to the one we'd heard from the manservant, though with a slightly more feminine timbre. I spun around to find Hel's handmaiden, Ganglot, standing behind us. She was young, and strangely beautiful, yet also somehow made of stone like the man outside. She stared at me with those same hollow, empty eye sockets. "The goddess… is… impatient."

"Apologies," I murmured. "Please, lead us to her."

If we had to follow this woman, it might take weeks as slow as she moved, but I had no idea where in the palace Hel might reside. This entryway must lead to somewhere more official. Hel probably didn't entertain guests very often, unless the dead liked to pay visits and help her throw parties. I had to stop myself from letting out an anxious giggle at the thought.

"I… cannot… lead you…" Ganglot told us in that halting manner she seemed stuck using. With excruciating slowness, she lifted a hand to point at a hallway leading off into the darkness. "Go through… that… corridor…. She will… be… at… its end…"

"Thank you." I tried to remain kind despite my nervousness. This was merely a handmaiden. She had no control over any of this. For all I knew, Hel watched how we interacted with her servants.

By now, my heart was hammering against my ribs like a dwarven blacksmith beating out a sword. I thought my ribs might crack under the pressure. At the end of the corridor was a final door, just as intimidating as the gate and the front door. It was not made of obsidian, at least, but instead of polished ebony, and when I reached towards the bronze door handle, the door creaked open on its own.

"You came," hissed a soft voice, as if speaking to an injured child.

I swallowed hard around the searing ball of paralyzing fear that had scraped its way up my throat. Gunhild stood so close behind me that I could feel her body heat through my clothes. Loki trailed a few feet after her, almost an afterthought. Hel lounged on a massive canopy bed with silken, deep purple covers. The curtains surrounding it were a matching hue and fabric. It was surprising to see the pop of color after the overwhelming amount of black.

"Yes, mistress." I took a knee before the bed and she draped a pale hand over the side for me to kiss her knuckles. She smelled, as always, of rotting flesh, and I had to stop myself from gagging as I took her freezing hand in mine and pressed my lips to it. "I have brought what you required of me."

"And you have brought friends as well, it seems," Hel said, glancing with an annoyed look to Loki before her chilling gaze settled on Gunhild. Gunhild looked so terribly out of place, all flaming copper hair and shining blue eyes. She was too much color and light for the underworld, and one nearly had to squint to bear it. Hel *did* squint, though I doubted it was due to Gunhild's appearance.

"Yes, you know Gunhild already. And Loki too." I stayed kneeling before the bed but released Hel's hand to keep the corpse stench from permanently taking up residence in my nostrils.

"Rise, child, I do not care who you brought with you." Hel flicked her hand at me and so I rose as commanded, with my hands respectfully clasped behind my back. I wanted to scrub them clean of her scent but all I could do was stand obediently before her. "You brought the armor?"

"Yes, mistress, I did." I removed my pack and set it carefully on the black basalt floor. I still hesitated to give Hel the armor, but what choice did I have? I had trekked through half the Nine Realms to acquire it at her bidding, and it was the only way to free Eryk from the fate I had condemned him to with my selfishness.

"Then give it to me," she hissed, her sibilant voice growing louder. Was that a smirk twisting her full lips? Or just the way the shadows in the room fell across her shadowed face? It was hard to tell with only meager lamplight and the occasional flicker of lightning through the high windows.

I reluctantly pulled the helm from the bag first. The dwarven-crafted silver flashed even in the darkness, as if it created its own light. I passed it to her waiting hands, and she snatched it away from me greedily. Once she had it though, she merely set it on the silken bed sheets beside her and looked back to me for the rest.

I took out the falcon cloak next. The white feathers fluttered despite the stillness of the air. This she grasped as soon as I brought it close enough for her reach. Once it was in her hands, she sat up to wrap it around her shoulders. It looked rather out of place in the gloom that surrounded her and was much too beautiful to be wrapped around the wraithlike goddess. But she seemed pleased with it, and that was all that mattered now.

Her eyes flitted back to my bag, but I did not reach into it again. I was loath to give away this last piece, which hung delicately around my neck. Not because it could bend people to my will or make them fall at my feet in adoration, but because I did not wish her to have the same effect. I didn't want to imagine what would happen if people found the Goddess of Death herself irresistible. It couldn't lead to anything good.

"You *did* find Brisingamen, didn't you?" Hel sat up further, her dark eyes piercing sharp as the obsidian that had cut me. The room seemed to grow even colder, and a dreadful silence settled over it when I didn't immediately answer or turn over the necklace. It felt like we had been buried alive with her in this tomb of a palace.

Would Eryk ever forgive me if I changed my mind? If I didn't give the amber and gold necklace over to the goddess, I might never forgive myself. Then again, I might not forgive myself for whatever Hel did after she had all the pieces in her possession, either.

"Yrsa," she snapped, "Give me Brisingamen! Do you not wish to see your beloved? Do you not wish to save him from Nastrond?"

"Yes, of course," I said finally. Gunhild held her breath, almost as if she hoped I might say otherwise.

With trembling hands, I managed to unclasp the delicate necklace and pull it from where it had hung for the last couple of weeks around my throat as I traveled from Jotunheim back to Armvind. I could almost feel its power leave me when I took it off. I gritted my teeth together and handed the necklace over to Hel, who gave a wolfish grin and immediately fastened it around her own throat with much steadier hands than me.

"Thank you, Yrsa. You have completed your task well," the goddess said, her voice almost a purr. It set the hairs on the back of my neck on end.

"Now will you take us to Nastrond to retrieve Eryk?" I hated to beg, but she had left me no choice.

"Yes, we can go to Nastrond," Hel said, twisting the gold links of Brisingamen's chain between her ghostly fingers.

"To get Eryk, though, right?" I couldn't imagine she would let me come all this way and then go back on her word. Oaths still meant something, even to the gods, didn't they? I glanced at Loki, but the trickster god looked as concerned as I felt.

"We'll see." The words came out of Hel's lips in a sing-song tone that made my stomach dip dangerously, like I had taken a bad step down a flight of stairs and was now falling to my death. "Come, we'll go now."

"You promised, mistress. You promised that if I brought you the armor, you would free him. That was the deal." Instead of fear, anger was beginning to creep in on me. I likely would have let it loose on her were it not for Brisingamen tempering any negative emotion I might feel toward her.

"Watch your tone with me, Yrsa," Hel warned, stabbing a finger at me. She climbed from the bed and stalked over to me. She didn't seem to mind that I was a head taller and quite a bit more muscular than her.

"I promised nothing. I made an offer, which you accepted, but that is not the same as a promise."

"How? How is it not a promise? It was an offer I accepted. It was a verbal contract!" My voice grew shrill and cracked on the last word as I let my emotions get the best of me. If it hadn't been for Freyja's necklace, I might have attacked Hel as she drew closer. Her corpse-breath in my face caused me to shy away despite my anger.

"Did you sign something? Did I swear an oath? I think not, little Valkyrie. You may see Eryk, yes, to see that he is safe enough, but otherwise, you will have to go on your way." That wolfish grin returned to her face and distorted her features.

I reached out in a panic to try to grip Brisingamen or the falcon cloak and rip them from her possession, but she vanished from my grip, appearing in the doorway as I spun around. With Brisingamen around her throat, it would be much more difficult to win any battle against her.

"You cannot have the armor *and* keep him," I growled at her, stalking across to where she stood. She only vanished again, then reappeared outside the room. Trying to chase her down was foolish. I couldn't stop myself from trying to reach her though, to steal back the armor or even attack her for going back on her word. It was like swimming upstream in a flooded river to go against Brisingamen's power.

"I can do whatever I like, Yrsa, and you cannot stop me. I am a goddess." She smirked and turned around to keep walking away from us. Her bare feet barely made a sound against the basalt floor of the palace, though she left a trail of rotten slime behind her as she walked. "Now, do you not wish to see Nastrond and make sure your warrior is still... well, not alive, per se, but not simply... gone?"

"Loki, do something." I ignored Hel's taunting and turned to face the red-haired trickster with a desperate plea. He held his hands up and shook his head.

"I can't get involved."

"Can't or won't?" I was seething with anger. My limits boiled over like an unwatched pot. My hand went to the sword sheathed at my hip as I considered whether I could murder the Goddess of Death.

"Can't. It was the deal you chose to make with her. It was your choice to believe her, to bring her the armor. The gods do as they please. There was no oath." Loki sighed and shook his head, but after a moment looked over at Hel with a disapproving frown. "And you. You should be careful how you handle this whole deal with Yrsa. You tricked her and it seems very likely you'll pay for it."

"I dragged him to Nastrond personally from the place-between, you know," Hel said with a wicked laugh that sounded like dead leaves rustling down the corridor. Obviously, she didn't care to heed Loki's warning. "Oh yes, your little friend there knows all about that place. She's lucky I didn't drag her to Nastrond as well."

"She is manipulating you, Yrsa," Gunhild said, coming to lace her fingers through mine. "Don't listen to a word she says. Just…"

"Just what?" Hel asked, eyes widening with something akin to amusement. It was a strange expression to see on her usually emotionless face. "What is she to do? Try to kill death herself? I think not. No, she will turn around with her little tail between her legs and limp back to Midgard to live out the rest of her miserable little life. Maybe you will stay by her side, if she doesn't bore you with her sobbing over the warrior. Little fools, all of you."

"Enough." My voice was raspy with raw emotion. I would make her take me to Eryk and then deal with her once we were there. It was the only solution I could think of. "Take me to him."

"No." The word was so simple, so unexpected, that I wasn't sure how to react. I blinked and stared at her with my mouth hanging open on words that wouldn't form into anything more than a garbled cry. "Go home. Or… well… back to Midgard. Valhalla won't have a traitor like you."

It took all my strength to pull my sword against the urge Brisingamen brought to fall at Hel's feet in worship, but I somehow gathered the strength to draw it with a metallic hum and swing it with all my might. Hel flicked her hand again and the world around us contorted like war-paint running in the rain.

I was on the floor suddenly, the world around me tilting precariously as if she had flipped it on its head. My sword had skittered off into a corner and out of reach. Hel stalked over and stepped on my wrist as I reached for it. The odorous slime that oozed from her feet, corpse-like and rotting, was like acid on my skin, burning the soft flesh at my wrist as it soaked into it.

I jerked my hand away and crawled across the ground to get my sword, which Gunhild hurried to and kicked over to me. Hel grabbed me by my tangled blonde curls and dragged me backward. I had gotten the heavy sword in my hands though and twisted out of her grip to slice at her with the blade. She leapt back, but not before the sharp edge caught her across the middle.

"Yrsa!" Loki called. I didn't bother to look at him as I struggled to my feet while Hel stared in shock at the ichor flowing from the cut across her abdomen. "You cannot kill the Goddess of Death!"

"Cannot or should not?" I bit out the words as I advanced on the goddess. "Because there are a lot of things I *shouldn't* do, but I guarantee you that I don't care about any of them right now."

Hel grasped at her stomach as she backed away. I didn't really think it was possible for me to kill a goddess, but Loki's tone and the way Hel reacted to my blade slicing into her made me think it might be possible after all. I advanced again, glancing at Gunhild who had drawn her axe and was ready to attack should I speak the right words. I gave her a brief shake of the head to call her off. This fight was between Hel and me.

"Should not, obviously," Loki snapped. "Think about what happens if the goddess of death dies. You can't just kill my daughter with no thought for the consequences!"

"What, you won't let me? Tell me what happens then," I growled, stabbing my sword toward Hel's abdomen again. I hoped to really do damage this time instead of just cutting into her skin. Her bottom half was a rotting corpse, the opposite of the beautiful top half. I might just sever the two halves of her and leave her bleeding on the basalt floor of her palace while I went to retrieve Eryk. She could probably put herself back together anyway, but at least that would delay her.

"Nothing happens, you foolish girl," Hel hissed at me, though she seemed concerned despite her insistence. "Nothing happens. I will end your pitiful little life, and that of your little shieldmaiden too."

"The gods are not immortal," I said, stalking towards her as she backed away. "They live forever, but they are not immune to death should someone manage to get close enough to kill them. Baldur died, didn't he?"

Hel's furious expression faltered, and she stomped once on the floor, which caused a small earthquake that set the palace itself rumbling and threw me across the floor. This time I kept hold of my sword, and Gunhild crept closer to help even though I didn't want her to.

"Loki, go back and get the helm from Hel's bed," I told the trickster. He hesitated, looking at me warily for a moment, but then rushed off in the direction of Hel's bedchamber. "The rest of the armor I'll take from her myself."

This time, I ran at Hel full tilt, my sword raised and ready to hack down in the soft spot in the crook of her neck. She ducked out of the way just in time. As she did, I lowered the sword and reached out with my free hand to snatch at the falcon cloak.

The feathers fluttered into my hand, as if I had summoned them to me, rather than just taking them from the goddess. I hurriedly put it around my own shoulders to keep her from getting to it. I just needed Brisingamen now.

"You foolish girl, you give that to me now or so help me...."

"So help you what? You'll kill me? You'll kill Gunhild?" I was almost amused at how unbalanced she seemed now. Her gaze was frantic instead of angry, especially as Loki hurried back down the corridor to get the helm and bring it to me. When I had it in my hands, I slid it over my hair and down over my face.

I discovered then exactly what the helm did, beyond protecting one's head from blows. A ghostly, glimmering version of Hel moved first, and then Hel herself followed seconds later in the same path. As the ghost of Hel began to move again, I understood what I had to do. I set my blade and spun just in time to catch her in the back with it. She cried out in some ancient language, falling to her knees.

"Her head!" Gunhild shouted. I couldn't cut off the goddess's head though. Loki's apprehensive grimace gave me pause. He had a point that killing the goddess of death was likely a terrible idea. I wasn't blind to the possibilities of what might happen if I killed her. Would nobody ever die from then until the end of time if I did that? Or would someone else, someone worse, take her place?

"Surrender, Hel," I said instead, standing over her with my blade leveled at her throat.

"I will do no such thing," she hissed, gripping at my ankle to try to pull me down. She had been weakened with my strike to her back and had little effect on my balance.

"You will, or I will sever your body in two and leave you to figure out how to put it back together while I go about my business." I lifted my sword again, ready to do just that should she choose not to heed my words. She closed her eyes and winced as she anticipated my blow. I wasn't sure I would be able to make good on my threat without taking Brisingamen from her, but she didn't have to know that.

"I surrender!" she gasped as I brought my sword down to cut her in two where she laid. Odorous black ichor seeped from her wounds across the basalt floor of the palace. I barely had time to stop my blow, and the sword came to a rest against her middle without piercing too deeply. "I surrender."

Her last words came out in a whimper, and she fell onto her back. Her dark hair spilled out around her head like waves on a beach, and she closed her dark eyes against the pain of what I had done to her already.

"We need to lock her away," I told Loki. "You know the palace; how do we do that?"

I kept my sword drawn and ready to strike should Hel change her mind, but the gleaming ghosts predicting everyone's actions did not show her moving, so I wasn't too worried. Loki's ghost, on the other hand, knelt at Hel's side to check her injuries. Before he could put that thought into action, I stepped between the gods and shook my head.

"You tried to kill my daughter." Loki's expression was accusatory, but I found it hard to care.

"She would have killed all of us, if we let her, including you. She lied to me. Broke her promise. And you are defending her? I thought you of all people would understand," I turned away and reached down to pull Brisingamen from Hel's throat. For now, it would stay tucked in my pocket. "Bind her, somehow, and put her somewhere she won't escape. I don't care what she does once we're gone. Once Odin and Freyja hear of her plans, they won't let her come after us. I'll give the armor to Freyja myself."

Gunhild came to my side and looked me over for any injuries. I had hit my head hard when Hel tossed me away the first time and bled from a wound above my left eyebrow. The blood stung my eye when it dripped into it, and Gunhild gently wiped that away with her sleeve. My leg had also twisted at an uncomfortable angle during the earthquake she had caused, and I limped a little now, but it was nothing that would slow me down too much.

"You're alright?" Her expression was etched with concern. I nodded and looked back down to Hel, who still lay on the floor trying to catch her breath. When the ghost predicting her movements shifted to get away, I put my sword back to her throat.

"Loki, I swear to the gods, yourself excluded, just bind her already." My head hurt and my anger was rising with each throb behind my eyes.

Rather than respond, Loki vanished.

My heart dropped so rapidly to my stomach that I thought I might vomit. We would truly be in grave danger if he had left us behind for my attempt to kill Hel. Once again, I had led Gunhild to her death, it seemed.

"Now your only salvation has gone, what will you do?" Hel smirked up at me, so I pressed my blade harder against her throat until a bead of ichor pooled around the tip of the sword.

"He'll be back," I said, though I wasn't confident he would.

"Are you so sure? You tried to kill his daughter; do you think he'll be grateful for that? Let me go and I'll spare you. You can even have your little warrior." Her voice was wheedling, but I didn't believe for a moment that she'd do what she said. She'd already lied to me and manipulated me before. I wasn't stupid enough to fall for it again.

"He will be back. He doesn't even like you," I insisted. Her little smirk and manipulative tone annoyed me and made my head hurt worse.

"And if he isn't? What will you do then? I think you'd be smarter to let me go my own way. Give me the armor, take your warrior, and we'll call it even," Hel offered.

"If you move before he gets back, I will cut your rotten head off and feed it to Nidhogg when I go to Nastrond," I growled. Feeding her head to her own dragon seemed an apt punishment. "Now. Shut. Up."

Hel shrugged and closed her eyes. Thankfully, she was wounded enough that she couldn't just vanish like she normally might have.

When Loki finally returned, I breathed a long sigh of relief. I had genuinely thought he was gone for good, punishing me for what I had done to his daughter. He carried heavy iron chains with shackles at the ends, though he didn't look happy with the idea of chaining Hel.

"Thought I wouldn't be back, did you? Serves you right for not listening to me," Loki said, glowering at me.

"I did listen. She's not dead, is she? Just help me bind her," I said.

Gunhild and Loki set about shackling Hel, who hissed and spit at us like an angry cat. I kept my blade to her throat to keep her still at least. The ichor pooling from her wounds ate holes in our boots. Once she was fully shackled and there was no chance she could escape the chains, I sheathed my sword.

"Where can we put her?" I asked.

"We'll chain her to the bed." Loki's expression was distraught. "I am sorry it came to this, Hel. But you did it to yourself. I did warn you."

"Oh, shut up. This is your doing too. You could have kept them from coming here to begin with," Hel hissed at him. "Some father you are."

"That definitely doesn't make me want to help you, you know," Loki told her with an injured frown as he helped me to drag her down the corridor back to her bed. A trail of ichor and rotten slime followed us.

"Do you know the way to Nastrond from here?" Gunhild asked, trying to distract from a fight between Hel and Loki.

"I don't, but I assume Loki does." I glanced at the trickster, who looked up from glaring at Hel to nod. "See? We'll be fine."

Hel gave a dark laugh that made my stomach turn. "You will still have to get through Nidhogg to get in. I wish you every bit of luck with that."

"Can we gag her?" Gunhild asked.

"No need." I barely spared a glance at the goddess. "We'll be on our way as soon as she's bound. Then she can scream her lies to the rafters and it won't matter."

I focused on looping the chains through the bedposts once we got her to the bed. We didn't bother lifting her onto it. She could rage from the floor. The entire time, she shouted curses at us. She was too wounded to do much besides that, and the helm I still wore told me she had no intention of doing more.

Once the goddess was shackled to the bed and Loki had enchanted the locks to be unbreakable except by him, I glowered back at Hel.

"I wish you nothing but the worst, mistress. May you rue every moment of what you've done to me. May you rot here, filled with your lies and hatred," I said in a quiet, even voice. She spat at my feet and writhed in her chains, so I turned away and stalked out of the room with Gunhild behind me.

Loki stayed behind long enough to lean down with a grim expression and murmur some final words to Hel. "You've done this to yourself, daughter. If you behave, then I'll return eventually to free you."

She spat at his feet as well, and then began to sob pitifully as he closed the door.

"I'm sorry, Loki," I told him. When he looked doubtful, I repeated myself. "I'm sorry. I am. I never would have had it come to this. She has earned her fate, though. Even you must see that."

"I do. I don't have to like the consequences." Loki closed his eyes at the sound of Hel's shrieking from her prison. "Come, let's go get your warrior."

"How do we get to Nastrond from here?" I asked as he started to walk away.

"We cross the plain and the river, then we have to face Nidhogg or try to sneak past him," Loki said vaguely. "It will be a long journey. Do you intend to wear the armor all the way there?"

"If something happens and we have to fight Nidhogg, I might need it."

"Suit yourself," Loki said with a shrug.

"Freyja will be glad to have it all back when we are done," Gunhild said.

"I'm happy to return it to her. Now come on." I motioned for Loki to lead the way, and we took off out the front door of the palace, past the handmaiden who had barely moved from where we had left her. She seemed unaware of what we had done to her mistress. Or at least unbothered by it.

Chapter Forty Eight

WE SET back out into the darkness of Helheim's vast, deserted plain. This time there was no road to follow, though Loki seemed to be confident about his direction.

My thoughts wandered in the darkness. Had I chosen poorly by keeping Hel alive? What might have happened if I had killed her? Would Eryk be happy to see me? The path to Nastrond would have been easier with conversation, but we were all quiet. Gunhild must have seen the grave expression creasing my brow. She squeezed my hand and bumped her shoulder against mine.

"I wonder if Freyja will restore you to Valhalla when you return her armor to her," Gunhild said. I hadn't even thought of that. If Freyja did offer to let me return home, then that would mean leaving Gunhild. I wasn't sure I could bear that. She was a part of me now, a piece of my heart that I couldn't live without.

"Who knows?" I didn't want to consider that yet.

"Unless something happens between now and when you return the armor, she'll send you back to Valhalla. It's only fair, right? Will you still go back if she offers you a choice not to?" Loki asked from up ahead. He paused and turned to look back at Gunhild and I, hand in hand.

"I…" I wasn't sure of the honest answer to that question, and I think Loki asked for that exact reason. "I suppose I will have to make that decision if it's offered to me. Let's not get ahead of ourselves."

"It's something you should be ready to answer." Loki's gaze shifted to Gunhild. Her expression was clouded, her eyes on our clasped hands. "I think your shieldmaiden might be bereft if you leave her."

"I would be bereft too," I admitted, tapping out a pattern on the back of her hand with my thumb. "I don't know what I would do. What would become of me if I stayed in Midgard?"

"I assume you'd become mortal and the two of you would grow old together and die one day." Loki seemed perplexed at the idea, his expression curious and open. "I suppose you'll know for sure once the choice is offered. Come on. We have a warrior to save."

He started off again, more hurried this time. I quickened my pace to keep up and gripped Gunhild's hand more tightly to pull her along with me. The flashes of lightning grew more intense with each step we took, until the sky was almost constantly lit, though thunder never followed. Up ahead, I could hear rushing water, and we soon approached a wide river with a rickety bridge spanning its violent currents.

"The river Gjoll," Loki murmured. "We'll have to cross. Careful on the bridge. It's not steady."

We paused to look over the side of the rushing river below as we crossed. It was so loud that we wouldn't be able to hear each other speak. The whole bridge swayed as we walked on it, as if the violence of the river made it less stable.

When we reached the end of it, the sky darkened more, and we found ourselves surrounded by an almost impenetrable fog. I reached out for Gunhild's hand, and was tempted to grasp Loki's as well, simply so we wouldn't get separated.

"It reminds me of the place-between," Gunhild said in a hushed voice, which was quickly eaten up by the fog. I gave her hand a reassuring squeeze and pulled her forward, closer to Loki.

"It's very similar—another in between of sorts, that leads to Nastrond. Come, we're safe as long as the fog lasts, but when it parts, we'll find Nidhogg," Loki warned us.

"Can we sneak around him, do you think?" I asked. If we could simply slip past the dragon without him knowing, and then do the same as we escaped with Eryk, that would make life much easier. Then again, when had any of this quest been easy?

"Unlikely. He's larger than you realize." Loki's calm tone belied his concern. "His body stretches almost entirely around Nastrond. I don't even know how we'll defeat him, much less sneak past him."

"Do you think the Hel-cakes will make a difference?" Gunhild asked.

"Let's hope so. He used to be fond of them." Loki looked doubtful. It certainly didn't inspire confidence in our task.

We walked for a mile or two through the murky night of Helheim until the thick fog started to dissipate. My heart sped up as I anticipated the sight of the mighty Nidhogg. If we couldn't get past him, after everything else we had overcome, this whole journey was for naught.

"Gunhild, get the Hel-cakes out," I told the shieldmaiden in a soft voice. She nodded and dug through the pack we had brought to pull the small tin of them out. There were only half a dozen small brown cakes, dotted with currants and smelling like honey, and I hoped that would be enough.

Soon, there was a deep grumbling that shook the ground beneath our feet. A sulfurous smell permeated the dense air around us and made us cough.

"Who goes there?" echoed a growl from the distance.

"Loki," called the trickster. He seemed as confident as ever to the undiscerning eye, but I could see the tension in his movements even through the parting fog. His back was rod straight, and his jaw was clenched against the possibility that Nidhogg might attack. "I have an errand to run in Nastrond for Hel."

There was a snuffling sound, as if Nidhogg were sniffing the air around him. "You brought shieldmaidens?" The dragon sounded perplexed.

"Long story, but yes." Loki appeared more concerned by the minute. "But I also have brought Hel-cakes for you as a peace offering. Hel recommended the recipe herself."

"I do like those..." the great beast thundered. Even its quietest voice caused the ground to shiver. I shivered as well, afraid of what might happen when the Hel-cakes weren't enough.

"Then we will give them to you and you will allow us entrance into Nastrond?" Loki requested. The tension in his posture had drained a little, but it came back as the dragon growled.

"I think not. Hel does not send anyone to Nastrond that she expects to return from it. You will have to stay if you decide to enter," the dragon rumbled.

"No, that's not really an option, we have to find a warrior that she promised to the Valkyrie here," Loki said in a wheedling tone. "It was part of a bargain they made. Freyja's lost armor in exchange for the warrior."

"Prove it," said the dragon with finality.

"I can tell you the story, if you like," I volunteered. Hopefully, this was the sort of obstacle that could be convinced with a good tale. "A story of a quest along with some Hel-cakes is a fair deal, right?"

Loki's gaze shot over to me and shook his head firmly. The desperate look on his face made me think it was a mistake to speak to the beast at all. Great glowing eyes were suddenly turned on me, the pupils gleaming as if they were made of fire itself, visible even through the fog. I grimaced but stepped forward so that I was face to face with the creature.

Its head alone was the size of a house. The eyes were so high above me, it would have been impossible to see them without the fire contained in their pupils. Shining teeth the size of a troll flashed in the darkness, reminding me that this dragon could snap me up in one bite and not even have to chew to get me down its gullet.

"Tell me the story then, Valkyrie," Nidhogg growled. "Tell me and I will decide if you are telling the truth. And in the meantime, you may give me the cakes."

"They are small, I fear. I was not aware of how large you would be," I said, though I held out my hand to Gunhild for the tin of cakes. "Hopefully, they will still be satisfying."

"Well go on then," he said in a slow voice. The sound of metal against metal grinded out into the night as Nidhogg shifted his head lower so I could give him the cakes. His mouth opened wide, larger even than Arnbjorg's house in Jotunheim. I stepped forward with a deep breath, which I regretted as I inhaled the sulfurous fumes exuded from his mouth. Once I was close enough to be eaten, I opened the box and carefully emptied the fragrant Hel-cakes onto the dragon's tongue which had slithered out of its gaping maw in anticipation of the treats.

I stepped back just in time. The dragon's mouth snapped shut so quickly that I almost went down with the Hel-cakes. Gunhild jerked me toward her, keeping me out of harm's reach. Ending the quest as dragon-fodder was not how I wanted to finish things.

The Hel-cakes were so small by comparison to the great Nidhogg, that we couldn't even hear crunching as he swallowed them. Merely a gulp as he devoured them whole. Smoke crept from his giant nostrils as he hummed a rumble into the night.

"I fell in love with a warrior," I began, which caused those great, flaming eyes to open and shift to my face. He didn't' seem to have heard much of love before. Certainly not in Nastrond. "But instead of sending him to Valhalla when he died, I spared him and kept him in Midgard instead. I did this many times, because my heart belonged to him. And his belonged to me. We spent every night together."

I paused, and once again that metallic grating echoed around us as the dragon shifted to look at me better. "Go on," the dragon prompted. That had to be a good sign, right?

"One night, while we were together, a great wind blew into the bedroom where we were, and when I looked up, Hel stood there, as ominous as ever," I said, trying to make the tale interesting while sticking to the truth. I was not a good liar like Loki. "She told me I had been disobedient and would have to pay a price. That price was for the warrior to be condemned to Nastrond and for me to be exiled from Valhalla."

Telling the tale all over again brought a painful lump to my throat. We were so close to retrieving Eryk though, and I couldn't stop now, even if the tale filled me with sadness and regret. The dragon grumbled and I continued.

"Hel made me an offer, a deal, that if I were to find the lost pieces of Freyja's armor and give them to Hel, that she would let me have the warrior back. So, now here we are," I said. What if the dragon recognized the feather cloak and the helm?

"You gave the armor to Hel then?" asked Nidhogg in that deep roar of a voice that sent a shiver down my spine.

"I did," I replied. It wasn't a lie. I had given it to her. I had just taken it back as well.

"Why has she not accompanied you here?" Nidhogg pressed, and I tried to stand my ground.

"Hel is very busy, you know that," Loki said. Nidhogg's eyes flared, and he hissed angrily at Loki for interrupting.

"It is as Loki said. She had plans for the armor, so she is putting those into action," I said, trying out a lie. I hoped the dragon wasn't very observant, or at least not good at sensing deception.

The fire blazing in the dragon's eyes simmered down a little, as if he was satisfied, and I breathed a small sigh of relief. Perhaps my story and the Hel-cakes had been enough. He might let us pass now. I tried to tamp down the hope that was building in my chest.

"And so now you are here, wanting to enter Nastrond to bring this warrior back to Midgard, even though no one leaves Nastrond. Not ever," Nidhogg completed my story for me.

"Yes," I agreed. "May we pass to do so according to my deal with the goddess?"

The dragon's metallic scales scraped against each other again, but this time it was to reveal a gate beyond the massive coils of the beast's enormous body. Did this mean we were allowed to pass? I paused, and shifted the helm on my head, paying attention to the ghosts of future actions that it showed me.

The golden ghosts of my trio moved toward the gate as permitted, but then, out of nowhere, Nidhogg struck at us, fire erupting from his maw and engulfing us for a brief moment before he snapped us up with those razor-sharp teeth and we disappeared. My heart sank. This was all a trick. How would we get through if he intended to simply eat us when we tried? It seemed I would have to attempt to fight him after all. But how did one defeat a dragon so large he stretched around an entire realm?

"Well go on then," Nidhogg said gently, though steam flooded from his nostrils, filling the air with the putrid scent of sulfur. "You may pass."

Loki began to step forward, and Gunhild moved to follow, but I grabbed them both and pushed them behind me with a slight shake of my head. Hopefully, they understood that I was protecting them, but Loki gave me a sharp look, and Gunhild simply looked confused.

I reached in my pocket and put Brisingamen on, before looking up at him again. I was hyper-aware of each piece of armor and what it could do for me. I would need all of them to survive should Brisingamen fail to convince the dragon to let us pass.

"Are you sure?" I asked as I took a step forward to see if the prediction changed.

"Of course. You gave me Hel-cakes and told me a story; why should I not let you pass to fulfill the deal you made with the goddess?" Nidhogg asked, but the prediction barely changed, only an extra moment of hesitation added to Nidhogg's movements. He still enveloped us in fire and then ate us as we burned to death.

"You could have just told us no," I said, unsheathing my sword. Nidhogg's eyes flared again, and he reared that massive head back in preparation to strike. Fire bubbled in the back of his throat with a crackling sound. "Get back!"

I hissed the word *"fljuga"* which caused me to suddenly soar into the air. Pure instinct told me the correct word to use, as if Freyja herself had whispered it in my ear in a time of need. It took me a moment to control my flight, but then I was high above Nidhogg, sword drawn and ready to pierce whatever might be penetrable. My actions distracted the dragon enough that as he turned to look at me, Gunhild and Loki darted out of the way.

Thankfully, a dragon his size could not move with any speed or grace, and as he released his fire toward me, I simply darted out of the way. I then allowed myself to plummet, sword outstretched, to try to bury it in Nidhogg's flaming eye. As I plunged downward, he unleashed another volley of fire, which elicited a worried shriek from Gunhild. She tried to run forward to help, but Loki held her back.

I took off upward again, the helm showing me just where to fly to stay out of the flames. They were close enough that I could feel the scorching heat of them as they singed the feathers closest to the fire. Once the fire abated again, I swooped downward and sliced my sword into one eye, which burst outward in flames. That wasn't enough to kill the dragon, but it was half-blinded now, which was a start. I flew just out of reach again, so that I could regroup and think of a method to end the dragon.

The dragon roared and snapped his fangs at me, sending a shockwave through the air that threw me back and almost sent me plunging to the ground. I managed to catch myself just before I crashed to earth and shot back up in time to bury the sword in the soft spot between Nidhogg's eyes, driving into his brain at the perfect angle with a sickening, wet crunch.

The great beast toppled to the ground with a massive thud that caused the world around us to shake. The walls of Nastrond shuddered with the defeat of the dragon, who nearly fell on Loki and Gunhild. They scurried out of the way just in time, and as I landed before them, they looked at me with wide, unbelieving eyes.

"You… you just defeated a dragon the size of a mountain!" Gunhild shouted as she ran to throw her arms around my neck.

Loki chuckled and patted my shoulder as if I had done the easiest thing in the world. "She's a Valkyrie," he said as he stepped around the smoldering carcass of the dragon. "Of course she did. Congratulations. Shall we go get your warrior?"

"Yes," I said breathlessly. "Let's go get him."

Chapter Forty Nine

The arching walls of Nastrond, the realm of the dishonorable dead, were made of criss-crossed rib cages of gigantic serpents. The bleached bones curved around each other until there was no way to see inside. Frozen air roiled outward as we stood in the doorway. The hissing of snakes crept out of the entrance, warning us of the dangers inside. I shivered, though whether it was from the cold air that poured out or from the knowledge of how awful it would be inside, I was unsure.

Above the persistent hissing came the sound of painful howls, screams, and other dreadful noises indicating a greater, more awful level of torture than I had expected. The thought of Eryk being subjected to such horrors made me hurry inside despite my fears.

Gunhild hesitated but followed me in, and Loki huffed a sigh before doing the same. Our breath clouded from our mouths. There was a splash at my feet as I stepped foot inside the skeletal city, and I looked down to see a greenish-black liquid floating across the floor about two inches deep. It had an acid reek to it that made my eyes water and I recoiled into Gunhild, who nearly fell as she caught me.

"Venom," Loki whispered as he steadied us both. Were we supposed to whisper here? Would that protect us from the snakes that writhed in the ceilings and dripped their venom bit by bit onto Nastrond's occupants? "Be careful where you step. It will be painful if it gets on your skin."

"Noted." I stepped forward, fighting the urge to run away.

The whole wretched place was lit by dimly burning oil lamps hanging from the bones above. I kept my eyes on the ceiling even though it was disturbing to see the mass of snakes twisting in and out of the bony rafters. It was better than catching a face full of venom. It was almost like a dance to maneuver between the fonts of fluid that dripped constantly from above.

"Where would Eryk be? This place is huge." I whispered to Loki, whose nose was scrunched in disgust at our environment. He looked around, as if looking for something in particular, before gesturing for us to follow him.

"He won't be with the murderers or adulterers, I don't think. Even Hel wouldn't subject him to that," Loki explained. "Probably with the oath-breakers. That's this way, I think."

"You think?" Gunhild echoed. "I don't want to just wander around until we find him. We need to know we're going to the right place."

"Look, shieldmaiden, I'm doing my best. If it weren't for me, you wouldn't have the first clue where to start. Be grateful I'm subjecting myself to this despite your attempt to kill my daughter," Loki snapped, voice still low. It was difficult to hear any of our whispered voices over the hissing and howling. I put a hand on his arm and gave Gunhild a look to subdue her. The last thing we needed was for Loki to abandon us. We'd never escape this place if he did.

Gunhild just sighed, and Loki took off with the same dance-like movements to lead us through the entry of Nastrond and deeper into the realm. Our boots sloshed through the venom on the flooded ground as we walked. Eventually, Loki turned down a narrow corridor, leading us away from the constant sounds of agony. I took this as a good sign that at least Eryk was not being tormented like the others.

The corridor morphed into a tunnel, and we noticed fewer snakes as we walked. Their venom dripped less and less as we traveled as well, until we reached a great arched doorway marked with runes. Rather than waiting for Loki, I took a deep breath and stepped through the threshold.

Instead of snakes hissing, the rattling of chains echoed through this chamber. Along the walls, men and women were shackled, spread eagle, so that they could not move. Was this where Eryk had been this whole time? A stab of guilt struck me. I scanned the faces of each prisoner who called out to us for help. Should I try to free them all? That would upset the balance, and for most, the Norns had determined that they should be here. Even if I didn't like it, I couldn't very well destroy the world itself just because I hated seeing people in this condition.

"Eryk?" I called, afraid to shout his name. The chamber was long and seemed to stretch out before us for miles. The ages were filled with oath-breakers who had been sent here upon death. How cruel to chain them up for eternity for something so simple!

I continued walking, scanning dirty faces to see if I recognized one, and called out Eryk's name every few yards. Loki and Gunhild trailed behind me, as there was no point in them looking. They wouldn't have recognized his face to draw my attention to him, anyway. After several minutes I called again, and this time, I could have sworn I heard a response.

"Yrsa?" A small voice came from somewhere on my right, a few yards away from where I stood.

"Eryk?" I rushed forward, inspecting the grimy faces of those I passed until I found a familiar one. I nearly collapsed as I saw how thin and pale he was. His face was caked with the greenish-black residue of venom. He nodded and his shoulders and head drooped for a moment as I approached.

"I thought you wouldn't come," Eryk admitted in a raspy voice. How long had it been since he had spoken to someone? That sting of guilt came again as I wondered just how long it had felt for him.

"Of course I came," I said firmly. "I couldn't leave you here. I just… I had to find all the armor Hel commanded me to bring to her in exchange for your freedom. It took a long time. I'm sorry."

He nodded, swallowing hard. His eyes didn't meet mine, though they did wander to Gunhild for a moment. Loki had tucked himself off to one side, out of notice. I wished Gunhild had done the same. Eryk seemed curious, as if he wanted to ask who she was, but then his gaze finally met mine.

"Thank you for coming now, at least." He shifted and the chains rattled and clanked with his movement. "Do you have any water?"

"Oh. Yes. Of course." I gently lifted the flask Gunhild brought me to Eryk's lips. He drank deeply, the water dribbling down his chin and leaving a streak of white skin, cleansed of the venom, in its wake.

"Will you get me down from here?" Eryk asked when he was done. He still avoided my gaze. I couldn't have faulted him if he was angry at me. It was my fault he was here, even if it had been his choice too to avoid death for so long.

"Yes, yes," I said, and reached up to the shackles to try to remove them. There were no locks on them to be picked though, no closure of any sort. They were sealed around his wrists permanently. "Loki? Any idea of how to get these off?"

"Must I do everything?" Loki asked with a huff. "Move."

Loki pushed me out of the way and set about muttering to himself as he took hold of the shackles. Eryk winced as the metal scraped across the raw skin of his wrists but remained stoic otherwise. I had hoped he would be glad to see me.

After several minutes, there was a soft hum and then a clunk as the shackle on Eryk's left wrist fell. Shortly later there was another clunk as Loki released his other wrist. I had to catch Eryk as he fell. His legs were too weak to hold him up after being chained there for so long. Finally, he shoved me away from him and leaned against the wall. I wasn't sure how to react to the almost violent action. It felt like a betrayal to what we had shared, but I tried to understand how he must feel after months in the pit of Nastrond.

"I'm sorry it took me so long." I took a step closer and lifted a hand to brush a lock of dark hair from his eyes. He shied away though and refused to let me touch him. "You know I would have gotten here sooner had it been possible. We had to subdue Hel and slay a dragon just to be here."

"At least you're here now," Eryk said, his voice colder than I expected. Something twisted in my stomach to know he was so disappointed in my efforts to save him.

"I know it's my fault you were here, but..." I wanted to shout at him that we had *both* chosen the path that had led here, to blame him too, to make him see that I had done so much to save him, but I bit my tongue.

"Yrsa has conquered much to be here," Gunhild murmured, stepping closer to me. The way Eryk looked between the two of us made me wish she hadn't. Maybe I should have left her outside for this part.

"Yes, I'm sure. But… it's been *years*," he said bitterly. After a moment, he muttered almost inaudibly. "Never mind. I'm glad you're here now."

He finally came closer and pressed a kiss to my cheek. I wrapped my arms around him, though the passion with which I might once have greeted him was as dulled as his reaction to me.

"Yrsa?" Gunhild said my name so gently that it made my heart ache. How did I choose between her and Eryk now? "We should be going. We still have to retrieve the dwarf's staff."

I had forgotten about that altogether and closed my eyes. This gods-forsaken quest wasn't over yet. It felt like it would never be over. Eventually, I opened my eyes and forced a smile as I looked to Eryk.

"Here, let me help you walk. We have to get out of here, get back to the main part of Helheim and try to find this staff," I said. He stiffened a little as I went to pull his arm over my shoulder and pushed himself up off the wall without my help. It stung, but there was nothing I could do to subdue his anger at me for not coming sooner.

"I can do it myself," he said with a lift of his chin.

"Come then," Gunhild said, nodding toward where we had come from. "We should go."

"Yes," I agreed. "We have to find Merrymaul."

We headed back down the endlessly long corridor, careful to avoid the venom dripping from the ceiling. Those chained there barely had the energy to call out to us for help as we passed. I had no choice but to ignore their pleas. Their punishment was their fate, and I couldn't reverse that. Eventually, we made it to the door. Eryk paused to look back into Nastrond's depths for a long while, before he turned to limp past us out of the cursed site.

Chapter Fifty

I FOUGHT the urge to look back over my shoulder at Nastrond as Loki led us away and back into the fog and toward the river. Eryk limped along, but refused my help any time I tried to put an arm around him and get him to lean on me. As we walked past Nidhogg's smoldering corpse, Eryk barely gave it a second look. It was as if my defeat of the massive creature meant nothing. A bitter taste filled my mouth; I had done so much, only to receive a dismissive glance.

The only reason I could think that he might refuse my help was that his pride got the better of him after so long in a powerless position. I kept my head down and eyes on the ground ahead of me. The walk seemed to take less time than before, and I was glad for that.

The fog eventually dissipated and revealed the decrepit bridge over the rushing river.

"We're almost there." Gunhild was suddenly next to me and took my hand in hers as we trudged across the swaying bridge toward the palace rising up in the distance. Loki cleared his throat and jerked his head in Eryk's direction. I quickly let go of Gunhild's hand and offered to take Eryk's. He seemed almost begrudging as he took it but then smiled when I looked at him in confusion. I felt like I was being torn apart, my love for Gunhild warring with my love for Eryk.

Something felt very wrong though. Eryk's hand was loose in mine, not gripping it back. He didn't look at me when I glanced over at him, even when I paused to look at him more closely. He kept walking until I pulled him back. For a moment, he leaned close, as if he intended to kiss me, but then he froze, his lips a mere inch from mine. I opened my eyes to pull back and look at him.

"Is everything well?" I asked him. Something seemed to break inside him, and a disgusted expression distorted his features. "What? What's wrong?"

"I was right," he said with his lip curled in derision.

"Right about what?" I asked, voice brittle.

"Whether it was worth it to pretend I loved you to gain immortality. It didn't work and look where it landed me. Even if you have come to *rescue* me now." If his other words hadn't been so hurtful, I might have cringed at the sarcastic way he said the word "rescue." That word barely registered. It hurt much worse to hear that not only had he never loved me, but he had used me to become immortal.

No matter if I had found Gunhild or not, no matter how I loved her, the betrayal still took its toll on me. I gritted my teeth, my stomach twisting on the knowledge that everything I had thought we shared was a lie: every affectionate word, every moment of passion, and every dangerous moment I stole to be with him. None of it had meant anything to him. Before I could stop myself, the rage at his betrayal overwhelmed me.

"How dare you? How *dare* you tell me you love me, promise me you want nothing more than to be with me forever, let me spend almost every night *in your bed*, and now? Now you tell me you never meant it?"

My voice rose louder and louder as I let my fury free, my hands clenched so tightly at my sides that I thought they might break. Before I knew what I was doing, my fist was colliding with Eryk's jaw. His head snapped back with the impact, and he stumbled away, his mouth agape in shock.

"I don't..." Eryk mumbled out as he managed to stand straight again. I shoved him hard so that he fell to the ground with a stunned expression.

"You say it wasn't even worth it? What do you take me for? Some foolish, love-struck girl, happy to be strung along just so you can live forever? You've got the wrong woman for that. You're a vile, selfish, little boy and I regret ever meeting you. I regret saving you. How dare you!" I spat these last words at Eryk and then turned away.

Loki gave a low whistle, stirring me from my wrath. He and Gunhild both stared in awe at me, while Eryk merely lay on the ground, gritting his bloodied teeth together as if he shouldn't have to tolerate me speaking to him in such a way.

"I'm happy to take him back if you want," Loki said after I took a shaky breath and let it out in a slow exhale.

"No," I snapped. As much as it hurt to learn the truth, I couldn't erase all that had happened. I couldn't erase that I had fallen in love with him, or that I had sworn an oath to rescue him. And I couldn't erase that he had betrayed me after everything I had overcome to fulfill my promises. The words that came out next were seething, but deadly quiet. "I made an oath to rescue him. So, I will. No matter if he lied to me about everything. We will get him out, and then we will get to Midgard where he can... do whatever he pleases, I suppose. Perhaps die in battle and go to Valhalla as was planned for him all along. Come on, we have to go."

Eryk didn't move, though. I scowled, my back straightening and my muscles tensing, ready to let my rage flow again. Gunhild placed a hand on my arm, though I wasn't sure if it was to comfort me or to keep me calm.

"What will you do? Refuse to come with us?" Loki asked in disbelief.

"I could," Eryk replied with a defiant lift of his chin, though when he glanced from Loki to me, there might have been a bit of fear in his eyes.

"That would be awfully stupid," Loki pointed out. "But I'm happy to chain you back up and leave you here for eternity with that attitude. Do you realize all she's been through to get to you? Everything she has fought just to be by your side again? And now you act like this and tell her you don't love her and never did? I'm tempted to leave you here whether either of you want me to or not. Ungrateful wretch."

Eryk's eyes widened at Loki's threat, and he glanced at me for a moment. Did he soften a little, or did I imagine it? He sighed and returned his attention to the trickster.

"No, don't leave me here," he begged. He got to his feet warily, as if afraid I'd just shove him back down again. I wanted to. "I'm sorry. You're right. I'm being ungrateful."

"That's what I thought," Loki said. "Worthless worm. Should have left you chained to that wall, little bastard." We didn't have time to berate Eryk any further. We needed to get the staff regardless of what he may or may not feel for me.

"Tell me where to go, Loki," I said finally, the rage finally ebbing a little.

"This way," Loki said as he led us around the massive palace, until we finally saw the halls of the dead gathered like ravens in the distance. There were so many, dozens and dozens of them, that I wasn't sure how we would ever know which one might house Merrymaul.

"Any idea how they're divided?" I asked Loki, who shrugged.

"Probably by their station in life. Slaves and servants in one, average men of different sorts in others, kings and jarls in the largest I would think. Valas should have their own, considering how sacred they are. Look for the one that is decorated like a seer's home would be." Loki pointed off in the distance where we could hear wind chimes jingling and see blue bunting hanging from one of the large halls.

With my target in sight, I released Gunhild's hand and increased my pace. I wanted this to be over as soon as possible. I wanted to be out of Eryk's presence, and to get Freyja's armor to her so that I could move on with my life, whatever that may look like now.

Gunhild and Loki hurried to keep up, but Eryk struggled, so we had to pause for him to catch his breath. I finally removed Freyja's helm and the falcon cloak and put them away. Brisingamen stayed where it had been for most of the time since I found it—around my neck. I felt better then, with the hope that it would make it easier to get the staff from Merrymaul.

Eventually, we reached the hall where the valas and seers and oracles would be housed, its blue bunting bright even in the darkness. Bits and bobs of amber and glass and gold were strung up to jingle, though there was no breeze here. I looked to Loki for guidance, and he motioned for me to knock at the giant, blue wooden door.

I lifted a hand, but before I could knock, it opened, and a wizened old woman stood looking up at me with clouded eyes. She seemed to recognize me and stepped back silently to gesture for us to come into the grand hall, which was brightly lit despite the gloom outside.

"You're looking for the dwarven vala," the woman croaked. "They'll be in their chambers, expecting you."

"How?" I asked before I could stop myself.

"We were seers above, and now we carry on below, it's just a little less useful here," the old woman said with a raspy laugh. "Come, it's this way."

"Thank you." I bowed my head as I followed her down the corridor. She knocked at the door, which was decorated with runes that I recognized from Nidavellir, and an even smaller, more weathered looking vala answered. This must be Merrymaul.

"Greetings, Valkyrie, do come in," the dwarf told me as they glanced at the others. "They can wait outside. I think you and I should talk alone, don't you?"

"We'll stay right out here." Gunhild gave my shoulder a reassuring squeeze which made Eryk raise an eyebrow. The dwarf offered a knowing smile and stepped aside to allow me to enter before closing the door behind us.

"Come now, have a seat." They led me through the cluttered chamber, which seemed like a normal seer's cottage now that we were inside. Charms hung from low wooden ceilings, and the whole place smelled of fragrant herbs. A merry fire crackled on the stone hearth, and a pair of comfortable looking chairs sat in front of it, facing each other. It hardly felt as if we were in the underworld at all.

I took a seat in one, and Merrymaul sat in the other. Their gaze seemed to look through me rather than at me. I squirmed with discomfort and tried to tell myself that they already knew what I was here for, so there was no need to do any convincing. Either they would give me the staff or send me away without it.

"Emberthane and the elders sent you for my staff." They picked up a cup of aromatic tea. "They finally realize the worth of my teachings, so many centuries later."

"Yes, they do. They are doing very well now with them. Everything is voted on, and everyone is equal. I was quite impressed. If only humans could take up the same ideas."

"I am impressed too, but it's by you, not by my descendants." Merrymaul reached over to put two fingers under my chin and lift my face. "You've come an awful long way. It's a shame that boy is too selfish to see what you've done for him."

I wasn't sure at all how to respond to that. The sympathy and understanding of what I had faced over the last several months was enough to make me release a shaky breath. Merrymaul chuckled and shook her head ruefully.

"Well, you've found a better love anyway, haven't you?"

I hadn't thought about it that way. As I thought about it in earnest now, I realized she was right. Gunhild loved me not because I was a Valkyrie and could spare her from death, but because I was me, and I made her happy when we were together. And she made me just as happy. I couldn't deny that I had loved Eryk, but now that love didn't seem to compare to how I felt for Gunhild. It was a relief to realize what I had gained despite everything it felt like I had lost. I looked back up at the dwarf after a moment or two to think.

"I did. I just have to bring your staff back to Nidavellir, and then Freyja's armor to her and I can…"

"You can go home?" Merrymaul supplied when I trailed off. "Freyja might be convinced to let you stay with your shieldmaiden, if that is what you want. You will just have to ask when she comes to retrieve her armor from you. Either way, you've done well, and should be proud."

"Thank you." It was freeing to hear that I had made the right choices, and I basked in Merrymaul's approval. It was not an experience I was treated to often. "Do you… that is… will you give me the staff to return to your people?"

"Oh, that old thing? Of course. What do I need it for? It will mean much more to them than it ever did to me," the vala told me with a toothless grin. Without meaning to, I breathed a heavy sigh. It released all my remaining fears, and I felt lighter than I had since before Eryk had come into my life and turned it upside down. "Let me go get it for you."

They eased up to their feet and toddled off into another room to shuffle and thump around. After a few minutes, they returned with a gnarled oak staff in hand, jewels hanging from its knotted crest. Blue ribbons wrapped around its length, which was taller than them and almost as tall as me.

"Bid my descendants peace and good fortune from me, yes?" The dwarf handed the staff off to me and patted my shoulder. "Now, let's get you out of here, shall we? Just follow the river to the root of Yggdrasil. You can go find a new home with your shieldmaiden if you convince Freyja not to return you to Valhalla."

The dwarf led me back to the door of their chambers and pulled it open, showing that my group was still waiting patiently outside. Except for Eryk, who tapped his toe in annoyance as he waited.

"You got it!" Gunhild's eyes sparkled as vibrantly as the jewels hanging from the staff's tip.

"We did, yes, now let's get out of here before Hel gets out of her shackles." I tugged Gunhild's arm, and Loki shoved Eryk in front of him to get him walking. "Merrymaul said to follow the river to Yggdrasil's root, and we should be able to travel to Midgard from there."

"Then let's get out of here, I need some sunlight, don't you?" Loki said with a grin.

"Sunlight sounds like a dream at this point," I admitted. My laugh sounded foreign to my ears. When was the last time I laughed? I couldn't even remember. I held out my hand to Gunhild, who happily took it. Eryk huffed and followed behind us, muttering angrily to himself. It hardly seemed fair for him to be upset about it when he had betrayed me so terribly, but I couldn't find it in myself to care anymore.

We followed the river for several miles until we finally saw the roots of a mighty tree rising into the lightning-illuminated clouds above us. I hadn't seen Yggdrasil since we visited the Norns. It seemed so different in the darkness, lit only by the occasional flash from above.

"Do we just climb it?" I asked. I circled the great tree, looking for some way to climb, until I came upon a stairway that seemed to be embedded into its gnarled roots and up its trunk. It disappeared into the clouds high above us.

"How am I supposed to climb stairs in my condition?" Eryk asked.

"Well, I'm not carrying you," Loki told him. "So, either you climb, or you go back to Nastrond and pout."

"Ugh. Fine." Eryk stomped over to the tree and stepped onto the first step, which seemed to glow as he put his foot on it.

"Ooh, that's a good sign, right? Maybe we won't have to climb as far as we think?" Gunhild asked.

"Guess there's only one way to find out," I said with a shrug. "Go on then, next foot, Eryk."

Eryk scowled, clearly unhappy with being the one to carry out this experiment. He took a deep breath and put his other foot on the next step. This one glowed as well for a moment before a flash of light blinded us and a strobe of power sent me, Gunhild, and Loki flying backwards. We landed in a pile, and when we looked up, as the light dimmed, we saw that Eryk was gone.

"I assume that means he's in Midgard." Loki clambered to his feet and reached down to help Gunhild and me to ours. "Brace yourself next time. I'll go next. Then you two try to go up together if you can, so you're not separated wherever we end up."

"Good idea," I agreed, taking Gunhild's hand in mine tightly enough that my knuckles turned white. She didn't shy away but gripped back just as hard. "Go on then. I'll see you on the other side."

Loki nodded, and Gunhild and I set our feet as the trickster stepped one foot up and then the other. The light and power came again. We were knocked back a couple of steps like before, but we didn't fall this time.

"Ready, sunshine?" I asked Gunhild after a deep breath. She nodded and closed the distance between us to kiss me. I kissed her back, hoping it wouldn't be the last time, and then led her to Yggdrasil's root. "Together, yes? One, two, three."

We both stepped up, one foot then the next, onto the tree, and the light enveloped us. The last thing I saw was Gunhild's face smiling at me.

Chapter Fifty One

THE BLINDING light that surrounded me slowly faded, and I was left standing in a field with Gunhild's hand still in mine. As predicted by Merrymaul, it was summer in Midgard now, and the warm sun shone high above us. Birds sang cheerfully as they flitted around, and butterflies floated over the wide field of colorful wildflowers we had arrived in.

Gunhild turned and threw her arms around my neck, laughing as brightly as the sun. I picked her up with my free arm, despite my pack weighing me down, and spun her around before setting her on her feet again. As I became more aware of the world around us, I noticed Loki standing nearby with Eryk, who looked rather more like he belonged in a stormy sea than in a summer meadow.

"Looks like Yggdrasil took us right to where we needed to be," Loki said, coming over to clap me on the shoulder. "Does this seem familiar to you?"

"No, where are we?" I asked, looking around to get my bearings.

"Just outside Armvind."

"How in the world?" I tried to puzzle out how we had ended up here, rather than anywhere else in Midgard. I would at least have expected us to end up with the Norns at their place by the tree.

"The magic of Yggdrasil. Remember, it's an instrument of fate, just like the Norns. It knows where we are meant to end up." Loki laughed, and pointed to Eryk, who looked so out of place among our joy that in any other situation I might have felt sorry for him. "I think we should probably get him a horse and send him on his way."

When I turned to Eryk, he wouldn't even meet my gaze. "We got you back to Midgard. Do you think you can find your way home from here?"

"Do I have any choice?"

"You sound like a child," Loki said. "She's gotten you out of Nastrond and you're going to quibble over where she brought you in Midgard? Please. Grow up."

"Loki… can you take him back to his village? It's called Austruna—it's due west of here, on the sea." It was a big thing to ask of the trickster, but I didn't know how else to get Eryk home. I certainly wasn't going to take him myself. That would take well over a month, and I would have to deal with him the whole time.

"I can, I suppose," Loki said, sighing heavily. "Though he probably won't thank me for it, even if it is a huge favor."

"Please, I beg you. You can join us back here afterwards, yes?" This time I was not afraid to beg.

"Fine, I'll do it. Come on, lad. Say your goodbyes."

"Goodbye, Eryk," I said, when Eryk didn't immediately look at me to say it himself. Though I found myself hating him, I reminded myself that even though he was young and selfish and stupid, I had once loved him, even if my rage had burnt that love out like a wildfire in a drought-stricken forest. I couldn't wish him ill no matter how much I might have liked to. "I wish you the best. I did what I promised."

Eryk looked like he was about to say something awful, but Loki swooped in and grabbed him by the wrist before he could. Both vanished without another word. Part of me was grateful that Loki kept that pain from me, but another part wished I could know what other hurtful things he might say. I might have earned at least some of them.

Once Loki had gone, I dragged Gunhild into my arms to claim her lips with mine. I needed to feel something that didn't hurt, and I knew I could count on her to give me that something. My pack dropped to the ground as I pulled her to me. She melted into me as her own pack fell beside her. Her relief as she held me close was palpable, though she didn't relax entirely. There was still unfinished business.

As we held onto each other, the rage that was left in me finally seeped out. My shoulders lowered, my jaw unclenched, and even my breath felt like it came easier. It was such a respite from the anger I had felt, that I couldn't help but kiss her again, out of sheer gratitude.

The sound of a throat clearing interrupted us, and I pulled away from Gunhild with flaming cheeks. She was just as pink and looked with a guilty giggle at Loki, who watched us with a raised eyebrow and a shake of his head.

"Inseparable, the two of you. Come, let's go into the village and see how they've been doing without us. We can bathe, eat, and rest. We've earned it, I think. Eryk is safely back in his village. He didn't have much to say about the whole thing. Not even a thank you out of the boy. Ingrate."

"He's young, and he's had a rough time," I said, which earned me a skeptical look from both Loki and Gunhild. I didn't really believe my own words.

"He should be glad he was rescued," said Loki. "You could have just left him there and gone back to Valhalla as Hel offered."

"Loki is right," Gunhild agreed. "But he's where he wanted to be all along, so let's just... move on?"

"Right. Move on." I took a deep breath, inhaling the scent of wildflowers and fresh air. I would never look at Midgard the same again after this journey. "Loki, can you do me one more favor?"

"What's that?"

"Can you take Merrymaul's staff back to the dwarves?" I offered him the staff and he frowned as he took it.

"You'll wear me out this way, but I suppose it does have to be delivered." He pulled an elf-light from his pack, along with a small, heavy pouch. "Take these. The elf-light is for the jarl, the bag is for the little girl. You promised her dragon scales, right? Those are from Nidhogg."

"You're my hero, Loki. Truly. We'll see you in the village. I expect to eat supper with you tonight." I kissed him on the cheek as I took the elf-light and the pouch. He patted the top of my head and grinned, then popped off to go back to Nidavellir. When he had gone, I retrieved my pack and held out a hand to Gunhild once she had picked up her own. "Let's go greet our friends, yes?"

"Yes," she agreed, giving my hand a squeeze. "They'll be so happy to see you."

Chapter Fifty Two

WE BARELY MADE it to the gates of Armvind before a tiny body catapulted into my legs with great force. Despite her size, Hjordis nearly knocked me off my feet.

"You're back! We missed you. Do you have stories to tell me?" Hjordis shrieked delightedly. I laughed and knelt before her, though her mother appeared soon after and scolded her for attacking me.

"It's fine," I assured Signy with a warm smile. "Hello, Hjordis. We weren't gone that long, were we? Luka will be back soon as well. We have a gift for you, but I was hoping to take a bath and give it to you at supper. Would that be alright, or do you need it right this second?"

"It's been almost a month. I suppose adventures can make you lose track of time," Signy said with an amused smile. "You can wait, can't you, Hjordis?"

Hjordis gave a big sigh and nodded after a moment.

"Good girl," I said. "We'll see you at supper then and tell you all about the dragon we slayed."

"You promise?" the little girl asked.

"I swear it on all the gods," I replied with a wink.

"Good. Then we'll see you at supper," She took her mother's hand and Signy gave me a grateful smile.

"We are very glad you've returned. I'll let the jarl know you're back. Do you remember where the cottage is? It's still available for you." Signy said gently.

"Just like we never left," I said. "We'll see you after we've had our baths."

Signy nodded and headed off with Hjordis. Gunhild took my hand, and we went to the small cottage where we had stayed before. I opened the door and felt the weight of my quest lighten significantly as I stepped inside and dropped my pack by the door. It felt like home. I wondered if Gunhild and I could stay, if Freyja didn't send me back to Valhalla when all was said and done.

We moved around the cottage in comfortable silence as we prepared to bathe and rest before supper. We each took a nap while the other got cleaned up and changed into clean clothing. I felt like a new person once my hair was washed and my clothes were fresh.

"I should probably summon Freyja after we eat," I said softly as we curled up together in bed before supper. Nothing was urgent at this point, other than getting the armor back to its proper owner, and even that could wait a little longer.

"So soon?" Gunhild asked, voice trembling a little.

"I don't want her to think I was keeping the armor for myself. It's the right thing to do."

"Right." I could tell from her flat tone that she hated the idea, and I hated it too, but I couldn't avoid it. "I suppose I can't stop you."

"No. Unfortunately not. But I promise, if I have the choice to stay, I will. I would never leave you if she let me keep you."

"You have to do what's right. Don't worry about me. You're a Valkyrie. You belong in Valhalla. I just wish it didn't have to be so soon." Gunhild tucked her face into the crook of my neck, and I felt warmth against my skin as her tears fell.

It made me want to never give Freyja the armor. Or at least make Loki give it to her without me. But that was a task I couldn't trust him with. The armor had already tempted one god; I couldn't risk that again. I had one last duty on this quest, and I was determined to fulfill it, no matter the consequence.

After a long while basking in each other's presence and memorizing the experience in case it didn't last, a knock came at the door. I didn't want to answer, but we couldn't ignore the world forever. Gunhild nudged me to get up, so I huffed and got out of bed. Loki greeted me with a cheerful grin as I opened the door. I offered a tired smile.

"The staff has been delivered to the dwarves as promised. They were very grateful and sent their thanks and congratulations on completing your quest. Hakon said to tell you hello, and that he was disappointed you didn't return it yourself." Loki looked past me as if he wanted to come in. I didn't step aside though, so he just pouted. "The jarl is expecting us at the hall for supper. He's excited to see you and hear about your adventures. Are you planning to go?"

"Yes, I suppose we have to," I said as Gunhild came to stand at my side. I could put off calling Freyja, but it needed to be done before anything could happen to her armor. I hesitated even to leave it in the cottage without someone there to guard it.

"Well, come on, they're waiting for you." Loki said, turning to go. I stepped back into the house to get the gifts for Hjordis and the jarl and then followed Loki and Gunhild to the mead hall.

We were greeted by cheers and slaps on the back as we entered the hall. Everyone seemed so happy to see us. I had expected to be in a better mood now that everything was neatly wrapped up for the most part, but that one little remaining task nagged at me. I managed to put on a good mask, though, and greeted everyone with cheer. Gunhild seemed even more muted than myself, and I hated to see her that way.

"Yrsa! Gunhild! Luka! You've returned triumphant I hope?" Leif was so overjoyed to see us that he gave us each a tight hug. I squirmed as little as I could and smiled as he released me.

"We have, yes. We come bearing gifts," I told him, lifting the bags that contained the elf-light and the scales for Hjordis. "Should I give yours to you first, or shall little Hjordis receive hers first?"

"Me!" cried Hjordis from where she sat by her mother. Signy hushed her as she gave an embarrassed laugh and murmured to the little girl to be patient.

"You should definitely give little Hjordis her gift first," Leif said, gesturing for the child to join us. She hurried over with shining eyes.

"Because you were so kind to us when we arrived, and because you were very brave to stay here with your mother instead of running away with us for an adventure, I have brought you something very precious indeed." I knelt before her and pulled the pouch of dragon scales from the bag.

"What is it?" she practically squealed as I placed the leather pouch in her hands.

"You will have to open it and tell me what you think is inside," I said, offering an encouraging smile.

She very carefully unlaced the top of the pouch and dipped her fingers into it, pulling out two of the iridescent black scales, each of which was the size of my hand. They were metallic and smelled vaguely of sulfur.

"Are these… dragon scales?" she asked, her voice hushed in awe as she stared at the precious treasures in her hand. "They're heavy!"

"They are. And they aren't just any dragon scales, but scales from the dragon who guards the gates to Nastrond, where all the bad people go when they die," I explained, unsure how much she knew of the cosmos. Both Hjordis and her mother looked in awe of the gift, their eyes wide as they gazed at the scales.

"You will have to put those somewhere very safe and special," Signy told her daughter as she looked over her shoulder at the scales in her hands. "Tell Yrsa thank you."

"Thank you!" Hjordis bounced on her toes.

I got back to my feet and turned to Leif. From my bag, I pulled the melon sized elf-light, still glowing that eerie blue color that it had ever since we stole it from Alfheim. The jarl came closer to inspect it, his eyes as wide and child-like as Hjordis's had been.

"This is what they use to light Alfheim," I said, offering it to him. "You can use it to light your chambers, or somewhere sacred."

"This is truly a spectacular gift. More than worth the horses you took." Leif took the light and turned it over in his hands curiously. "How does it work?"

"Fungus," Loki supplied. "They've used them for centuries. The whole city is lit with them. Particularly beautiful at night."

"This will have to go in one of our shrines to the gods," Leif said. "Thank you. You have honored us."

"We were in your debt and still are. You have been so kind and gracious, we could hardly fail to show some symbol of our gratitude," I replied.

A small crowd had gathered around us, trying to get a glimpse of the elf-light in Leif's hands. The light cast a blue hue over the jarl's features, making him appear as otherworldly as the elves had. Var appeared among the crowd and winked at me before turning to Leif.

"Why don't you let me take that, young man. I'll see it gets somewhere safe, yes?" she told him with authority. She gently took the light from him and headed off to take it to a shrine.

"What will you do now?" Leif asked after she had gone. "After you eat, I mean."

"I have one more task and then I will likely be gone. Could Gunhild stay though? And Luka?"

"You can't stay too?" Leif asked, brow furrowing.

"I would like to, but I may have to return home," I admitted. "Time will tell, I suppose. For now, we may enjoy some good food and good mead. My task can wait until after."

"We weren't prepared for your arrival, so I fear there is no great feast awaiting you," Leif said with a small frown. "I hope venison and roasted parsnips will be sufficient."

"They will be far more than sufficient. We'll be grateful for anything hot and fresh."

We talked of adventure and excitement as we ate, with lots of laughter and good cheer. It was refreshing to finally feel the weight of Eryk's demise lifted from my shoulders. I barely even wondered what he might be doing now. It wasn't my problem anymore, and that was a relief all its own.

Despite the relief, I still dreaded what came next. It would be an honor to return Freyja's armor to her, and an honor to be restored to Valhalla if that was how she chose to reward me, but I didn't want to leave Gunhild behind. Gunhild babbled about our adventures and Loki cracked jokes, but I was quiet, focusing on what came next.

Eventually, the food had been devoured, the conversation ran quiet, and Leif and the rest of the community left to go about their business. I had no choice but to finish my final task. I couldn't summon Freyja without saying my goodbyes though.

"Loki," I called. "Will you come with me?"

Gunhild and Loki both looked up from what was left of their meal, and Loki offered a perplexed frown. I led him over to an unoccupied table where we sat across from each other. It took me a moment to find the right words.

"I wanted to thank you. We couldn't have finished this quest without you," I told him, which earned me an amused smile. "I'm grateful not just for your assistance, but for your way of keeping our morale up while we completed our tasks. You kept us laughing. I will forever be thankful, wherever I end up."

"You silly thing, you don't have to thank me," Loki said with a chuckle.

"And you forgive me for what we did to Hel?" I asked worriedly.

"She really didn't give you much choice. I don't like it, but I don't blame you for it." He squeezed my shoulder and smiled. "It was an honor to watch you accomplish everything you set out to do. I'm quite confident you could have completed it without me coming along. I was just there to enjoy the ride."

"Either way, I'm grateful. I wish there was some way I could repay you," I said.

"Don't be a stranger?" he suggested.

"If I'm in Valhalla, I won't be able to visit," I pointed out. "And even if I'm here, I won't always know where to find you."

"You've summoned me before, I'm sure you remember how to do it again. If you ever need someone to make you laugh, or to play a trick on someone, I'll be there. I promise."

"I'll keep that in mind. I guess this is goodbye."

"You know I don't do goodbyes, Valkyrie. I'll see you later. I hope you get what your heart desires. Whatever that may be." Loki held out a hand, palm up, and I took it and gave it a squeeze. "Good luck. And remember, nothing is ever as serious as it seems."

"I'll remember," I promised. My gaze drifted to Gunhild who was picking at an apple tart and trying to give us our moment. She looked up in time for our eyes to meet and smiled a little sadly. "I should go tell Gunhild goodbye too."

"She'll be in Valhalla one day, I have no doubt," Loki assured me. "Now go, don't keep me here and make me cry, sweet Valkyrie. I've got a reputation to uphold, you know."

"Of course. Can't have the trickster god weeping, can we?" I teased. He grinned at me, gave me a wink, and wiggled his fingers before hopping up and heading out of the mead hall to leave me with Gunhild.

I wandered back over to her with a deep breath to fortify myself against this goodbye. I knew it would be difficult, but this felt like the most impossible part of my quest now that I faced it.

"Can we take a walk?" I offered a hand to help her up.

"Of course." She took it and got to her feet. "We can go to the meadow."

"That sounds perfect," I agreed.

The meadow burst with even more color now that the sun was closer to the horizon. It wouldn't set completely this time of year, but it still streaked the horizon with brilliant pinks and purples. Gunhild's hair shone an even brighter copper than I was used to, her eyes sparkling in the evening sun. It could have been tears that made them glitter so.

"This is goodbye, isn't it?" she asked, her voice trembling a little.

"Most likely." My throat felt tight. I pulled her into my arms, holding her tightly to me as if I could keep her if I refused to let go.

"Maybe we can just say… until next time? Instead of goodbye? Like Loki does?" she suggested, her face buried against my shoulder.

"Yes, let's say that. I like that much better. It's less final." I pulled away a little and tucked a beaded braid behind her ear. "If nothing else, we'll see each other again when you come to Valhalla. But you must promise that you won't come for a good long time. I want you to live a long, full life."

"I don't want to live a life without you." Her voice cracked, and she swallowed hard. A tear slipped from the corner of her eye, and I leaned forward to kiss it away.

"You must. You must be brave, as you always are. You must fight to become a little old woman, with children and grandchildren surrounding you as you die of old age. Promise me you will," I told her firmly.

"I'll do my best, though I really don't see children in my future."

"Then lots of friends, at least. People who love you as much as I do. Because I do. I love you more than anything I have ever loved."

"I don't want you to go. I know you must, but I'm not ready." Her lower lip quivered, and she hiccupped a sob that she tried to hold back. I couldn't hold back my own tears when I heard her cry.

"I can't put it off; I have to do this. You know that." I traced her cheek with my fingertips, swearing to myself that even if I were in Valhalla for an eternity, no matter what else I might forget, I would never forget her.

"I know. I don't have to like it though." She cupped my face and then pulled me to her to press her lips to mine. "Until next time, then. Go summon Freyja. Go where you've belonged this whole time. Don't let me be selfish."

"You have never once been selfish. Not ever. I love you. That will never change." I kissed her one last time and then let her go. "Come back to the village with me to get the armor. I'll go to Var's to summon Freyja."

She took my hand, and we walked ever so slowly back to the village, dragging out what might be our last moments together as long as we could.

Chapter Fifty Three

VAR OPENED the bright blue door to her cottage before I could even knock. Did seers always know to answer the door before someone knocked?

"I was wondering when you would be here." Her expression was sympathetic. "You've said your goodbyes then?"

"I have. May I use your home to summon Freyja? It seems like the most appropriate place." I had removed Brisingamen and placed it carefully in the pack with the rest of Freyja's armor, which I held in my arms as I stood on Solveig's doorstep.

"Of course you may. I've got everything prepared for you already," she said. It reminded me that she wasn't just any vala, but also a goddess in her own right.

I stepped inside as she moved out of the way and went to where she had set up a circle of candles in the center of the main room.

"I'll leave you in peace." Var said. She closed the front door and slipped out of the room, where she had placed all the tools I would need to summon the goddess of love and war.

I went to the circle and took a seat in the middle, pulling each piece of armor from the pack and setting it within the circle. The room smelled of roses and lavender. A pitcher of mead and a horn mug sat at the head of the circle facing the crackling fire on the stone hearth.

With a deep breath, I poured the mead into the mug and began to sing a song to summon Freyja to Var's cottage. It was hard to get the words out around the lump in my throat. Hopefully, the goddess wouldn't notice how choked my voice sounded when she arrived. If she arrived.

"Freya, Goddess, Warrior, Queen,
Patron of love, war and sorcery
Bring us love and light this eve
Give us wisdom, make us free
With Brisingamen, Fjodfeld, and Gull-hjalm I call to thee"

Eventually, there came a soft rushing sound, accompanied by the chiming of bells. When I opened my eyes, Freyja stood before me, a golden aura emanating from her.

"A Valkyrie, how curious," She tilted her head to one side. "Are you the one who was exiled?"

"Yes," I squeaked. She was even more beautiful here than in Valhalla because of how ordinary everything else was surrounding her. "I summoned you to give you back what is yours."

"Oh? And what might that be?" She did not take her gaze from my face until I gestured to the armor sitting on the floor in the circle of candles. Her eyes widened, then flicked from the armor back to my face. "Is that... what I think it is?"

"It is. Brisingamen, Gull-hjalm, and Fjodfeld," I picked up the amber and gold necklace to offer to her. "I found them, on a quest to redeem myself to Hel, and thought it would be best to return them to you."

"I see. Will you tell me about this quest?" Freyja asked. When she shifted to kneel before me, so that we were on eye level with each other, my mouth dropped open and my eyes widened. A goddess kneeling was shocking to begin with. But that she put herself on a level with me, a disobedient Valkyrie, took my breath away.

"It is a very long story," I admitted.

"I would like to hear it, so that I may properly determine your reward for bringing me what has been lost for so long," Freyja said in a melodic voice.

I started from when I fell in love with Eryk and kept him from Valhalla until the moment when I summoned her. The story was no longer painful to tell, the guilt and remorse for the pain I had caused Eryk were gone. All that was left was sadness that I had to leave Gunhild after everything we had gone through together.

"Tell me more about this shieldmaiden who joined you on your quest," Freyja requested when I had finished my tale. I searched her expression for a reason why she might care.

"She is the bravest person I ever met. She wanted to join me, and I allowed it, because a quest such as mine is a lonely prospect."

"And you fell in love." A warm smile curved Freyja's full lips. "Don't hide that part from me, child. I know love when I see it. Your eyes give you away when you speak her name."

"Oh. Do they?" My cheeks flushed. I should have expected the goddess of love to know that I had fallen for Gunhild. "Yes. I love her. More than life."

"I'm glad you found real love on your quest. So you would know that what that boy offered you was not real." To my surprise, the goddess reached out a glowing hand to touch my cheek. Her touch was warm and gentle, and I couldn't help but lean my face into it. "But it is time for you to go back to your place in Valhalla, don't you think?"

The idea of going back brought tears to my eyes. My place was in Valhalla, and I couldn't refuse to go if that was where Freyja wanted to send me. I had to let her do what she thought was best—she was a goddess after all.

She stood again and held out a glowing hand to me. I took it and rose to my feet. I was about to go back to Valhalla, the thing I had wanted more than anything. But now that it was within my reach, now that Eryk was saved *and* I was going to go home, it physically hurt.

"Hmm." She looked at me curiously, her head tilting as she regarded my glassy eyes. "You would stay here then? In Midgard? With her?"

My eyes must have lit up, because the goddess laughed. It was a musical sound that rang through the small cottage. She took my hand in hers and turned it over so she could trace the lines on my palm.

"You don't belong in Midgard anymore," she said thoughtfully. I watched her fingers over my palm, wondering if she could read the lines there and knew what my future would be. But of course she did.

She was the one with my future in her control. She could take me back to Valhalla, or she could leave me in Midgard. She was right, though. I technically didn't belong here anymore.

"No, I don't," I agreed, with an obedient nod as I stared down at her finger still grazing over my palm. My voice was a little choked, tears threatening now that I knew the inevitable was coming. I would never see Gunhild again.

"You were always meant to find her, you know," Freyja told me, as if she read my mind and knew I was thinking of Gunhild. "The Norns wove it in their tapestry. You found each other as you were always meant to. I couldn't really separate you now, against your will. Even if you don't, technically, belong here."

I opened my mouth to respond, but nothing came out beyond a helpless little laugh, much less musical than Freyja's. Was she really offering to let me stay in Midgard with Gunhild? She sighed and released my hand.

"Can I... can I stay then?" I finally asked, too afraid to even hope she would say yes.

"I think..." She looked back up to my face finally. "I think that Hel is the only one really concerned with balance and the order of things. Life and death and orderliness is not my domain. I'm more of the passionate type—love, war, magic—you know that."

"Right," I agreed, unsure if that meant I could stay or not.

"If staying here is your true desire, and you are making that decision out of love, then I can hardly deny you," she said finally. "We will miss your presence and song in Valhalla though. One day you will return to us, though. With your shieldmaiden."

"I will miss Valhalla too. But I would miss Gunhild more, I think," I admitted.

"Then stay in Midgard. Live a long life, and when it is time, I shall bring the two of you to Valhalla myself, yes? Regardless of whether you die in battle." Freyja's offer was astonishing, and I hardly knew how to thank her for it. I merely bowed my head deeply and fought back the urge to grin like a fool, the tears forgotten now.

"You are too kind," I managed to say. "Thank you."

"Go see your shieldmaiden. Tell her your news. Oh, and tell that trickster I'm grateful he helped you instead of the usual mischief he gets up to. I hope he's learned a lesson in there somewhere."

"I'm sure he has, though you can hardly expect him to change his ways altogether," I said. "But I will tell him."

"I will see you then, in many years I hope, and we will welcome you when the time comes. Take care, my Valkyrie. And thank you for restoring my armor to me."

Freyja stood, picking up her armor, and then began to glow so brightly I had to close my eyes or be blinded. When I finally opened them, she was gone and the only remaining light was from the fire. Her departure had blown out all the candles.

Var came tottering out of a back room a moment later and wordlessly put away the candles and mead. I stood and helped in silence though I was about to burst with the news.

"You should go," she said after we had put everything where it belonged. "Your shieldmaiden is probably in pieces somewhere. She'll be glad to have you back."

"She never lost me," I pointed out, though I was beaming at the idea of returning to Gunhild's side with the good news. No matter how I tried, I couldn't stop smiling. Var laughed and reached up to pat my cheek, before turning me toward the door by the shoulders.

"She thinks she did. Go tell her. Celebrate. You've done everything you set out to do and got out of it better than you hoped."

"I did, didn't I?" I had wanted Eryk back, and to return to Valhalla. But now I knew that all I ever needed was a home with Gunhild. "Thank you for allowing me to use your home. I'll be sure to tell you goodbye when we leave."

"You could always stay in Armvind," Var pointed out. "Leif would welcome you, as would the others. And it's peaceful here, with no battles to fight. A good place to grow old together."

"Perhaps we will." I smiled at the idea. "If we do, then I'm sure I'll see a lot of you. Take care."

Var laughed and sent me on my way. As I stepped out into the summer evening, the vivid colors fading into a soft lavender hue, I felt lighter than I ever had. Like I had been freed from invisible chains that had bound me for years. I couldn't help but take off at a run through the village to get back to Gunhild.

When I reached our cottage, I didn't bother knocking. I threw the door open and shouted for Gunhild. A shuffling and sniffling came from the dark bedroom, and she poked her head out. Her eyes, red from crying, widened as she saw me.

"You've already said your goodbyes," she said, her voice hoarse. "I don't think I can handle another, Yrsa."

"I'm not saying goodbye," I replied, offering a small hopeful smile as I opened my arms to her. After a moment of realization, she barreled into me, pressing kisses all over my face.

"What? You're not? Were you not able to summon Freyja?" Gunhild asked.

"I was. She let me stay," I said simply.

"What did she say? Was she angry that you had her armor? Was she pleased you gave it back to her? Are you staying in Midgard then?" Gunhild had a million questions, and I laughed as I tried to think of answers.

"I can't answer everything at once, sunshine. But yes, I am staying in Midgard. With you."

"This is the best news of my entire life! I will give a thousand offerings to Freyja!" She was so excited she seemed to vibrate with happiness.

"We will. She was very grateful that you had helped me. She said she will take us both to Valhalla when we die. Whether it is in battle or not. As a reward," I said as I pulled her into my arms.

"What an honor," Gunhild said, her eyes widening at the news. "It's so strange, you know."

"What's strange?" I asked.

"Do you remember the first time we met? On the fjord?"

I thought back to that day when I had made the decision to fight for Eryk, and how she had been at the fjord too. She had faced a difficult decision of her own that day, facing down her own mortality and the idea of ending her own life.

"Yes, I remember. How could I forget?"

"When I saw you that day, I knew you were there for me. That I just… belonged to you. In a way."

"Well, the Norns weave what is to be. It might have been the tug of fate we both felt that day." I let her go and took her hand, leading her to the bedroom. I wanted nothing more than to curl up in bed with her and sleep, completely peacefully, for the first time in ages.

"Fate. I never believed in it, you know. But I do now," Gunhild said.

We settled in bed together, our legs entangled, and our bodies pressed close. I never wanted to move from here, unless it was to find other adventures with Gunhild. But just growing old with her seemed like the perfect life after everything we had been through together.

"I do too. To think, everything led us to this. Every awful, horrifying step was always to bring us here. I would do it all again, you know. If it led right back here." I rested my forehead against hers and closed my eyes.

"And I would always, always come along."

THE END

Trigger Warnings

This book contains scenes that may depict, mention, or discuss: Blood & gore depiction, Knife, sword & axe violence, Loss (death), and Suicidal ideation.

About the Author

When Victoria Jansen isn't writing, she works as a family law paralegal. She lives with her husband, their grown child, and their deeply beloved but not-so-bright dogs. She enjoys crochet, karaoke, and reading speculative fiction.